3

The Spur & The Sash

Middle Tennessee, 1865

~ A Novel ~

The Spur &
The Sash

Middle Tennessee, 1865

~ A Novel ~

Robert Grede

Three
Towers
Press

Published by:

Three Towers Press
1288 Summit Ave. Suite 107/115
Oconomowoc, WI 53066
Tel: (608) 576-9747
Fax: (262) 565-2058

Three Towers Press is an imprint of HenschelHaus Publishing, Inc.
Please contact the publisher for permissions and quantity discounts.

ISBN: 9781595980922

Publisher's Cataloging-In-Publication Data
(Prepared by The Donohue Group, Inc.)
Grede, Robert.
The spur & the sash : Middle Tennessee, 1865 : a novel / Robert Grede.
p. : ill., maps ; cm.
ISBN: 978-1-59598-092-2
1. Soldiers--Tennessee, Middle--1849-1877--Fiction. 2. Nashville, Battle
of, Nashville, Tenn., 1864--Fiction. 3. Man-woman relationships--Tennessee,
Middle--1849-1877--Fiction. 4. Plantation life--Tennessee, Middle--1849-1877--Fiction.
5. Love stories. 6. Historical fiction. I. Title. II. Title: Spur and the sash

PS3607.R44 S68 2010
813.6   2010928066

Cover design by The Czycz Company Inc.
Photographs courtesy of the author.
Illustrations by The Shepherd Express.

Printed in the United States of America.

For Dad

PROLOGUE

This book begins with the Battle of Nashville, December 15 and 16, 1864, the single most decisive victory of the Civil War. At Nashville, Union General George H. Thomas, the "Rock of Chickamauga," swept Confederate General John Bell Hood's Army of Tennessee from the field, nearly obliterating it in the process. (Thomas's battle plan, still studied today by military strategists, is considered a masterpiece; his unique use of cavalry, a key part of his offensive, presaged the mobile tactics later used during World War II.)

After the battle, both armies moved on while the wounded were left behind. Many Yankees wounded in the battle were forced to convalesce amid the staunch secessionist inhabitants of Middle Tennessee. It is against this backdrop that the story unfolds.

THE BATTLE

For nearly four years, the Union, with its huge population of fighting men, abundance of food, clothing and shoes, and its massive superiority in manufacturing, had been pounding and grinding and breaking the backs of Rebel resistance. Early in the war, the South's superior generals had bettered the North's inexperienced military leaders. But the tide turned after Gettysburg. By December of 1864, Union General Ulysses S. Grant had Confederate General Robert E. Lee and the Army of Northern Virginia under siege near Petersburg, Virginia, and General William T. Sherman, after taking Atlanta, was somewhere in Georgia— no one knew exactly where—carving up the Deep South, facing little opposition.

Having lost Atlanta, and with no hope of stopping General Sherman's huge force, General Hood and 40,000 desperate Rebel soldiers marched north in one last dramatic effort to destroy Sherman's supply lines, retake Nashville, held for two years by the Union Army, then turn east and link up with Lee at Petersburg. General Thomas, in command at Nashville, had General Steedman's army to the east of the city, and generals Wood, Smith, and Schofield and their armies to the south, with General Wilson's division of cavalry on the far west flank. Thomas intended to stop Hood.

The Rebel army deployed in a line south of the city and awaited the Federal attack. Having far fewer men at his disposal than Thomas, Hood reasoned that defending a position would allow his force to deplete the Yankee attackers, then roll right through Nashville in a follow-up counterattack.

On December 8, 1864, all was ready. Bad weather, however, intervened. That night, a terrible storm of ice and freezing rain coated the city, rendering General Thomas's attack impossible. The ice storm lasted three days. Union leaders in Washington grew impatient; Grant threatened to relieve Thomas unless he attacked. By the 14th, under a warming sun, the frozen ground began to melt. Next morning, Thomas struck.

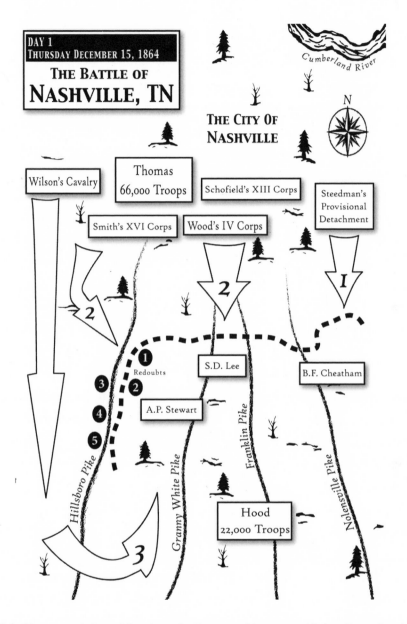

DAY 1: After several days of freezing rain, the ground lay covered in ice. December 14th brought a thaw and, on the morning of the 15th, Thomas sent Steedman against the Confederate left (1) in a feint, then sent Wood and Smith hard into their center (2), while Schofield remained in reserve. During the early fighting, Wilson's cavalry rode clear around the breastworks, dismounted, and attacked from the rear (3). Redoubt #1 was the last to fall, and the Confederates fell back to a row of hills further south.

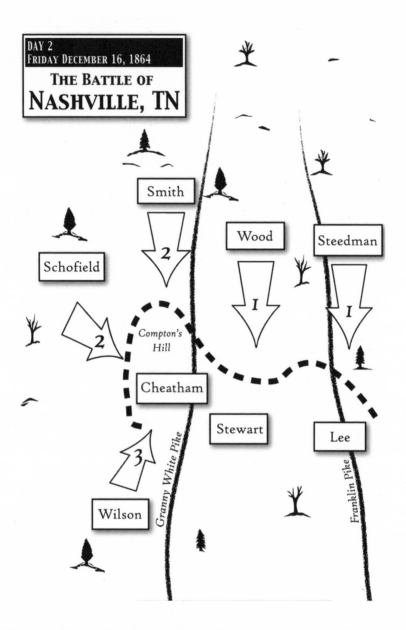

DAY 2
FRIDAY DECEMBER 16, 1864
THE BATTLE OF
NASHVILLE, TN

DAY 2 Thomas again sent Steedman against the Confederate right flank, followed by Wood in the center (1). Both were quickly repulsed. Schofield joined the fight and, with Smith, attacked the Confederate left flank (2). Hood transferred troops from his right and anchored his stand on Compton's Hill (later renamed Shy's Hill after its defender, Confederate Colonel William Shy). Wilson's cavalry again outflanked the Confederate line (3), and the rout was on.

A simple plan: after a feint by Steedman on the enemy's right flank, Wood and Smith advanced on the Confederate left, swinging like a great wheel with Wood at the hub. The Eighth Wisconsin Regiment, assigned to Smith's Corps, attacked Confederate General Stewart's men, who anchored the Confederate left in a series of redoubts. At the same time, Wilson's cavalry rode around behind the enemy's left and fell on the Confederate rear.

The strategy worked perfectly. Men of the Eighth Wisconsin were among the first to overwhelm Redoubt #4, among the first to reach the Granny White Pike. Everywhere, Confederate works were overrun; more were surrounded or cut off from retreat; dozens of artillery pieces and hundreds of prisoners were taken.

During the night, Hood's army, its ranks decimated by casualties, desertions, and capture, regrouped a few miles south of the battlefield. Hood anchored his left flank on Compton's Hill (later renamed Shy's Hill for Confederate Colonel William Shy, its gallant defender), a rocky, wooded prominence rising 400 feet above the surrounding area. This became the lynchpin of the Rebel position on the following day, December 16, 1864. Among the defenders were Tennessee infantry regiments, many of whom were from parts of Middle Tennessee.

Smith spent the morning positioning troops around the hill, then attacked from the north while Schofield came from the west. Wilson's cavalry again circled the hill, dismounted, and attacked from the south. By a strange quirk (military strategists still argue the point to this day), the Rebel works were placed too close to the peak to be able to fire down upon the attackers as they climbed. Until the final hundred yards. This became the killing field, where fighting was so intense that soldiers could not walk without stepping on the fallen.

It was late afternoon when the Confederate position was finally overrun. Remnants of Hood's army retreated south on the Franklin Turnpike, General Nathan Bedford Forrest serving rear guard. Yankee cavalry pursued the fleeing Rebels, the Eighth Wisconsin followed in support, and the last major battle of the Civil War ended with a dramatic Union victory.

General Hood did not wait long at Franklin, but burned the bridge over the Harpeth River and moved further south, General Wilson's Federal cavalry in close pursuit. For three days, the Confederates fled through sleet and snow, a forlorn army discouraged and defeated, the men hungry, mostly barefooted. By December 19th, after another day of fire-and-fall-back against Wilson's cavalry, the last of Hood's men crossed the Duck River at Columbia.

On a chilly Christmas day, General Forrest and the Rebel rear guard lay in wait for the pursuing Federal cavalry. In a series of feints and maneuvers, Forrest successfully routed the pursuers and captured several field artillery before again withdrawing south. It was the last effort by the Federals to impede the Confederate retreat.

Hood and his men crossed the Tennessee River into Alabama and Mississippi where the armies dispersed. The invasion of Tennessee, the South's last great aggressive military action of the war, ended in bitter failure. Confederate battle flags would not wave in Nashville; Hood would never reach Kentucky to recruit more soldiers for his depleted army; he would not have his grand march east through the Cumberland Gap to link up with Robert E. Lee at Petersburg. By late January, General Hood was relieved of his command and the armies he led were reassigned to other generals. The Army of Tennessee effectively ceased to exist.

The Eighth Wisconsin Regiment continued as far south as the Tennessee River, but had no further contact with the enemy. New Year's Day, 1865, was spent camped near Pulaski, Tennessee, at a crossroads the locals called Goodspring.

THE SETTING

Early white settlers first came to the Tennessee Central Basin around 1800. Some were soldiers of the American Revolution who had been granted tracts of land by the nearly bankrupt government of North Carolina as payment for their wartime services. Others had purchased land in the hope that a treaty with the Indians could be arranged and the area opened for settlement. In 1806, much of Middle Tennessee was bought from Cherokee Chief Old Black Fox. The area included all lands stretching from the Duck River to Alabama.

While Nashville, on the Cumberland River, was the capitol city, many settlers were attracted to rich farmland further south, in Maury County along the Duck River. Columbia became the center of commerce, former President James K. Polk its most famous citizen. Before the Civil War, Maury County boasted 20,000 inhabitants, with Columbia its largest city.

During the War, the area was occupied at various times by both armies. After Nashville fell to Federal troops, the city became a major provisioning area because of its strategic position as a transportation hub.

THE PEOPLE

Most of the area's inhabitants believed in states' rights, but few held slaves, and in January 1861, Middle Tennessee voted to stay with the Union. After the shooting started, however, heritage and politics prevailed and Middle Tennessee, including Maury County, voted to secede. Many men joined the Confederate Army, twenty companies from Maury County alone.

Political leaders were staunch secessionists. Those who remained loyal to the Union were banished, shunned by the aristocracy and working class both. One such man, Samuel Mayes Arnell, remained an ardent Union man throughout the war, for which he amassed a small army of enemies. Tall, slim, and dour by nature, he was not a gifted speaker and did not win many to his point of view. But after the war, his efforts helped Tennessee become the first Southern state to reenter the Union.

Andrew Johnson, too, was from Tennessee. An adept stump speaker, he championed the common man and vilified the plantation aristocracy. Johnson chose to remain in the United States Senate after Tennessee seceded, which made him a hero in the North and a traitor in the eyes of most Southerners. In 1862, President Lincoln appointed him Military Governor of Tennessee, and in 1864, the Republicans, in a pointed effort at reconciliation, nominated Johnson, a Southerner and a Democrat, for Vice President.

When Abraham Lincoln was assassinated on April 14, 1865, Andrew Johnson became the 17th President, and the arduous mission of reconstructing the South passed to him. Lincoln's vision for a reunified country included no plan to punish those who had seceded, and Johnson dutifully made an effort to fulfill his predecessor's vision.

Politically, this meant allowing the Southern states to rejoin the Union as accepted and equal partners with the Northern states. From a human perspective, it meant replanting farms left fallow, finding homes for countless refugees, confirming the rights of Freedmen, and resurrecting local governments in courthouses whose inner recesses had been gutted and records destroyed by occupying armies of both sides.

Lincoln's plan had been to offer complete amnesty to anyone who would take an oath of loyalty to the United States. If one tenth of a Southern state's voters took the oath, they could re-establish state government and be represented in the U.S. Congress.

Radical Republicans, brilliantly led and ruthless in their tactics, remained embittered by Lincoln's murder and suspected it had been conspired by the Confederate government. Their supporters were not disposed to be generous to the conquered Confederacy, and favored punishment over reconciliation.

Andrew Johnson was earnest and well meaning, but lacked Lincoln's political savvy and willingness to compromise. Long unpopular with Southerners, Johnson's strong belief in states' rights (and fair treatment of the defeated and destitute former Confederacy) made him equally unpopular in the North. To compound his woes, he had to deal with the problems created by six million newly freed slaves who couldn't read, had no place to live, and few means to remedy either.

Johnson was not up to the task. After just four months in office, he had aggravated all sides of the Reconstruction issue. He narrowly escaped an impeachment attempt by the Radical Republicans and was replaced by Ulysses S. Grant on the Republican ticket in the 1868 election.

THE STORY

Rummaging through my father's dressing room many years ago (I must have been looking for some clean socks), I came upon a cloth sack wrapped loosely with old twine.

Carefully undoing the string, I discovered a long, ribbon-like piece of satin, deep red with a generous fringe. With it was a worn piece of gray metal in the shape of a U with a studded piece at its base.

Curious, I asked my father about them. He said they were just some family heirlooms that had belonged to my great-great-grandfather. I asked if that was the same guy riding a giant black horse in a picture on his office wall. The same, said my father, and then he started to tell me one of his many stories, something about how they were given to my forefather by a woman he met, some woman who had liked him and helped him recover from some wounds he had received in some war or another. Seemed like an interesting story, but I was barely a teenager and history to me was whatever happened yesterday.

Over the years, I came to appreciate my father's stories, especially those of my ancestors. He would share bits and pieces from time to time, stories he had heard on his great-grandfather's knee, anecdotes he gathered from his grandparents, family lore passed down through his parents, my grandparents.

Later, as I acquired an appetite for history, I remembered his telling me of ancestors who had fought in America's Civil War. So I began to study their exploits, the campaigns in which they had fought, the great battles of Shiloh and Corinth, Pea Ridge and Peachtree Creek. I begged my father for thrilling stories of screaming cannon, bugles calling for a dashing charge across a battlefield, the heroic adventures of my great-great-grandfathers.

Sadly, my father knew little about their battlefield exploits. But he did know a good deal about what happened to one ancestor in particular after he had been wounded. He slowly began to tell me a story about George Bosworth Van Norman, my great-great-grandfather, a story of passion and atonement, of honor and sacrifice amid the anarchy that was Middle Tennessee in 1865, a story about the spur and the sash and how George came to have them.

This is that story.

*I*n *The Spur & The Sash*, I make every effort to remain true to the historic times. Despite the many hours of research to assure the accuracy of historical fact, however, this remains a work of fiction. Wherever possible, I have used memoirs and letters, diaries and accounts of events written by the people who lived them to either support or refute the version in my family's oral history.

The characters, with the exception of George Van Norman and his fellow members of the Eighth Wisconsin Volunteers, are fictional. The voices of the characters, their reflections and responses to their experiences, are as I would have you know them.

The ability to create this story from bits and pieces of oral history would not have been possible without the vast assortment of books, archives, and Internet web sites available on the subject, testament to the affect the era still holds over our nation. Without the continuing interest in America's Civil War, this mountain of detailed historical references would not exist.

Robert Grede
Milwaukee, WI

CHAPTER ONE

Columbia, Tenn. July 31, 1865

The brakes chuffed and the whistle blew, and Sergeant George Van Norman stepped aboard the train at precisely noon. An old man in a sodden green uniform approached, his toothless grin beneath a pillbox cap. "This here's the South train," he said. "Ain't you headed the wrong way?"

George just nodded, shook the rain from his hat, and found a seat alone near the back of the car. Outside, the brakes chuffed again and the car lurched and the station moved slowly past his window. A sign drifted lazily, as if in flight: **COLUMBIA, TENN.**, and he stuffed his haversack and small case beneath the bench. He folded his wool coat under his arm and tried not to think about the morning—his journey to the train station, the ambush on the road, the death of his friend. A pungency rose from his woolen uniform like medicine, familiar, the smell of wet leaves in October rain. He breathed deeply and let the fragrance roll about his mouth.

The monotonous kick-kack, kick-kack of the iron wheels beat a steady tempo, a gentle throbbing both inside him and distant, dulling him into stupor. He stared at his ghostlike reflection, a mask over the panorama that had been his home, and he saw there a hundred tomorrows, his life in the South.

His injury had healed, his scar fully hidden. With the war over, he should be going home. Sweet celebration with his family, red clapboard

I

house and picket fence, the smell of his mother's cooking, and the boisterous laughter of his sisters. He tapped his fingers rhythmically on the wooden seat as though gently laying each thought there in cadence. This image he held in his head now seemed faint and faded as an old tintype. His sisters were married and moved away; his brothers were gone, too. The Wisconsin farm was his parents' home, not really his. Not anymore. Not after this.

The train slowed for the next station and George looked up from the bench where he had arranged his thoughts. On the platform stood itinerant citizens and men in uniforms of both armies. Young soldiers slapped one another on the shoulders amid a chorus of laughter and farewells. For many, "home" had become their regiment, their families the men with whom they had wandered like nomads through four years of drill and dysentery and war. Now, three months after Appomattox, regiments disbanded. Soldiers scattered like milkweed in the wind. Going home.

A boy of nine or ten hawked newspapers and George leaned from his window and tossed him a coin. The boy ran alongside and handed George his paper as the train pulled from the station. "Thanky, mister," he shouted, and faded from sight.

George opened the Nashville paper: July 28, 1865, three days old. Headlines spoke of Reconstruction and the Freedmen's Bureau and much that had happened while he recuperated, waiting for orders to return to his regiment. Conviction of Jefferson Davis, Trial of Mary Surrat, Confederate Senators Censured. The end of the war had brought no end of hostilities. Northern Politicians led the condemnation, attacking unabated all things Southern, hurling invectives like minié balls. No voice carried the Southern Cause as no Confederate state had yet been allowed to rejoin the Union. And so Southerners' pleas fell scorned and unheeded.

He turned the page. News of returning soldiers and messages from families searching for their loved ones mingled with advertisements, everywhere, advertisements:

**Aetna Insurance of Hartford, Connecticut
(Losses Paid in 46 Years over $17,000,000) ...**

**Special shipment of medicines for
diarrhea and dysentery ...**

**A large assortment of prostheses with technological wonderments
to replicate natural movement ...**

Two benches in front of George, crude wooden crutches lay beneath the seat of a passenger missing a leg, a young man not much older than himself, casualty of some battle, who could not afford the luxury of technological wonderments. George laid his paper aside.

Seven months had passed since he had last been with the men of the Eighth Wisconsin. After the battle at Nashville, the regiment had been on the move chasing Rebels through Tennessee and Mississippi and Alabama. George had been left behind.

Now, it was nearly August, and he was to finally rejoin his regiment at Uniontown, a small town along the rail line west of Montgomery, Alabama, a thousand miles from home. The conductor's words echoed in his head and the irony of heading further south was not lost upon him: heading south to rejoin his regiment so that he might muster out and return north to his Wisconsin home. Or to the planta-tion, a Southern plantation—a farm anywhere else, but Southern pride, insistent upon propriety, called them plantations—where a woman waited for him, a woman of the same Southern aristocracy and pride. And he, a Yankee, having chosen to live as a Southern aristocrat, was headed south, only to muster out and return north to a Southern life. He sat bewildered, as if these thoughts mocked him.

Across the aisle, two men wore gray kepis in a casual fashion. They eyed him curiously, the triple chevrons and polished buttons of his blue uniform. George nodded, wondered for a moment in which battle he might have opposed them. They nodded in return, and one asked to read a page of his paper. George passed it to him and the man said, "Much obliged, Billy." The other soldier tipped his cap.

It was a small thing really, and yet it served to kindle a faith, a belief that there may exist a salve that could bind this Great Wound. It suggested hope, and George could not contain a smile. "Pleasure, Johnny," he said, and tipped his hat, one soldier to another, a mutual respect for the fight, if not the politics.

How does one begin rebuilding a whole country? Everywhere, talk of Reconstruction rose and fell, as if by its mere mention the nation might right itself. It seemed a task too large to comprehend and George feared it was just as Judge Wilson had predicted: Reconstruction was merely Northerners' justification for their incursions south. It was a word used by Carpetbaggers who sought wealth and power from the ashes of what once had been a powerful and wealthy country.

Carpetbaggers! Those steely-eyed Northerners he had seen on the streets in Columbia, who tipped their hats and beamed their oily smiles as ladies of Southern culture bustled and fretted and stepped aside. Living in the South, George would be branded with the same stick. He, a Yankee, one of the very same Yankees who so recently had been killing their sons and husbands, who now sought a life among them, would acquire the moniker as easily as a recruit his nickname. Yet he sought no wealth, no power. His motive for remaining in the South the noblest of all motives: love. His love for a woman, the Judge's daughter. He wanted only to return to the plantation, marry her, and live the life of a gentleman farmer, raising crops and children with equal fervor.

The kick-kack tempo slowed once more. At a crossroads, two old women dressed in black stood watching as the cars crept past; in a field, a farmer, shoeless and emaciated, tilled the muddy earth; children played "war" with sticks in an empty yard, lobbing mud cannon balls. Crisscrossed by rival armies scouring and pillaging, burning what they could not carry, Middle Tennessee lay wounded and pitiful, and he shut his eyes to the sight of it. It did not look like a place to fall in love.

After what seemed a long time, George returned to his newspaper. One item in particular startled him. The war, just three months over and already Confederate regiments were reuniting:

> **Surviving members of Shy's Battalion**
> **of the 10th Tennessee to meet**
> **at Barlow's on Church Street Sunday next.**

It had been Confederate Colonel Shy and his Tennesseans who had defended Compton's Hill at Nashville. George rubbed his moustache where it hid the scar. His luck had been strong that day. But for some, the Fates held no sympathy.

CHAPTER TWO

Outside Nashville, December 14, 1864

Jacob Aney had seen the enemy campfires, red eyes in the twilight, unblinking and unrelenting, waiting. Weeks of bitter cold and freezing rain had finally given way to a south wind and the icy shield encasing the armies had thawed. The waiting was over. It was time to go to war.

Wind buffeted the walls of his tent, flapping an unsteady rhythm. Outside, the Union army lay hibernating. It would awaken in the morning, groan and stretch out the stiffness, come to consciousness with a raging hunger for battle. It was time, that moment when the hands of the Great War God would snatch him up and send him reeling beyond the Evangeline.

But Jacob Aney would not follow, not this time. He closed his eyes, groping for a vision, and it came to him then, fuzzy at the edges as if a dream, but tantalizing and close. It was Christmastime and his family was gathered at a table eating bratwurst and sauerkraut and potatoes with hot bacon. Afterward playing cards, the air filled with profane language and raucous laughter, his mother would shake her head, half disapproving, half amused. She hadn't wanted him to go. He was her "little boy" and wasn't one son in the Army enough? His father had spoken of duty to farm and family, not to the Army, and wasn't it Abraham Lincoln's war after all? More than anything, news of heroism at Gettysburg had convinced Jacob he should be a soldier.

It had been a mistake.

Jacob was not like his older brother. James Aney was strong, decisive, and dedicated, a good student, always up at first light, never complaining, a leader. James had always jumped the highest, run the fastest, caught the biggest fish. It was as if God favored James, had given him more ability than other men. No, Jacob Aney was not like James. Jacob understood his place in the grand scheme of things, understood that he was a follower, not a leader. And so Jacob had followed his brother to war as soon as he had come of age.

His first few months had been nothing but drill. Sergeant Van Norman had vowed to make the new fish into fighters "even if it killed them." Van had shouted at them in rhythm: "Halt-Kneel-Ready-Aim-Fire-Load!" It was difficult to reload while kneeling, the ramrod harder to wield, powder and shot charged at an angle. So they practiced "by-the -nine's": "Load-Hand-Tear-Charge-Draw-Ram-Return-Prime-Hup! Load -Hand-Tear-Charge-Draw-Ram-Return-Prime-Hup!"

Jacob Aney had marched and drilled and cleaned his weapon and practiced the skills of war for months on end. Mostly, he had marched. Through Tennessee and Louisiana and Mississippi and back through Louisiana and through Mississippi again, trudging and tramping over hideous terrain, swamps and bayous of stinking, mud-sucking, reptile-filled waters. Vines creeping like snakes poised to strike, moss reaching from trees as if to strangle, biting flies, mosquitoes everywhere. Worst of all was the smell. Rotting vegetation had its own foul stench that penetrated the head and dulled the brain.

Disease lay waste to the regiment. Soldiers fell ill with camp fever, befouling themselves on the march. Or they simply sat and stared blankly at some unseen horror, their faces pinched and drawn. Others came down with "Southron sickness," a disease Yankee doctors had never seen, never treated. Jacob had watched as a friend grew delirious and suddenly vomited, his face the color of old fish. Many a mother who had wept with pride when her son marched bravely off to war would be ashamed to learn that he died, bowels tied in knots, from some bloody flux.

At first it seemed like some fantastic sport, marching and drilling, as if in preparation for a make-believe dream-game. Until Pleasant Hill, Jacob Aney's first taste of war. Two minutes and he had witnessed a man's head taken clean off by a cannon ball, another man disemboweled by canister. He had nearly died himself when a Confederate soldier shot at him from point-blank range. But the gun misfired.

That had been an omen, a test. And, having survived the test, Jacob Aney vowed he would survive the war. He conceded it was not in him to be a hero. He felt no hatred for this enemy, found no satisfaction in the fight. He had made his decision carefully, logically. Valor in battle, he reasoned, held no great honor. What was honor if you could not live to enjoy it? Only survival mattered. He thus judged himself neither brave nor cowardly, but felt a satisfaction that he, among all others, understood this great Truth. In his misery, this offered a certain contentment.

He moved his legs, tried to relieve the stiffness. But the cold crept up from the muddy ground, through the rough wool of his army blues, past the taut gristle and bone, to clutch at his heart. He slapped his arms and blew into his hands for warmth, clouds of vapor dissipating on the canvas walls.

Outside his tent, nothing moved. The camp was quiet, soldiers tucked away in their soggy tents, getting what sleep they could. No sound but the dripping of melt water in steady tempo, marking time. His brother had drawn guard duty and would not return before sun-up. Tonight was the night.

Jacob Aney shivered once more, checked his bedroll and the things he had rolled up in his blanket: pocket knife, canteen, some hardtack, and most importantly, civilian clothes. He peered outside once more, glanced down the long rows of tents to where a small fire still smoldered. Its coals gave a dim glow, scarcely enough light to avoid bumping into tents or stumbling over stacked rifles that dotted the camp. Clouded skies, no moon or starlight—these he judged would make travel difficult, but would also hide him from curious eyes.

A man snored softly in the next tent. Time to go. Jacob snatched his bedroll, and scurried out of his canvas cell. He walked casually down the long row of tents, past the fire glow as if he were just another soldier out to relieve himself, then quickly slipped between a stand of trees. He began walking briskly across a muddy lane, then darted into the woods. Deep in the forest, he stopped, took off his blue sack coat, then stripped off his trousers and uniform shirt. Shivering as he donned the rough work clothes, he put on a long, black kerseymere coat, stuffed his uniform under an old log, and disappeared into the night.

Early morning, December 15, 1864, Private Jacob W. Aney, Company I, Eighth Wisconsin Volunteers, deserted.

CHAPTER THREE

Outside Nashville, December 15, 1864

A bugle wailed and two lines, elbow to elbow, surged forward. To either side, men grunted or cursed or prayed, their voices boorish and bestial, angry animals on the hunt. Through the rows of smoke, stabs of bright orange and red appeared and Sergeant George Van Norman leaned into the bedlam. Noise filled his head and tore at his nerve—boom of field cannon, crack of musket fire, a too-familiar "pock" sound, followed by the scream and the curse, the cry for "Mother!"

To his left, Private Ole Anderson raised his rifle. The gawky Norwegian chased the Battle Brotherhood bareheaded, his white-blonde hair flying in the wind. The boy's weapon jumped and he began to reload. "This is good, eh, Mr. Van?" He grinned, white teeth in sharp contrast to the soot on his face. "We are winning, eh?"

George shouted, "Give 'em hell, man!"

Corporal Mike Mansion bit off a cartridge and rammed it down the barrel. "He's got the fire in him, don't he, George?"

"Plenty," George shouted. "If he'd just keep his head down."

His words were lost in the mayhem as he plunged toward the line of smoke. The first Bluecoats began tumbling over the abatis, stabbing with their bayonets, swinging their rifles like clubs, men possessed as if by demons, clawing in frenzy. Screams of triumph and conquest for the victor, panic and pain for the vanquished.

George charged alongside Mike Mansion, up and over the earthworks, and fell among Rebels huddled below the ramparts. One thrust his bayonet and George parried it with the butt of his rifle. A musket banged close, and he felt the scorch of barrel flame burn his cheek. He brought his rifle around, fired into the face of one defender as another swung, a stinging blow crashing into the side of his head.

His eyes danced. He felt himself drifting into a deep warmth as if he lay hidden in a blanket of eider down. Spinning into the blackness, he floated in the dreamless sleep of the happy drunk, peaceful and still. And quiet, the utter absence of noise.

Then, "George!" He stirred to the sound of his name. "George!"

Roused as if from deep slumber, things around him began to take form: mud and sticks, an arm waving, a face he thought familiar. George blinked, tried to sit, and the pain struck like a hammer blow. He pinched his eyes. His head felt as if it hung on rusty hinges, every movement a struggle, pain coursing down his neck and into his arms strong enough to make his eyes water.

He fell back and Mike Mansion called once more, "George, you going to be all right, eh?"

George nodded slowly and rubbed his neck, then sat up.

"We have them on the run, we have, George." Mike Mansion grinned. "Have them on the run. Those Minnesota boys come in just yelling and hollering and scared the beejesus out of them." He started to laugh. "Brushed them clear back to Georgia, I'll wager."

George held his head, a knob forming hard as a knuckle above his ear. "Forgot to keep my damn head down," he said. His throat felt constricted by knobs and thistles and he had difficulty keeping his chin from bobbing against his chest.

"Ain't no holes in you except the ones God intended, eh?" Mike Mansion said. "No tin cup for Mr. Joosten just yet." Since Corinth, Sergeant Joosten, the regimental quartermaster, had marked each casualty by tying the victim's coffee cup to the supply wagon. The clatter of dozens of tin cups had long-ago ceased frightening the mules.

"What's the good word?"

George mumbled, "Fit as a fiddle..."

"...and fat in the middle," Mansion finished, grinning.

Musket fire lit the air, sporadic and distant, and it occurred to George that a battle raged somewhere else, too—he had somehow imagined that it all took place directly in front of him—and he slowly regained his feet. He retrieved his rifle, but found the stock broken, then fetched another from the muddy ground. He checked the bore, ran his thumb along the priming cap. Satisfied, he loaded it slowly and deliberately. He took nearly a minute.

"Looky, somebody's darling here," Mike Mansion said, pointing to the one with no face. "He's got rags on his feet. And this other one's got no shoes a-tall." He shook his head. "It's a wonderment is what it is, George. We're wrestling with one ragtag bunch of Rebs, eh?"

George nodded stiffly. He made a conscious effort to look at the dead man, imagined some hollow voice coming from the bloody face, and he struggled to keep from striking at it.

"Yes sir, brushed them clear back to Georgia," Mansion said, still grinning.

George marveled at his friend, at the pure joy he found in the fight. For Mike Mansion, war was a grand party. Nothing surprised him. Nothing frightened him. He was the soldier George wanted to be.

"Dress the lines!" came the shout.

Mike Mansion shouldered his rifle. "Damn, now that we taken this dirt, I'd have thought we might set here a spell," he said.

A bugle sounded and George took deep breaths to blow out his mouth. He stepped around the faceless body, somebody's darling, and cursed at the dead man for the miserable cold, and for the god-awful war, and for the ache George had in his head.

THEY ADVANCED THROUGH AN OPEN stretch of waterlogged grassland where the wind shivered the puddles and fog clung to the low places. Far above the smoke and haze, George heard battle noises, but in their part of the field, it was strangely silent, and he drew a long breath. His head throbbed and his shoulders ached, but he was, for the moment, safe.

As they marched, the men gestured and cursed and shouted epithets, scathing insults, directed and personal, daring the enemy to show itself. Their faces held huge grins, battle euphoria, exhilaration at having survived the initial charge. George grinned, too. War, to be sure, was a terrible thing. Like sin, it was wicked and evil. But like sin, it also held a terrible attraction. General Lee had been heard to say that it was a good thing war was so terrible lest we come to enjoy it.

Beside him, the men walked in two ragged lines, their boots sucking at the muddy ground. "Keep your head down, men. Johnny could be anywhere." George said. "And find yourself a hat, Mr. Anderson,"

The company followed the retreating Rebels along the Pike, the tramping of their boots muffled by thick woods. Late afternoon sky streaked dimly between the pines where shadows fell to deep gray. They stepped carefully and spoke only in hushed tones. The Rebel army might be miles away, or just over the rise of the road.

George held up his hand and stopped, and the men bunched up behind him. Low boom of cannon sounded in the distance. He tipped his head but could hear no other sound except the men panting, curtains of breath about their faces, as if it might hide them from whatever lurked behind each bush and tree, every curve of the roadway. He raised his arm once more and the men moved forward, a crouching walk, watchful, searching, their heads darting side to side in pendulum fashion. One step, two steps forward, he counted absently in his head.

At a hundred steps, George stopped and the men stopped. He tipped his head and felt his legs tense, his fingers grow stiff. A soft breeze high in the trees played a rhythm against the constant tapping of melt water dropping from the sodden limbs, a sound he imagined like that of the sea, placid and calming, a sound that contained its own heartbeat, this wet darkness breathing among the trees. Another ten steps. He peered once more into the gloom.

Then came a sharp pop and Will Pooler screamed and knelt in the mud. George dove for cover. Others froze, searching for the source of the sound. Ben Entriken quickly dragged Pooler off the road. Mike Mansion leapt a ditch and dropped beside George. "Monkey," he said, their term for a hidden marksman. "Watch for the puff of smoke when he fires."

"Hell, man, I can't see anything," George said.

Another musket report and another soldier fell. Those men still standing in the road scattered; others fired blindly into the woods. Ben Entriken again raced from cover and dragged the man into the brush.

"Ben's goin' to get his arse shot off, he keeps that up," Mike Mansion said. "You see any smoke?"

George shook his head. Too dark to see much of anything.

"Me, neither," said Mansion.

George listened, strained to hear the faint scrape of metal as the "monkey" reloaded. From somewhere behind him, Will Pooler cursed his wound, his pain diffused in a tirade of words unfit for muleskinners.

"Watch for his smoke," and Mike Mansion leapt over the road running hard, head low. Another crack and a musket ball clipped the leaves by Mansion's shoulder. He crawled beneath thick pine boughs, removed his hat, and waited. From above came a faint noise, the sound of metal on metal. "In the trees!" Mansion shouted. "He's up in the trees!"

Two dozen rifles sounded a staccato rhythm and a moment later, a musket clattered to earth, the stock shattering. Then a body landed hard, groaned once, and lay still.

The men began to emerge from their hiding places. Ben Entriken knelt beside the Rebel, a young boy not more than sixteen, while the others made an excited circle. "He's finished," said Ben.

Suddenly, another musket fell heavily at George's feet. He jumped in surprise, aimed his rifle into the thin foliage, and shouted, "Come down, Johnny, or die in your tree."

"Don't shoot. I'm coming down, but I'm coming slow," said a voice from above.

Men gathered beneath the tree as the Rebel soldier dropped to the ground. He wore no coat, his brown homespun clothing in tatters over a body lean and hard. His hair hung long and twisted around sloping shoulders, his beard greasy and knotted. Flesh, pale and wrinkled, fell away from cheekbones protruding like darts through canvas, his eyelids inflamed, red-brown and swollen.

Lieutenant Sherman Ellsworth approached the circle of men. "What do you have there, Sergeant Van Norman?"

"Rebs, sir," George said. "Couple of monkeys up a tree."

Nearby, the boy lay in spasm, blood bubbling at his throat as he tried to draw breath. His eyes stared and his small body stiffened convulsively before lying still. The older Rebel knelt in the mud and leaves and gently placed his hand on the boy's shoulder. "You stupid kid," he said softly. "We were home, Jimmy. We were home."

Lieutenant Ellsworth peered at him in the dying light. "How old are you, soldier?"

The man stood slowly, still looking at the dead boy. "Be forty next week," he replied.

George picked up the old man's musket, examined the breech. It was unloaded, the breech cold. It had not recently fired.

Ellsworth spoke to George. "Sergeant, you found him. You take him back to wherever they're gathering prisoners."

"Yes, sir." He shouldered his rifle and took the Rebel by the arm.

"Take Corporal Entriken and the wounded with you. Then join up with us later." The Lieutenant looked down the road in the gathering darkness. "We'll put in for the night right here," he said. "Can't see anything anyway."

The men drifted into the woods and George began to return along the Pike with Ben Entriken and the two wounded men, Will Pooler and Jake Rutherford. Pooler held a rag to his injured hand and mumbled curses as he walked. Rutherford's belly wound was superficial and had already stopped bleeding. "Must have run into some mighty tough hardtack, eh?" he said. "Bounced right back out."

Will Pooler said to the Rebel, "What's your name?"

"Noah Turner," came the reply. "I stayed behind because I didn't want to go back south. I live just over yonder," he said, pointing. "That was my cousin Mildred's boy who was killed back there. We planned to hide out 'til you passed. Looking to get home is all, same as you."

"Only place you be going is prison," said Will Pooler.

George stepped between the two men before Pooler could say more. To the victims, concealed marksmen were cowards, the lowest form of life, hiding in ambush, waiting for a man to step into their sights. They were hated and feared by soldiers everywhere.

"I'm sorry you boys got hurt," Turner said, staring hard at the earth as if to hide there. "Jimmy always was a lively one for a fight. I expect you all will need to recuperate some, I mean with your wounds and all. You boys might see your homes before I will." He looked toward the trees. "And I can damn near spit on my own fields from right here."

They walked on and the darkness collapsed around them, each man oblivious, exhausted, in motion but not noticing. After a time, Will Pooler began to whistle.

George marched beside the ragged Rebel captive, an older man, thin as a rail. Even this miserable prisoner knew the war was over. He had lost, given up. Why couldn't the generals see it? It was as if the Union wanted to punish the Confederacy, make it suffer for its insolence. At the basest level, it seemed revenge dominated the average soldier's actions.

That afternoon, they had launched themselves at the throats of those resisting and the gray line had split and broken, the Rebels scattering before them. One man in gray had knelt as if in supplication, blood spreading into the pine needles beneath him. Another man leaned against a tree holding his stomach, his face a bleach of death as his entrails spilled between his fingers.

Yet for some, it was not enough.

One young soldier had taken aim at a wounded Rebel who was raising his one good arm. George had knocked away the boy's gun at just the moment he fired.

"Why'd you go and do that?" the boy asked.

"He's surrendering. You don't shoot a man who's given up." The boy, no older than fifteen, had baby-fat cheeks and full lips curling as if he had sucked a lemon. "Where's your unit? Fall in and march, soldier!"

"Seems to me we came here to shoot Rebs," the boy had grumbled as he trudged off. "Can't rightly win this war unless we shoot some Rebs."

Generals and politicians found them inconsistent, war and compassion, especially General Sherman, who preached that killing was the path to victory. Make the secessionists feel the pain of war, its malice and its injustice and its devastation, and the sooner the war would end and the sooner everyone could go home. And maybe the General was right. In the larger sense, maybe unrelenting and unmerciful killing was the way to win a war.

But not this time.

A DISTANT SCREAM, HOLLOW AND FORLORN, pierced the dense woods. Through the trees, faint light traced the outline of the hospital tent. Lanterns, like great fireflies, hung in the darkness, illuminating deep craters dug by cannon shells and trees cleaved at angles, their stout limbs cast away. Lying between stumps, horses and mules lay stiff and unmoving, their eyes milky and dull. Unburied soldiers, pale yellow in the lamplight, lay in rows as if on parade.

George led the party off the road to where two men squatted at a campfire, eyes staring blankly. Without looking up, one said, "Hospital's across the road there, and prisoners get took straight away, a few rods up the Pike. Look for a ravine."

George nodded and to Ben Entriken, he said, "Get some coffee. I'll meet you back here soon as I can," then led his prisoner up the road.

Walking by the light of campfires, they came upon a company of Michigan men laying in for the night. George managed to find coffee and offered some to his prisoner. The man who called himself Turner wrapped long fingers around the tin cup. He wore socks on his hands, holes cut for fingers and thumb.

"Real coffee." Turner breathed the steam rising off the fresh brew. "Been a long time since I had real coffee," he said. "Thank you, Sergeant. You're a good man."

George stared into the campfire where wet tinder snapped and hissed as if in argument with the flame. His head filled with anxious thoughts and he tried to bring them into focus. Three years of war come to this: dead horses and dead soldiers and an old man who wore socks on his hands to keep from freezing. Grant and Sherman preached callous, relentless killing. But someday, George reasoned, this war would end and we would have to live with these people, do business together, maybe even fight together against Mexico or France or somebody. Brutality bred a thousand tomorrows full of resentment and loathing. It was a future he wished no part of.

"How far is your home from here?" George asked.

"A couple miles, if I was a bird."

They wandered into the dimness beyond the firelight, descending into a narrow gully where prisoners huddled by a campfire. A trail through thick trees marked one end of the ravine. "Some great partridge and pheasant hunting off that way there." Turner nodded toward the trail. "And those woods have deer and even a bobcat or two."

George watched the other prisoners gathered by the fire, their heads bent low, hands to the flame. No hats, no coats. Most were in rags. Many had no shoes. A winter made more brutal by chance and circumstance. He closed his eyes and tried to imagine what hope looked like, and some dark murky channel that ran from his sense of duty to the core of his soul began to erode.

"Show me," he said.

Turner cocked his head, stared at George for a moment to weigh his words carefully, to be sure of their meaning. He looked over to where the Rebel prisoners gathered in silhouette against the campfire. Then he turned and walked down the trail into the woods.

George followed. They slipped between hickory and pine that closed over them like a great hood until there were shadows between the shadows, and George stopped. "Mr. Turner?" He waited. No reply save the whisper of darkness and the waving of the leafless trees.

George turned and walked out of the woods.

AT THE HOSPITAL TENT, A SKINNY YOUNG soldier sat against a broken caisson. He wore the familiar shiny, black stovepipe hat of the Eighth Wisconsin. George drew near and the man looked up. "Sergeant Van Norman?"

George recognized the long nose and square jaw of Private Ed Mason, Company K, and he nodded. George liked the man, son of a butcher. Shared the sausages sent by his family. Mason had often sung with the men, a high windy voice that hung in the air. George said, "What you got there, Private Mason?"

"Caught a spitfire in my leg," said Mason. "Not too bad, though. In the front, out the back, eh? Doc Murdock patched me up. I'll be up again in a week."

George slapped him on the shoulder as Ben Entriken emerged from a tent. "Hey, there, George. Ed here is waiting for the wagon to take him to town." Ben stood smiling in the yellow glow of the lanterns, both hands wrapped around a steaming cup of coffee as if it were a sacred urn. "You'll have to go back on your own," he said. "They're short-handed here. They want me to stay and work in the hospital."

"Where's the fun in that?" George said.

"Damn sight better than watching after you," he said. "Besides, Doc Murdock needs the help."

"Yes, but does he have my charming personality?"

"You take care yourself now, eh?" Ben said.

George made his way down the pike, the road no more than a dim path. Great rucks of men and munitions lay scattered in the forest and fields. Riders in the darkness chased him from the road and nervous pickets hailed him. Thick limbs shivered overhead and he quickened his step, his thoughts buried beneath the barren branches. He felt no guilt in allowing his prisoner to go free, a decision derived of circumstance. The man was but a tiny part of a vast army, a soldier who had lost the will to fight, trodden beneath a greater injustice, a man who simply longed for home and hearth. It was a small consideration, one George deemed of insignificant consequence in the grand strategy. And wasn't the war almost over anyway?

George walked steadily toward a light dimly visible in a clearing. He stepped carefully through the camp where the ground was strewn with sleeping men. In the glare of a small campfire, Corporal Billy Craven, steam rising from his thick hair, sat telling a story.

"…and Stosh is stuck being the cook because they all want to go hunting, eh? And so the hunters decide somebody complains about the food, he has to do the cooking. So Stosh takes the dead moose and cuts it up and makes a big soup and he throws in some gristle and some bone and even some part of the tail. Finally, he takes a handful of moose shit and stirs it up in the pot. Boys come back from hunting to eat supper, first fellow takes a taste and spits it out quick, and he says, 'This tastes like moose shit ... good, though.'"

Ole Anderson shook with laughter and Mike Mansion grinned broadly. George said, "If there's an audience somewhere, Billy will be telling jokes."

"Heya, Van!"

George sat and Billy Craven poured him coffee, steaming and thick. "What's this, Billy? Some more of your moose shit?"

"Looks like it, but doesn't taste as good," said Billy Craven. "Where's Ben?"

"Stayed to work in the hospital."

"Good spot for him," said Mike Mansion. "You see anyone else from the Company back there?"

"Just Ed Mason. Leg wound. He'll be all right."

Mike Mansion scratched an ear and brushed his rain-soaked hair from his eyes. "Glad they won't have to find a new tenor for their quartet," he said. "Ed has a good voice, he does."

"I'd miss his sausages from home," said Billy Craven. "He give me some once, eh? Mighty tasty!"

"Mr. Anderson, I picked this up at the hospital." George tossed him the familiar regimental dress hat, the Hardee hat, this one pierced neatly through the crown with a hole the size of a button. Anderson donned the hat with a toothy grin .

"Looks good on you, Swede," Mike Mansion said. (The company called Anderson "Swede," despite his Norwegian heritage. "It is easier to say than 'Norwegian,'" explained George when Anderson protested the insult.)

Mike Mansion rummaged through his ammunition pouch until he produced a small piece of swabbing, wrapped it on his ramrod, and cleared the barrel of his rifle. "You think them Rebs is high tailing it for home, George?"

"I would." George rolled up the collar of his woolen greatcoat. His mind fell upon the events of the day, the marching and the killing and the yellow lights of the hospital tent, shoeless prisoners standing in the frozen mud, and an old man with socks worn over long fingers holding a tin cup. Yes, that's what he would do, go back to Iowa County in the rolling hills of western Wisconsin. "Hell, man, time to turn in," he said. He poured the dregs of his coffee onto the ground. "There is plenty of work to be done in the morning."

Beyond their fire, silence filled the deep forest, eerie after the day's struggle, an army at rest, calm but not calm. A reverence. The firelight cast a pallid glow that made the woods lucent, as if ablaze. The trees stood out more solidly than by daylight, each branch pink and luminous as the moon, each twig and bud unique to every other. The men, too, were different in this light, their eyes red against their dusty yellow faces. George pushed a long branch into the fire and carefully set his rifle against a log to keep the barrel clear, then lay down and put his head on his arms. He closed his eyes then, and their muted voices surrounded him, comforting him and reminding him he was safe, that while he rested, men were busy holding the peace. And toward these disembodied sounds, his heart knew a moment of love.

George folded his hat over his ears. Sentries and messengers passed furtively, men stumbled in the darkness, soldiers searched for their units or maneuvered down the line. George did not hear them.

Noise seldom disturbed his sleep. He came from a large family, the youngest of ten children, sleep skills learned amid the bedlam that was home, the room he shared with older brothers, Michael, his mentor, and Junior, his tormentor. Junior, who claimed that Pa liked him best; it's why he was the namesake.

George's job for as long as he could remember had been to fetch water from the spring. Rain or shine, summer or winter, George tumbled out of bed, slipped on his brother's hand-me-down boots, snatched up the wooden bucket, and walked the fifty yards to where clear water bubbled out of the earth. That always amazed him. Where did the water come from? He had asked Junior once, who told him cow piss had filled up the earth like a sponge. All their walking around squeezed it up out of the ground. Pa gave them both a licking when George finally explained why he refused to wash up before supper.

Pa was born Jacob Van Norman, 1794, in Stroudsburg, Pennsylvania. After working land near Elmira, he moved to Wisconsin in '54 with his growing family. George was 12. Pa bought a farm, became a prominent Methodist, and got elected to political office. If asked, he would say, "I am a businessman," and farming was the family business. Jacob Van Norman had six sons and four daughters and they all worked the land.

Iowa County, Wisconsin, in summer was the prettiest place on the planet. Rich fields stretched for miles, their furrows rolling like a calm sea; cherry trees and apple trees exploded pink and white; sky a shade of blue he had never seen anywhere else. And thunderstorms! They would come up in an instant, sky suddenly smeared black with thunderheads rumbling horizon to horizon, pastures blasted with brilliant bolts of light, chased by thunderclaps that shook the shutters and rattled the dishes. Long slanting curtains of rain soaked the land, the fields shiny in the gray light.

And then the thunderstorm would pass, leaving deep puddles for splashing, earthworms everywhere. The sun would come out, and the birds would all talk about it, gather in the treetops and play their private system of phonetics: the "conk-a-reeeee" of the redwing blackbird, the "coo" of the mourning dove, the "rat-tat-tat" of the woodpecker. He could almost hear the tapping, "rat-tat-tat. Tat-tat-tat-tat."

"George!" Mike Mansion shook his shoulder. "Wake up, eh? Time to dance!"

A bugle confirmed it and the men were on their feet. The tat-tat-tat became sharp reports of muskets, and the peace of home dissolved from sleep to soldier.

Batteries on the summit of a wooded prominence called Compton's Hill awakened in the morning light and began a booming chorus, each shell screaming like the wheels of a rusty train as it gouged grave-size trenches into the earth. Musket fire to the south carried a staccato counterpoint. At the Pike, officers shouted orders and the men fell into step in a dragging weariness. Heads hung forward and shoulders stooped. George hefted his rifle and trudged alongside. Billy Craven, still buttoning his britches, hurried to keep up.

The roadway quickly crowded to overflowing as the army assembled for war. Beside them, white-topped wagons, driven by raving teamsters, swaggered like sheep. A caisson rumbled past, its horses already slathering and sweaty in their exertions. Orderlies and couriers lunged about, pushing aside those who seemed to be on less important errands. In a clearing behind a log home, Federal guns stood in a line, blazing and howling like devils on parade. George gaped as the huge monsters belched proudly. Great gouts of smoke spit fifty feet or more from the gun muzzles and scattered burning scraps of wadding to hiss on the icy ground. From a dozen places, fierce explosions blasted the hill, just two seconds from muzzle flash to target, showering its defenders.

"Must be hell up there," he muttered.

Billy Craven shouted, "Lamppost!" Artillery shell glimpsed in flight.

"Enough of them to light New York City, eh?" replied Mike Mansion.

They halted in a ravine and a soft rain began to fall, then heavier, some mixed with snow. Sleet turned the land to mud and the men huddled together in sodden groups. Teeth chattered a clicking noise between cannon blasts. Hours passed and they hunched under makeshift shelters of blankets and tarps as the rain fell at angles. Sporadic gunfire sounded from the east, skirmishers trading rounds near the Granny White Pike. Still they did not move.

"Hurry up and wait, eh, Mr. Van?" Ole Anderson shouted over the cannon noise. "At least in the woods there we was out of the rain. Now here we sit and soak like herring in a barrel, eh?"

Mike Mansion grinned at the big man and at the sprig of white-yellow hair that stuck through the hole in his hat. He said, "Keep your socks on," the men accustomed to tying socks to gun breeches to keep their powder dry. "You'll hear the hornets soon enough."

Finally, the shout, "Form up!" echoed down the line. A bugle sounded "Forward" and they began to climb the steep hill. George clambered across wet rocks and slippery footing, crouching low, the air alive with the familiar buzz of musket balls, the occasional ping on stone. Cannon shells ripped through the trees with a brittle noise; branch pieces and whole limbs fell like rain in their path. Men stumbled and lurched and scampered up the rough terrain. Many found shelter in the steepness of the slope where Rebel breastworks were behind the brow of the hill. Others fell in ragged heaps, tumbling and turning until coming to rest against stone or stump.

George pushed himself over rocks and fallen timber, Mike Mansion at his elbow, Billy Craven beside him. The steepness fought him. Whistling ribbons of fire stung the trees and pierced the ground. He came upon a dead soldier, his glassy stare a warning, and George strained to hug the earth as he climbed.

He reached a low shelf and scrambled over slick ground to a break between two boulders. Mike Mansion shouldered him aside and charged through the gap. Instantly, the hill warped and buckled in a blast of fire and smoke, and a great weight fell upon him. Barbaric noises and fierce bawling and the wail of a bugle all blended into a loud humming and George felt he might drown, bucked himself from under the heavy weight, and gasped. Mike Mansion lay in a grotesque heap, with a face but no face, his features black and distorted. George gagged. A choking spasm gripped him with a terrible strength, and he clutched at his throat and tried to spit but could not.

Another volley from the abatis and bits of stone slapped his face. He heard a low keening where Ole Anderson lay, and George scrambled to drag the boy behind a rock. "Swede!" he screamed above the noise. "Where does it hurt?" He began to loosen the man's coat buttons in search of a wound.

"My legs, Mr. Van. Feel kind of mushy." His head lolled lazily on the wet ground. "And I lost my hat."

George pushed the man's coat tails aside, searching, but could find no wound. "You're going to be all right," all he could think to say. Anderson made a feeble whining noise like a wounded dog. His head bobbed weakly, and his eyes were glassy and gray. George cradled the boy's head and felt the sticky wetness, a gaping wound bleeding in a deep red pool. Ear-splitting crashes and interminable thumpings made him dizzy and he could think only to retrieve the boy's hat and wrap it gently over his bloodied skull.

Another volley sounded and more men rushed forward, hurrying, screaming for victory or death, no compromise, no remorse. George stood, and a thunderous crash burst the trees, turning bits of splintered wood to lethal missiles. A hundred needles punched his face, and he reeled and fell to his knees, deaf to his own scream. With mud-covered fingers, he probed the wound across his cheek, located the offending splinter, and pulled it through his lip. His tongue wedged in the jagged hole and blood oozed into his mouth, salty and thick.

Officers shouted, urging the men forward with profane words. George went to stand, staggered, balanced on his rifle, and turned up the hill … and fell back again, his ears exploding, the taste of burnt wood on his tongue. His vision shrank and he was sucked below a great wave of blackness broken by tiny bubbles of light, pinprick stars that darted and danced. He reached to grasp one and hold on to keep from drifting, but the stars burst and he fell into a deep numbness of mind and body, alert but inert and not caring.

Around him, there was movement and jostling, the angry buzzing of wasps and long periods of silence, until at last he felt the pain, searing, as if from a branding rod. Across his chest, he suffered a crushing weight thick with leaves and limb and he reached to brush it away but could not. Rolling to one side, he saw an arm—a human arm—at the side of his face. He tried to push it away, and the arm moved. He flexed his fingers, and the arm's fingers flexed.

He saw and he understood, and he thought: "I am not dead."

CHAPTER FOUR

West of Nashville, December 16, 1864

I t wasn't the cold that woke him. It was the noise, a low growling outside his tent. But there was no tent. He remembered then.

Jacob Aney had wandered blindly in the darkness, searching for the Cumberland River. It was his plan to find a boat, smuggle aboard, and make his way north. He had seen no one, heard nothing. Just the wind and the trees and the cold. He was tired and hungry and wet, his long black coat little comfort. With the promise of more foul weather lurking under thick clouds, Aney had stretched out beneath the sheltering boughs of a tall pine, his bed made from wet needles. It even smelled like Christmas, he thought as he fell asleep at last.

Now fully awake, Aney pulled his heavy black coat about him, and the low growling came again. He stiffened, listening, but heard no sound. No birds were yet awake. Not even the wind stirred the pine branches above his nest. The fusty smell of wet earth filled his nostrils, and the musky odor of moss, too, snugged about him. He sat up slowly and pushed aside the pine branches.

Before him lay a low field dotted with scrub oak trees bent back to the earth as if struggling to free themselves. They leaned motionless; no branch or leaf moved. The tall grass, too, stood perfectly still as if waiting for matins. Across the field, he could make out a small building, a henhouse, in the mist. Where there were hens, there would be eggs. The growling sounded once more and he realized it was his stomach, its

28

cries of hunger amplified in the stillness. He rose then, and hunched his shoulders as he dashed across the open meadow. Just as he reached the henhouse, the rooster crowed and that set the dog to barking. The door of the house opened a moment later, and Jacob Aney missed his chance for an egg breakfast.

He trotted quickly back through the meadow. Hunger dogged him, his hardtack eaten hours ago, the growl in his stomach urging him to find nourishment. Time enough then to sleep in a thicket somewhere out of sight, maybe find an old barn or cooper's shop. He jumped a split-rail fence, the first he'd seen in days. Most fences had been stripped for firewood by one army or the other. It was small comfort to know he must be far away from the armies and the fighting. Nothing around him but woods and hills and the odd field that once had been plowed but now lay fallow.

He emerged from a thicket, and a ramshackle old house loomed out of the hazy dawn. He thought to circle wide around it until he saw the corncrib on the far side. Making his way along a stand of trees, he managed not to wake the dog or the rooster or any other animals that might give him up, grabbed two fistfuls of cob, stuffed them in his coat, and grabbed two more. Better than nothing. Just enough to keep him until he could smuggle aboard a boat headed north. Then home by Christmas.

If he could just find the damned river.

Climbing a steep grade, he came to an open area where movement caught his eye. He ducked into the tall grass, then poked his head up. Below him on a sandy swale were a boy and his 'coon dog. Must have been downwind, or the dog was no good, because it never barked. Aney steered clear around them, beyond a thicket, ran down a steep slope all the way to the bottom, and stumbled in water up to his knees. He grabbed at a tuft of wet grass for balance and sat heavily. His boot caught in the swamp muck with a slurping sound as if it meant to eat him.

"Hell of a way to find a river," he muttered and retrieved his boot.

The dog found him there, its long blue-gray body rigid, sniffing, curious, the boy with his gun likely not far behind. The dog stood stiffly, watching him, and Jacob Aney stared at the dog and considered what had to be done.

He held out his hand and rubbed his fingers together, made kissing noises with his lips. "Here, boy," he whispered. The dog snuffled once, its head bent low. "Here, boy," Aney said again.

The hound took a step toward him, and Jacob Aney put the knife in its neck, ripped forward to cut the throat before the dog could yelp. It fell to its side, shook its head slowly as if to shed the hurt, then lay still. He quickly stuffed it under the water, rinsed the blade, and scrambled for higher ground, keeping low in the reeds.

Far off, he heard the boy call, "Here, Jack! Come on, boy. Where you at?"

CHAPTER FIVE

Near Lynnville, Tenn. July 31, 1865

George awoke to the sun in his eyes, the kick-kack of the train beating a steady rhythm. He felt light-headed, as if the train car floated on the wind, hovering over farms where jagged lines of clotted grasses and misshapen weeds lay wilted against black earth. The train glided past a ramshackle house. On the crooked porch, a man leaned on crutches, one pant leg folded back and pinned. Past another house, a shed bent nearly sideways, empty. Slowly past the horse corral, empty. Past another field, empty. Beyond it, more fields, empty.

No animals could be seen. Horse, oxen, mule—all had supplied the Union Army long after the soldiers had moved on to Georgia and Alabama. George had heard about the Bummers, foraging squads who simply plundered a place empty, then moved on and took everything at the next farm: prosperity, faith, hope. Rape of the land. Supply depot for the Western Theatre. Breakdown of social order at every level. Anarchy inevitable. This was true throughout the South. But it seemed that nowhere had it rendered such ruin as in Tennessee.

George had a curious mind, one that needed reason and value in all things. For each cause, there must be an effect. For each credit, there should be a corresponding debit. Victory had been won. The cost lay before his eyes. He began to understand why these people held such contempt, such pitiless hatred, for anything Yankee. Their hate would not abate easily.

Seated across the aisle, two men talked in high tones. George heard the word "Wisconsin" and cocked his head to listen. Taken prisoner at Pea Ridge, the taller fellow had spent most of the war in a prison camp near Sparta. "Damn fine country," he drawled. "Half the year, anyway. January there was so cold, your spit froze afore it hit the ground."

George laughed to himself, until the man said, "Reckon I might go back, though. Good farmland there, and nothing for me here. The missus run off with some scalawag, thinking I was dead. Hell, I tried to write her, but no mail was going through."

What quirk of fate, George thought, this Confederate returning to Wisconsin, while George intended to stay in the South. How casually our destinies are set—as if chance taken by pitch-and-toss—that we should arrive at such meaningful verdicts in such random manner. A question of philosophy and geography.

He worried what his mother and father might think of him, what they might say to change his mind, if they would say anything at all. Would they even recognize him? He had left Wisconsin a skinny pup. Now the face staring back at him from the train window was an older man, his jaw line longer, cheeks heavier. He had grown a half foot and was bigger than he remembered any of his brothers. Their memory of him would be different in others ways, too. When he had enlisted, he held opinions that were, he admitted now, a product of his parents' views and prejudices. He still believed in his country and its aims; faith in the Union had not waned over those four years. But the war had not been the grand adventure he had once thought. It followed no reason or preconceived plan, but often took pointless and random paths. It offered no pity, no compromise. It had taught him the hardness of living, the finality of dying.

A few seats in front of him, two middle-aged women talked in hushed voices. The one in the blue bonnet craned her neck around, like an owl, to look at him, then quickly turned back. George felt grateful to be returning to the company of the regiment. Only a matter of hours now. Had it really been seven months?

* * *

South of Nashville, December 17, 1864

On Compton's Hill, he had awakened in darkness, a slow arriving of head and hands and fingers, sensations dulled by silence and strain and the smell of cordite. He heaved himself against tree fall, a trunk broken and twisted, and slowly fitted his shattered arm into a makeshift sling fashioned from a ramrod and a torn shirt. A heavy rain pelted his face and soon washed away any fog his mind had used to blunt his pain. George pushed his back to the shattered trunk until he could gather his feet beneath him and wander off the hill.

He came to a clearing where men, blood stained and grim, passed him without notice, their faces glowing as if lit from within. They crowded together in stern postures and uttered no sound. One walked with aid of a stick, his bare toes dragging a bloody trail. Another moved as if in a trance, the gray pallor of death upon his face, his lips curled and biting. In the distance was the sound of voices and George followed them to a road where officers shouted orders, teamsters cursed at their mules, and orderlies unloaded wagons carrying wounded soldiers. Beneath a stand of leafless trees, a flag of torn yellow bunting, a green letter H in the center, waved over the large hospital tent. Inside, dozens of soldiers lay on tables and makeshift cots. Several wore Confederate uniforms. The smell of decay, like old meat, hung heavy in the still air as the rain drummed against the canvas walls.

An orderly pointed to a stool and George sat. The surgeon was a tall and round-shouldered man with full whiskers matted against his ruddy cheeks. He wore a leather smock black with dried blood. Bending over a wounded man, his grim face reflected the lantern glow, a dullness in his eyes as if Death had wrestled with him. From a table laden with equipment, the surgeon chose a long knife, lifted his foot, and stropped the blade across the sleeve of his boot. He examined the wounded man's arm that no longer looked like an arm, and drew a circle clear around the shoulder with his knife. Blood oozed, then spurted, and the surgeon busily tied knots. Moments later, George heard clearly the rasp of saw, brittle and numbing. An orderly in bloodied shirtsleeves cast aside the severed limb. It fell atop a heap of arms and legs, a pool of red-brown liquid draining from the pile, spreading across the dirt floor. Soldiers brought more wounded and the surgeon stepped forward, wiped his hands on the soaked leather apron, and reached for the saw with its blackened teeth, and George cast his eyes away.

Outside, more wounded lay on boards and makeshift cots. Orderlies walked briskly among them as if searching for answers in the darkness. More wounded arrived on carts. Still more stood about, their faces pinched as if biting sour candy, their eyes staring at nothing. George held no fellowship with the spectral figures, did not belong among them, did not feel remotely akin to them. From a passing orderly, he snatched a strip of gauze. "Hab you seen the Eighth Withcobbin?" he asked.

"What?" The man looked at him as if he had uttered gibberish.

"The Eighth Withcobbin Reg'ent." The words tumbled from George's swollen lips.

"Some fellows with them same stovepipe hats were headed down yonder." The man pointed and George trudged off in search of his friends.

From a cavalry captain, he learned his regiment had marched on without him, chasing Hood's men. At daybreak, George hitched a ride on the caisson of an artillery blacksmith, the steaming forge warming him as he cradled his arm on the bumpy road. The gray-bearded blacksmith sucked salt candies and spoke in broken English, his German accent thick and guttural. George, his upper lip in heavy bandage, spoke not at all. They gestured and pointed and mimicked great stories and worldly accomplishments, and George felt a kinship with the older man.

The forge rumbled past wagons loaded with injured men, steam rising from their open wounds, their moans and cries fading as they passed. All around were the remnants of war. Scattered among the frozen joe-pye weed lay the detritus of the Army of Tennessee: discarded haversacks, muskets broken and abandoned, a wagon wheel, its shattered spokes like hungry teeth in the wind. Rebel prisoners, sullen and brooding, filed north in long lines. Many were wrapped in blue blankets stamped "U.S."

At each stop along the Pike, the husky blacksmith set to work with intense concentration, firing the forge until it glowed a particular orange. Hammer and tongs brought form and function to iron scraps and oddments. The smithy shaped tools and repaired transport for grateful soldiers and citizens alike, while George sought news of the regiment, following their path further south as they chased General Hood's fleeing army.

At Franklin, they rattled across the Harpeth River on a rough plank bridge. Through a thin veil of fog, they could see broken war machines lay scattered indiscriminately across a broad field. The smithy stopped the forge on a small rise and sat gaping. Bones rooted up by swine lay bleaching in the raw December air. Resting half buried in the frozen ground, a rotting shoe sprouted a skeletal foot. A grinning skull rose from the earth on a pale neck bone still sporting a silk cravat tied in a fashionable knot. The scene had a nightmare quality, a haunted place where some mad beast of Hades made sacrifice to Moloch. George's companion swore harsh epithets and hurried his mule for some distance.

The two men spent Christmas Day at a tavern in Spring Hill. Dropping into a heavy oaken chair, George slowly removed the bandage from his lip and hurriedly discarded it. Beer felt cool upon his tongue. The smithy offered George sausage from his haversack and said, "*Frohe Weihnachten.*"

George nodded and said, "*Danke.*" The smithy smiled broadly and they drank long into the night.

West from Pulaski, at a crossroads the locals called Goodspring, George bid the smithy "*Auf Wiedersehen*" on the first morning of the New Year. There, in a low meadow, were scattered tents and soldiers wearing the familiar Hardee hats, and his wounded spirit lifted at the sight of them. He stuffed his sling under his shirt and hung his thumb on his belt to hold his throbbing arm. Rubbing the scar over his lip, he felt the coarse bristle of beard.

Billy Craven spotted him as he strode into camp. "Well, looky here, you guys. Hello, if it ain't Mr. Van." Men squatting by their campfires stood to greet him. "Come to call just like a preacher on a Sunday."

George nodded to each of the men in turn, exchanging greetings, boisterous and renewed. A slap on his back gave a sharp sting to his arm, but did not quell his enthusiasm. George was home and so it did not matter.

Ben Entriken emerged from his tent. "Where have you been, Van? We thought we might have lost you." He spoke in a reluctant tone, as if admonishing a favorite child. "Good to have you back among the living." Ben shook the hand George proffered, then said, "Say, Ed Mason asked about you. Before he went up."

George blanched. Just a simple leg wound. He had not expected the man to die. His mind brought forth a brief vision of the surgeon and his blackened saw.

"He gave me something for you," Ben said, and ducked inside his tent.

"I thought he wath gonna bake it," said George, struggling with the words over his scarred lips.

Ben emerged with an envelope. "There was little they could do," Ben said as he toed the muddy ground. "Infection. Had to take off his leg. He died the day after Christmas."

George sat on a small canvas stool, opened the letter clumsily, and found another folded inside. The first, poorly scribbled by the dying man: "George," it said. "Take this to Racine when you get home. Good work there for you." It was signed simply, "Mason." The second was a letter of introduction to Mason's father, a businessman in Racine, Wisconsin.

Reading the words, George tried to picture Ed Mason, skinny, brown hair curled over ears that hung on his head like open doors. Ed Mason, who had sung in quartet around many a campfire, who had shared sausages from home. One tin cup the quartermaster should not have hung on his wagon.

George carefully refolded the letters and tucked them inside his shirt. He left his kit beside Ben's tent and wandered onto the meadow where the matted grass lay trampled into the muddied earth. George hunched his shoulders to the chilling wind and imagined he could hear *Nelly Bly* in high harmony beneath the brittle grinding of the surgeon's saw.

He came upon the canopy of a large dust-colored tent. Inside, Lieutenant Sherman Ellsworth conferred over a map table with Major Bartlett and other officers George did not know. Ellsworth's thin face topped a long neck, and his hair hung in thin strands. "Hi'ya, Van!" he said. "What's that hanging from your nose? You get yourself a pet mouse?" His eyes crinkled and his head bobbed when he talked.

George tried to smile, one side of his mouth refusing to cooperate, a lopsided grin. "Good abbernoon, thir." He saluted stiffly. "Thergeant George Van Norban rebording for duty. And it's a bustache, sir, or at least it's a thtart."

Bartlett returned his salute. "Let us finish up here, Sergeant, and maybe we can find some way you might be useful." He returned to his map.

"Yes, thir." George saluted once more and turned to go.

"Find yourself a spot on the line, George," Ellsworth called after him. "And get yourself some food. I'll catch up later."

George wandered among tents laid out neatly in company streets. Soldiers squatted on sawed stumps or camp stools to play cards or write letters. In a small meadow, recruits drilled by the nines. "Load-Hand-Tear-Charge-Draw-Ram-Return-Prime-Hup. Load-Hand-Tear-Charge-Draw-Ram-Return-Prime-Hup."

George sat at a long wooden table in the open-sided mess tent. He mopped his hardtack in bacon fat and gingerly sipped coffee from a tin cup, its steam rising in soft plumes. The smell of wood smoke filled his head and he breathed it in great gulps. He turned to the sound of boots slogging in the soft mud.

"Hi, George," Ellsworth said. "Find a cozy spot for your kit?" The lieutenant laid his hat on the rough slat table, gently blocked it with his knuckles, then dabbed a smudge with his thumb. "Well, pack it up again," he said. "The major has a mission for you. Detached service." Ellsworth reached for the coffee pot, poured, sipped carefully from his steaming cup. "This war is all but over, George. General Sherman is in Savannah. Grant has about whipped the Army of Northern Virginia. When Lee surrenders, Washington fears many of the Secesh may just go into the hills and keep on fighting." He put down his cup. "It's our job to protect the locals."

Ellsworth swung a leg over the bench before continuing. "There have been reports of bandits and bushwhacking all over Tennessee. It's a mess. Barns burned, livestock stolen, people robbed and beaten. Some have been killed." He paused, dabbed another smudge from his hat. "Worst thing is some of it is being done by our own, George. Yankee foragers. And some deserters, too." He took a piece of paper from his coat pocket. "A prominent landowner has asked for protection."

George stared, his mouth agape. Protection?

"I know it sounds crazy, but landowners are the ones who will have jobs for the soldiers when the war ends. If we are to have peace, there has to be a way of life for the Johnnies to return to, something to keep them from taking to the hills and fighting on for who knows how long." He unfolded the document and set it beside his hat. "These are your orders," he said as if reading the page. "You are to proceed to Columbia and once there, to procure victuals and outfit for an indefinite stay at a plantation about twenty miles northwest." He looked at the document. "A place called Elm Grove."

George took the paper and began to read.

Ellsworth said, "Forrest has been spotted just across the river. We could move any time. You're not..." he hesitated. "You're not fit for fighting, George," he said, quietly. "This will be easy duty. You just have to wear your uniform, guard the plantation, and protect it from rowdy foragers and the like. You can have a real bed, clean linens, even a hot bath when you want it."

George stared at the orders, tried to measure its message in his mind.

"I understand how you must feel, George," Ellsworth said. "And when your arm is better, you can rejoin the regiment." He put aside his coffee and stood. "In the meantime, you guard the plantation and stay out of trouble. And this place—Elm Grove—might be right nice." His conviction seemed lost in the telling, his words plaintive, tentative.

George had grown accustomed to life by routine and schedule. The regiment was his home, the company his family, the army his security. It had been an easy transition from growing up on a farm: awake before dawn, exhausting chores, and long days of routine. Same as the army. Even battle had its manifest habits: extend the lines, engage the enemy, flank and forward and oblique as required until the position is overrun and the enemy beaten. Standing guard over some wretched Rebel farm would mean unfamiliarity, a departure from customs acquired over a lifetime. Protecting landowners, those aristocrats with their slaves and their pompous politics; they were the ones responsible for this war, not the poor working men who were made to fight it. They were the ones who had strutted and swaggered and boasted of a quick Southern victory. And now they demanded "protection?" There promised to be nothing routine about such duty. George felt overcome by a wave of disappointment. This was not the homecoming he had expected. His mind reeled in frustration and he struggled to control his thoughts, to keep from pounding a fist into the wooden table and uttering words that would fall bitter and resentful. He deliberately filled his lungs with the crisp air and held it for a moment.

"Day after tomorrow is soon enough," Ellsworth said quietly. "Draw whatever gear you need from the quartermaster in the morning."

George nodded, folded the paper, and put it in his pocket. "Habby New Year, Sherm," he said.

CHAPTER SIX

West of Nashville, December 16, 1864

Jacob Aney saw the face of his mother and she was laughing, her chin bobbing lazily, her voice low and throaty, rumbling in rhythms like deep drumbeats. He saw his family at supper, sausages on the table and packages wrapped in ribbons, a Christmas dinner with James and Pa holding court, their laughter muted as if from behind closed doors. Beyond them, through an open window, came the sounds of rain and wind battering the shutters in long cadences. The rain began to flood a meadow, a meadow of still grass and bent oak trees. The meadow washed into a marsh where it became a bog, and from it, a dog slowly rose to the surface, its eyes yellow and staring. It rolled its head to him and growled menacingly, a snarling rumble like thunder.

Jacob Aney woke to the sound. He tried to swallow but his lips stuck shut, pine dust thick on his tongue. He turned to rise, felt cold iron on his cheek, and saw the muzzle of a hunting rifle. Behind the blackened barrel, a young boy wore a Rebel cap with the brim half torn, well-worn butternut coat and pants, and flimsy shoes tied with twine. His hair was matted under his hat and his face was dirty, deep gray eyes hidden beneath half-open lids.

"Whoa, there, young man," Jacob said, rolling away. "Aren't you being a bit unfriendly?"

He tried to sit up but the boy nudged him with the barrel. "You a Yankee?"

Jacob Aney eyed him a moment, then looked around, searching the woods for sign of any companions, but could find none. "Yes, I am," he said from his elbows. No sense in denying it.

"Why you dressed like that? You look like a preacher," said the boy.

Aney looked at his clothes, feet poking from his trousers like overripe corn, his long black coat parted at his knees like the wings of some wounded bird. Nothing for it, he decided. Best to just brass it out. He sat up. "That's right," he said. "I have come here to preach the righteousness of our Lord, against the evils of war, and for the goodness of the peoples of this great state of Tennessee." It was the kind of thing his preacher back home might say.

The boy stared at him, probably hadn't been to church in a while. "Why's a preacher sleeping on the ground? In the middle of the day, too. Don't traveling preachers sleep in churches or folks' houses? And them brogans is soldier boots," he said. "Yankee soldier boots."

"Well, now, that's right observant of you, my young man. Right observant," said Aney. "But if you just let me show you my papers, I can prove I'm a preacher."

As he clambered to his feet, Jacob Aney swung his foot and kicked the muzzle aside. He lunged for the boy, knocked him over, and snatched the gun. The boy fell hard and Aney stood over him. "What's your name, boy?"

"Buck," the boy said, rubbing his shoulder. "Buck Turner. And I ain't no boy." He stood up. "I's old enough to shoot Yankees."

"I'll bet you are," said Aney, eyeing the old weapon. Then he deftly dislodged the priming cap and handed back the gun. "Here. A preacher has no use for such things. But I don't like them facing my way, just the same."

Buck snatched it. "I'm going to join up soon as General Hood gets to here," he said. "Kill me some bluecoat scum, just like my brother."

Thunder rolled through the meadow once more and Jacob Aney began to gather his few belongings. "Your brother?"

"Yep, his name's Jimmy."

"And you say he's with General Hood?"

"That's right, and he's killing Yankees as we stand here. You can hear 'em." And the boy pointed.

Thunder no thunder at all, but the rumble of cannon, hundreds of them. A massive battle raged beyond the distant hills.

"That's Nashville over yonder," said Buck. "And them are Hood's cannon. Giving the Yankees a good going over, I'd say, by the sounds of it."

Aney eyed the boy. "How do you know those are Rebel cannon, young man? They could be Yankee cannon giving it to General Hood."

Buck grinned. "Cain't," he said, and tugged at the brim of his cap.

"They could be."

"Cain't."

"Why not?"

"Just cain't." The boy turned and began to walk through the low brush, keeping to a path only he seemed to know.

Aney followed. "Sounds like Yankee cannon to me," he challenged.

"Cain't," said the boy without turning around.

Aney hurried to catch up. Cannon thunder continued, sometimes rising, pausing, then rising again. "Yep, that's definitely Yankee cannon," he said.

Buck stopped, turned. "Cain't be," he said. "'Coz we pissed the shells."

"You what?"

"We pissed the shells," Buck said. "When the supply trains come down from up north, they set for a spell on the west river track. Me and my friend, Pitch, we hopped the cars and pissed the shells. Makes them rust up good so's they cain't fire." He said it like "far."

Cannon thunder grew louder and Aney looked at the sky. Kid piss and cannon shells? Sergeant Van Norman had never taught anything about artillery. But if Union cannon could not support the infantry, the attack was doomed. Hood could take Nashville and keep going. There was nothing to stop him all the way to Chicago. War might go on for years.

"One of them bluecoats caught us up as we was leaving the train, but we outrun him." The boy grinned, his face animated. "Big fat Yankee with his belly flopping and bouncing, trying to run after us. Me and Pitch almost gave away our hidey hole, we was laughing so loud. Had to stifle myself just to keep still." Slapped his thigh. "Hah, we must have drunk half a barrel of spring water working up to it, but we went back and pissed them shells again later that same night. That was two days afore Saturday."

Jacob Aney leaned against a gnarly oak. Cannon thunder seemed at once far away, sometimes directly overhead. He took off his forage hat and shook the water from the brim, thought again about the river, where he might get on board a boat, head north. Maybe this boy could be of some use, and he tried to work out in his mind how to do it, how to get help from this young boy with the baby face and the old man's eyes. "When was the last time you were in church, my boy?"

Buck stared at the ground. "Been some time, I suppose. Our preacher went off to the war like everybody else," he said. "He used to tell us Bible stories, all about how God was on the side of the righteous. He said God rides with General Lee."

Jacob Aney didn't know what to say to that.

"You ain't seen a dog around here, have you? I was 'coonin' with Jack—that's my dog—but he ain't come back."

"I'm sure he'll turn up," Aney said.

"Yeah, he's probably to home already. I best be getting, too. Ma'll have supper on the table." The boy turned up the path. "You, too, Mr.

Preacher Man. More rain's a-coming and you look like you could gain by getting out of the weather."

Jacob Aney smiled. "How far is your place?" he asked.

"Down yonder," said Buck, and he disappeared through the brush.

FROM THE SMALL CABIN'S LONE WINDOW where she prepared supper, Mildred watched the preacher step into the yard and her sodden dishrag dropped to the floor. Had he come to tell her news of Jimmy? She had had no word from her son for nearly six months, but she knew he was with Hood and the Army of Tennessee, and knew they were camped somewhere near Nashville. It had entered her mind that Jimmy might find his way home, if only for a short spell.

A right good boy, oh, yes, but he was a handful to be sure. To some, he was a peck of trouble, sharp-tongued and short-tempered, like his pa. Just like his pa. It was why she loved him, worried for him, but hoped it would make him a good soldier.

Now here come a preacher, though not one she recognized. Behind him, she could see Buck, her other boy, spirited like Jimmy, but a smart boy, and dependable. Wonder what he's doing with a preacher? They seem to be talking, friendly enough. She bent slowly to retrieve the fallen rag and wiped her hands.

The cabin door opened. "Good evening, ma'am." The preacher tipped his broad-brimmed hat.

He was polite, she thought, and he was smiling. But he wasn't from around here. Talked like a Yankee. Surely he would not bring bad news about Jimmy.

"Your boy and I were just discussing the wonderful smells coming from your fine home."

Just like a preacher, Mildred thought, full of baloney and his hand out for a meal. And him with the nice hat and the fancy coat.

"I found him sleeping in the woods, Ma, over by the creek. Says he's a preacher."

"Your son has been most helpful, ma'am," said the man, "And most entertaining, I might add. He has regaled me with several enthralling stories."

Regaled? Damned Yankee, using high-faluting language. Mildred shifted her weight in the doorway, thinking hard about the man who stood before her. He is a man of the cloth. Probably had some schooling. Despite hard times, we ain't so bad off we can't be civil. Best to ask him to set for a spell.

He thanked her and she looked him over, his hat all dirt crusted, pine needles like pinfeathers mud-stuck to his trousers. "You might like to wash up by the well pump. Buck'll show you."

"That's right cordial of you, ma'am," he said, but she had already closed the door.

THE PREACHER SAT AT THE ROUGH-HEWN wood table, smiling as he admired the bowls of warm food—potatoes and turnips and salt pork and fresh eggs, hard-boiled. He picked up the bowl of turnips and heaped a ladleful on his plate, then began eating. "Tell me, ma'am, do you know anything about shipping on the river, when the boats come and go and such?"

Mildred thought about this. Here this fellow says he's a preacher, and yet he's stuffing his mug without so much as a nod of his head to the good Lord. He don't act like no preacher; don't even have no Bible. What's a preacher want to know about boats? Could be he's maybe a bushwhacker? Plenty of them around these parts, fellows who roam the roads looking for an easy meal. They take whatever they can, leave you for dead. She had heard talk. Scavengers and such who will just as soon cut your throat as look at you.

"Only boats on the rivers are Yankee gunboats," Buck said as he served himself a helping of potatoes.

Mildred said, "Maybe you'd like to say a prayer over the food, Mr. Preacher." Buck put down his fork and stared at his mother.

"Yes, of course." The preacher set down the basket of cornbread, carefully folded his hands, and bowed his head. "Dear Lord," he began. "We thank you for all this fine food and for your son's good health, I mean for Mildred's son here, Buck, rather, and for her health, too, and for all the animals here at this fine place that give of themselves for this fine food and the good earth where they grow the crops and also please give good weather so the crops can grow and give more food later." He looked up, first to Mildred, then to Buck, as if wondering whether it sounded as bad to them as it did to him. "Amen."

Buck looked at his mother again, then began to eat, chewing noisily. Mildred wondered how a preacher couldn't even say a decent meal prayer. She frowned at Buck, caught his eye while the preacher was busy slathering jam on his cornbread, and gave a quick shake of her head.

Buck caught the look, nodded. He asked the preacher, "Can you recite some scriptures? I always like to hear them stories about Daniel and Goliath. Or that one about Noah and the whale."

The preacher stopped his chewing and looked at the boy, then at Mildred. He smiled and said, "I'll be happy to tell you a Bible story. But why don't we finish our supper first?" He returned to his plate.

Buck stopped eating. Mildred's eyes grew wide. There was a scraping noise as Buck pushed away from the table, and the man was in motion. Buck and the preacher both dived for the rifle standing by the door, but the preacher shouldered the small boy aside and grabbed the weapon.

Looming behind him, Mildred wielded a carving knife, long as her forearm, and Jacob Aney swung the gun like a club. She folded over and fell, groaned once, and rolled to her side. The preacher brought the butt of the gun down hard on the side of her head and she lay still.

TIED UP, THE BOY SLEPT FITFULLY on the narrow bed. The air was chilly and the small fireplace gave little heat. The boy's mother lay on the floor in the dim light, hours and she had not moved. Probably dead by the looks of her, but Aney did not want to touch her to find out. It was not that he had meant to hurt her, but they had forced him. They weren't believing his story, and they weren't willing to help him find a boat.

Aney considered returning to the regiment to warn them of the rotten timing fuses, of the boy with his overactive bladder. But he doubted there was anything to it, and they would simply arrest him anyway, throw him in the stockade. He had no choice but to run, try to find the river, maybe steal a small boat and paddle downstream to the great Mississippi. Then, catch a steamer, or talk his way aboard a hospital ship heading north. North, and home.

Aney sat against the cabin wall, the boy's old rifle over his knees, his mind filling with preparations and plans. At first light, he would take some food, maybe the carving knife, and make his way north and west until he found the river. By the time the boy shook loose, or someone came by and found him and his mother, Jacob Aney would be far away. Christmas in Wisconsin. Warm fire, colored candles on the table, and gifts under the tree, maybe sing Christmas songs.

He wasn't sure what awakened him. His eyes opened and he sat alert, searching the room. The woman lay where he had struck her; the boy slept, tied into his bed. A soft "thunk" against the door and he was on his feet. He turned to the small cabin's only window where he cast a dim reflection, his own eyes staring back at him. Again, a noise outside, soft scratching as if a cat, by habit, sought shelter for the night.

He checked the musket prime and slowly opened the door. Darkness outside complete, he could see nothing but his own shadow from the firelight winding down the path. One more look inside, checking on the boy, and he turned…

He had not taken a step when he felt a soft scratch across his neck, tried to cry out, but heard no voice. The musket fell and he grabbed for his throat, stared in shock at the blood, warm and thick on his fingers. His chin fell and he glimpsed a knife, its handle gripped by long fingers wrapped in socks. And then the muddy ground came up and struck him, and he rolled, looked up to see only blackness, and amid the blackness, even the blackness ceased.

CHAPTER SEVEN

Watersmith Plantation, January 2, 1865

Two men emerged from the main house. One was tall and rangy beneath a long black coat. He walked easily, yet with serious purpose. The second was larger and heavier, a great brute of a man with long arms that swung in wide arcs. In his hand, he carried a chicken leg that he chewed between strides. Bits of skin and gristle fell to the earth as he walked.

William Slive thought best when he ate. Food seemed to put his body parts to rest so his mind parts could get to figuring on things, make them solid in his head. Thinking came hard to Slive. It was his way to ponder on things, weigh the good parts and bad parts, seeing how people might prove useful, how outcomes could favor William Slive, then go ahead. Eating always helped.

His mind now turned to his missing mule. Some coloreds had been seen that same morning, walking on this same road. "Damn niggers! They stole my mule." He spoke in guttural tones, the sound like two rocks rubbing together. "If I catch them, they'll need wings to save them. That's for damn sure."

His tall companion spoke with an easy drawl. "We'll find your mule."

Slive narrowed his eyes and weighed the value in the man's words. What kind of person could this one be? Scalawag? Deserter? A thief like all them others who have come around of late? This fellow looked like a preacher, what with that big black coat hanging past his knees, and the black hat. But he looked undependable-like, sort of shifty. The type you never know what he's thinking.

Slive stopped at the open door of a barn gray with age, the boards warped and bent like old paper, "Uppity niggers is what they is." He slammed the barn door, rocking it on its rusty hinges. "Damn! We give them everything they need. Then they goes and takes what ain't theirs."

The property was in a sorry state, crops all gone, and no help around to plant more come spring. Yankees stole anything they got their Yankee hands on. Now niggers taking stuff, too. Slive had even seen some coloreds squatting on his land, his own land. Uppity niggers! The mule was his. He wanted it back. Simple as that.

The man in the long coat spoke evenly as he stepped toward the rail fence at the end of the dirt path. "We'll find your mule," he said again, and he squatted on the muddy ground to pick up a clod of hardened dirt.

His hands were covered in socks to protect them from the weather, and when his coat fell open, Slive saw a long knife at his belt.

"Been gone just a few hours by the look of it," the man said. "Where do you keep the horses?"

Slive squinted to where the man stood gazing up the road. "Got 'em hid," he said, and he turned on his heel to lope back toward the barn.

Horses were scarce in Middle Tennessee. Those not taken by Confederate cavalry had been confiscated by Yankee foraging parties. But he was William Slive and he knew how to outsmart both armies. A shed by the barn appeared to be a part of the main structure, but it had a separate entrance, and room for two horses behind a false wall. Slive felt a certain smugness in this deception. Horses he had.

Now, it was his mule he wanted, and moments later, both men were mounted and galloping north on a muddy trail that cut through thick forest of beech and old oak, a road known for centuries as the Natchez Trace.

CHAPTER EIGHT

Giles County, Tenn., July 31, 1865

K ick-kack. The train lurched over a newly built trestle, and George righted his hat. Across the aisle, a woman in fine silks sat with a man in starched shirt and fancy tie. The man stared at him under heavy white eyebrows. George felt their animosity wash over him, a seething current just below the surface of Southern decorum, where a mix of pride and resentment drifted beneath their restraint.

George took off his hat and put it on his lap. These were not his people. He worried that he might never know what it was to be one with them, to mix with them, befriend them, gain their respect, and accept their kindnesses. The Judge had hoped that whatever bitterness they held might fade in time. Maybe in a year, he had said. Maybe.

The train slowed on a grade and trees darkened the dusty windows. George's reflection startled him. His hair lay matted, and deep shadows across his face foretold a future of labor and anguish. His shirt had dried to a stiffness that chafed, and he hunched further into his seat. Outside, the clouds gave way as the sun fell below the tree line, and the land took on a brownness as if he were looking through an old stereoscope. The squalid countryside had somehow melted into the brown landscape. In their drab greens and browns, these forest and fields looked like any forest or fields anywhere.

A lone horseman rode alongside the slow-moving train, and George nodded when the man tipped his hat. He had a scrubbed look about him, whiskers trimmed, a crease to his trousers. When he turned his horse, George saw the carpetbag behind his saddle. It had a red design and looked new.

George sat up. Was that how others saw him? "Painted with the same brush," the Judge had said. Was George Van Norman just another carpetbagger come to pillage the people of Tennessee? George peered at the rider as if he held answers, but the man veered onto a wooded path and the brownness took him.

Lieutenant Ellsworth had done his best to reassure him, but when George left the regiment, he suffered an uneasiness that stayed with him on the road to Elm Grove. He had no idea what to expect, so he left Columbia with just a week's provisions, alone and abandoned without the next rank on his flank, reserves at his back. He held his injured arm carefully, a throbbing with every movement. His .50-caliber rifle lay in its scabbard, but he feared the consequences if he had to use it. His arm was too weak to support the heavy stock and too fragile for close fighting. The only horse that could be spared limped badly, one of the 2nd Iowa Battery's old caisson carriers that had been wounded at Nashville. The animal, unaccustomed to carrying passengers, seemed more edgy than George, and her uneven gait made him queasy so he walked alongside.

He wound his way through the Duck River Valley, past fields gone to sedge and cedar. The moist air clung to his skin and he felt a chill that ran to his boots. High above him, large birds, dozens of them, wove a lazy pattern, gliding and plunging soundlessly against a sky of deep pewter, dull and overcast.

The leafless trees twisted in ellipses, their garish limbs stark and throbbing. Each creak and crackle of branch and bough held mystery, each cluster of bush some secret enemy. Every shadow summoned imagined evils—bushwhackers or brigands, devious hooligans or scattered remnants of Nathan Bedford Forrest's cavalry. And he, gallant knight, plantation peacekeeper, had come to slay the beasts! "Hell, man!" he muttered.

Who were these bushwhackers and bandits? And what drove them to steal what little remained in the countryside? It did not take long to guess at the reasons. Easy liberty and license had grown commonplace, as if by right. What had begun as simple pity for hungry soldiers—a cup of water or a warm supper freely given—had quite easily led to begging. Foraging, condoned by both armies, had led quite naturally to stealing. From begging food to stealing food to stealing other things were easy steps.

Soldiers were but one of the lot. The colored people, newly freed and homeless, were forced to provide for themselves for the first time. Hundreds roamed the countryside. Many interpreted freedom as the right to take what had been denied them for so long. He had heard reports of some who ransacked their masters' homes, even killed their former owners. Simply for the pure freedom of it.

Beneath the covering sky, more birds circled in the still air. He watched them, curious. On a ledge high above the sunken road, an old oak stood crooked in the mist. Hanging from a limb were great sacks of grain or coal, two of them. Big black birds darted in and out, squawking.

George stared at them, wondering exactly what he was seeing, until the smell hit him like a fist, and he retched. The birds scattered at the sound. High above his head, a colored man and woman hung from a gnarled limb, hands tied behind their backs, bodies bloated, blackened tongues poking from their mouths. The man was stripped to the waist, chest crusted with blood.

A moment of fear gripped him and he cocked his rifle and peered into the woods. Nothing. No sound but his steady breathing. Kerchief to his mouth, he tied his horse to a branch and stepped forward to read

THEF

carved across the man's swollen torso.

What manner of beast would defile another human being like this? Where in the heart of a man did such hideous cruelty abide? In battle, the enemy was decided, the battle lines clearly drawn. Despite its brutality, war had rules, conventions, principles. This gruesome atrocity sustained his worst fears and he cursed wild epithets for what seemed like minutes.

A light wind came up and he coughed, the foul odor of decay seeping through the kerchief, palpable and repugnant. Perched safely above the morbid scene, a murder of crows kept wary vigil in the oak branches.

George took a long breath, then stepped beside the tree and slashed at the hanging rope with his knife. The man dropped from the tree and fell in a heap. The birds scattered, screeching and flailing into the early-morning sky. George steadied himself and slashed at the second rope. The woman fell atop the man.

Kerchief again to his mouth, he examined the bodies. Inside the man's pocket, he found a train schedule for Pulaski Station. Nothing more. He rolled the bodies into a shallow depression and clumsily covered them with dirt and rock, then laid a large tree limb to keep the animals away. Before moving on, he removed his hat and bowed his head. Two crows landed near the grave and sat quietly as if to pay homage.

* * *

Hickman County, Tenn., January 5, 1865

George led the mare up a winding path overgrown with weeds and thistles. Beside him, a fence bordered the driveway, many of its rails missing or broken. Further along, he saw piles of rock strewn about a field, with many more stones partially hidden in deep grass.

The path curved beneath twin rows of elm that formed a high arch of leafless limbs. Beyond the trees, the big house, hidden at first by a roll of the land, came into view. Red brick, it had wide stone steps leading to a porch framed by weather-stained pillars. Twin gables revealed a third story. Shutters, their missing slats like spaces in bad teeth, framed rows of tall windows to either side of the door. To one side and set well back stood the stable, long and low, its paint blistered in chips the size of flapjacks. Further west, the path continued to where a row of smaller buildings lay among dense undergrowth.

George hitched the mare to a post at the front of the house and stood for a moment. All around were signs of abandonment and decay. It might have been a prosperous farm not unlike many in Wisconsin, but it had been allowed to deteriorate for lack of labor. Chores he had so dutifully performed back home stood begging here. Boards needed paint. Weeds choked the garden. Neglect lurked everywhere.

A soft breeze rustled the naked elms as he walked up the stone steps and rapped on the great oak door. He waited, but no sound came from the house. As George lifted his hand to knock once more, the door opened. A huge man stood before him, black as toast, one shoulder brushing each doorframe, a striking figure clad in faded evening coat and matching pants. A small tear at the knee, neatly sewn, matched another on the same elbow. The man wore no shoes and his large feet were gnarled and twisted, the toes bent at angles.

"May I help you, sir?" the man said, his voice deep and measured as if he expected an echo.

George said, "I'm here to see Mr. Malachi Wilson."

"Your calling card, sir?"

George stared for a moment, then shook his head. "I'm sorry, I don't have one."

"Then, whom should I say is calling, sir?"

Whom? A colored who says *whom?* This immense figure in formal attire at this isolated farm in god-knows-where Tennessee? *Whom?* George squared his shoulders. "Please tell him the United States Army," he said.

"Yes, sir." The door closed and George waited under the broad portico as a thin fog gathered on the lawns. *Whom?* he thought, and found himself grinning, his lip still tender where the splinter had pierced.

When the door opened once more, the man stood aside and said simply, "Come."

George stepped into a lofty arched hall with fluted pilasters, flowered wallpaper in muted tones, and rich mahogany furniture on a thick carpet in twisted patterns of red and gold. Ahead was a long staircase climbing to rooms left and right from a hall that ran to the back of the house. A marble side table covered in books stood along one wall. Beside it, a woman's parasol rested in a leather stand. Through double doors to his left he observed a dining room, its long table lined with chairs.

"Your hat, sir." The servant held out a gloved hand, the tips of two fingers neatly darned where they had worn through.

George removed his hat and handed it to the man, who took it under his arm and gestured at an open door. George entered a long and narrow room, dimly lit, its tall windows heavily draped. As the door closed softly behind him, he smelled the ripe odor of tobacco, as if it had permeated the furnishings. On the floor, a thick rug spread across the polished planks in navy and gold patterns. The walls were covered in wood the color of creamed coffee. Behind a broad writing desk piled deep with papers and books, a man sat hidden in shadow, a shock of white hair revealing his position.

"Please come in," said a voice firm and throaty that cut the air like a foghorn. "My name is Malachi Wilson." He rose, a man in his early fifties, heavy-shouldered so that he seemed to stoop, a broad open face close shaven and deeply lined. He was not a large man, but his intensity gave the impression of someone who was. "What can I do for the United States Army?" he asked.

George drew himself to attention. "Sir, you wrote to U.S. Army headquarters at Nashville regarding deserters and highwaymen at large in this area. I have been instructed to provide you with protection. I am Sergeant George B. Van Norman of the Eighth Wisconsin Veteran Volunteers, Army of the Republic, at your service, sir."

The man smiled, and deep lines framed his mouth. "Well, well, Sergeant. That's very good of the United States Army to send out troops to protect me from thieves and the like," he said. "I'm not sure there's much left here to protect, mind you, but it's quite noble of your army nonetheless."

Wilson spoke in clipped sentences, words fairly bursting from his lips, tart with energy. Not the slow drawl George had expected.

"How many men do you have with you? I daresay, I only have accommodation here in the main house for half a dozen or so, maybe a few more if they don't mind crowding. You, of course, may have my quarters for yourself. It's the largest bedroom, and looks out the front of the house. The rest of your men will have to be content with the stable. It's quite large and should not be much of an inconvenience; the animals have all been taken anyway. Just the same, if you…"

"Begging your pardon, sir," George said. "There's just me, sir, and I'll sleep outside where I can best keep an eye on things."

Wilson gaped. He stepped to the large window, pulled aside the heavy drapes and peered outside, then looked again at George.

"If you don't mind, sir," George said, "I would ask you to assemble all the persons of this plantation on the front lawn in one hour's time."

Wilson said nothing and George turned on his heel. At the door he thought of a question, one that troubled him, exactly why he did not know. But he paused, rubbed his lip, and probed the thick scar with his tongue. "Mr. Wilson," he said. "Can you tell me what happened to the feet of the man who let me in?"

Wilson met his gaze and spoke in measured tones. "He was beaten," he said, "by his former owner."

GEORGE WAITED BY THE FRONT PORTICO, its grand pillars flaking paint chips, the railing twisted and gray from lack of care. Weeds lined the steps and grew in great clumps in the roadway's center. A faint breeze brought voices and a group of colored people walked slowly up the road, led by the giant houseman. A moment later, Wilson emerged from the house with a small boy.

"This is Jesse, my son," he said, and he ruffled the hair of a tow-headed boy who scuffed his boots in the dirt. "This is Eb, our house servant, whom you met." The big black man, his deformed feet planted firmly, nodded slowly. "And this is Mitsy, our cook, and their children, Silas and Chryssy." Silas, about 15, tall and gangly, smiled, white teeth gleaming in his brown face. Chryssy was younger—probably five though she might claim seven—and had her hair tied in an array of brightly colored bows.

"I's a flower," she said. "My name is Chrysassimum."

"Chrysanthemum," Mitsy corrected her.

Wilson smiled and looked off toward the barn. "Yes, well, that's everybody, Sergeant."

A long-eared mutt loped through the mud, then wiped its wet nose on Jesse's trousers. "This here's Jeff Davis," said the boy. "He's my dog." The rangy brindle hound closed his eyes as Jesse rubbed his ears. His long tail flapped against the boy's leg.

As they watched him, it occurred to George that he must appear just as much a novelty to them. Nevertheless, a question nagged at him, and he searched about in his mind for the right words. "Are there any other servants on the plantation, sir? Anyone missing?"

"No, Sergeant," Wilson said.

"I came upon a colored couple just down the road. Wondered if they might have come from your place, that's all."

Wilson eyed him carefully. "At one time, we had over thirty slaves working this land. They all lived down in the quarters," Wilson said, gesturing toward the row of ramshackle cabins a few hundred yards past the house. "When war broke out, I offered manumission to any who would take it. Most of them left last season, right after your army arrived." He paused and George felt a cramp of pity for this man, his dignity held without pretense, without regret.

"There is no one to do the work anymore," Wilson said. "All the men are gone. In the army or dead. I do what I can, and Jesse here helps out. But without even a mule, we can't break the dirt to plant."

Bitterness hung thick in the air and George broke from Wilson's disheartened look by casting an eye about the property. What he saw confirmed the man's remarks: broken fences, peeling paint, untended fields. George understood farms and the constant attention required of them. "How many acres do you have here, Mr. Wilson?" he asked.

"It's not a big place," Wilson said. "There are just the 400 acres you see here." He made a sweep of his hand. "And another 300 or so scattered around the county that we work from time to time."

"And what is it you grow here?" George asked.

"Nothing much anymore." He gazed toward the graying sky. "At one time, all the land that's workable was working, or resting to be put to work another year. Over there, we grew cotton and corn. Back there, we had tobacco, good tobacco, as good as any in Middle Tennessee if you don't count the Roberts' place. There's a pair of drying houses behind the ridge, but they are in pretty bad shape." He idly hitched his hands in his pockets and said nothing for a long moment, his eyes fixed to a spot on the ground as if remembering another time. At last he said, "We can take a walk around if you like."

George nodded. Even with dozens of workers, he realized it might take years to bring this farm back to capacity. "What sort of problems have you had from the citizenry?" he asked.

"Citizenry?" Wilson misunderstood. "We are the citizenry. What you see here is the last of a dying way of life. Without workers to tend the land, without slaves to till and plant and harvest the crop, we have no way to make a living. Your Mr. Lincoln and his army have seen to that." His face became flushed, his Ts and Ps fairly bursting from his lips. "All the crops have been stolen, and all of the animals. Our way of life has been taken from us, Sergeant."

"I beg your pardon, sir," George said. "I have been ordered here to protect this plantation. I need to know what sort of problems I might expect."

"Last week, a Yankee foraging party took the last of our horses." Wilson's voice grew raspy as it gained force. "They also took a sack of potatoes and a barrel of corn meal we used to feed our chickens."

Jesse said, "They took our chickens, too."

"Your army has methodically confiscated anything we couldn't hide." Wilson's voice rose and seemed laced with invective. "We've lost over twenty horses, a dozen mules, a pair of oxen, chickens, turkeys, ducks, and goats." He ticked them off on his fingers. "I filed a complaint to your army, and they sent me you."

"Yes, sir." George didn't know what else to say.

"We've had robbers, too. They took what the army didn't, a bushel of early apples, some silver from the house. Killed one of our neighbors, the Roberts." Wilson looked at Eb. "Deserters even broke into the slave quarters and took their blankets and clothes."

George wanted to ask whether the deserters were Union or Confederate, but thought better of it. These people had suffered all the deprivation and destruction that could be inflicted by two warring armies shifting and twisting as they maneuvered across the landscape, like a tornado sucking anything of value in its vortex. "It will not happen again," he said.

Wilson looked straight at George "Thank you, Sergeant Van Norman," he said correctly, courteously, without conviction. "We appreciate any help you would be willing to render."

The others dismissed, Wilson led George behind the main house. He walked casually, his arms thrust into his suit jacket. He pointed to where they had grown wheat and corn and tobacco, the orchards, the vineyard—fields that now lay fallow, buried under layers of detritus.

"Over here was a pleasant little garden, with lanes and vistas, and an arbor of scuppernongs," Wilson said. "Those are fruit trees over there. The apple trees still give apples, but we get fewer than ten bushels a tree now and have no one to pick them."

George studied the land as they walked, the pitch of it, its grit and texture, and imagined fields bursting with greens and yellows. Odors, too, were familiar: loam from the fields, balsam from a windbreak, and tree box used to outline the garden beds. Through late afternoon, the two farmers talked dirt. They spoke of plowing it, planting peas in it for feed, how corn depleted it if you planted it year after year. Then there was gully mud and swamp muck to be hauled as compost—even with dung from the barn and the peas plowed under, every acre needed a hundred loads of compost a year. It had been a long time since George had talked farming. He found comfort in it.

On a small promontory overlooking a narrow stream bubbling and churning with spring run-off, they paused to appreciate the view, long shadows cast by the setting sun.

"This creek wanders its way a few miles before it flows into the Duck River," Wilson said. "That building over there's where we boil sorghum for making syrup." He nodded toward a lone wooden building, spaces between the boards lit by the fading light of evening. Suddenly, he turned to George. "Not all Southerners favor slavery, Sergeant. A man has to decide why he fights, and I wanted it clear—in my own mind and that of my family's—that we were fighting to defend our right to self-government, and not for any self-interest. That, young man, is why I granted freedom to our people."

George nodded. It was not a question he had asked, but one whose answer he was grateful for knowing. It was the Great Debate, and it eased his mind to know the colored people who had remained had done so of their own choosing.

They walked in silence through a canopy of barren tulip trees and hemlock, past the smithy's house and the poultry yard, and the rustic cabins of the former slaves. Alongside the dirt path, George saw more rocks scattered in the mud.

"My son and I planned to build a wall along this lane," Wilson said. "It was going to run all the way past the house, out to the main road." He stooped to pick up a heavy, yellow stone, examining it as if it held answers, or perhaps questions. After a long sigh, he dropped the stone and walked on.

AS THE DUSK DESCENDED INTO NIGHT, George strung a rope between two trees near the stable. He tied his tent halves and tried to stake them, awkwardly stretching the canvas sides with his injured arm. After his third curse, he sensed rather than saw the man standing beside him.

"Would you like assistance, Sergeant Van Norman?" It was Eb, his disfigured feet spread like giant pods in the grass, his immense shoulders higher than George's eyes, and his broad face the luster of ebony in the fading light. The man knelt and began to drive the stakes that held the canvas into the ground.

"I guess I'm a little clumsy," George said.

"How did you come to injure your arm, sir, if you don't mind my asking?" Eb's voice was rich and deep, like mahogany amidst a cord of pine.

"Battle at Nashville," said George, reluctant to tell anyone a tree limb had fallen on him, and not brazen enough to make up something more glorious and heroic.

Eb asked no more questions, but George's head swam with them: Why hadn't Eb's family left with the other slaves? Where was Wilson's wife? Whose parasol was that in the house? Together, they finished erecting the tent and George stowed his gear. Eb paused for a moment when he saw the rifle.

"It's all right," said George. "Here. Take a look. It's a rifled musket, fifty caliber."

Eb hefted the heavy weapon easily, felt the smooth finish of the barrel, the burnished wood of the stock. "Slaves are not allowed to have firearms," he said, and gently laid the weapon on the ground cloth.

"You're not a slave, Eb, not anymore. You heard Mr. Wilson, what he said about President Lincoln? It's true. You're a free man. You can go where you please, do as you please. You don't have to stay here anymore if you don't want to."

"I understand the ramifications of the Emancipation Proclamation, Sergeant Van Norman. I have some education. Judge Wilson saw to that when he took me in." He gazed at the house for a moment, then slowly turned back, like a giant tree stirring in a stiff wind. "Elm Grove was very beautiful once, before the war. There were parties and festivals and the laughter of children. It is good land, fertile and abundant." He looked at George. "It will be a good place to live again, when this war is over."

"Judge Wilson?"

"Before the courts were disbanded," he said. "He appointed the sheriff and the road overseers, decided where bridges should replace fords, where schools are needed, and who should stand for Assembly. The Judge is, or rather was, quite important."

"I see." With Federal troops had come martial law, and the local court system had been shut down. "But you could have your own farm, Eb, your own land, work it yourself. You could..." He saw Eb frown, and he stopped.

"I am not a farm hand, Sergeant Van Norman. I am a house servant. I do not toil in the fields."

Even among the lowest classes—and you couldn't go much lower than slave, or even former slave—there was a caste system. It was beneath a house servant to do manual labor in the fields. George said, "Well, Eb, I toil in the fields. Before the war came, I was a farmer."

Eb scratched his head as if trying to understand where Sergeant Van Norman fit in the scheme of things.

"You said children. Does Judge Wilson have more than the one child?"

"He did," Eb said. "Master Frederick was killed at Shiloh. We learned how Frederick helped drag another man behind some shelter, and took a bullet in the back. He was just nineteen." Eb looked again at the house. "I'd best be going now. Good evening, Sergeant Van Norman."

"Good evening, Eb. And thank you."

Eb nodded, then turned and slowly walked to the house, his gait part shuffle, part hop.

GEORGE FOLDED HIS COAT AND PILLOWED his head against the hard ground. He lay in the shelter of his tent and listened for the familiar sounds: Ben Entricken mewing quietly to the camp dog, the snoring of Mike Mansion in the next tent, the men bustling about as they readied for sleep.

But all George heard was the quiet of the night, the murmur of the elms, the far-off hoot of an owl. This was enemy country, and he longed for the sanctuary of his regiment, of his friends. He pondered where they might be, if they were thinking of him. Jesse Cole and Billy Craven, Ben Entriken and Sherman Ellsworth. Sandy Cluxton had fallen that first day at Nashville. So had Joe Henry. George wondered if Ole Anderson had recovered from the head wound he had suffered at Compton's Hill. He knew that Mike Mansion had not.

Mike Mansion was the first boy George had known when the family moved to Wisconsin in '54. Mike had shown him which fishing holes would fill a string, how to gut a catfish for the best eating, how to tie a fly so the trout couldn't tell the difference. Chest like a tar barrel and arms thick as logs. Fishing or baling hay or splitting a face cord, Mike Mansion had no equal in Iowa County. Everybody liked Mike. Girls, too. But Mike could find no words for a woman, couldn't bring himself to ask Molly Johnson to dance at the Apple Harvest Cotillion, his pie face flat as a tin and red as a cherry. He had stood before her holding his hat and looking at his shoes for nearly two minutes before he turned around without a word and walked away.

But Mike Mansion would not be with the regiment.

Ben Entriken would be there. Ben had been George's closest neighbor. They had spent long winter nights studying arithmetic and grammar lessons, long summer days swimming in the Pecatonica. Ben and he had once built a raft of heavy oak timbers. Weeks they spent shaping boards with an adz, nailing them together, adding a sail made from an old bed sheet, and a wooden box for "secret stuff." They christened their ship "Excelsior" and dragged it to the shallows to launch it in the turgid water, where it promptly sank. Like a rock. His father told him he should have used pine boards, but at thirteen, George hadn't known the difference.

Ben was small, a head shorter than George, with a little potato face and sloped shoulders. Bigger boys would have picked on him if he hadn't been so likeable. He still was. Ben could walk through camp and acquire friends the way a dark suit gathers lint. Ben actually listened and actually cared and made you feel as if the whole miraculous day would have been far poorer were he not in it. In camp, Ben befriended the new fish, volunteered for post duty, saved scraps for the camp dog. Compassion could not be drilled out of Ben Entriken.

Mike Mansion and Billy Craven lived just a few miles away from the Van Norman farm. They all met every Saturday in Dodgeville to spend a few pennies at Robertson's Market on Spring Street, then sit on the river bridge and eat licorice and talk about girls with pigtails, the Methodist corn roast and sausage festival, and the big catfish Mike once caught that pulled him in the water and nearly drowned him.

George rolled onto his side and sought to imagine his home, a reunion with his family, his mother bustling about the kitchen with his sisters, his older brothers working the fields with Pa. And then he thought of Elizabeth. Yes, Elizabeth. While on furlough in Madison, George had gone to the hospital to visit a friend. It was evening and a single lantern was the only light in the room. Until she walked in. Her golden hair framed a face that fairly glowed. She took his breath. His friend introduced her as his sister, and after a polite howdoyoudo, she asked if he would be going to the Daughters of the Union Auxiliary cotillion.

George soon found himself shuffling about the dance floor, his hand upon her back, carefully but firmly guiding her among the other couples. She amused him and he tried to amuse her, too. Mostly he just looked at her. All silken skin and saucy smile, a voice like a comedy. She knew things: history, politics, the piano. She didn't just read; she read literature. A few hours of nonsense talk interrupted by bursts of laughter, and George had been besotted. He'd talked plain with her, told her right out he was going to marry her as soon as the war was over, though they were laughing about something at the time so he didn't know if she took him seriously. Didn't know himself. On the walk home, when she had first kissed him, he had held onto her then, felt her breath in his ear, her warmth against his thighs. He remembered how he had held her as if she possessed the answer to questions he had not yet begun to consider, held her as if on the other side of her kiss there could be a new life.

He thought about these things as he waited for sleep: the softness of her neck, the hollow of her back, her face as she held her arms up to kiss him, the touch of her lips. It was these—the piano, the laughter, the kiss, a life—these that George tried to hold in his mind. And these things that began to fade from his thoughts. He reached to grasp them but could not move his arms. He thought to struggle for a moment, but found he could not remember what it was he meant to grasp. After a time, he began to snore softly.

HE DID NOT KNOW WHAT AWAKENED HIM. Still dark, hours yet before the dawn, George sat up and listened for the faint sounds of camp, the steady breathing of the man in the next tent, the hiss of green wood on a campfire. But silence surrounded him, so stark and intense it was almost hurtful, and George felt his heart pounding in his chest, a moment of quick terror when he did not know where he was, or why. Absently, he probed the deep scar above his lip, remembering then—beyond the canvas of his tent—the plantation, the house, and Judge Wilson.

He lay back and waited for his breathing to slow. On the verge of sleep once more, another sound alerted him, this one clear, from the side of the house. With the barrel of the rifle, he slowly pushed aside his tent flap and peered into the darkness. There, by the stable, he saw something move, just a shadow in the dim moonlight. He tried to swallow but found his mouth dry and realized he was panting. He crawled from his tent to peer between bare stems of honeysuckle, but could see nothing. Then, from deep in the shadows, another movement. A man stooped and seemed to root in the dirt. After a moment, the man stood and hopped a few feet, then stooped again.

George stood up. In a clear voice, he said, "What are you doing here at this hour, Eb?"

The big man turned toward the voice in the darkness. "Is that you, Sergeant Van Norman?"

George shouldered his rifle and stepped around the hedge. "It's the middle of the night, Eb."

"I was looking for something," he said. "But I am sorry to have disturbed you." He turned to go.

"Hold on there, Eb. What brings you outside at this hour?"

The big man gnawed on his lip and shuffled his distorted feet. His old cotton nightshirt hung below his knees and wafted gently side to side. Then he leaned forward and said, "I'm looking for potatoes," and he opened his hand, revealing three small spuds covered in mud. "Silas says he found some potatoes here yesterday, some we must have missed at harvest. I was looking for more."

"I see," said George. He looked toward the house. "Eb, what food stores are here at Elm Grove?"

"The Judge would not like me to reveal the plantation stores, sir."

"I'm supposed to guard this plantation. Don't you think I should know what it is that I am protecting?"

Eb seemed to take a long time deciding about this. Finally, he said, "This is for today's breakfast. In the larder, we have one ham, some baking flour, apples preserved, and a pail of hickory nuts. We don't go hungry—there are always duck and fish in the river—but the rest must last us until the Judge sells another heirloom." Eb sat against the stable wall and George sat beside him. "Truth is, I don't think there are many heirlooms left. He hides things in various places in the house—beneath a loose board in the parlor, behind some books in his study. All the silver is up behind the crown molding. I find things from time to time. Never took any, mind you, but I am the house servant and I keep the place tidy, I do. So I see things."

George sat. "What kind of heirlooms?"

The big man measured his words carefully. "Some silver, a tea set, a ring belonged to Mrs. Wilson, some ivory brushes. Nice things. Folks around here can't pay much for such things, but I imagine they fetch a fair price in Memphis or Nashville."

George sensed a great confidence had been shared. Eb, who seemed to revere Judge Wilson and his family, had revealed information another man might use to advantage. Eb seemed to trust that George was not such a man.

A sudden noise in the underbrush, and George scrambled to his feet, levered the rifle clumsily, the stock in the crook of his injured arm. Loping from behind a low bush, the mud-brown dog, long tail waving like his personal battle flag, sidled up to Eb, and George resumed his seat.

"Hello, Jeff Davis," said Eb. "Out for your evening stroll, are you?" He stroked the animal's long, floppy ears.

George petted the animal. "Jeff Davis?"

"The Judge named him," Eb replied. "He says President Jeff Davis is basically good, but not so smart." Eb smiled, his teeth white against the night. "Same as the dog," he said.

CHAPTER NINE

Hickman County, Tenn., January 7, 1865

Morning sun spilled through the sparkling glass and splashed onto the oaken floor, warming her bare feet. She parted the fine lace curtain and peered from her window.

Below, on the lawn, was a Yankee soldier, and the idea made her shudder. His uniform was precise and imposing. His head sat squarely on shoulders broad and weighty. His hair escaped in coffee-brown waves from beneath his hat. He walked with purpose and bearing, as if he owned this place. Which he decidedly did not. His confident swagger frightened her and she hurried to the door, examined the lock, and twisted the catch.

Here were Yankees come to her doorstep, come to steal and debase and despoil. And God knows what else. As if we weren't deprived enough—too little food, money not worth anything anymore. There was nothing to buy anyway. Blockading had stopped all trade. New Orleans was closed; nothing came up river to Memphis anymore, no fashionable clothing or bolts of bright green and blue satins. Local newspapers, such as they were, had little of real news—no Times Picayune, no idea what was au courant in Paris. And frankly, she admitted, there was not much reason to care. There were no balls to attend, no parties, no way to flirt with the boys or stir the envy of her friends with her colorful attire.

She considered the parts of this dilemma. Her life seemed completely devoid of flavor. Old friends seldom came to visit any more. Too dangerous these days, what with highwaymen and the like. You needed an escort to go anywhere. Minnie Waters visited from time to time from Pulaski, but less often now that her aunt had passed on. The aunt had been a bitter old woman who had left her land to that horrid overseer rather than her kin. A disgrace is what it was. And after all that Minnie had done for her in her aunt's dying days. Staying with her and nursing her and comforting her while she wasted away, getting meaner and crazier with every passing day, the way it was told. No one ever figured out what ailed Mrs. Waters. Some said she had the consumption, but the doctor said no. Some said that overseer had poisoned her slowly but surely. Minnie said it was just bad nerves and heartache after her boys died.

Well, if grief was a disease, half the county should be finished. Nearly everyone had lost someone. Strophes of *Nearer My God To Thee* had been heard in every churchyard, in every hamlet, in nearly every home. In this one, too.

She looked from her window once more, and imagined she saw her brother, his brown hair flying in the wind as his spindly legs carried him on some errand or another. Lost in a peach orchard at a place called Pittsburg Landing—two years since they had received the terrible news.

Now she imagined another soldier, handsome in his uniform, with golden hair to match his epaulets. Tom Harden, her Tom, who had written diligently every week, but from whom she had heard no word in over a year.

She turned from the window and began to pace, her head bowed forward as if she scrutinized each step. Despair clutched at her heart and she fretted for counsel, someone to guide her in these dark days. There were bandits on the road at night and Yankees on the road by day. Free coloreds roamed the highways, no pass required. Disgraceful. So her friends stayed home, and so did she. Would this war never end? she wondered. And when it did, what would her world be like under the dirty boots of these Yankee invaders?

She sat at her small pinewood desk and opened a side drawer. Counsel must be taken where it can be found, she reasoned. Mother, who had so often faced the same loneliness when Papa ran the circuits, who had so often counseled her on lonely days. That was it, really. More than anything, it was the loneliness, no one to talk to, no one to share the little everyday joys: geese flying, honeysuckle in bloom, a log burning in a fireplace. These were humble pleasures. She could find happiness in humble pleasures. She knew this in her heart. If she just had someone with whom to share them. Gathering paper and ink, she dipped her pen and began to write.

> *Dearest Mother,*
>
> *As you would want, I remain grateful to God for his tender mercies. My faith continues undiminished despite circumstance. "He will stir up the hearts of others to minister to their necessities."*
>
> *Yet these times try my soul beyond measure or relief. As if the war were not cruel enough, the land teems with deserters and highwaymen, thieves and free Coloreds, each sinking deeper than the next into pits of depravity. I fear there remain but few patches of my soul not brutalized by humanity's bottomless capacity for evil.*
>
> *Only with utmost restraint do I accept His most recent trial, a Yankee in our yard and on our doorstep. Such disgrace is difficult to endure. There is little comfort or consolation when our person is not ravaged if our homes are*

defiled. What could bring His wrath in such grievous fashion as this? Driven into this very ground?

I worry for all that is strange in the world. One man wrote Dixie for his wandering troupe of minstrels. Then Mr. Lincoln's Republicans made it their campaign refrain. And now it seems to be our anthem. How does one man, by singularly proclaiming its emancipation, revoke the right to own property bought and sold for hundreds of years as the will desired? Today, that Devil's own mercenary has been sent to protect the gates of our personal heaven. Job himself could not have endured more.

If I glory, I glory in my woe and that is not your way. I follow your example; there is none better. "We that knoweth to do good and doeth it not to him is a sin." You remind me still.

So I will do as you would have me do, no matter the aversion or shame. Emulation becomes adoration becomes

Love,

&

Pale sunlight filtering through the leafless trees made a lacy pattern on the paper, and she folded the letter carefully to put away in her drawer with the others.

Chapter Ten

Noah Turner sat with his chair braced against the wall in a darkened corner of the parlor, his black kerseymere coat draped over his long legs, a tin cup of warm chicory in his hands. He had been in motion since the battle and it felt good to rest. As he sat, his thoughts wandered to dark things, the dark line of Yankees overrunning his position, hiding with Jimmy in the treetops as the Yankees walked beneath them, then scuttling down a dim trail to escape captivity, and now this dusky parlor in a gloomy house with a man whose heart lay in dark places.

These memories plagued him, clamored for attention, and his heart groaned under the strain. It was not for self-pity. The capacity for pity had long ago left him. There was a time when his companions' deaths from battle or disease had caused him to weep like a child. Then, for a time, he had actually felt contempt for the dead. How devious of them, escaping the horror, cheating those who remained to fight. Now, he simply lay adrift in a vast sea of indifference. He saw the faces of friends and comrades who had died fighting for the Great Cause and could feel only shame for himself because he felt nothing for them.

The war was lost. This did not disturb him so much as it did others. Large landowners would suffer the most, those for whom slavery had meant prosperity. Noah Turner had never held slaves, and so the loss would affect him less.

Noah's anxiety came from simply not knowing what the future held for him. Where could he go? How would he eat? The questions nagged at him, not because he doubted his own capacity for survival, but because he simply feared that which was unknown to him.

He rubbed at the rough socks he wore to protect his hands, tried to scrape at the flecks of blood that lay crusted in the wool. Noah had lied to the Yankee sergeant, the young fellow who had let him go. It had not been his home that was near the battlefield. It was Jimmy's. Jimmy's mother, Mildred, lived there with Jimmy's brother, Buck. When he had reached the house, it was late, well past midnight, but a light still glowed from the lone window. Inside, he had seen Mildred on the floor and Buck all trussed up. He had also seen the legs of a man, a gun resting by his side. Noah idly patted the long, slender fascine knife at his belt, and he remembered. Buck said the man claimed to be a preacher, but his papers showed he was a Yankee from Wisconsin. Noah had taken the dead man's coat, and wore it still.

He had buried Mildred, said a few words. Probably best she would never know about Jimmy. Buck, bitter and angry, had wanted to run off and join up right then. It wasn't until Buck had promised to stay put and watch the farm that Noah headed west again, toward his boyhood home, to visit Pa, maybe see Jenny. But between Yankee patrols and the Home Guard, he had been forced into hiding. The Army of Tennessee probably listed him as missing. But when that Yankee sergeant had let him go and Noah did not return to his unit, Noah Turner became a deserter. If they caught him, they would put him back in the lines, probably with some unit from Texas or Georgia where he didn't know anybody. If the Yankees caught him, it would mean prison in Maine or Minnesota or some godawful place with snow drifting past his knees. So he used the roads cautiously.

A few miles west of the Natchez Trace, on a cold and starless evening, he had met William Slive, former overseer, now owner of a rundown plantation he called Watersmith. Slive had asked no questions and Noah had offered nothing. When he was given a spare horse to ride, Noah had supposed Slive to be a man of influence; only the armies had horses.

That night had been cold and the ground covered with snow and ice. The sound of cavalry drove them from the road, forcing them to lie in an icy ditch until the patrol passed. Afterwards, as Noah prepared to mount in the dense undergrowth, his horse spooked and bolted. Noah had watched helplessly as the horse galloped away, the rhythm of its running on the frozen ground fading after a mile or so. Slive had cursed him, his epithets wicked and cruel. But the man had taken him in and fed him, and so Noah Turner had offered to help William Slive recover his mule.

That had been a week ago, and Noah's face became tense as he thought on it. He had agreed to help Slive track the riffraff, but took no part in their killing. A colored couple, uncomprehending, completely bewildered at Slive's wrath, had claimed the mule was theirs, bought from a teamster further south. They had shown Noah a train schedule, claiming it was a bill of sale. Swindled because they couldn't read. Slive had recognized the mule, said it came from Watersmith, pistol-whipped the man and clubbed the woman, tied them up and hung them quick as that. The man was still twisting while Slive carved up his stomach.

Noah stared at Slive beside him, asleep in the chair, gap-mouthed, making coarse throaty noises. His clothes were sturdy but well worn and dirty. A blackened leather vest torn at one corner covered his stout belly. Baggy butternut trousers were tucked into boots of once-fine leather, now cracked, the heels turned over. His coarse hair was a bottle brown, the stubble of his beard a darker color, like coal water, his lipless mouth turned to a permanent sneer by an overgrown mustache. Cruelty hung about him like a rude odor and tension clung to everything he did.

Stuck firmly into the arm of his chair, a knife blade reflected the dim firelight. In that reflection, a stab of fear took shape and form and Noah began to wonder. What type of man was this? Slive, former overseer, ruthless and rash, who saw other men simply as chattel, who measured their value only as they served his interests, a means to an end. The lowest white man can look down on another man if it makes him feel sufficiently superior. Slive seemed to take special pleasure in it. Perhaps Slive thought it a condition required of an overseer. Yet Noah had known many overseers who were firm while remaining fair in the doing. Thinking on it now, he could not imagine Slive among them.

What Noah feared most was the man's cunning. As uneducated as the next poor farmer, Slive had proved shrewd, using his assets as coolly and cleverly as any commanding officer Noah had known. Slive had demonstrated stealth and skill avoiding the cavalry patrol, and an intimate knowledge of the terrain.

The fire cast a soft glow on the peeling paint of the ceiling and for an instant, Noah Turner saw the couple hanging, twisting in the wind high above the road. He grimaced, eyes hard with anger at the memory. Being a partner to Slive held no profit. Noah understood this. A partner inspired trust. And trust was wasted on a man like Slive. Noah vowed to separate himself from William Slive as soon as he could come by a horse.

Tonight, Slive's plan was to surprise a small party of Union cavalry and steal their horses. Slive called it an act of war, but Slive was no soldier, and taking Federal horses was risky. Get caught with army horses and they hang you. Slive said he had that part figured out. He just needed Noah to help in getting them. Said Noah owed him for losing the other horse—no mention of retrieving the mule. For himself, Noah just wanted a horse, binding and legal if it all worked out.

A knock on the door. Noah climbed to his feet while Slive pushed past him, knife in hand, his sheer bulk moving as easily as a bear's. A man stood in the doorway. He wore a little round hat that he removed with both hands as the door opened. He nodded to Noah and Noah nodded in reply.

Slive called him Coogin, no first name, and he stood a foot shorter than Noah but wider by half. His worn woolen shirt strained at its buttons and his tattered cotton jacket carried the spatter of tobacco juice. Dirty blue trousers barely retained their striping, which had long since faded to dull purple. His pallid face was flat, as if it had been stepped on when he was a child, his upper lip bowed in its middle, giving his tiny mouth the shape of a horse's shoe.

"We leave at midnight," said Slive. "We'll head north to the river. There are cavalry on the roads, and we could be easy pickings if we're not watchful. Go and fetch the horses."

Coogin looked at Noah, then at Slive. He picked up his dusty brown bowler and popped it atop his head as if corking a jug. "Horses," he said, his voice high and windy as a woman's.

When the door closed, Noah tipped his chair forward and said, "Five-step threat."

"What you say?"

"An old army saying." Noah recited, " 'Fart, start, fumble, stumble, and fall down.' A term we used to describe a fellow who don't think too good."

"A little tetched in the head is all. Got kicked by a horse when he was a young'n, and he weren't too bright to begin." Slive laughed, a sound like sand in a wash pan. "Kind of like a new coon hound. Stroke him now and again, he pretty much does what I tell him."

Noah nodded, thinking: "Sit, Coogin. Roll over, Coogin."

"Little fellow, but strong as a horse, worked here when the war come. Spent time in the ranks, but just come home one day." Slive walked to a sideboard that held some papers and began riffling the pages. "I expect he had some trouble. Time to time he can't remember his left from his right. Bobby Lee needs boys who can march."

"Bobby Lee needs more than that," said Noah.

Slive ignored the comment and thrust a paper at Noah. "What's this say here?"

"Looks like a bill of sale of some kind. Except it's blank."

"That's right." Slive snatched the paper and tucked it in his shirt. "Bobby Lee needs horses, too. Good ones, like them ones Yankees been stealing from folk." He took the remaining pages and walked across the hall to the study.

Noah stood slowly and helped himself to chicory from the pot. It brought to his mind the last cup of real coffee he had tasted, compliments of the Yankee sergeant who had captured and released him.

Slive returned, and Noah asked, "What kind of work does Coogin do for you?"

Slive bit the end of a hand-rolled cigar, opened the fire door of the stove, and spat. "Not nearly enough," he said. He held a stick in the fire until it caught, then brought it to his cigar and inhaled in short puffs. "He helps in the smokehouse during season, other odds and ends." Slive sat heavily on a ratty, overstuffed chair by the sideboard. "When the old woman died, I got this place, and he took my job as overseer. Nothing to oversee anymore with the slaves all gone."

Noah wondered about the way things were, the way Slive had taken over Watersmith when Mrs. Waters passed on. "Mrs. Waters give you legal title and all?" he asked.

"That's right," Slive said. "All registered at the county courthouse."

Something still not right, so Noah said, "I thought the courthouse closed after the war started."

"Did," and Slive's ash fell to the frayed carpet. "Yankees process all the legal papers now, and I filed the deed in Nashville. Even used a Yankee lawyer to be sure it stuck."

"Ain't Mrs. Waters got no kin?"

"Just a niece that come round, made a pest of herself. Mr. Waters got killed at Vicksburg and her boys died with General Johnston. So I was the only kin she had, took care of her, took care of this place. Watersmith is a fine plantation and soon as this war's over, it'll be finer still."

"How'd it get the name, Watersmith?"

Slive ground the stub of his cigar on the stovetop and laid the butt on the sideboard. "Miss Smith married Mr. Waters."

Noah watched as Slive bent forward in his chair, covered his face with his hands, and jerked his head. When he sat up again, his left eye was squinted shut; he held a glass eyeball between his fingers. Noah flinched, sucked air. "Can you see with that?" he asked, first thing that popped into his head.

"Hah! It's just glass, you old gump. Can't see with it, can't do nothing with it." He laughed, a low guttural noise. "Pull it out to scare the niggers now and again. Give them the evil eye, so to speak." Laughter deep in his throat made him cough and he spat on the carpet, rubbed it with his boot. "Once, I told this old nigger I was going to keep my eye on him." He laughed harder. "And I put this in his pocket. You should have seen him. Jumping and hollering. He shucked off his buckaroos and ran into the field." Slive slapped his leg and nearly tipped over the sideboard. "I worked him bare naked all day."

The door swung open and Coogin entered. One hand cradled his silly round hat. The other pulled on his fleshy ear as he spoke. "Horses," he said.

Noah uncurled his lanky body from the hardwood chair and shrugged into his coat. "How'd the old lady die?"

Slive dropped the eyeball into his shirt pocket. "She just died," he said.

THEY RODE INTO THE WESTERN PIEDMONT for nearly three hours, following a winding trail that twice crossed the Natchez Trace. Thick clouds like oversized cherubs played hide-and-seek with the moon, throwing shadow patches. A mile past the rail bed, they crossed the icy waters of Leiper's Creek at a gravel bar choked with willows, and dismounted. Coogin stayed with the horses while Noah and Slive scuttled through the underbrush and began crawling along the muddy ground. They crept over a grassy hill and Slive nudged him and pointed. Across the eerie moonscape, Yankee tents dotted the banks a hundred yards upstream. Slive removed his hat and Noah thought to do the same, tucking it into his belt. They peered through the darkness into the narrow valley below. A gray ribbon of water shimmered in the scattered moonlight. The sky cleared and he could see a dozen horses grazing on the near side, more on the far bank. Remnants of a campfire smoked on the bluff.

Slive tapped Noah's shoulder and pointed toward the streambed. Moonlight revealed the dozing Yankee picket, and Noah nodded. Slive made signs with his hands. He would slip around to the right. Noah should do the same to the left. More hand signals and Noah nodded, understood. With no further word, Slive edged to the right, down the embankment, and disappeared, swallowed by the darkness. Noah moved off to the left, sliding quietly down the muddy slope.

A horse whinnied, and Noah paused, saw the picket raise his head. He waited in a thicket, shivering as a stiff breeze whipped at his hair, until the soldier again rested his chin on his chest. Noah crept closer. Ten yards, five.

The sentry looked up as Slive, appearing from the darkness, said quietly, "Good evening, soldier. Do you have a light for my cigar?"

Noah said, "Here, let me help there."

The sentry spun to face Noah, and Slive was on him. Noah crossed the last few feet in time to catch the soldier as he fell, no sound, just dead weight, knife handle sticking from his neck. Slive stooped to remove the blade and wiped it on the dead man's coat, then pawed the man's pockets and came away with some bills and a pocket watch on a thin gold chain.

They collected half a dozen horses, loosely looping thin ropes around their necks. Noah followed Slive as they led the horses up a slippery path. Clouds drifted in front of the moon, leaving darkness amidst the brush. Noah stepped carefully, fearful of any misstep in the gloom. Close by his ear, a horse snorted and he felt the steam billowing from its muzzle. At his feet, his moon shadow was suddenly visible on the slope and at that instant, a whistle sped past his ear, followed by the sharp crack of gunfire.

Slive shouted, "Go, go, go!"

More "pock" sounds filled Noah's ears as bullets bored into the hillside around them, rifle reports lost in the wind rolling down the narrow valley. A shout came from his right. Bluecoats were on his side of the river. More gunfire. Noah slipped in the mud, falling headlong while Slive deftly mounted the nearest horse and began riding, trailing two horses behind. Noah regained his footing and flung himself over the horse nearest him, wobbled there a moment, then slid off on the far side, landing on his back in the soft mud.

A shout and another rifle cracked. More shouting came from below as Yankees closed the distance. Noah fumbled in the darkness and bumped into a horse standing over him. The others bolted in the melee and he heard the sound of their cantering.

Noah began running, leading the remaining horse. Out of the darkness, a huge fist snatched the thin rope from his grasp. "Ride, damn you," Slive screamed. "This place is swarming with Yankees. You can't walk out of here!"

Noah said into the darkness, "I never rode without a saddle."

Slive swore. "Fine time to think of that."

More shouting and gunfire and Noah stood watching Slive and the horses' backsides disappear in the darkness. Galloping horses from behind drove him to cover. He plunged into the dense woods and immediately lost all bearing or direction. Branches reached for him and vines and creepers tugged at his arms. His feet caught in brambles and twisted roots, and he kicked at them as he ran. He cast about for some path, but could find none. The dim moonlight was made murkier by a draping of limbs and clusters of leaves too stubborn to have fallen.

Horses sounded to his right and he charged left. Another shot sounded and he skidded to the ground, sensed his hat being plucked from his head as he fell, but thought he remembered his hat tucked in his belt. He had a dim sense of cold leaves and mud against his face, and the smell of moss and dirt filled his nostrils. And then the dimness became complete.

THE FIRST RAYS OF DAWN BURNED FROST from the trees, melting and dripping and forming rivulets on the ground. Birds awakened the forest, the distinctive coo of mourning doves punctuated by the raucous bawling of crows. A jackrabbit peeked from its warren, darted back again as Noah Turner groaned once and rubbed the knot over his brow, big as a biscuit. He retrieved his hat from his belt and slapped it atop his head. He flinched at the effort, let out a long breath, and slowly climbed to his feet. The crows beat wing and were gone.

He staggered a few tentative steps, working out the stiffness in his bones. His arms and face were scratched from his headlong flight through the tall brush. Now, deeper inside the woods where there was more space, great pines left brown needles to muffle his steps. Sunshine fell in narrow shafts through the thin foliage and warmed him. The forest gave him assurance, hiding him, while it crowded with life. Birds discussed his every step in odd rhythms. He surprised a squirrel as he rounded a stand of hickory. It dropped its nutty treasure and scampered up a tree, then poked its head cautiously round a high limb and chattered at him with vex. Noah felt an air of fulfillment at this demonstration. The laws of Nature were with him. Sensing danger, any wise creature will drop its booty and seek shelter from an overpowering force. Noah felt renewed and plunged on through vines and bushes that parted as he passed.

He emerged onto a field overgrown with tall grass and scrub cedar. In the distance, a house nestled in the shade of red oak—huge trees that he remembered as saplings—a wisp of smoke climbing from the stone chimney. Large windows framed the center entrance and a wooden porch ran along three sides, its pine boards long faded to gray. Drawing closer, he saw an old man on the porch, razor thin and stooped, leaning against a broom rather than it against him. He was bare-headed, bald front to back, with strands of white hair cascading over his ears in thin streams. Noah called out, "Pa," and the man lifted his head. As Noah came near, the old man stepped into the yard. Noah slowed to let the man see him.

"Hello, and who are you?" The old man scratched his forehead, shading his eyes.

Noah stepped closer and gently touched the man's shoulder. "It's Noah, Pa."

"Noah?" The old man showed no fear, but no comprehension.

"I'm Noah, your son. I've come home."

"Hello, Noah. Won't you come in?" Pa hunched his shoulders as he made a rounded turn and strolled leisurely to the house. Noah followed.

Before he stepped onto the porch, the door burst open with a loud bang and a woman fairly flew into his arms, her legs wrapped clear around his thighs. "Whoop de doo!" she cried, and together they danced and chattered and laughed and cried for a whole minute.

The old man watched under the shade of the porch for a moment, then sat on a three-legged stool, leaned against the wall, slowly un-sheathed his knife and began to whittle.

"Oh, Noah, Noah, Noah, Noah, Noah, Noah!" She stepped back to look. "Noah, Noah, Noah," and ran again into his open arms.

They laughed and giggled and he spun her through the air. A twisted pile of chips gathered beneath the old man's stool.

"God almighty, it's good to see you!" she said.

"Good to be home, Jenny," Noah said. He admired her as she danced barefoot, her cheeks sunburned and tight, eyes the color of dry grass, her auburn mane bouncing on her shoulders in time to her sentiment.

"How long can you stay this time?" she said.

CHAPTER ELEVEN

Maury County, Tenn., January 12-13, 1865

T he road wound over a low rise between hills, and George let the old mare—Eb called her Bessy, and George had begun to call her Bessy, too—have her pace. Near midday, he stopped where a spout-spring bubbled from the hillside, the water feeding a hollowed gum log. Dismounting, he filled his canteen, let Bessy drink her fill, and listened to the noises of the woods: the gentle wind-rattle of leafless branches, a log-cock's pounding tattoo, the drum of a grouse. It took him a moment to remember that somewhere, the war raged on. Men marched and fought and killed one another. Somewhere else. Here, the war had taken pause. He corked his canteen and remounted, then lingered to watch a ground squirrel watching him watching her watch him. "Hah!" he shouted. And the squirrel dashed to a tree.

Beyond a wooden bridge that spanned a shallow creek was a row of clapboard houses, the outskirts of Columbia, Tennessee. George followed the Iron Bridge Road past neat picket fences surrounding tidy little yards where lilac bushes waited to bud. On a veranda, an old woman working a butter churn waved at him, and he tipped his Hardee hat. At the train station, a soldier pointed to the Union encampment.

Following the river, his shadow bobbed along the shoreline where the evening sun gilded the turgid water. He came to the familiar rows of tents, baked orange as if roasting in the twilight. Several figures huddled by a small fire and George dismounted.

"Hello, yourself," said a soldier, squinting against the setting sun. "And who have we here, eh?"

"Sergeant Van Norman, come to raise some hell!" George said.

Ben Entriken stood. "Why, you one-armed water rat, how have you been getting along without me?"

"Managed to tie my own shoes last week," George said. "Is the Major here? Where's the rest of the regiment?"

"Chasing Hood back to Alabama. A few of us were sent here for supplies. Be leaving again tomorrow. Why don't you stow your kit. You can hitch your tent to mine if you don't mind the snoring."

George hobbled Bessy beneath some peach trees and had begun to stack arms from habit when he noticed his rifle did not match the others. "What's this?"

"New Spencer repeater," Ben said. "Just got mine from the sutler." He retrieved it, hefted the stock. "See here? Loads seven rounds. Work the lever here, cock it, and pull the trigger." He demonstrated. "Easy, eh?"

George hefted the weapon, pulled on the trigger guard, dropped the breechblock, and ejected a cartridge. He ran his thumb along the barrel, eying the sight piece. Self-contained cartridges. Seven rounds, no reloading, that fast. George stared at the weapon he cradled in his arms. In every lifetime, there are bursts of insight, moments of enlightenment profound and absolute. A wave of awe enveloped him: the overwhelming capability of this technological wonderment with which a few men could unleash the firepower of a full company—all here in these bits of wood and metal and Yankee engineering. The thought fixed in his mind that now the South must surely surrender.

"These are what those cavalry boys had at Nashville," Ben said. "Ask in town. You can get yours from one of the sutlers." Ben took a tin cup off a nearby tent pole. "Let's get some coffee. I'll catch you up, eh?"

Walking between tent rows, stark white in the dusk, they talked of pranks and parties and pretty girls they had once known and who surely missed them now. Lies fell upon lies that neither believed, and so they served as fuel for kinship, nothing more. And that was enough.

"They call farms 'plantations' here," George said. "The owner is polite. He even offered me his personal 'boodwar,' as he says it. Hell, man, I didn't want to sleep in his damn house. I've been sleeping on the ground for three years." George sipped his coffee. "They don't have much to guard. Not even much to eat. Some soldiers—Yankees, too—have been thieving in these parts. So they don't trust me much."

"Can't say as I blame them for that," Ben said.

"The house servant, Eb, seems all right. Talks like he's King of England or somebody. 'Whom should I say is calling, my good man?' I walk around the place, wondering what in hell's name I'm doing there. The house must have about forty rooms—well, twenty anyway—but it's pretty much empty. Eb says the owner has to sell off the valuables just to eat. By the look of things, there isn't much left to sell."

Ben nodded. "It's happening all over Tennessee. We're the invaders, the conquerors, and some fellows feel it's their right to take whatever they want from these folks. 'Spoils of war,' they call it." He shivered, perhaps against the chill night air. "And it's not just a few eggs or a chicken or two. I've seen some with carpets, furniture, fancy clothes, and jewels, eh? One fellow from Company D has a silver tea service, uses it for coffee. Even the Major has been wearing a silk top hat and sporting a gold-tipped cane. He looks like a dandy."

George said, "It will be a long time in healing when this war is finally finished." He took a swallow of coffee. "Tell me about the regiment, Ben. It's lonely out there with no one to talk to but my horse," he said. "She's a good listener, but her stories are only 'half-assed'."

"We haven't seen much action since Nashville. Right now, they say Hood's somewhere near Corinth." The word hung there, and Ben dumped the last of his coffee on the ground. "The other night, we got bushwhacked by some horse thieves. Lost a fellow from Company B."

At Ben's tent, George added his fly and unrolled his blanket. Stretching out, George found the cramped quarters comfortable despite the crisp night air. "What do you hear from home, Ben?" he asked.

"Well, Ma wrote that the farm is doing poorly and the barn needs painting and the cows keep wandering over to the Olafsson's pasture and the chickens are dying of some disease she doesn't know what. She wants me to come home." He laughed. "She has no idea what our life here is like. She seems to think it's a grand gathering of boys, laughing and having fun. Of course, she wrote it before our little party at Nashville. Mail's kind of slow in getting here. Supply lines are stretched thin, from Nashville all the way through Kentucky, back to Chicago."

"I don't get mail where I am," George lamented. "I'll ask in the morning."

"Sergeant Joosten can tell you where to find the postmaster. See the paymaster and collect your pay, too."

George fell asleep wondering how much pay he had coming, and what he might do with it.

AT DAYBREAK, GEORGE QUIETLY LED BESSY to the riverbank, mud trails in the wet grass marking their path. His eye rested upon a row of ducks paddling in the shallows, their water rings speckled with early sunlight. The fowl swam and pecked and flustered and gossiped to one another in muffled tones. Suddenly, one fat mallard lifted from the raft and flew pell-mell into the sky, and George watched until it was lost in the mist rising from the river. He struggled to decipher the sweet pain that held his eye, this simple line of ducks, each so near, yet so close to being so far away. Behind him, Ben slept soundlessly, his tent among many tents ghostly in the mist. Without saying a word, George uttered his good-bye.

In Columbia, people bustled from building to building, going about their morning chores, conducting business and trading stories with neighbors. Faint smoke billowed from an alley, carrying with it the odor of burning steel; a loud banging confirmed the blacksmith hard at his forge. In Courthouse Square, two old men sat whittling on a pine bench. A woman dressed in black peered into shop windows. The butcher held an animated conversation with a customer while absently twisting the neck of a chicken. Buggies and wagons and carriages of all models crowded the muddy streets. It could be any city in Wisconsin, or Massachusetts, or South Carolina. The war seemed a distant thing.

At the paymaster's, George collected his wages and stuffed the bills into his haversack. He also discovered three letters at the postmaster's and buried these in a coat pocket. At Emma Jones's Café on Garden Street, he found a seat at a wobbly table near the window and ordered coffee from a woman with a broad grin and gaps between her yellow teeth. She said things like "Hey-ho," and called him "Partner" and he liked her immediately. When his coffee arrived, he tipped her generously and was rewarded with a "Hey-ho" and a yellow grin.

He opened his first envelope eagerly and recognized the gently slanting script of Elizabeth Atkinson. His hand quivered with a nervous weakness as he carefully read her words. But disappointment quickly embraced him as she delivered only banal news of a sheltered life at Mount Holyoke: heavy snows last week, a gathering of charades with friends, plans to tap her uncle's maple trees for syrup. She never once mentioned the war except to say, "George, be careful." It was signed, "Love...," but George recognized that to be an affectation and not what he preferred it to mean. He tugged at his moustache and tucked the letter back into his pocket.

The second letter, a brief missive from his mother, carried news of home, the successful harvest, his sister's brief illness, and his father's activities in local politics. It aroused in him reflections upon a life that seemed a distant memory, and he laid the letter aside.

The last letter came from an address he did not recognize. Greetings from O.F. Mason, President of Cudahy Stockyards. It was an invitation to discuss employment following the conclusion of hostilities. He read slowly. Stockyard business… negotiations and transactions… advancement opportunities… Edward strongly commends… The cheery voice and round laugh came to him then. George remembered eyebrows with a peculiar jump and jerk when Ed Mason sang harmony, his voice floating above the camp, strains of *Nelly Bly* in high tenor. A "spitfire in the leg" is what he had called his injury. But a butcher took off the leg, and Private Ed Mason died just after Christmas.

Outside, blowing bits of sleet and snow tapped against the windowpane as if chanting. George put aside his coffee and sat, shoulders hunched, and re-read the proposition, examined the words individually, searching for meaning behind the sentences. He drummed his fingers upon the wooden table and thought of things he wished he had said to Ed Mason.

An old woman entered the store and a gust of wind burst in behind her, rustling his papers. He opened again the letter from his mother and he saw her animated face glowing in the light of the kitchen stove. An overwhelming sadness engulfed him as if a great weight had fallen upon his chest, and he struggled to control his breathing. The loss of his youth balanced poorly against the loss of Ed Mason's life. He quietly folded the pages and stuffed the letters deep into his haversack. "Hey-ho" offered more coffee but he declined, tipped his hat, and braced for the cold.

Along Bridge Street, at Jamison's Comestibles and Merchandise, he purchased books, pins, bolts of cloth, and toys of a curious nature. At the train depot, he secured a buckboard, and at the sutler's, he collected a Spencer repeating rifle. He wrapped it carefully in coarse sacking and laid it in the wagon.

It was early afternoon before he started for Elm Grove. Bessy strained against the harness, pulling the heavily laden wagon as it pitched and swayed in the icy ruts. A soft snow began to drift from the gray skies and wet flakes dotted Bessy's flanks, disappearing into her coat like mice in a hayloft. George loosed the reins and she plodded on, ignoring the interlopers. The wind began to stiffen; it swirled snow and sand into tiny brown tornadoes. Icy flakes struck his face like glass shards and his eyes stung. Beneath a long wooden bridge, its planks covered in a thin coat of ice, the water swirled in frosted eddies. Snow skated on its surface in tight figures.

His arm ached from shoulder to palm, as if the blood ran more sluggish inside him, and he held the painful appendage close against his side to keep it steady. The wagon plunged forward and the dull throb in his arm grew to a deep grinding, as if a mill wheel were operating against him, his arm pinioned in the thwarts. His thoughts fled to his predicament, his duty to protect Elm Grove, and the bitter voice of ridicule assailed him. The Judge had asked for protection. His property lay in ruin from foraging—hell, stealing, call it what it is—by the Union Army, his family terrorized by bushwhackers—Southerners mostly, the man's own neighbors reduced to banditry. And the generals, in their infinite wisdom, had sent the Judge one man, one lone soldier with a broken arm.

"Hell, man!" He cried out to the ice and to the wind and to the uselessness that overwhelmed him. He rummaged in his mind, seeking some excuse for hope, a shelter from his self-pity, and he came upon his letters. He tried to inhale relief from their pages, but the wind sent up a breathless howling and the words dissipated in the vapors. The detachment he felt from his family, the emptiness of Elizabeth's wooden prose, and the noble gesture of Private Ed Mason, as inspirational as any preacher's sermon, reminded him that affairs could be altered too easily by circumstance or the flick of a surgeon's saw.

When at last the wind began to abate and the snow ceased and bits of sun began to dapple the treetops, George settled in for the long ride to Elm Grove. The wheels crunched forward, snapping the ice-frosted snow, and mist hung in the low places, hiding the bases of trees that stood tall and sharp against the blanket of white. High above, thick branches, glazed with ice, threw shimmering points of light as if from a shattered mirror, glittery and dazzling. The place had a moony look about it.

George crossed Leiper's Creek and found fresh hoof marks guiding his path, just two sets of horse tracks, no cavalry patrol. After a short distance, the tracks abruptly left the road, leading into the woods. At a sharp tug on Bessy's reins, the old mare halted and the wagon rolled to a stop. He sat for a moment and rubbed his arm. Snow dripped slowly from branches overripe with melt, making a soft drumming noise in the snow crust. Bessy stamped her foot and waited. The tracks ran up a steep embankment where they disappeared behind a high rock shelf. George undid his sling and reached for the rifle. Crouching, he dashed from tree to tree and rock to rock. His footfalls made raucous noises as he crunched through the snowcap and a startled squirrel leapt to a tree and vanished, appearing a moment later to curse him from a high limb. George peered over the rock shelf and saw a narrow meadow bordered by a steep hill, its slope dotted with cedar clinging between the rocks. At the base of the rise was an opening, the mouth of a cave where two horses stood deep in shadow, motionless, riderless. From George's perch, he could see no brand on their haunches. But a McClellan saddle, compromised by ropes and makeshift bridle, lay to one side.

He eased away from the ledge and hastened back to the road. He threw his rifle into the wagon and cursed through gnashed teeth. Bessy side-stepped uneasily. His arm throbbed and there passed through his mind a profound annoyance at his frailty, the notion of retreat abhorrent. He had seen it at the Red River campaign, the only defeat the regiment had known. Retreat invades the spirit and poisons it. It plays little games in the mind, ones in which all odds favor the oppressor, and all hope vanishes. It is a serpent that must be strangled before it swallows one's principles.

He jumped again from the wagon and gathered several large stones, carefully placed them one atop another, gathered more and piled them, too. Melting snow dripped noisily about him as he admired his work, a three-foot gully wall marking the trail. After a few moments, he clambered back into the wagon, snapped the reins, and Bessy began to trot, heading west again for Elm Grove.

GEORGE PASSED BENEATH THE ARCHING ELMS of the plantation road where melt water rained from the bare branches and soaked his clothes. He pulled Bessy to a stop beside the main house and hailed "Halloo!" Mitsy opened the kitchen door as he dropped a barrel of flour on the stoop. Behind her, Eb and Jesse stood gawking.

"Come help me, will you, Eb?"

They dragged boxes, sacks, and barrels into the house. Eb hefted a sack under one arm and a barrel under the other while Jesse and Silas wrestled a barrel through the door. Chryssy danced and clapped her hands over her head. Mitsy scurried about, organizing dried beans and desiccated vegetables, a massive slab of bacon, salted beef in kegs, sacks of potatoes and cornmeal, and barrels of parched wheat and parched corn for hominy. Stores of all kinds covered the kitchen floor.

"This is for you," George said to Mitsy, and he gave her a bolt of blue gingham cloth neatly folded in squares. "And this is for Chryssy." A roll of red velvet ribbon appeared from his haversack. Chryssy snatched at it and her mother scolded her. But George smiled broadly, and Chryssy giggled. To Jesse, he gave a wooden bear that raised its limbs when a lever was pushed. "It feels just like Christmas," George said, and he nearly shook with laughter. The last package was wrapped in paper and tied with string. "For you, Silas." He handed it to the boy. "It's a book by Nathaniel Hawthorne."

The boy eyed the package with unspeakable wonder. "I has heard of Massah Hawthorne," he said. "The Judge, he let me read his books. I has read Massah Dickens, and Longfellow, and Eliot. I's named Silas after the story by Massah Eliot."

The boy's enthusiasm earned a crooked grin from George.

"Can I keeps it, Ma?"

Mitsy nodded. "Thank you, Sergeant. It's his first book."

For a moment, George did not understand her meaning.

Mitsy said, "We borrows from the Judge time to time. But we always gives back. Mizz Jane, she teach us to read, afore she pass on. She done teach us poetry and music and art and geography. I can find Japan on a map. And I can play the piano in the parlor. A little bit, anyways. Silas, he play the bania. And Chryssy draws pictures." The child dipped behind her mother at the mention of her name. "But we ain't supposed to own books."

Everyone owned books. Among his neighbors and friends, George had not known a house that did not have books. The Entrikens had books of poetry and books about kings and castles and faraway places. Billy Craven's folks had almanacs going back twenty years and magazines of all sorts. But slaves were forbidden to read. In his giddiness, it had somehow left his thinking that Eb's family was different than his, that the color of their skin somehow separated them from other people George considered his friends. He had not appreciated this distinction, and it disturbed him that it should exist.

George stared at the crevices in the board flooring as if he were searching for words within their cracks. "I'd like to hear you play sometime, Silas," he said, and turned to go.

"Massah Van?" Mitsy spoke softly. "Thanky," she said.

CHAPTER TWELVE

Watersmith Plantation, January 21, 1865

E ven from afar, Watersmith had a sickly look. The driveway, rutted and heaving, wound aimlessly toward the house. The hedge that ran alongside had large gaps, limbs hung loosely from twisted hickory, rusted tools lay indiscriminately about the lawn. The big house itself settled crookedly into the earth, its portico tilted to one side as if limping, its roof slanting rakishly.

It had been a long walk from the farmstead and Noah Turner loathed the task that lay before him: beg Slive for one of the horses taken on their raid. A horse meant more than simple transport. It held the promise of plowed fields and bountiful harvest, of food for himself and Jenny and Pa. He'd walked a long way to reach Watersmith, only to beg a horse from a horse thief. And a clean bill of sale, too— legitimate—if Slive could deliver it.

He walked into the big kitchen where Slive sat alone in a rough wooden chair eating his supper, elbows braced against the painted table. Surrounding him, cupboards hung open, and pots, pans, and dishes of all sizes lay about the countertops, crusted with debris; the pine flooring stank of old grease. When he leaned back, Slive's half-buttoned shirt failed to cover his ample belly.

Noah scratched his chin, his fingernails raking rough stubble. "I do recall them Yankees was shooting at the both of us." He despised his own petulance, near choking on his words. "Had to be half a dozen horses. Just wondering where they went to, is all."

Slive said, "I got them well hid." Bits of food lodged in his rough beard. "Going to sell them to a fellow I know over Memphis way. Pays good for horses." Slive mopped at a bowl of turnips and gravy with cornbread, and stuffed it in his mouth. "Besides, seems to me you ain't so good with horses. First one I give you got away, I'm remembering." He gulped a long draft from a bottle of sorghum whiskey, swallowing noisily. "And them ones we just took? You let yours get away again." He stood, wobbly, the chair leaning to him.

"Spring's coming and there's plowing to be done," Noah said.

"Well, you just have to make do, same as everybody." Slive waddled to the side door, flexing his suspenders like wings ready to take flight. He nearly fell off the step and his boots slopped along the muddy path to the privy.

Noah sensed opportunity. He needed a horse. And while treachery came hard to him, he did not like or trust Slive, and held no loyalty. He had no plan, but was aware that one could be in the making. That he would be placing himself at great risk he had no doubt. Slive was as formidable a foe as any he had seen in combat. Yet, he concluded, it did not matter. He needed a horse. All these thoughts took place in the instant Slive stepped through the door of the privy.

Three strides, quickly into the study, to the desk, Noah fumbled through papers, searching. Phony bill of sale documents must be here somewhere. The drawer stuck and he heaved. Nothing. Another drawer. Nothing. The bookshelf. Nothing. No papers, empty but for a few books. Books? Slive didn't read books. Noah lifted them aside and spied a large metal plate against the back wall, iron handle at one side. Across its front in peeling gold letters: "John Tann, Ltd., Reliance Patent Guarded Lever Locks." He grasped the handle. Dust and flakes of rusty iron crusted in his palm like gnats on parchment. It did not budge, and Noah concluded it had not been turned in years. Slive probably never got the combination from the old lady. He slid the books back into place.

Noah quickly glanced out the window. Slive was still at the privy.

Once more to the desk, shuffling through papers. Still nothing. Damn. Where then? The chair. He tipped it and it slid unevenly across the old carpet. The carpet! One corner was torn and curled under. Noah lifted it, rolling it back. Underneath, he found a board rubbed smooth at one edge and pried it up with his fascine knife. In a small hollow he found money, a revolver, and sheaves of papers. He shuffled through them quickly, found the blank bills of sale, stuffed one inside his shirt, left the rest, and carefully replaced the carpet.

He made it back into the kitchen just as the door opened. "Coogin get a new horse?" Noah asked.

"Coogin works for me." Slive wiped his fingers in the folds of his shirt and sat heavily in the old chair. "What he gets, I gets."

Noah paced the wooden floor, boards creaking beneath his worn boots, as he tried to find an angle, struggled to think of some leverage. "Hope you're not keeping them in that shed there. Them Yanks'll find them for sure."

Slive tipped the bottle to his lips. Whiskey dribbled across his beard and left tracks in the dirt of his neck, as if worms sought shelter in his collar. "Them horses is well hid, and that's where they is staying." He sponged cornbread through his bowl, then sucked the last swallow from the bottle. "Got me a little hiding spot," he said, his voice raspy and sour like old cider. "An old cave. Caught me some niggers in it once. They was running and that's a fact." He squinted through the alcohol haze and tilted his chair against the sideboard, his contentment evident, contentment with his hiding spot, and his stupor, and himself.

Noah said, "I ain't got money to buy one. Army ain't been paying for over half a year."

Slive grinned, bits of turnip between amber teeth. "Army don't pay deserters now, do they?"

* * *

Maury County, Tenn., January 23, 1865

Karst topography confused and misled travelers unfamiliar with sinkholes and caves along the Duck River drainage, the land perforated by tunnel and crevasse. Carbon dioxide and rainwater gave way to carbonic acid that percolated to underlying limestone. Dissolved it. Over millennia, large chambers and long passages had formed.

It took Noah Turner two days to find it, sleeping in dense woods, traveling by night to avoid cavalry patrols. Noah knew several subterranean hollows where Slive could hold horses, but after two days of feeling his way at night and hiding by day, he had exhausted his knowledge of the area's caves. Discouraged and hungry, he spread his bedroll in a hollow of scrub oak for a quick nap in the last hours of daylight, resigned to return to Jenny and Pa as soon as darkness was complete. No food. No fire to attract attention. Just a season of fallen leaves and a kerseymere coat against a January Tennessee freeze. He pulled his collar over his ears, and settled his shoulders into the damp earth.

A flurry of air jarred him upright. He rolled to his knees and brought his eyes to focus. In the murky twilight, bats flying silhouettes against smoky blue western skies suddenly dived and disappeared into the ground as if they never were.

Noah blinked hard and stood up. "What the hell?" Bats, once there, then gone. He thought his mind was playing tricks and he resolved to discover the deception. Three loping strides up the slope and he peered over a ridge of rock he had supposed to be the remnants of an old fence line. There, a crack the size of a grave opened in the earth, the bottom of which he could not see. The gaping void exhaled a soft breeze that puffed the hair from his forehead. He gathered his bedroll and kit and peered into the dark cavity, its rocky walls slippery with mud and ice. A test pebble quickly disappeared, rattling off the walls in its descent.

He sat staring into the hole, weighing options and outcomes. This might lead to the cave he sought. But it was dark and he had no light. A broken limb in this isolated hole would deliver a slow and piteous death. For a long time, he did not move.

Dusk crept over the sky from the east and darkness settled upon the hillside. Stars began to glitter against the pale indigo sky. As he huddled there against the evening chill, his mind turned inward. He thought of the great upheavals and squalling misery he had overcome, the black passions and red blood he had survived. He had been to the edge of the Great Abyss, and he had escaped. There were good reasons to rejoice at this. He thought of Jenny and Pa, their struggle to scratch against the bitter repression that had settled upon the land. They needed him, and they needed him alert and able-bodied. But to be of any use, he needed a horse. He stared once more into the pit, as if the answers lay inside.

In the end, the matter was decided for him. Horses galloping on the valley road—either Yankee cavalry or Confederate conscripts, neither welcome company—drove him to cover. He dropped his kit, heard it tumble downward, and then lowered himself carefully through the gap, probing for a foothold. Grimacing and cursing, he slipped, his boots skidding on shale and limestone, bat shit and mud, his shinbones colliding with rock, his head banging against what he did not know. He landed hard on the limestone floor, and there he lay, unconscious, insensible as one who has suffered a beating.

A single ray of light across his vision woke him. He sat up, cracking his head sharply in the confined space. A deafening rumble filled his ears and he realized he was cursing, the noise echoing about his head like rolling thunder. With a twisting motion, he got up on his hands and knees, blinked hard, and examined his surroundings. An opening behind a row of hanging flowstone led to a large chamber. Crawling deeper into the cave, he found himself upon a narrow shelf above the main floor of a deep cavern. Light against the far wall came from behind a curtain of rock, evidence of another opening. Below, in the dim light, stood horses, six of them by his count, their heads bent forward as they nibbled at hay strewn in a line.

With a rope, he might climb down from his window above the cavern. But he had no rope. He shinnied back up the crack and popped his head into daylight. And quickly popped into hiding again before warily peering over the edge of his hole. There, not ten yards down the hill, stood a man, small and slim, boyishness in the hang of his shoulders. He wore tattered plaid and homespun twills over cobbler's brown boots. Noah watched the man untie his waist belt and hunker in the scrub oak, backside up.

Without hesitating, Noah took three quick strides and wrapped an arm over the startled squatter. "Who are you?" he hissed, his well-worn blade at the young man's throat.

"Gaaaah," came the reply.

He released his grip, stepped into a crouch, the long knife poised. "Who are you? What are you doing here?"

The man coughed and rubbed his throat. "Henry Carter. And I'm a-tryin' to shit."

"What outfit you with?

"Cheatham's Corps, Georgia Sharpshooters," said Carter.

Noah Turner dropped the knife to his side, but continued to eye the young man warily. "Pull up your pants, boy."

Carter tucked and tied. "Who are you and what do you mean fretting a man like that?"

"These are frightening times, Mr. Carter," he said. "Name is Noah Turner. Fell out at Nashville. Been hiding out since, same as you."

"That's a fact," said Carter. "I'd like to get back to my outfit but them Yankees keep getting in my way."

Noah guessed Carter to be a skilled thief by the look of his hand-made boots. He was probably making little effort to rejoin his unit, wherever it might be. If he was trying to get home to Georgia, he was truly lost.

Carter began to talk freely and Noah formed opinions, as a man will, from his words and the look of his eyes. Carter lamented the woes of the Rebel army and spoke of his hatred for President Lincoln, Radical Republicans and abolitionists, niggers and Freedmen, and anything Yankee. Raised in DeKalb, Georgia, Carter had spent his life the son of a gentleman farmer, cultivating tobacco and cotton, attending parties and the theatre and chasing eligible women, and some who weren't.

Noah Turner had seen too many like Carter, one of the South's own, a member of the "landed gentry." Carter was an ineffectual little turnspit with a pride that small men so often assume, lacking all reverence or virtue, one of those people who never stood when he could sit, never sat when he could lie. Work was considered disreputable among such types. Negroes did most of the work. Labor was not fit for a gentleman.

That was not true among Noah's neighbors. Here, farmers were thrifty and hardworking men. Few owned slaves. Most Tennessee men had their own farms and worked them by themselves or with family. It was loafing that was disreputable here. Noah took pride in this distinction.

Many white men were poor. Carter was not poor. He simply possessed a poverty of spirit. Men like Carter had little except their white skins of which to boast. So they hated coloreds and abolitionists with equal spite.

Noah said, "When were you last with your regiment?"

Carter dropped his eyes. "Not since some time before Christmas. About two months now, I'm guessing."

"Any idea where the Army is?"

"Headed south last I saw them, fast as they could go." Carter undid his trousers, preparing to squat once more. "Say, old-timer, you got anything to eat?"

Noah sucked his lip. Carter was of no use to anyone, not even to himself, hungry and scared and running from the war. Noah felt a remote pity for the man's misfortune, an empathy for anyone whose only future lay in the war coming to an end before he did. Perhaps they shared a certain similarity in that. Yet this was Noah's country, his people. An old-timer, yes, but wiser for the experience.

Pity was cheap, survival dear. "No," he said.

* * *

Hickman County, Tenn., January 24, 1865

Noah Turner chose wisely: a tall roan mare with a splash of white on her forelock, a horse traded, though he did not know it, first from a Menomonee Indian named Billy Willow near Lake Winnebago to a trapper named Wick. The trapper had lost her in a card game to a wandering minstrel from Terre Haute, who sold her to a Tennessee farmer, who gave her to his son for training. Yankees took her from the farmer, and the boy went off to Virginia with A.P. Hill. Noah Turner and William Slive had taken her from the Yankees. Noah simply called her "Red."

He and the beast took to one another easily, the sensation of being astride a horse growing familiar again after years of marching. The saddle had been among several in the cave and it, too, proved to be a good choice, with long stocks well suited to his height. A snaffle bit rested softly in the mare's mouth.

She responded to a soft hand—touch of heel to flank and the horse turned sharply; lean back in the saddle and the animal slowed. When he urged her forward at a brisk trot, his legs gripped lightly to her great barrel. There would be no hiding from Yankee cavalry or Confederate provosts on the road home. Wearing the long black coat taken from the Yankee deserter at Mildred's, Noah looked like a preacher. A spare hymnal from the Cumberland Presbyterian Church and a Bible from the abandoned rectory completed his disguise. The horse was accounted for, too. Noah had the bill of sale neatly folded in his haversack, signed by a fictitious Colonel Butler. Sounded like a Yankee name.

When he reached the house, Jenny greeted him with infectious enthusiasm, her eyes glowing like nuggets in deep water. "You old husker, what you dressed like that for?" She pulled on the broad lapels of his coat.

"Bless you, my child," Noah said, and she grinned and dragged him into the house.

Supper was okra soup, tender pods sliced and dried a season ago, lima beans, jellied yams and baked cornbread with lusty smells that caused his belly to growl with impatience. Pa sat at the plank table and stuffed a worn cotton cloth under his chin. The old man had a bony face, ears like urn handles, his long nose wedged between dilute blue eyes, and thinning hair running down his face and neck. He stared at nothing, gently rocking in his stiff-backed chair.

"Pa, would you like some soup?" Jenny asked him.

He looked at her as if seeing her for the first time. "That would be fine," he said. She nodded and ladled soup into his wooden bowl.

"Such a feast," said Noah. "You have outdone yourself, Jenny," and he eagerly dipped his spoon into the steaming broth.

The old man spoke to no one in particular. "Ma should be home soon."

Jenny nodded and passed cornbread, smiling at Noah. The remainder of the meal they ate in silence.

Later, after Jenny had seen her father to bed, she sat in her nightdress by her bureau. Noah stood in the open door of the little room, his arms folded, admiring his sister. The mirror reflected an oval face with auburn tresses parted to one side. Brown eyes framed a long nose that lifted at its tip; her mouth was set wide across a square jaw. Farm work had made her arms lean and well muscled, her skin taut and faded a musty tan, and though the work had not been kind to her hands, her face remained youthful and reflected easily the goodness that lay within.

Men called her "handsome." A fine figure of a woman, she always had been. She could outrun, outride, outwit any man. Self-sufficient and self-reliant. When her husband, Gordon, died just before the war, she moved back to the family farm. She sold the little general store for half its worth at the time, but a fair trade or better once the war began.

Jenny had looked after their father, and for that alone Noah was grateful. She had tended a small garden and managed to hide the chickens from scavenging parties of Yankees and Rebels alike. A small crop of white corn and potatoes was barely enough to keep her and Pa, and how she managed, Noah could not imagine. "You have a good face," he said aloud.

She turned and smiled, color rising in her cheeks. "It is so good to have you home. You don't know how lonely it gets here. No one comes around anymore. Even the neighbors think he's crazy." Her shoulders slumped and she rested her elbows on her knees. "Sometimes, I think I'll go crazy, too."

"Maybe you should get away for a while. I can keep an eye on Pa. It would do you good to visit friends for a few days."

Her eyes widened. "I hadn't thought of that. Yes, now that you're here to watch after him, I certainly could. I haven't had a chance to visit with anyone these days," she said. "I've been wanting to see the Dandridge's again, and pay respects to Minnie Waters."

"I have to take a ride up to see Buck at Mildred's old place. Why don't we talk about it when I get back?" He sat on the edge of her rough

-hewn bed, the same one Pa had made for her as a child. "Does he ever have good days, days when he recognizes you, knows your name?"

She nodded. "He does, but he slides in and out. Sometimes, in the middle of a sentence, he'll stop and forget just what it was he was saying. When I try to remind him, he'll get angry, like I'm poking fun. Or worse, he'll just look at me and grin, and I can tell he has no idea who I am. Just the nice lady who takes care of him. Then, it may be a week or some before he remembers anything again. It's so sad, but Doc Bertrum says there's nothing we can do." She stood and stretched her arms over her head. "'Hardening of the brain,' he called it. I guess it means the blood doesn't get to his head like it should and so he doesn't think as good as he's supposed to."

Noah breathed deeply and scratched the stubble on his chin. "I'm sorry I couldn't be here to help, Jenny. You've been a saint, and that's for sure, taking care of him and all." He stood to go.

"Stay and set a spell, Noah." She reached for him, clapped her hands. "Tell me everything that's going on. What's the news?"

He found a spot on the floor at the base of the bed and she snuggled down beside her bureau, as if they were still children. "Not good," he said. "Sam Hood's whipped, been replaced, and rightly so. The man's a butcher. There's talk of Forrest somewhere south of here, near Pulaski. Some say he may be trying to get behind Nashville, ride a Jeb Stuart 'round the whole army, but I think that's just talk. Officially, I'm a deserter, escaped from the Yankees—paroled, really—but I'm making no effort to get back to my unit. So I don't get much news on what's happening anymore."

"If you're a deserter, so is half the county. Webb Garity is back, and Tommy Hampshire. Lang Doty was spotted out at his mother's farm just last week."

Noah listened as she recited names of more boys he had known all his life, men now, returned from the war. He imagined them hardened and bitter and mentally worn out, tired of the lousy food and the lousy

Yankees. Tired of losing. God knows, he was. The war was lost, and if the generals didn't know it, the soldiers did. He said as much to his sister.

"What's going to happen to us?"

Noah paused before answering, as if posing the question to himself for the first time. The truth of it was, he didn't know. "Some folks are talking about heading into the hills and fighting on. All over the South, small bands could hole up and never get caught. The war could drag on for years. Others are just waiting to see what happens with General Lee. If he can break out of Petersburg and join up with Joe Johnston, they might still have a fighting chance."

Jenny idly played with her hair, twisting curls around her finger. "I sure hope you don't take to the hills. Colored folks are everywhere. Bandits and bushwhackers have been making trouble in these parts. Pa and me can't rightly protect ourselves. We've had plenty stolen just these past few months. You go fighting up in the hills and who knows what might happen to us."

"Let's pray I don't have to."

"Lord, have mercy on General Lee," said Jenny.

NOAH TURNER SLEPT, A SHAFT OF light tracing cheek and nose, stealing between curtains drawn but not drawn, edging, dancing, a life its own, time etched by sun's rising, across his brow and beyond, reaching, searing, as it touched his eye. He blinked and turned over, his head lost in down and linen. And sleep, gentle sleep.

Rolling over, eyes wide now, the olfactory awakening what the light could not, he sat up, joints spitting and scraping, sinew on bone, the ravages of age and bad food and years of hard living. Disorientation gave way to familiarity and affection. And home. "Damn, that girl can cook," he mumbled.

"Hey, Noah, that you?" Her voice somewhere in the back of the house, punctuated by the clatter of metal on dish. "I got biscuits cooking, and some eggs, too, nice and hard just the way you like them."

"Damn." He bolted from the bed and ran like a scalded dog for the kitchen, boots and britches in hand. Rising late into the mornings now, army regimen gratefully forgotten. Then it was outside into the chill air, chores just like old times: draw water from the well, feed the chickens, mend a hasp on the barn door. A sharp axe made quick work of oak logs felled years before. Home. War and marching and sleeping on the ground became distant memories. How easily man adapted to life's extremes, to hardship and terror and grief. And yet how easily he slipped back into routine of "Home."

After chores, he walked the property and admired how well Jenny had managed—vegetable garden in neat rows, cordwood neatly stacked, chickens well fed and fussing about the yard. Footfalls crunched on earthen clods and he turned to see Pa, barefoot, no coat, a shovel in one hand, and a wooden bucket in the other. His breath came in puff-cones of fog that were swallowed by the chilly air. "I told Ma I'd dig some potatoes afore supper," he said. Ma, dead these past twenty years—the consumption, they had said—wanted potatoes for supper. Noah stole a glance at his father and for a moment, he could appreciate all that Jenny had endured, Pa's memory as faded as old fence boards.

"Let me help you," said Noah.

Together they hoed the muddy ground, digging in places no potatoes had ever lain, moving on after a few shovelfuls. Stooping low, Pa picked up a rock the size of his fist, turned it round, spat on it and wiped it with his sleeve, then dropped it in the bucket. Jenny will have trouble cooking that one, thought Noah.

Slowly, as if polishing glass with his feet, Pa shuffled to the potato patch, one corner of a broad field beyond a low swale. Noah wrapped the old man in the preacher's coat, and held him then until Pa said, "Thank you, Noah."

Noah could not help but smile. "It's good to be back home, Pa. Been a long time." His thoughts hurried, prospecting for a connection, trying to hold the moment. "The fighting is almost over now, Pa," he said. "I expect more of the boys will be coming home."

"Jenny could use the help working the field, you know."

"You're right, Pa, she sure could." He waited, but Pa moved on. "How have you been feeling of late? You getting around alright?"

Pa straightened, stared blankly at his son for a moment, his watery eyes reflecting the pale gray sky. "Feet are cold," he said.

Questions just too much for his fragile mind, thought Noah. Bucket half full, they headed for the house. A final attempt: "Pa, I deserted from the army. I'm sorry."

"You're a good boy, Noah. Always were a bit of a rascal—couldn't tame that out of you—but I expect you done your part. War'll be over soon."

Noah stopped still and watched his father slowly tramp into the house, his bare feet dragging clumps of mud and bits of leaf. He ran then, so as not to lose an instant, so grateful, so rare. He burst through the door and stumbled over the preacher's coat clumped on the floor where Pa had left it. He fell hard and his bucket clattered and potatoes spilled in all directions on the unfinished boards.

Jenny rushed from the kitchen, chintz apron wrapped around her like a present. "What on earth?" Wiping her hands in the blue checks, she bent to retrieve the bucket.

Noah said, "He's having one of those good days you was telling me about, Jenny." Thunk of potato in the bucket. "Called me Noah. Knew your name, too. Knew about the war." He snorted. "Called me a rascal."

Jenny, wide eyes peering over the hand on her mouth, squatted like a duck fresh from the pond. They held each other then, and laughed. Potatoes speckled the floor. And one rock.

CHAPTER THIRTEEN

Hickman County, Tenn., January 24, 1865

A crisp wind battered the window and she hurried to close the drapes. An icy current whipped at the eaves and chilled her bones. Her shawl lay on the side chair and she quickly wrapped it over her slender shoulders, shivered, and went to the small tinderbox to gather more oak chips to spread on the smoldering coals.

Locked in her chamber, barricaded in this icy box, she waited, a prisoner in her private rectory, safe from marauders and malcontents and the godless heathens from the North, but unguarded from the more rapacious enemy: boredom. Dull days with little to do and evenings that seemed to linger for an eternity. No one to talk to, no one with whom to share her isolation. No news, no letters, hardly any conversation with another human being at all, unless you counted the yawping of an 11-year-old child. She lived a captive in her own home, as if she were the criminal rather than that blue-bellied scurvy camped outside her door.

In her distress, she lamented all that had befallen, and all that might have been. If only this war had never come at all. If only Bragg had followed up after Chickamauga. If only Hood had smashed through the Yankees in front of Nashville. Too many "if onlies." They haunted her thoughts.

But one stood out to torment her above all others. If only Tom were here. If only he had come home as he had promised. Golden Tom, hair blond as winter wheat, uniform of deep gray with gold brocade at collar and cuff, and golden epaulets. Over a year had passed since his last letter: "Billet outside Chattanooga... home by Christmas." Had he survived, there would have been time for him to send word. Where had he fallen? Was it quick and painless? Or had he lingered on the field, waiting for the relief that could only come in death?

She began to pity herself and her mind tumbled in agony and despair. She felt trodden beneath the wheels of an iron injustice that rolled over her with utter disregard. Abandoned in her tower, with little hope of reprieve, she sat, head bent over her knees, body racked with sobs. No noise, nothing to alert the enemy. Just heavy weeping, tears dotting the floorboards between bare toes. Her metal-gray shawl spilled from her shoulders to puddle on the floor.

"Oh, Tom," she cried out, but then caught herself. No noise, she remembered. It was the rule.

Outside, the wind blew steadily, rattling the arched window, rustling the heavy damask drapes as if in sympathy. Slowly, she retrieved her shawl, swung it about until it enfolded her. She opened the drawer of her desk, withdrew paper and ink, and began to write.

Dearest Mother,

What makes the wind blow? What color is Tuesday? Is this tree a boy or a girl? Inquisitive as always, I beg inquiries from you still. Where is the joy we once knew? Why must God take our innocence? Will we never again be at peace?

Perhaps it is peace that lies in the grave, for only the grave can hide us from all things terrible. Perhaps only Tom and Frederick truly know peace now, for they cannot be hurt more deeply by the future than they have been by the past.

And you. Has it been three years? A thousand days since you last graced this home, held this child — as I was a mere girl then — spread your joy and animation to all whom you touched with your warmth and dignity?

Injury befalls those who remain; it is the living that must endure the loss. As Father has endured his, I endure mine. Do you remember Tom? Such a dancer, you once remarked, such grace. It served him with society, but alas, not so well in the field. Graceful Tom, my love, my betrothed, as much a part of me as my arm.

Yes, of course! An arm, an appendage! Just as a man may lose an arm and yet survive, endure, not whole, no, but his life continues.

You have salved me once more. Such comfort you instill, never failing to console. Your countenance exudes that for which I am most blessed, your

Love,

&

She gripped the shawl tightly about her shoulders as she slipped the page into her drawer.

CHAPTER FOURTEEN

Elm Grove Plantation, January 25, 1865

T he invitation was delivered formally as George put polish to his boots. The uneven footfalls were unmistakable. T-galump, t-galump.

"Good morning, Eb," George said without looking up. He set down his boots and folded the blackened rag.

"Sergeant Van Norman, sir, the Judge requests the honor of your presence at dinner this evening," Eb said in *basso profundo*. "May I relay your reply, sir?"

George stood up. Dinner? An invited guest in the master's home? "Hell, man! I mean, yes. Thank you, Eb. Please tell the Judge I will be there at five."

"The invitation, sir, is for seven o'clock. Dinner is to be served at half past the hour." Eb turned and shuffled back to the house.

"Yes, of course," George said to his back. Farm life had always meant early supper. Apparently not at Elm Grove. A lopsided grin rose to George's face and his head swam with the implications. Dinner with the Judge held great promise, a signal, an opportunity, a beginning. Not acceptance, no, not yet, but one of recognition, acknowledgment that a Yankee, too, may gain redemption. George was to serve as Ambassador to the Court of Judge Malachi Wilson. Carrier of the cross of righteousness, of the Noble Cause. These thoughts uplifted him, and for the moment, George felt sublime. He put his boot polish and rags with his kit and stowed the haversack in his tent.

Since arriving, he had seen little of Judge Wilson. On one occasion, a chance meeting in the orchard, George had found the man sitting on treefall with a cigar and glass of brandy. They had exchanged banalities and watched the sun sink behind gauzy clouds of purple and orange. One thing the Judge said had struck George as odd. When George muttered something about the colorful sky, Judge Wilson had said, "Beauty is as you find it, Sergeant, a matter of philosophy and geography." George replied that he didn't know much about philosophy, but he thought the geography looked about as pleasing as any Wisconsin sunset he had ever seen. And then the Judge had laughed. George hadn't aimed to be funny.

The Judge's young son, Jesse, was even more remote. A sickly boy, he spent most days in the house. Occasionally, George could see him in his robe, pacing inside a third-story gable, talking to himself.

Even if the Wilsons were not congenial, Eb and his family gave George companionship. Silas was clever and industrious. George had seen him shape a makeshift wheelbarrow from some wire and nails and spare parts he had salvaged from an old apple cart. Silas spoke about books, about knights and kings, the heroes of quests and fair damsels. He seemed especially partial to a book about Greeks and Trojans and a fellow named after General Grant.

Eb was special. Everything about him seemed a contradiction to George's way of thinking: a disfigured giant, powerful but gentle, earnest but aloof, an educated black man. Eb was curious about history and politics and the war, and spoke knowledgably about each. When assuming his duties as house servant, he was formal and curt. But when he engaged George in conversation, he was just as affable and compelling as Ben Entriken or Billy Craven. George thought, "He is a colored man. He is a former slave. And he is my friend." And the thought fell comfortably upon him.

George snugged his feet into his freshly polished boots and prepared to make his daily trek about the property. Each day, he traversed the length and breadth of the plantation, peeked in every copse of trees, surveyed every field gone fallow, examined every hedgerow, every building. Despite its rundown appearance, Elm Grove was a magnificent estate, its fields laid out logically and efficiently, buildings spaced for maximum utilization, trees planted to offer shade during the hottest months and provide a windbreak during winter. Someone long ago had envisioned Elm Grove as it could be, had planted the plants and built the buildings and today, when it should enjoy its finest years, it sat empty and uncultivated, its opportunity wasted.

He stumbled as he reached the drive that led west from the main house. Lining the roadway, dozens of stones lay half buried as if a great crowd slept beneath the mud and only the tops of their skulls showed. George stooped to pick one at random, hefted it, and dropped it again. He chose another, roughly the same, about the size of a cannon ball. Strewn here and there were a few oblong shapes as big as his arm, limestone, quartz, and sandstone, white and tan and brown. They lay only along one side, as if dropped by some ancient glacier that had decided to retreat rather than cross the road.

He walked through a narrow hollow down to the bubbling stream where he stripped and, despite the cold, prepared to bathe in the shallows. He set his coat and shirt on a boulder, carefully hung his trousers over a low bush, and sat on a sandbar in the chilly water. Here, surrounded by the soft melody of the wandering current, his mind drifted to thoughts of home, to the banks of the Pecatonica and the family farm, the big white two-story house, warm biscuits and sausage on the table. Water rushing over the rocks became the babble of his brothers and sisters. Home. Three years of his young life had been spent as a soldier, marching and drilling and loneliness, occasional moments of sheer terror. Three years of war, the last year a succession of victories, as the great wealth and industry of the North slowly ground the Confederacy into submission. George thought of his new rifle, of the victories it would represent. This war will be over soon, he thought. The nation will be reunited and we can all go home. Northerners and Southerners alike will once again be simply "Americans" and the great healing can begin. He splashed water on his arms and face.

What is it that brings men to fighting? Surely it is not a natural human inclination. Somewhere in time, man had chosen to be aggressive, to master his surroundings. And so he had invented weapons: clubs, sharp sticks, hurled objects. Man was pushed to kill, a learned skill. George understood that drill and discipline and training made men effective killers. Yet he had witnessed otherwise on the battlefield. Given time and truce and temerity, scattered firing by the pickets would cease and the men would laugh and joke with the enemy and barter small luxuries. It stood to reason that, if left to their natural impulses, men would stop fighting and again live as men.

George tossed a pebble and watched it disappear in the current. He took comfort in this line of thinking. He had noticed as a child that when boys fought, they were often better friends afterward. And with war's end, this hating should cease as well. But George was not so sure. Benevolence is easily proffered when one is the conqueror, and so Yankees might easily forgive and forget the atrocities of this war. But when the fighting ended and the country united, George wondered if the South could ever stop hating the North. It brought to mind the resentment of a wayward child trying to escape the overbearing parent who refuses to allow it to leave. The parent will welcome the prodigal child's return, but the child's resentment will remain.

He stepped from the stream and dressed quickly. Despite his bath, he did not feel refreshed. The question continued to nag at him: What good can stand against such hatred?

Along the road, he paused and stooped to retrieve a stone, then stacked it upon others waiting in line at the edge of the field, waiting, as if they, too, longed for the war to end. He lifted another into place, then another, larger stones on the bottom, flat stones along the top. Atrophied muscles in his arms ached in protest, but he plunged onward.

He hefted a heavy boulder and dropped it in place, more stones lifted and laid, edges plumbed with a stick, another stone on top and another at the base. The sky shimmered and the sun came out and baked his shoulders, warming him. A fever of sweat glistened on back and forearms swiftly stacking heavy stones in a burst of fury and frustration and rage at three years of war and wasted time and living he had lost.

And the wall grew by rock and yard.

It was a beginning, this dinner invitation, a gesture of appeasement, and George Van Norman surged with eagerness. He felt capable and proud. It was required that he affect a proper dignity. It was his duty to perform with respectability and correctness. No talk of politics, he decided. It was an argument he had no hope of winning. Some people will hold their opinions, and others felt bound to convert yours. George did not know which the Judge might be, but he had no desire for him to regret his hospitality. Best not to talk of politics.

Dress uniform long since abandoned in the conduct of war, George resolved to make the best appearance his meager belongings would allow. He pulled on his tunic, polished his buttons, and ran a cloth over his boots once more. Mustache full and neatly trimmed, hair parted and combed, George walked up the broad front steps promptly at seven, took a deep breath, and knocked.

Eb, in his tattered black suit and dusty tie, greeted him at the door and ushered him into the dining hall off the foyer, his shuffling gait resonating softly off the rich mahogany. The room had high ceilings that answered his every movement with a thin echo. Along the outside wall, painted shades with scenes of dancing couples and horse-drawn carriages covered windows between massive damask drapes. "May I take your hat, sir?" Eb said.

George handed it to him and grinned, enjoying the ceremony. With a bow, Eb left the hall and George suddenly noticed the table setting, heirlooms that had somehow escaped sale or theft. On the pressed linen cloth sat a silver candelabrum, its light glinting off fine sterling and cut crystal glassware. Ornate trays held candied fruits and fancy breads—delicacies he had seen only in magazines.

"Good evening, Sergeant, and thank you for coming." Judge Wilson strode into the room with Jesse and stood by the head of the long table. "Please sit here." He gestured to a seat beside his own.

Drawing out the heavy wooden chair, George suddenly stopped. Into the room came a woman, slim and erect, her dark hair piled high to emphasize her slender neck. She had the bearing of a princess, whether from intent or natural demeanor he could not tell, but he consciously made an effort to close his gaping mouth.

With a sweep of his hand, Judge Wilson said, "Please, won't you be seated?"

George knew enough not to sit while a woman stood, but this did not register in his conscious mind. More, it was the unexpectedness. Clearing his throat, he said, "There's someone here I have not met."

She wore a long dress of rich velvet the color of blue spruce, her slender waist tightly cinched. Her eyes were the violet of an oyster's inner shell with an intensity that made them glimmer in the candlelight. George had never seen eyes like that before.

Introductions made, Jesse held her chair as she took her seat, the rustle of petticoats a recital. The Judge led the group in a brief prayer of thanks, careful to make no mention of politics or events of the day. Mitsy scurried into the room and set a platter of steaming ham on the table as the Judge held forth on various topics ranging from oil wells in Pennsylvania to camels in the Crimea. George sat quietly, mesmerized not by the Judge's incessant banter, but rather by his daughter. For daughter she was, hidden on the third floor from prying eyes and men of ill intent, of which there were many about, and of whom he had been considered one.

Her name was Eva.

"No insult was meant upon your person," explained the Judge. "We simply could not chance any…" he paused, "… unwholesomeness until we could better determine your intentions."

Another brimming pot appeared and Mitsy left again by the kitchen door. As George spooned wild berry sauce onto yet another biscuit, the Judge said, "It was most kind of you to share your provisions with us, Sergeant." He gestured to the platters laden with cornbread, dried peaches, and candied yams. "The army must have an abundance of stores to afford such luxuries as these."

"You are quite welcome, sir," said George. "Mitsy makes them look far better than they do in camp."

"Please pass the salt," said Jesse.

George passed a silver shaker.

"That's the pepper," said Jesse. "I want the salt."

"I'm sorry," said George, and offered the matching silver shaker.

"We were taught to pass both when you ask for one or the other," Jesse said.

"Perhaps Sergeant Van Norman does not share the same table rules where he comes from," said Judge Wilson.

"I come from a large family," said George. "We couldn't all fit at our table, so we ate in shifts."

Jesse said to George, "Why do you talk like that?"

"Like what?"

"You clip your words like you're in a hurry," the boy said. "And you talk through your nose."

Eva started to giggle, then quickly covered her mouth.

"I talk the way I talk," George said. "I'm from Wisconsin and that's how we talk."

The Judge said, "Sergeant, tell us something about Wisconsin."

George raised a linen napkin and wiped his mustache self-consciously. "I grew up on a farm much like this—only not so big—with nine older brothers and sisters."

"Are they Yankees, too?" asked Jesse.

"Well, Jesse, I suppose we're Yankees because we come from the North, but only two of my brothers are in the army." George did not like this turn of conversation. "We all moved to Wisconsin from New York when I was about your age. My father is a civil servant, just like yours." He groped for other things they had in common. "And we live on a farm and raise crops and tend the animals and do chores just like you."

Mitsy cleared the dishes and George continued. "My brothers and I all worked around the farm. My job was to fetch water from the spring every morning before sunrise. During the harvest, I worked in the fields picking corn and wheat. Sometimes I had to dig potatoes, but mostly that was my brother's job.

"On weekends, I walked into town and bought licorice at the store with some pennies my pa would give me. Or my friend, Mike, and I would go fishing or hunting for squirrels or raccoons. Mike once caught a catfish that was so big, it hauled him into the water. He nearly drowned." He caught Jesse smiling. "I guess you could say the fish caught him."

"I go fishing sometimes. I have a fishing pole Papa made for me. Silas and I have a special spot," Jesse said.

"I once caught a mess of trout in our creek," George said. "We had fish dinner that night, all twelve of us."

Jesse said, "I caught sixteen fish once, all in one day. Mitsy cleaned some for dinner that night, and we smoked the rest."

"Maybe we can go fishing together some time," George said.

Jesse looked at his father. There was an uncomfortable silence for a moment until the kitchen door flew open and Mitsy entered carrying a pie, her hands wrapped in towels against the warm pan. Immediately, the room filled with an enchanting aroma, part bakery, part sunshine, part home, all fragrant and delicious.

"This is Mitsy's specialty," said Eva, her first words of the evening. "It's hickory nut pie," she said, her voice deep and silky, like warm maple syrup. "She and Silas pick the nuts from our shagbark trees."

"I help, too," said Jesse.

"Yes, you do," she said. "The nuts are very hard. In the fall, we all sit together breaking out the meat. Mitsy makes hickory nut cookies and pies all winter long."

"Except one winter," said Jesse. "The squirrels got them."

"We discovered we had a hole in our roof," the Judge said. "Cletus and I fixed it, though. Cletus was one of our…" He paused. "… people here. Good man."

George spooned a portion of pie into his mouth, chewing noisily. Eva stared at him, probably out of the same curiosity he had for her, or perhaps in objection to his crude table manners. He paused and wiped his moustache carefully. "Sure is good pie," he said. "I'll bet Mr. Lincoln doesn't even get such good cooking." Immediately, he realized his mistake, invoking the name of the President, loathed by all loyal Southerners.

Before he could change the subject, Eva spoke. "Tell us news of the war, Sergeant Van Norman. What do you hear from your friends in Washington?"

Jesse said, "Has General Sherman burnt all of the Carolinas like he did Georgia?"

Eva said, "Has he exterminated all the animals, too, as Sheridan did in the Shenandoah? Or does he limit his destruction to just homes and barns?"

Jesse again, nearly shouting, "How many men have you killed, Sergeant Van Norman?"

"Children!" called the Judge, gesturing with his fork like a conductor silencing the orchestra. "Sergeant Van Norman is our guest. And I remind you he was kind enough to provide us with much of what we are eating here this evening. Please show some courtesy."

Eva peered at the table. "I'm sorry, Sergeant Van Norman. You have been most generous."

George slowly wiped his mouth once more, then dropped the heavy linen carelessly on the table beside his plate. "I was wounded at Nashville fighting Rebels disloyal to the Union," he snapped. "My regiment moved on, and they sent me here. You know more about the course of the war than I do." To Eva, he said. "I have no friends in Washington. And no idea where General Sherman might be." He looked hard at Jesse. "And I never shot any man who wasn't shooting at me."

"Please excuse my children's behavior, Sergeant," said the Judge. "Ever since Freddie was killed, they have been excessively bitter."

At the sound of his brother's name, Jesse stood. "May I be excused, Papa?"

"Yes, you may," said the Judge. After the boy had gone, he said, "We all loved Frederick deeply, no one more than I. But the boy there was hit particularly hard. They were very close. Since then, Jesse has asked me many times if he could join up. He tried to run away once. Fortunately, some of your cavalry took kindly to him and returned him to me unharmed." He shook his head. "No man should have to bury his children," he said quietly.

George braced his elbows on the chair arms and clasped his hands. He stared at a spot on the table linen, a heaviness in his stomach that had nothing to do with the food. After what seemed a long time, he rose, thanked the Judge for his hospitality, ventured a nod to the self-important daughter, and returned to his tent in the side yard.

THE NIGHT WAS WARM, THE FIRST VESTIGES of spring on the wind. Dotted by constellations, the galaxies spread a great path of glitter, illuminating the night sky. George lay on his bedroll, flexing his arm, willing the strength to return. He was angry with himself and with the outcome of his dinner with the Wilson family. Not at all as he had hoped, it could not have gone much worse. He was about to draw the canvas tent flap when he heard familiar footfalls.

"Good evening, Eb," he said, crawling from his tent.

"A mighty fine evening it is, Sergeant Van Norman," Eb said in his rich timberwood voice, his bare feet splayed across a large patch of grass beside George's tent. "Sergeant Van Norman? May I ask something of you, sir?"

George stood. "What is it?"

"Sir, I should like to ask you not to go too hard on Miss Eva and the boy. Master Frederick was a fine young man. My boy Silas and he were very close." Eb played with the buttons on his muslin shirt. "Young Jesse can be … peevish time to time. And Miss Eva can be hard on folks, too. Sees things as black or white right now. You understand my meaning?"

George nodded. Many recruits saw the war with the same sense of good and evil. At the shouted command, they sprang forward in pitched fever of hate. After the battle, this savage madness would linger, as if an evil spirit had made camp within their souls and decided to remain. They might find fault with companions for petty grievances, or kick the camp dog for simply being underfoot. With all that had transpired against his hosts here at Elm Grove, their fever-hate might be long in cooling.

"I have seen a lot in my time, good and bad," Eb went on. "I can tell you, sir, there is too much ugly in this world."

George nodded. "I've seen some myself, Eb."

Eb said, "I expect you have, Sergeant Van Norman. I expect you have."

The wind rustled the elms. Shafts of light from the windows angled across the lawns, and the night air breathed warm against him. "Mind if I ask you a question, Eb?"

"You want to know about my feet?" Eb smiled, teeth gleaming against the dark. "I confess, sir, I heard you ask the Judge."

It was not the question he had in mind, but if Eb were willing to speak of it, George would willingly listen. He missed the amity of his friends in the regiment and welcomed the conversation.

"Former owner beat me, sir, or rather the owner's overseer," Eb said, and he began to unbutton his shirt, fingering each wooden button carefully, rolling his broad shoulders. He turned slightly, and George could not control an audible gasp. Scars crossed the man's back as if plowed in deep furrows. "I had a different woman then," he went on, buttoning his shirt. "Her name was Florence, after the city where she was sold." He gazed into the distance. "We had a family, two little girls. Lived a good life at a place not far from here. Flo worked in the kitchen. I was learning to be a blacksmith."

George nodded, eager for Eb to continue. It was more than simply a need for talk. This was new for George. Eb was the first black man with whom he had ever spoken at any length.

"That's how they broke my feet, with hammer and anvil," Eb said. He sucked air through clenched teeth. "One night, I heard noise coming from the barn, saw Flo with the overseer, wrestling with him." Eb paused, turned away. "Nothing I could do," he said and dropped his head. "Nothing." He wiped his hand over his face. "We left the next day. No plan, really. Just packed a few things and lit out after dark. They caught us in a few days." He waited for a moment, said nothing. Somewhere in the distance, an owl cried. "Flo died not long after they sold our girls. I managed to hang on, but I was no good to anyone. The Judge, he bought me, put me to work as a house servant. He and Miss Jane taught me to read. That was—let's see—about nine years ago now," he said. "Nine years."

George sat quietly for a moment. A hundred questions filled his mind, and he carefully chose those to ask first. "How old is Silas?" he said.

"Silas is fifteen, sir," Eb said. "Chryssy is our daughter. Silas's father is a fellow named Cletus who used to work here. Cletus... well, Cletus was a good field hand, but something of a wanderer, sir, if you catch my meaning. The Judge was quite fond of Cletus," Eb said. He plucked some blades of grass and rubbed them between his thick fingers, spoke his next words carefully. "Though Silas is not of my blood, it does not mean he is not my son. I raised him as my own and I know him as my boy." He spoke almost in a whisper. "When Cletus left, he tried to take Silas. We argued on it."

George watched as the big man clenched and unclenched his giant fists, like animal traps opening and snapping shut. George said, "Tell me about Eva, Eb."

A smile creased the big man's ebony features and slowly spread like ripples on muddy water. "She is the belle of the ball and the queen of the county. Yes sir, the pride of Middle Tennessee, she surely is."

A deep croak came from his throat sounding like a broken limb in a thunderstorm. George assumed it was laughter, but could not be certain.

"She held the envy of every woman and the heart of every man around these parts. One in particular, a Master Thomas Harden, was the one she chose. But he has not been heard from in some time." Eb scratched his chin, peered into the blackness of the night as if trying to remember. "A fine boy, came from a good family. But the Judge seemed to have his doubts, thought he was a bit..." Eb groped for the word. "'Fragile' is what the Judge called him. Sickly at times, maybe." Eb paused. "I got on with his man servant. He's the one told me Master Tom was lost. Struck Miss Eva right hard, it did." The wind rustled in the trees and around them were night sounds. "It's happening all too frequently these days."

George nodded, thought of the many loved ones left behind. Somebody's darlings.

"The Judge dotes on her, as did her mother, Lady Jane," Eb went on. "And young Jesse—well, he lost a brother—he is very protective of his sister. It was his idea to hide her in the attic. Now that you're here, well, it seems the Judge trusts you, Sergeant. And I think he sees something in you, sir, if I'm reading him right." He stared hard at George, a furl on his brow like a shade drawn over his deep-set eyes. "She is a willful young woman, sir. You be careful!" And he grinned broadly, and George could not help but grin, too. "Do you have family, sir?" Eb asked.

"A big family back in Wisconsin. Some of my older brothers and sisters are married off. Others have gone their own way." He scratched at his mustache. "The fact is I don't really know what to expect when I get back to Wisconsin. So much has changed."

Eb nodded. "I have come to mistrust my feelings for kin," he said. Somewhere near the stable, an owl's cry was swallowed by the night. "The Judge has been very good to me and I expect I will stay on. Silas can go if he wants, and I will miss him. But leaving home is part of growing up. Don't you think?"

GEORGE SLEPT BENEATH THE CANVAS TENT, darkness close upon him like an abyss, without moon or starlight. No sound, not even that of raccoon or possum or their fellow nocturnals. No swift or swallow, barn owl or squab disturbed the air. No drifting zephyr to come or go, nothing to disturb limb or leaf, no drone of insect to rouse the senses. Looming beside him, the house, hushed and dim, stood amorphous as if draped in sheath or shroud. Asleep beneath twin canvas sheets, breath so weedy as to be soundless, George kept vigil within his slumber, peaceful and quiet. Sleep, deep respite. Sleep.

Then: barking dog, rattle of hoof on rock, violent slap on leather, curses and shouting and galloping horses jolted him into fear and he jumped, smothered against fabric, confused, his senses tumbled. Darting into darkness, his rifle at the ready, he followed the sound of retreating horses and shouted, he forgot what. He stood bewildered in underwear sewn from old muslin towels, chafing in the dank night air. A light appeared in the doorway of the house and he turned, squinting in the glow.

"What in God's heaven?" It was the voice of the Judge. He stood dimly outlined in nightshirt and robe, his waist sash unwrapping itself from its hastily tied knot. The light bobbed and weaved as it grew closer, brightening the distance between them, revealing to both the scant attire that covered the sergeant. A titter of laughter from the doorway was stifled by a "Shush." A woman's voice. Eva?

George retreated to his tent to gather his trousers and overcoat. His mind raced, sifting that which was fed by his senses. More voices. Shouts and lanterns traced arcs in the darkness. He heard barking in the distance: Jeff Davis.

"What's all the ruckus? Who were those men?"

"I'm sorry, Judge," George replied, clumsily staggering into his boots. "But I think we've had some visitors."

"Bushwhackers?" Judge Wilson looked toward the barn, sighing heavily. "What is there left to take?"

Silas came running up, holding another lantern that George took from his outstretched hand. "We'd better find out," he said, and marched into the shadows.

The heavy wooden doors stood open, lantern light weakly illuminating the great void that had once been a bustling stable filled with horses and bales of hay, stores of barley and corn, barrels of molasses and feed for cattle and chickens. Now it stood nearly empty, the stores long ago eaten or stolen, animals confiscated by one army or another. Hay littered the plank floor, scattered sparsely, not even enough to warm mice through winter. To each side, stalls sat gaping as if, while waiting for their occupants return, they had lost all hope. Along the front wall, a bench ran for twenty feet or so, topped with leather straps, scattered bits of hardware, shoe nails bent and useless, a Bristol brick.

As George and the Judge walked the length of the cavernous barn, more lanterns appeared at the doorway—Eb and Eva, Jesse and Silas—shedding more light into the corners.

"Some protection you are," said Jesse, shivering, barefoot on the cold floor.

"That's enough, young man!" The Judge spoke from the depths of the barn, voice of authority. He stepped around a stall, eyed the party gathered at the entrance. "Eb, please take the boys back to the house. We shall be along shortly."

"Yes, sir." One lantern disappeared into the night, dancing with Eb's bobbing gait, the boys following.

George stood in the doorway listening. The barking of the dog grew more animated. "Sounds like Jeff Davis is chasing them," said the Judge.

From afar, more barking, rapid and frantic. And then a gunshot, distant but distinct in the still night air. The barking stopped.

No one moved. They all stood, as if frozen. Toward the house, the lantern cast a soft glow on Eb and the two boys, their eyes pinpoints of fire staring into the blackness.

George leaned against the open door. Ineffectual Jeff Davis had ranted against the angry intruders, and the intruders had replied. It dawned upon him a striking parallel to the army's place in Middle Tennessee, intruders raging against the protestations of pride and Southern aristocracy. And for what? To preserve the Union? Or to pilfer the meager possessions of a people broken and despondent? All for God and country, and for a barking dog. Across the yard, George heard distinctly Jesse's weeping and he knew that somehow it was his fault.

His mood was solemn and subdued as the Judge and Eva followed him back into the barn. Their lanterns cast eerie shadows in the rafters. Dust hung in the glow. Finally, the Judge said. "We'll find him in the morning, bring him back here to bury."

"Does anything seem to be missing?" It was Eva who spoke, lantern light haloing her head, her robe shimmering with flecks of silver on crimson.

"Not much left here to take," said the Judge. "The barn has been emptied of feed since the animals were gone. What food there was has long been ..."

"Oh, no!" Eva gasped and held her light high over the long oaken bench.

The Judge saw immediately what was missing. "They've taken all our tools, and the last of our harness and tack."

"No. Look." Eva pointed at empty hooks on the barn wall. "My spur. It's gone." In response to George's curious stare, she said, "My spur. I wore it when I rode. It was my spur, my only spur." Eva seethed beneath a thin façade of decorum.

"One spur?" George asked.

"Only one spur is needed," Eva snapped. "'Spur the left flank, the right will surely follow.' General Forrest told me that when he gave it to me." She wrung her hands, her anger palpable in the musty barn air.

"General Forrest was a friend of mine before the war," said the Judge. "He was quite fond of Eva as a little girl. Taught her to ride. Gave her the spur."

"And now it's gone." She turned on George, eyes the color of the lantern light, decorum evaporated. "Where were you?" A wave of shame swept through him and he kept his thoughts unspoken as she shouted, "You were supposed to guard this plantation." Spittle flung on popping Ts and Ps. "Where were you?" She turned sharply, a whiskey noise of silk on silk, hay skittering under her bare feet as she bustled from the barn, her lantern swinging wildly.

The Judge put his hand on George's shoulder. Together, they slid the heavy wooden door closed, rusty casters whining in the stillness.

CHAPTER FIFTEEN

William Slive stood in the parlor, what had once been a formal receiving room with deep wool carpets and hand-carved oaken tables and chairs. On the walls were paintings of long-dead family members slightly off plumb—Smith family and Waters family, not a Slive among them.

William Slive had no kin, or none he knew about. He remembered his mother as a woman who washed laundry by day and entertained gentlemen by night. He recalled some of the callers, their top hats and canes and fancy handkerchiefs, old men who bribed him with sweets and patted his head until he fled to his room. She had died when he was ten or eleven, never speaking of any Mr. Slive. No grandparents, no uncles, no brothers or sisters, no Slives to hang on the walls. And so he left the Smiths and the Waters paintings hanging. They reminded him of what his past might have been.

Moonlight shone through the half-drawn draperies and dust motes swirled and eddied in the beams as the big man strode through the room. Today had been a good day. Slive had bills of sale on five horses, all signed and legal looking. The raid on the plantation had given him tools and outfits for some of the horses. He toted up in his head how much he might expect from the trader in Memphis, a tidy sum. Yes, today had been a good day.

Until Henry Carter told him about that Turner fellow.

Slive had found Henry Carter two days past. Short little whippet, still wearing his Confederate grays, just walking down the road like a dosey-doe. Simply another deserter, this one more worthless than most. First thing Carter had done was beg for food. Slive was always amazed how easy it was to make a hungry man your friend. A few scraps of jerky and a cup of chicory and Henry Carter fell in line like an unweaned pup. Slive had put him to work at the smokehouse first thing, chopping wood. Henry Carter had been at Watersmith for two whole days before he thought to tell the story of running into Mr. Turner at the cave.

"Bastard stole my horse!" Slive slammed his fist, shaking the oak table. "That's a hanging offense."

"I didn't know they were your horses, or I would have told you sooner," Carter said. "I followed him after he nearly skinned me alive. Saw him take her out of that cave, big old horse, bright red like a fancy dress. He looked right noble on it, too, if I do say." Carter thumbed his dirty slouch hat back on his head. "He didn't see me, though. I'm sure of that."

Slive stood over the much smaller man, made a determined effort to contain his wrath. "Just like I didn't see you neither, huh?"

Carter removed his hat to rub the brim between his fingers. "You're sneaky like a fox, Mr. Slive. I have to say. If you had been a conscript man or a Yankee scout, I'd have been done for, and that's a fact."

"Damn betcha, boy." Slive sat heavily in the overstuffed wing chair and picked a thin cigar out of the drawer of the sideboard, snipped the end with his knife, and stabbed the blade back into the sideboard. "How far did you follow him?" he asked.

"Couldn't keep up, seeing as how I was afoot." Carter looked at his boots. "He headed south on the trail and I lost him. Then I came onto you."

"How come you didn't say nothing about them horses two days ago? And how come you didn't steal no horse for your own self?" Slive eyed him warily.

"Them are U.S. Army horses," Carter said matter-of-factly. "Get caught with one, they're likely to stretch your neck, just as you said." He thumbed his hat once more. "Unless you have a bill of sale."

Slive ignored this. He struck a match, and sucked his cheroot, short-puffed until it lit, then blew a long stream of smoke. "Man said he had kin in these parts," thinking out loud. "Up north of here somewhere. If he was headed south as you say, that puts his kin somewhere between here and that cave." He blew another cloud of smoke and eyed his companion. "Where you say you was from?"

"Hot-lanta, heart of the South," Carter said. "But I have no home to return to since Sherman marched through and incinerated everything."

"Mm-mm. And what outfit you with?"

"Cheatham's Corps, Georgia Sharpshooters," Carter said proudly. "Best outfit in the whole C. S. of A. But I don't know where they're bivouacked right now."

Henry Carter spoke with an airy style. His accent sounded like money and every third sentence had a big word like it was his special gift to you. He spun his tale of woe; the longer he talked, the worse his story became. Lying came to Carter as easily as talking. No home, family killed or lost, his best girl raped by the cursed Yankees surely as they sat.

Henry Carter was a lazy feather-bedder. Slive had seen his like before, especially among the niggers, who always found an excuse not to work—a blistered foot or a runny nose or some nonsense—nothing serious, just enough to keep them out of the fields for a day. Lazy bastards! Henry Carter, too. Except Henry Carter was white. Talked like he had some education, too. Uppity white trash. Wearing fancy boots, not army issues that's for sure, probably stolen from somebody. Slive thought to steal them for himself, but saw they would be too small.

No, best to put Mr. Henry Carter to good use. Work around Watersmith, maybe help find that Turner fellow who seems to have this problem with horses—either losing them or falling off them or stealing them. And stealing horses was a hanging offense.

Chapter Sixteen

Elm Grove Plantation, February 2, 1865

E va brushed and separated rippled strands of her raven tresses with a tortoise shell comb, the one that had been her mother's. With languid strokes, she parted it into two lustrous hanks that she braided swiftly and tautly, then wound the finished braids across her head, and fastened them with strips of cloth. The mirror reflected her peach complexion on cheekbones smooth and efficient, no unnecessary curves or draws. She dabbed at the edges of her eyes, searching for the wrinkles she knew would come eventually, but found none. She nodded almost imperceptibly.

Paradox hung in the stillness of her bedroom, her mind darting from pride to pathos, self-satisfaction to self-recrimination, in humming-bird fashion. She naturally embraced her feminine aspect. Yet it was an irony that she, in the prime of her womanhood, sat sad as a ripe flower in a deep wood, her beauty fading without notice. No male emotions to stir, no holiday balls to attend, her best years fleeting, ephemeral, like the cool on the underside of a pillow.

And then there was Sergeant Van Norman, a contradiction she struggled to understand. He was, after all, a Yankee, the Devil in all his grand display. Sent to watch over and protect. Protect us from what? she wondered. Other Yankees, is what. Like trusting a dog to guard your pork chop, or crows to protect the corncrib.

Yet this Yankee possessed inveterate symptoms of decency. He had brought the food stores. There was that, she conceded. And he worked the land without prodding, without recompense. She had watched him once from her canary perch for nearly an hour as he worked with young Silas to build the rock wall, his muscles taut beneath his linen day shirt, his body limber and strong. He seemed to possess a demonic energy. Such was the contradiction: in Sergeant Van Norman, anything seemed possible. And him, a Yankee.

But could he be trusted? Papa seemed to think so. Otherwise she would have remained hidden on the third floor. Mitsy and Eb assured her he was kind and charitable, and the people always seemed unfailing when they took the measure of a man.

Eva replaced her comb and set the strips of cloth aside. From the mirror, her face stared back, her lips tight as if containing a moan of great despair. Yes, he had brought gifts and food for everyone, she admitted. But the food had been taken from the rich stores of the Union Army, which in turn had been taken, no doubt, from the surrounding countryside, her neighbors and friends. She followed this line of thinking to its source and concluded that she and her family had become little more than commoners accepting the fruits of another man's theft.

Her mind reeled at the notion and she paused to examine this assessment. Small voices in her head clamored at her and the light in her heart flickered with shame. Could she not accept a gift with grace? More of the paradox, she supposed.

She drew linen paper, bottle ink, and pen from her writing drawer, dipped her quill and nib, and began to write.

Dearest Mother

God must surely dwell in this revolution, as he resides in all the events of history. Can adversaries mutually claim that Providence dwells in their house, that righteousness belongs to them alone?

Wellington believed that the issue of every battle depended upon Providence. Yet Napoleon, his greatest adversary, declared that from the moment he crossed the bridge at Lodi, he felt that he was a man of Destiny.

Divine Providence bore this Confederacy, its Genesis a new form of government. Yet as the weather freshens, our collective dream withers into nightmare. Providence, it seems, has abandoned us. Had we foreseen the torment of our Destiny, we might never have entered upon this quest.

Is it destiny that begets heroes, applauded and hurrahed, who perform courageous acts with the eyes of an admiring world upon them? Or is it simply the opportunity, and not the man that is required for heroism. You often said that true heroes are not shaped by grand deeds, but by small ones, fashioned alone and in secret and in the every day.

I believe such a man sups at our table, eats of our bread – or rather we of his. A leader of men, he carries responsibility gracefully, humbly. He possesses a quiet courage, his magnanimity evident in the trifles.

Therein lies the paradox of the heart. He is the Devil's own emissary. Yet iniquity attaches to him no more than rainwater to fowl. Could such a man tempt the temptress? Is he the snake in this Eden? Or is he as ingenuous and comme il faut as he exhibits?

I long for your counsel as I tire from contemplation. Content for now, aspiring only to warrant your pride as you so warrant my

Love,

$\mathcal{E}$

She gently dabbed the quill in her ink rag and set aside her writing kit.

CHAPTER SEVENTEEN

Near Athens, Ala., August 1, 1865

The train moved slowly through open country, each kick-kack made specific by the slowing of the wheels, as if the carriages had grown lethargic in the night. The cargo of soldiers and civilians slept, hushed and still in the dimness before dawn. They did not see the heart of the valley, grasses heavy with dew in the half-light, nor the rows of cottonwood surrounded by snowy pillows of fluff drifting in the air as if swimming on an invisible river. On a grassy slope lay long swaggering rows of honeysuckle in deep lavender, the air heavy with their perfume. The lively colors and drifting odors were woven together in the fabric of the dawn, somnolent and content within the spirit of the place.

The great train lurched around a long curve, the wheels gnashing at the rails with a deep grinding sound. His newspaper tumbled to the floor and Sergeant George Van Norman awoke with a start. On the next bench, a small boy slept upon his mother's lap, her head leaning into the window stop, hat askew, mouth drooping, a tiny bubble at her lips as she snored softly.

Outside his window, the sun rose in shades of indigo and violet, shafts of gold escaping from the horizon, turning to green that which had been black. The slow kick-kack, kick-kack became a rumble, hollow and throaty. Freshly hewn timbers, bridge supports, filed past his window like soldiers on parade, dark and ominous against the purple sunrise. Below him, a broad river flowed turgid and brown. Huge bestial trees hung lazily over its banks, draped with moss that cascaded from the highest limbs. Starlings careened across the valley, quiet as dreams.

At a crossroads, a signpost pointed lazily: Corinth. It stopped his eyes. The name alone made George want to reach out and pluck the sign and throw it down in tall grass where it could not be found. Corinth. He remembered it as a place for dying, where his friend, Bill Illingsworth, had bled out on a grassy field, and where a dozen more of the Eighth Wisconsin were still buried. The grinding of his teeth sounded in his head and he forced himself to breathe deeply, ashamed that something so trifling could provoke such temper.

Now the place teamed with life, its fields covered in rich greens and yellows. Brightly colored flowers, names of which he did not know, blossomed alongside the dusty roads. Southern weather seemed good weather for growing things. He supposed, over time, one became accustomed to the oppressive heat. Perhaps the South really was another country altogether. Rich in culture, steeped in civility, famous for its hospitality and propriety, for living at a slower pace. He admired the Southern people he had come to know: the shopkeepers in Columbia, the Judge and his associates, Eb and his family. They displayed kindness and civility in full measure.

All save one: Slive, whose bitter cruelty remained a mystery to George's way of thinking. What circumstances could have rendered such poor result as he, a man ignorant of the causes, whose capacity for recrimination had no basis in reason? Slive seemed to have possessed malice beyond scope.

George sought logic in all circumstance. He held this idea on principle, deeper than opinion. Something in his blood. Somehow, even the most outrageous behavior of officers or Democrats must make some kind of levelheaded sense. He had always worked out the logic eventually, finding reason in even the most unthinkable behavior.

Yet he found none in Slive.

George lowered his Hardee hat and leaned into his seat. He closed his eyes and rocked with the gentle swaying of the train. But Slive invaded his sleep. He clenched his fists, furious at the man's intrusion into the sanctuary of his slumber. Slive must have been born cruel, some strange twist of fetus, come on a Wednesday, in the drunken part of the evening. George could find no other explanation.

What excuse existed for such wickedness? Others had endured without such depravity. Others had managed to persevere, even with their farms destroyed, their families uprooted. How had they muddled through? From where had their courage come? What guided such faith?

George remembered a story of two Nashville sisters who had lost their husbands to the war. They had no money and were forced off their land. They had no horse, but they had an old wagon and so they toted their meager goods to town for selling, pulling the wagon themselves. A wealthy merchant purchased their belongings and gave them jobs as cooks in his hotel and a room to sleep until they could buy back their household goods and find a home to live. In time, they did both. And the women were black and the man was white. The women's husbands had fought for the Blue and the man had been a Colonel of the Gray.

Cause and effect had no connection to such circumstances. Reason, disconnected, became lost. When dragged to the point of terror, strange things happened to people, some bitter and cruel, some beautiful beyond faith. Perhaps, then, understanding is not the prize, finding logic but a lesson in futility.

George preferred to side with faith.

The train rumbled and swayed, a gentle rocking, and his chin fell and his chest heaved. Cause and result. Logic and faith. Philosophy and geography. And Slive. Big and brutal…Slive. Kick-kack.

CHAPTER EIGHTEEN

Watersmith Plantation, February 2, 1865

On porch boards warped from sun and worn from traffic, nails poking through like spring crocus, William Slive stood broad-legged, arms across his chest, and surveyed all he possessed: the great Watersmith, three hundred acres of chaos where once there had been order, privation where once there had been plenty. Tobacco stains lay like wounds on his tattered flannel shirt. He kicked at the muddy clods that clung to his boots and contemplated his misfortune.

A tension grew in his mind, a fear that his world was changing and that he would be left behind. He would not get his fair share. There seemed to him too much to understand. The slaves, all of them gone. None to plant the spring crop, no harvest to hold Watersmith through the winter. What good is land without the hands to work it?

Freed by Emancipation, niggers roamed the countryside, wild and unnatural, animals that had once worked the land, but now had turned to thieving and worse. No one to direct them but themselves. Obedience and labor had turned to disobedience and sloth. Niggers became squatters, living off what few stores remained. Or worse, stealing what they couldn't have as slaves: horses and mules, jewelry and silverware, anything they could sell. Slive had heard of one nigger named Mad Henry who had trailed his master, an old man fleeing the Yankees with all his belongings, axed him to death as he slept, then fled with the plunder.

It wasn't natural, these niggers running around free. Slive held that slavery benefited the black race, and therefore society as a whole. Niggers required discipline, direction, control, and thus the "natural order" was preserved. Look at free blacks in the North, proof that the common nigger lacked ability to exercise freedom. These Africans, savages really, had been lifted up under the wings of Southern society, given quality in their lives, even if not equality. Without white supervision, Slive believed that niggers were doomed to extinction by natural selection. Just like that Darwin fellow said. Slavery at least gave niggers some security and made them useful.

Slive believed that man was motivated by self-interest, believed competition to be a healthy thing, those of talent and ability forever rising, the rest fitting into their rightful place somewhere below. Liberty was for the quick and the clever, the deserving. Put the rest to work and allow the higher born to pursue culture and learning, to the bettering of civilization.

Now they were all gone. Before Mrs. Waters died, all but a handful of the niggers had abandoned the property, the remainder gone before harvest, run off with the others after word of Emancipation spread, no way to get them back.

Slive stood alone, like a man at a grave, the rasping voice of Mrs. Waters stirring in his head, "Yes, this seems to be all in order," she said, adding her scrawl to the document. All in order, thought Slive. Watersmith had become a wasteland. No livestock, no crops, no niggers. Only a smokehouse, an empty barn, and a big old house remained of the once prosperous Watersmith. Yes, the house, furnished in a forgotten era, chairs of cherry and walnut, their upholstery faded, stuffing poking from seams; the walls of some wood or another, but chipped and cracked; wool rugs, stained and threadbare; tattered window shades painted with idyllic scenes between massive drapes tattered and faded. Fashionable funeral parlor.

"Let me die," she had pleaded. Mrs. Waters, who for three score years had been a loyal citizen, but a bitter thing to preserve when war came. Worse still to offer her family in the trade. She had lost her husband at Vicksburg, and her boys, Delbert and True, killed somewhere in Georgia by that animal, Sherman. "Let me go peacefully, and I'll give you land." Property lines extended with a forger's skill to include the whole before presentation to the Registrar in the stockaded State Capitol. All in order. Mrs. Waters dead, no will to be found. Minnie, the nosey little niece, none the wiser.

With the land, Slive had expected prosperity. But it had not come, and he reasoned it was not his fault. The world had conspired against him. Slive felt a growing frustration with all that had changed, his needs swelling into pressures until they broke through. Needs lead to change, change to action.

Larceny had proved more dangerous and more hard work than he had expected. He raided from Dickson in the north to the Tennessee River in the South, a broad range. But his neighbors were often worse off than Slive, and the pickings grew leaner. Nothing but tools and horse tack at the last place he and Carter had ransacked. Had to shoot the damn dog, too.

"Somebody's coming up the road, Mr. Slive," said Carter. The rider approached, his tiny round hat bouncing awry. Coogin dismounted, shuffled across the porch and stood in the hallway, his dusty bowler held firmly in both hands. He nodded to Carter, then turned to Slive. "Niggers," he said, and pointed up the road.

"Squatters?" Slive said. "Where?"

"Bottoms."

"Damn! The niggers have come back. Too many of them hereabouts. On the roads, on the trains, in the shops."

"There's niggers everywhere," Carter said.

Slive began to pace. "These are on my land!"

"Niggers stealing horses, living in white men's houses." Carter eyed the big man walking across the worn carpet. "It just isn't acceptable, Mr. Slive. Now there are some residing right here? Right on your property?"

"Stealing my food and God knows what else." Slive stopped pacing, looked hard at Coogin. "Squatters down by the creek, you say?"

"We should do something," Carter said.

Coogin let out a low guttural noise that resembled a growl. "Get 'em," he said, and he pounded his fist in his hand.

"Too many," Slive said. Twice Slive had found niggers living in woods below the creek, and twice he had driven them off. Back again a week later.

"We should do something to keep them out, for good," said Carter. "Make them want to leave."

Coogin pinched up his face and wiggled his arms over his head. "Shoo 'em."

"They are a superstitious lot," said Carter.

Slive squinted his eye and chewed his lower lip. Scare them off? Yes, that could work. Scare a few and the rest will surely follow. His mind began to foam and fester, rabid imaginings of ogres and phantoms, creatures of the night. His chest grew tight and fetid breath hissed through his teeth.

"Some sort of monster," said Carter.

"Swamp Wampus," said Coogin.

Slive's mind ran as a body restless, energy bursting with no focus. Thought and perception ricocheted inside his brain like stones rattling in a can. Scare all the niggers hereabouts. Yes! Scare them so bad, they run, take their families with them, head north and stay. He marched toward the massive window, tore the heavy scarlet draperies from their shafts, and stretched their seams aloft. His head swam with the possibilities. Scare all the niggers hereabouts. Let the Yankees have them. Yes, that's it! Make it stick for good. He tore the knife from his belt, laid the drapery against the sideboard, and made two slashing strokes that left deep gashes in the cherry wood. Draperies once again held aloft, and the eyes stared back at the three men.

"Swamp Wampus," said Coogin.

CHAPTER NINETEEN

On Watersmith Plantation, February 3, 1865

I t was a dark and uneasy place. Bats drifted among the shadows. A bending line of rocks hauled from beneath the plow marked where the trees quit and the brick-hard dirt began. In the ocher dirt, soft padded marks showed where the people had lain their feet, not once in passing, but many times, back and forth until the grasses were torn from the ground and dust filled the low places. Separate from the darkness, a small fire glowed and gave form and depth to the place. It burned with an unsteady shimmer and cast long shadows into the crown of trees where the bats grew to be gargoyles and every wing-shadow announced their coming.

The fire was the only light along the trail at the edge of the woods, a point of reference, a beacon. In its glow, a tall black man stood against the darkness. His face, neither young nor old, reflected the firelight beneath a wrinkled slouch hat. A noise from the road drew his attention, and he tried to peer beyond the fire dots in his eyes. "Hello there," he said, his molasses-and-gravel voice pitched low and raw.

A young woman walked toward the glow. She had small children with her, two boys who clung behind her, hidden but for their eyes.

The man said, "Where you all from?"

"From Miss'ippi," she said. "Near Yooka."

He looked at her as she held out her hands for warmth, a girl not more than 16, black as a horse's hoof, eyes half-slits of flame. She rocked from foot to foot and there was grace in her movement, though her body lay hidden beneath a heavy shawl, its flower pattern muted by the darkness. She wore no shoes.

"You all can have some supper if you has a mind to." He motioned toward a makeshift tent at the edge of the trees, a few twisted limbs serving as tent poles. Light from inside glowed through holes worn in the thin canvas. A washtub hung from a nail on a tree, and more blankets draped from low-hanging boughs. Lying in the dirt, a dog with rheumy eyes raised its head as they passed.

At the opening to the tiny tent, the man said, "This here's Alice." A woman squatting in the dim glow of a few candles stood and smiled at them. Her blue serge dress was ridged with manifold flounces, small feet showing from beneath.

"How you do, ma'am?" said the young woman.

"Pleasure," said Alice. "Please join us. We can put some more fixings in the stew."

"We has some yellow cornbread." A packet emerged from the folds of the woman's shawl. She put it on the wooden crate that served as a table. "And some sorghum molass, too." The smallest of the boys whined and pulled at her skirt.

"Why, thank you, child," Alice said. "And let's see what sugar we can find for your boys."

The whining ceased. Alice rummaged for a moment on a low wood shelf that rested on stones above the dirt floor. Jet bracelets glistened with each movement of her slender hands. "This be all right?" Alice held out sugar sticks and the boys' eyes grew wide.

"Yes'm, and thanky," the woman said.

"Thanky," mumbled the boys in unison. The smaller boy hesitated before snatching the stick from Alice's hand.

At the fire, the man poked the coals with his boot, added a few chips, and then swung aside a cast-iron kettle on its rusting hinge. He ladled bowls of stew and passed them. "They come all the way from Mississippi, Alice." To the woman and her boys, he said, "Guess you all be headed North?"

"That's right. Going North in search of education. Got kin in Ohio. We got a pretty fair education back there but didn't take to it none. We come to Ohio looking for the same thing that most darkies go North looking for now days."

They sat on the fallen timbers and ate from tin plates and drank from tin cups. The woman talked as she ate. Cornbread crumbs fell from her mouth and she snatched them up again, slowly rolling each one with her tongue.

"My momma's master, Captain Pakky, he died and my momma, her husband and us, we was handed down to Captain Pakky's poor kin folk. Captain Pakky own about fifty or sixty niggers, and all of them was tributed to his poor kin." Bits of stew hung in the corner of her mouth as she spoke. "Ooh wee! They was just a lot of us. Couldn't have us all, so they took my momma, her husband and me and my little brothers here from Mississippi to the Tennessee line last summer, told us to git. We had a wagon but it got broke, and honey, let me tell you, I walked all the way from Mississippi to right here."

"A long way for children to be walking," said Alice. "And them with no shoes."

"Me neither. We spent the winter in a house with some folk near the river. We lived with them in a log hut and slept on homemade rail beds with cotton, and sometimes straw, but mostly cotton in the winter."

"Where your ma and pa?" Alice asked.

The young woman gazed into the fire a moment and gathered her shawl closer. "Got theyselves killed," she said quietly. Embers danced on the night air, the wind swirling gently. "We was tending to our personals at a creek—it's my place to take care of these here young ones—and was fixing to rejoin my momma and her husband when we heard them horses coming and so we duck away. I hush the boys and them riders don't see us." The older boy began to cry softly. "We watch and they got to talking about our mule. That mule we done bought and paid for." She looked at Alice. "They hung our momma and her husband and they took our mule."

For a time, no one spoke but the fire, hissing as the pine logs slowly burned. "That was a few weeks back now. Been hiding in the woods since then, living with folks like you. You been most kindly and we be much obliged."

"We share what we can with other poor folk," Alice said. She gathered plates and returned to the tent.

The man idly drew lines in the dust with a poplar switch. He felt a kinship with the three squatting by his fire. Hope was all they had. "I work for the soldiers," he said. "They pay me for hauling what they need hauled. Lots of poor folk here-bouts. Most are heading north just like you and yours." He drew a last line, then tossed the stick into the fire. "Guess we'd do the same, but we don't have kin in the North. Got no place to be going to."

A sudden movement between the trees made him turn. Into the circle of light, an apparition materialized, then another, and another: three specters, huge and menacing, blood red in the fire glow that sent ghostly shadows against the trees. They glided across the clearing and stopped near the canvas tent. One phantom spread wings and spoke with a sound like rolling thunder behind a closed door.

"Behold! The holy specter of doom!"

The other ghost bent, dipped a torch into the fire, and held it high in the air.

"Beware of the savage Swamp Wampus!" The thunder boomed. "It lurks by the river. And it eats darkies. Beware! Heed this warning and flee for your lives!"

One of the boys screamed; the other hid behind his sister, white-eyed in the torchlight.

"The Swamp Wampus flies faster than a hawk. Its teeth are like knives—they tear off your arm in a single bite. His claws will rip out your eyes." And he held aloft an eye, glassy and staring in the firelight. The young girl screamed.

"Run!" cried the phantom. "Run for your lives!"

The black man stood transfixed as the monsters swooped through the camp, waving their torches in widening turns until one ignited a blanket. Flames licked up its sides. Another torch hissed in wicked arcs, sparks scattering into the trees. Some fell atop the makeshift tent where Alice hid, and its dry edges flared quickly.

The man ran to his home. "Alice!" A crack of whip and he fell to the ground, his face in the dirt by the horse's hooves. Horse hooves! Not phantoms, not monsters at all, but men on horseback. Beneath the folds of their long, red robes, he saw boots, cracked and dirt-caked. And something more, something familiar, a sheen of silver. A spur.

The man jumped up and raced to the growing flames as Alice burst into the clearing. Their eyes met and with a clasp of hands, they disappeared into the trees. Behind them, fire whipped their belongings to shards.

"Beware the Swamp Wampus!" Shrieking and shouted curses stabbed the air. "Run for your lives!"

The phantoms flew off with the wind, lit by the burning shreds of Alice and her husband's home.

CHAPTER TWENTY

Elm Grove Plantation, February 3, 1865

George found Judge Wilson on a promontory west of the castor bean fields. They watched in a compatible silence as the sun descended below the tree line, then walked together until they reached the house. "Brandy?" asked the Judge.

George nodded. "Thank you, sir. I believe I will."

In his study, the Judge removed a crystal decanter from behind a row of books, the volumes mere facades glued together to conceal a compartment. George sat in a large leather armchair as the Judge poured two snifters, and passed one to George. "I've been meaning to ask you something about that weapon of yours." Wilson settled into his chair. "Repeat action rifle, isn't it?"

George shifted uneasily. "Yes, sir."

"Beautiful piece of equipment." Setting his glass on a blotter protecting the smooth mahogany desk, the Judge gave the edge of the floor-to-ceiling bookcase a rap of his knuckles. A narrow door opened, revealing a gun cabinet. Eb's remarks about the home's hidden heirlooms took on new meaning. Wilson removed a muzzle-loading flintlock, hefted it, appraising its weight or its deadly effect. "This belonged to my grandfather," he said. "He marched with Andy Jackson. Not much good beyond fifty yards, though. Weapons today are so much more …" The Judge groped for a word. "… efficient."

George sipped his brandy, felt the liquid warm in his throat.

"Efficiency, that's the difference," the Judge said. "This one-sided efficiency will bring a quick end to the war. And all of Bobby Lee's dignity and valor won't mean a thing in the face of such … efficiency."

"Dignity and valor have been seen on both sides," George said.

"Yes, yes. Indeed Mr. Lincoln was quite clever when he offered up his Emancipation. Now the coloreds are free, although we are not." The Judge replaced the weapon in the cabinet. "I hope he is equally as clever once this war ends." He sat once more and removed a thin cigar from a canister on his desk, clipped one end. "What a glorious day that will be," he said. He puffed on the cigar, a match to its tip. Lamplight streamed through the halo of smoke that gathered behind his shock of white hair, and George wondered if reverent hymns might fill the air and angels suddenly cry, "Hallelujah." He sat in rapt attention.

"Mr. Lincoln seems to understand that the world demands cotton, and the South supplies it. Cotton is the money crop. Not so much here in Tennessee, perhaps, but throughout the rest of the South. Cotton alone represents half this country's exports—or did, before the war."

George looked at his shirt cuffs: cotton. His work trousers: cotton.

"And cotton takes labor. The South won't survive without labor, hands in the fields."

George considered this. Before the war, his family had tilled the land—corn and barley and alfalfa hay for cattle—and muddled through well enough without slaves. "The war may be over soon. You could hire the soldiers. They'll be looking for work." That had been the very crux of Lieutenant Ellsworth's argument when George had been assigned to Elm Grove.

"But without slaves, the economy is ruined. Whites will not work for the wages we would have to pay to make a profit."

"But won't everyone be in the same fix? I mean, all the other growers will have to pay the same wages. So everyone's costs will increase, won't they?" George had seen similar problems in Wisconsin when the price of seed went up. Farmers all paid the same for seed, so they all had to raise their prices. If your competitors also have higher costs, raising your price shouldn't hurt your sales, or profits. Everybody knew that, didn't they?

Wilson peered at George through the thickening haze, cigar clenched firmly to one side of his mouth. "Hah! Sergeant Van Norman, you are one smart fellow." He took another swallow of brandy, and savored it momentarily before he continued. "Your thinking neglects but one thing: finding the men who will do that kind of work. It's hot, dirty, back-breaking work, from dawn to dusk, and sometimes long after. Only the coloreds will do it."

"Begging your pardon, sir, but I have seen many a white man willing to do hard labor. And not just soldiers. I lived on a farm. Boys no older than ten or twelve hefting bales of hay from wagon to barn for fourteen hours." George tipped his glass once more and was surprised to find it empty. "Men are willing to work for a decent wage and a boss who cares about them," he said, gesturing with his empty glass.

"Steady, man, steady." Wilson stood. "I admire your passion. You might make a good lawyer some day." A final puff and he stubbed out his cigar in the porcelain bowl. "Maybe even a politician."

Lord, help the country indeed, George thought as the Judge poured more brandy. "I'll discuss your ideas with my colleagues—Mr. Arnell, Mr. Porter, Mr. Moore. We're beginning to make plans for the courts to reopen."

"Isn't all of Tennessee still under martial law?"

"Your soldiers are too busy to deal with land issues or petty larcenies. We need a legal system for deeds and torts, the transfer of property and the like. Your General Miller favors the idea."

Miller, in charge of the post at Nashville, dealt with citizens adjusting to life amid warring armies. Women and children needed protection, and the Union Army was too busy trying to kill their husbands and fathers to give it to them.

Outside the window, they heard shouting. George stumbled awkwardly as he leapt from his chair. His brandy spilled and the dark liquid seeped into the rich wool carpet.

"I APOLOGIZES, MASSAH WILSON." THE black man removed his slouch hat and addressed the Judge, then cast his eyes downward. "Didn't mean to bother nobody, sir." His voice was cold and raw as the winter air. "No, sir. Got no place to go to, that's all. House burnt up, cain't stay outside in the weather, Massah."

Judge Wilson stood at the door and squinted into the night air. "Cletus, is that you?" The man raised his eyes to his former owner. "Well, I'll be damned." Wilson hitched his suspenders over billowing shirtsleeves and stepped onto the portico.

"I ain't asking for no charity, no, sir." Cletus, field hand at Elm Grove for thirty years, had returned with two women, one no older than a girl, and two small boys, faces half hidden, bundled against the cold. He introduced the older woman as Alice. The others remained unnamed.

"You and your family may use your old cabin." The Judge led Cletus down the porch steps, walking in the glow of the lantern to the slave quarters.

George watched the small parade from the porch. Beside him, Eb stood strangely silent, the heat palpable off his body. "Tell me about them, Eb," George said.

Eb stared down the road until the group disappeared behind some trees. "Cletus come back, is all, Sergeant. He left, said he wanted a better life. Said staying here was for the weak. Said leaving was the only way to be free."

Eb retrieved a lantern from the hall—step-hop, step-hop, step-step-hop—and hurried after the Judge, the light bobbing unevenly in the dimness. A vague thought nagged through the brandy haze in George's head: Silas was Cletus's son. But who were the others? He shook his head again to clear it and felt a throbbing, as if he were being pummeled with fists. He leaned against the porch rail. Out of the shadows, two eyes appeared. "That you, Silas?" he said.

"Yes, sir, Massah Van." Silas said.

"Do you remember that man?" George asked him.

"That Cletus," he said. "Worked the fields. Head dryer, too." He pointed into the shadows. "I don't know the people he has with him. Never seen them before."

Inside, George stood his rifle in the corner and leaned against the sideboard. Cletus? Could he be trouble? His mind felt fuzzy and he had a hard time concentrating.

The Judge returned and slapped his arms and blew on his fingers. "You seem to have all the answers, Sergeant. What do you propose we do about the Negro problem?" Wilson asked. "What is the official army policy?"

Was the Judge seeking his advice? Or was he simply mocking? "What do you mean, sir?"

"The emancipated slave owns nothing," he said, gesturing down the road. "Because nothing but freedom has been given to him. No place to go, no place to live, no means to earn a living." His words came in bursts and his arms waved in dizzy fashion. "What are we supposed to do with Cletus and the others? We can't keep them here. We can't feed them or clothe them."

"Put them to work!" George said. "Plant a spring prop. Crop."

The Judge's arms stopped waving, and George concentrated on the man's words.

"They may be willing to work, but I can't pay them. We have no money until the crop is sold."

"Well," George said carefully. "Pay them afterwards, then."

"Sharecropping?" The Judge rubbed at his chin, his brow furling and unfurling. "They'll need seed, tools, living quarters. In exchange for a share of the crop." He rubbed more vigorously. "Ah, but we still lack horses and feed. We have no seed, either. And no money to buy any."

George said, "Hell, man, the army has all sorts at Columbia. Mules. Feed. Seed. Indeed!"

The Judge stared at him for a moment, and George wondered what he might look like to others. He tugged at his moustache and realized he was grinning.

"Mm-mm. Get seed on credit at O'Rourke's. Uh-huh, uh-huh. Start with the eighty acres in the hollow, corn on the north hills…I daresay, we may have something. Sharecroppers! It's worked in Europe. Though not with coloreds, mind you. Yes, Sergeant, this may solve a number of problems. We need to address the Negro issue—what to do with all the Freedmen who have no skills—find them a means to support themselves. And also allow us to continue to make a profit, of course."

The Judge suddenly turned on his heel and walked into his study. The door closed softly behind him.

George stood swaying, eyes fixed on the door, which seemed to have two handles—or was it four—until Eb spoke to him. "Perhaps it is time to turn in, Sergeant?"

CHAPTER TWENTY-ONE

Elm Grove Plantation, April 10, 1865

Awakened by wood smoke and the smell of bacon frying, George believed for a moment he was with his Regiment. Sleep disturbed at last, he came slowly to consciousness, pulled back the tent flap, secured it with a granny knot, non-regulation, and he did not care. He stretched, arms wide, and yawned. It was his favorite time of day. The sun had not yet appeared over the horizon; the birds were not yet awake. The quiet time, when nothing moved. It gave him a moment to pause and plan his day, to create structure by program and schedule. He could sink into routine the way some people would sink into warm bath water, and he felt sorry for those who lived by buzzing, blooming confusion.

George walked the property, his daily inspection, as he had nearly every day these past months. Survey the stables, inspect the drying houses, march through a small woods that protected the main house from northerly winds, behind the quarters and on to the creek (he pronounced it "crick" but the locals said "creek") where he washed. Over a mile each morning, a twenty-minute march.

Mitsy and Eb greeted him as they bustled about. Even Eva spoke to him occasionally, her words courteous, if aloof. After breakfast, he would sit on the portico and read a book from the Judge's library. From tolerance to acceptance, it had been a measured passage, and thus he slowly began the journey from feeling a foreigner to feeling a part of the plantation family.

To those beyond Elm Grove, he remained an interloper. When the Judge entertained visitors, George's tip of the hat and "Good morning" were returned with a perfunctory nod and a scowl, or a curt "Good morning to you, sir." Scars of hatred cut deep. Dred Scott, John Brown, the Missouri Compromise no compromise at all. He felt he was being held accountable for acts beyond his making. An accident of geography. In truth, George admitted his mistrust of them as well. Rumors of General Forrest and his men had been heard—nightriders waged raids on Yankee supplies—and George wondered if any of his neighbors might be sheltering Forrest's men in their homes.

This morning dawned warm and sultry, mists layered in the folds of the fields, and the dew soaked his pants legs as he made his way to the stream. He bathed in the cool water, the chill bracing on his arms and face. George was just reaching for his shirt when movement caught his eye. A doe, bigger than a cow, sipped from the shallows on the far bank. She stopped to look at George, tipped her head, her eyes seeing but unconcerned, and bent once more to the water. Suddenly her ears went flat. A flick of her head and she was gone, her white tail bounding through brush and thicket like a bouncing ball.

George wandered upstream, following the bank through alder and willow branches already thick with spring buds. He climbed a steep grade of sandstone and shale to where a long rock ledge, like some great metal strap, held the stream to the land. To the north, the strawgrass gave way to a line of cherry trees and dogwood blooming pink and orange across the horizon. He filled his lungs and the rich sweetness spilled into him where he held it just for the taste. At last, he let out a long sigh and descended the rocky slope by step and slide to the muddy banks of the stream.

"Hello, Sergeant," came a voice, milky-smooth, guttural and deep. Eva parted a willow drape and stepped lightly onto a large rock. She stood eye to eye with George, unblinking.

"Good morning, Miss Eva." His boots sank slowly into the soft mud of the shallows.

Eva bounded to another boulder, avoiding the muddy spots lest she soil her tight-laced buskins. "I see you have discovered my secret place."

She danced deftly from rock to rock, reached the base of the shelf George had just left, disappeared behind some alder on the landward side, and reappeared moments later atop the prominence. Her chintz skirt billowed, baring her narrow ankles and George felt a pang of loneliness, brief but sharp. "Didn't know it was a secret," he said as he peered up at her.

She squatted gracefully on the ledge, her thin arms wrapped around her shins, and said, "You come here in the mornings to wash. I've been right here most days."

"You mean you have been spying on me?" George tried to remember what compromises had been made, what nature had been observed.

"Don't you worry, Sergeant Van Norman. You were too far away for me to see anything." She grinned. "Much."

"You were watching me? Miss Eva, it is indecent to spectate in such a manner."

"Oh, keep your britches buckled, Sergeant." She laughed at her own joke. "There was nothing indecent about it." She laughed again at the double meanings.

George scrambled up the rocky slope amid a scatter of shale and loose stones. His feet flailed, fighting to find purchase, but failed at last and he fell back, breeches first, into the soft mud of the streambed. Above him, he heard belly laughing and watched helplessly as Eva nearly collapsed on her perch.

George righted himself and examined his clothes: perfectly clean in front; brown as tar in back. "Is it customary here in Tennessee for proper folk to find pleasure in another's misfortune?"

"Only a Yankee's, Sergeant Van Norman. Only a Yankee's."

She darted from her roost and ran further up the rock outcropping. George followed. Ducking behind the alder, he discovered the sloping series of stones, a step here, another there, like climbing a crooked staircase. Emerging onto the prominence, he found Eva gazing toward the sun as it escaped above the morning mist. There he paused to marvel at the look of her: shoulders erect, chin sweeping from her long neck, her eyes… God, her eyes!

"It is a beautiful sight, is it not, Sergeant?"

George stood mute.

"Elm Grove has been in our family for generations. My great-grandpapa came here from North Carolina. This land was payment for fighting with General Washington. See that hill over there? That's the north horse pasture—the fence is pretty much gone now—where we had some of the finest Thoroughbred horses outside Kentucky.

"And there?" She pointed. "There's partridge and wood duck in those woods yonder. I shot my own dinner when I was just twelve years old. Right there. Bet you didn't know I could shoot, did you, Mr. Van Norman? Been shooting since I was nine. Papa showed us how to hunt and fish and …"

A faint wind ruffled her hair and she brushed an errant lock from her eyes. He smelled her then, felt the sweetness at the base of his tongue, and he struggled to focus on her words.

"… climb a tree together and wait, sometimes for an hour or more, not saying a word, just watching. Once, a big buck came past, so majestic, like he was king of the county. Must have had fourteen points if he had a one. Big black spot on his forelock. Goodness, he was a beautiful animal. I just couldn't let Frederick shoot him. So, I shouted and the big buck skedaddled." Eva laughed, and George found he enjoyed the sound.

"That was four or five years ago now. I see that buck every now and again. Same one." She sighed. "Last winter, he came right into the corn field and chewed the stalks. I sneaked up and just sat by the shader and watched him."

George gazed at the cornfield and tried to imagine Eva seated beneath the lone shade tree in its center. He wondered how she had reached it undetected by the deer, wondered if perhaps he had misjudged her. Eva, all social polish and supercilious air, a venal repository of Southern vanity. Her beauty had not blinded him to her shortcomings, but perhaps it had to her virtues.

"I used to tag along when my brothers went deer hunting back in Wisconsin," George said. "I can shoot the wings off a mosquito if I have a mind to. That may be why they made me a sergeant. I teach the men how to shoot." He heard himself bragging and wondered about it. It was not in his nature to boast, but he found this woman interesting and wanted her to find him interesting, too.

"The Natchez Trace is over there," she said, pointing. Her hand was the color of peaches, her long fingers tapered and elegant. "Back that way is a mile of woods before you come to the Roberts's farm. They're our nearest neighbors, if you don't count Crazy Dudley. He lives in a cabin up yonder."

She pointed upstream, her delicate wrist effortlessly flowing from beneath the ruffles of her blouse. He sighed and tried to concentrate.

"…an old Indian trail," she said. "It runs all the way down to New Orleans. I was in New Orleans once. Papa took me there on business. But then the war came."

They sat in silence for a time as the damp air gently rolled off the creek bottoms. She waved away an insect, and he glimpsed an undergarment beneath the cloth of her neckline, the soft line of cleavage running straight from her bosom to a stirring between his legs that had nothing to do with the mud seeping though his trousers.

"I love this place, Sergeant, I dearly do. But I am fearful. What will happen when the Yankees come? Is it true y'all are going to take our land away? Keep some for yourselves and give the rest to the coloreds? Don't look so surprised. Yes, give it to the coloreds. That's one of the ideas being thrown around by your Congress. Why, General Sherman has already gone and done it. He divided up some land and gave a whole plantation to the coloreds who were slaves on that land. Can you imagine? Cletus and his pickaninnies living in our home?"

George had a vision of Cletus, seated behind the Judge's desk, his bare feet resting on the polished mahogany. "I can't really imagine anything like that," he said.

She sat on the grassy hillock and he stretched out beside her. "You Yankees go and set them all free with no thought of what to do about them." He was set to argue the point when she plunged on. "You all have problems aplenty with your free coloreds in the North. I've read about the poverty and the free blacks living like animals in your cities. Some have taken to rioting in the streets."

George had read of this, too.

"Some folks talk about sending all the coloreds back to Africa. Put them all on a big boat." She brushed the ruffles on her skirt. "Can't imagine how that would work."

"Liberia," said George. "It's called Liberia. It's a country in Africa, run by former slaves," he said, remembering his lessons. "About fifty years ago, some freed slaves returned to Africa, started raising families. They set up a colony with a constitution and everything."

She studied him a moment.

George said, "They seem to be just fine, so I've read."

"Oh? And what sort of commerce do they conduct in Liberia?"

"They grow cotton, I think. Maybe some corn." His history and civics and cultural studies came back to him, schoolwork that he had enjoyed only because it served as a welcome interruption from his farm chores. "Mostly they export timber." Groping, he tried to recall. "Mahogany and ebony and such."

"Mahogany and ebony? I see. Somehow, that seems appropriate," she said.

George tried to remember more, but did not know if it was important.

"You seem to know a lot about different things, Sergeant. What do you know about this Mexico business?" she asked. "Some say they may try to invade. Mexican ships have been spotted near Mobile."

She stood to throw a rock, her skirt billowing, shaping the outline of her limbs.

"So," George said, "do you think you'll do be doing the cooking when Cletus takes over Elm Grove? Maybe I could get a job as his houseman."

She burst out laughing and threw the rock across the water into the trees beyond, startling a flock of birds into raucous cawing, and something else. Music? Chimes? No. Church bells, remote, but clear and distinct. Church bells. And this was Monday.

JUDGE MALACHI WILSON STEPPED FROM the portico and breathed deeply. The April air smelled of life. The land had transformed from brown to olive to emerald. Chlorophyll burst from stem to leaf, pistil and stamen performing their intended tasks. Spring had come at last to Elm Grove.

Beneath the Gothic arch of elms, he walked along the stone wall. A scattered pile of rubble just weeks ago. Now high and straight, paralleling the stately row of elms for nearly fifty yards, half the distance to the main road. Sergeant Van Norman's handiwork, he mused. An industrious young man, that sergeant.

Wilson ambled across the front pasture where horses had grazed for decades, the ground now muddied by recent rain, rutted and overgrown, sprouts of Johnson grass and thistles in contest for sky and space. Boulders, pushed to the surface by frost and time, tripped the unwary. More rock for the wall, he thought, stepping carefully.

Suddenly he heard shouting and the screech of metal against metal. A rusting buggy carrying two men careened up the driveway, mud flying behind its wheels. More shouting and the driver lashed the flea-bitten nag that was his horse. Spotting the Judge in the pasture, he pulled up short. "Judge Wilson, Judge Wilson!" he shouted.

The driver dismounted quickly. One hand held his stovepipe hat atop his head as he walked briskly to where the Judge stood. "It's General Lee," he said, panting. "Word just came over the wire a few hours ago. General Lee has surrendered in Virginia."

Joined by his companion, together the men recited the news that on Sunday, Robert E. Lee had met General Grant at the small town of Appomattox Courthouse west of the Virginia capital. Lee's plan to concentrate his scattered command near Lynchburg, provision them, and march south to join with Joe Johnston in North Carolina had been foiled. Capitulation was complete.

"Joe Johnston is our only hope now," said the rider, a little man with boxy ears covered by graying hair that had once been the color of chocolate.

"There's General Forrest," said the first man. "He's somewhere in Alabama."

"And they're still fighting out in Texas."

Wilson absorbed this information, rubbed his chin, and delivered his verdict. "No, gentlemen, I think not. Lee was the keystone. If he has submitted, Johnston and the rest must follow." He paused to listen, and heard faintly the plaintive peel of bells, their volume rolling up and down in the heavy air. "What are the terms?" The Judge wished to weigh outcomes, repercussions.

"Very generous, it seems." Stovepipe Hat extracted a well-worn piece of yellow paper from inside his formal coat and began reading. "Yes, all soldiers are to be paroled, not sent to prison." He looked up. "Not even officers. No proscription of Confederate leaders, simply a laying down of arms."

Boxy Ears nodded. "General Grant is certainly not known for his generous…"

The Judge raised his hand, as if the pasture were his courtroom. "Paroled?" Soldiers could return home, back to their farms and their towns and cities.

"Yes, Judge, and it says here that officers may keep their side arms and personal property. No looting of the ranks by Yankees will be tolerated."

"There's rumor that soldiers can even keep their horses and mules to use for spring planting."

"Unconditional Surrender" Grant was not so shrewd as this, nor so judicious. Judge Wilson decided this must be Lincoln's doing. No hanging of Confederate leaders, no degradation of the vanquished. Allow the men to retain their mounts—a wise choice—to work the farms and grow food for the soldiers and their families. It signaled a return to normalcy, the beginning of the reconstruction of the democracy. Solomon could have been no wiser.

Wilson nodded, rubbing his chin. Lee had already discouraged his followers from the guerrilla tactics so many feared. No one would take to the hills and fight on. Veterans had fought bravely for him for four years, the last year in adulation for the man alone, knowing The Cause was lost. And Lee had told them to go home. Lincoln and Lee, two wise men serving their cause and their countries in equal measure. Yes, he thought, nodding again. This was the day he had been waiting for. This was a beginning.

The messengers mounted the carriage and prepared to depart.

"Spread the word, gentlemen. Spread the word," the Judge said. The carriage turned about and headed back to the main road. "It is a glorious day for the nation," he shouted, but they did not hear him amid the jangle of metal and the clatter of wheels rolling on the rutted gravel road.

From somewhere beyond the trees and the road and four years of war, Judge Malachi Wilson heard clearly the ringing of bells.

CHAPTER TWENTY-TWO

Elm Grove Plantation, April 10, 1865

George sat on the portico as the sun dipped below the auburn horizon, rays of gold and crimson hanging over the spot of its going. One torn cloud, like a blood-soaked rag, lingered and darkened as if seeping slowly into the wet earth.

He lit his lantern, turned up the wick, and bent over his writing paper to compose a letter home. Lee had surrendered. The war was over. He searched his mind for what it might mean and felt the voices tug at him—tent mate "Big Bill" Illingsworth at Corinth; Captain Estee at Vicksburg; Mike Mansion, his boyhood friend, at Nashville. Wind howled in the trees and cold air rushed up his nose and George felt the physical pang of shame, a sense of guilt because they were dead and here he was, still breathing.

Elm Grove, Tenn. April 10, 1865

Dear Mother & Father,
We have just learned of the armistice in Virginia, and I am grateful for God's will in sparing me during these past three years.

A beginning. Letter writing did not come easily to George Van Norman. He scratched at his lip and ran his fingers through his hair before returning to the page.

The Regiment is somewhere in Alabama and I have no
one to share the occasion. This is all right as I confess I find
no solace in the Event, no great joy. I would salute the noble
Cause, and gladly wave the Stars and Stripes, yet I cannot
help but feel a cold weariness for all that has come to pass.

It struck him then. No more fighting. No more soldiering. Muster out
and go home. Home? Where was home? Wisconsin? The Regiment?
Perhaps it was just a matter of philosophy and geography.

It seems so long ago now that we first gathered in
Belleville, so many of us proud and foolish. This great
Rebellion was a test. For the Honor of our loved ones, we
sought a cause worthy of our lives. We thought we had a
taste for Rebel blood. I have seen it now and have no taste for
it. It runs red as any Wisconsin man's.

Noise carried by the wind distracted him. Laughter and music came from
the slave quarters as they celebrated the end of the war and a new
beginning. Freedom. George wondered if Cletus or the others had any
notion what lay in store. Liberty did not guarantee justice. Yet to a
former slave, this new freedom must seem as if the very gates of heaven
have opened and God Himself has granted safe passage.

He tried to imagine himself as they were, slaves, told what to do
and when to do it, unable to travel beyond the limits of home unless
bearing a pass and promise of swift return. Hell, man, just like the army,
he thought. But no, even army duty must come to an end. Born a slave,
die a slave. Until now. The Proclamation had gone into effect January 1
of 1863, but emancipation had not been enforced. Until now. With war
ended, today, the slaves were truly free.

The spring is come and every yard is full of daffodils and
bright verdure. Yet the mood here is uncertain. Church bells

ring at one church but are quiet at the next. Freedmen
celebrate the joyous occasion, their dawn of Liberty. But they
have no plan where to go or how to make a living. I fear for
them, as some have become my friends.

After hearing the news, the Judge had ruminated on commerce and the practice of law while Eva had talked about soldiers coming home, seeing her friends again, and attending parties. He could feel no part of their emotion. He could only observe, as an anthropologist examines an ancient culture, their lives, so irreversibly changed by the war and its outcome, their shame, and their joy at its conclusion. And in this joy, their virtue.

A matter of philosophy and geography.

The citizens are subdued but seem privately relieved at
the conclusion of hostilities, though they would have wished
a different outcome, one more favorable to their mind. For the
most part, their hospitality has been without parallel. But
they are doubtful about the Future and fear pervades their
thoughts, fear of what price due for having been beaten. My
reassurances politely received do not lessen their worry. Such
is the mistrust of both sides for the other.

It is over and we must all go about our duty to rebuild. I
fear the consequences of soldiers returning to wasted farms
and poverty, of Coloreds without homes or jobs or direction.
Fear lies in the hearts of Unionist and Secesh alike. We can
only hope and trust in the wisdom of Mr. Lincoln to do right
by this Country.

I should be returning soon and look forward to that
joyous day.

From my heart,
George

He folded the paper carefully, slipping it into the envelope and sealing it. In a rush of wind, a barn owl glided past, its meal gripped tightly beneath its feathered breast.

CHAPTER TWENTY-THREE

Williamson County, April 16, 1865

Noah Turner rode high in the saddle as the big, red mare picked her way carefully over roads rutted by army wagon trains hauling supplies to a war now ended. He plodded north to Cousin Mildred's, to see Buck, help him plant the spring crop as Noah had promised. A half-day's ride through familiar country, across the pike to the Natchez Trace.

Approaching the house, he saw Mildred's grave by the side of the road where crocuses bloomed, poking through the ground like tiny bugles. A wisp of smoke climbed lazily from the cabin chimney.

Noah reined in near the door. "Halloo, Buck," he hailed.

The door opened a crack. White eyes showed, but no sound.

Noah waited.

From behind him, "What you want here, Massah?"

Noah spun in his saddle to face a man as black as a boot. He wore an eye patch, and a latticework of scars ran from the corner of his patch to his jaw as if he had been cruelly whipped across the face. He had on nut-brown pants held up by a rope loosely tied. A shotgun hung lazily in his long arms. It was the first colored man Noah Turner had ever seen toting a gun. He had heard of Yankee colored troops, though he never faced any. But this black man and his gun seemed an affront, or perhaps a sign of the changes that would soon be sweeping the South.

"I was looking for Buck Turner," he said, and sidestepped his horse to view both the man and the door. "He lives here. Or he did."

The door opened, revealing a short, colored woman not more than twenty or so. She stood on the spot where he had avenged Mildred's death by killing the preacher. It seemed ages ago, but had been just a few months. "We be living here now," she said. "Found this place. Nobody to home."

"That's right, Massah. Ain't nobody here when we'uns come."

Noah backed his horse once more. "Buck is my Cousin Mildred's boy. That's her grave over yonder." He pointed to the mound of fresh-turned earth. "Buried her a few months back. I left the place with her son, Buck."

"Heard tell of a boy lived here. He left though, afore we-uns come."

"Did you also hear where he went?"

The man shook his head. From the door, the woman said, "Joined the army."

Noah leaned forward. "He what?"

"Joined the army, become a Johnny Reb."

"But the war is over," Noah said.

"Yes, sir, it is, but he ain't come back," said the man, squinting his one good eye. "And we be staying here now."

Noah thought about this. "Did he leave anything in the cabin? Any papers or personal effects?"

"Nothing what all but a few chairs and a blanket or two."

"They is some paper and such in a box," the woman said. "I seen it in the barn." She shut the door and walked toward the barn. "Don't know what they say. Cain't read proper."

Dismounting, Noah followed her to the barn, wary of the man behind him toting the shotgun. The woman rummaged through some dusty shelves, pushed aside broken tools and bits of leather, and produced a small wooden box, handed it to Noah. He undid the hasp and opened the box. On top was a tintype of Mildred and Cousin Jessup taken before the war, the image of silver and purple faded like ghosts of the past. Beneath it, letters, the correspondence of lovers separated by circumstance, more papers, a marriage certificate, a list of goods, words faded to illegibility, a receipt for a horse, and a deed. Noah closed the box and tucked it under his arm.

"You're welcome to stay here," he said. "Times being what they are." He mounted his horse and turned up the road. The couple stood near his cousin's grave, watching him, until he passed from their sight.

The road wound lazily through thick timber cut by freshly-hewn fields. Noah appraised with an expert's eye the condition of the crops in each man's clearing, whether the rows were straight, the soil turned deeply. Farming was his true calling. This he knew. Hard work, good weather, and a little luck. He could make the land give up its wealth to him. Noah Turner smiled. He worried for Buck, but it was not enough to dim his spirit. There were opportunities within his grasp, prospects to be had.

At a crossroads, he waved "Howdy" to an old-timer driving a wagon, four children bouncing in the back, overtook a man and woman in a carriage pulled by a mule, nodded a greeting to the man and tipped his hat to the woman, her face hidden under her sunbonnet. Cresting a hill, he saw a lone man walking, old by the bend of his back and the drag of his gait. Above scarred boots, the man wore dusty coveralls patched and sewn at random intervals, a jacket decorated with remnants of blue-black piping. A rough blanket hung by length of twine around his neck. Noah slowed to match the man's pace and the man looked up with watery eyes. The face seemed familiar—a much younger man, only a boy really. Noah had known his family for many years. The boy, always prone to fat, had been thinned by undernourishment and the rigors of army life.

"Orvis? Is that you? Orvis Roberts?" Noah asked.

"Mr. Turner? Well, hello, sir," he said, his voice shallow and coarse as river sand. "Quite some time since I made your acquaintance, it is." His hair poked from his shabby hat like straw from mattress ticking and his once-fleshy face lay sallow and gaunt, soft skin hanging from wide cheekbones and a square jaw. "And how might you be?"

"I'm doing all right, I suppose, considering everything." Noah was astounded by the boy's transformation, the leaned form, frail and frayed like old rope. "Where would you be headed?"

"Going home, Mr. Turner. The war's over and I am glad of it."

Orvis was the first returning soldier Noah had seen since the news of Lee's surrender. Word had passed quickly house to house in hushed tones, neighbors gathering at O'Rourke's General Mercantile or the Reformation Baptist Church, quiet times for prayer and reflection. And a vow never to forget.

Noah dismounted. "I'll just walk along if that's all right with you," said Noah.

"Much obliged for the company." Orvis shuffled on, intent in the doing. "We have been subjugated, we have. Made to take a vow to the Union, I was." Backward-speaking habit, he had. "Why, I would fight no more for the Stars and Stripes than for an old horse blanket. Oath be damned, I say."

"They whipped us, Orvis," Noah said. "And they did the work thoroughly."

"Yes, they did that, all right. I have too much pride to surrender if we had not been so thoroughly whupped. But take the fight out of me, they can't. No, sir."

"I had enough of it," said Noah. "If I hadn't, I'd have fought on. But I had my fill of fighting. Now I'd like to try and get some seed and go to farming again." Noah believed in the righteousness of The Cause, thought he had done all he could to make it triumph. But arguments in favor of secession made no difference anymore. All of that had been settled against them in the court to which they had appealed. The South had been beaten, badly beaten. And now, having submitted, he did so in good faith. "What will you do now?" he asked.

"Go home." Orvis hitched his thumbs in his belt, hauled up his drooping drawers. "Go home and see if my mam and pap are still there. Maybe get some clothes, go back to bookkeeping. Make some money somehow." He swiped his hands together. "But I will swear no loyalty oath to President Johnson." He spat the words. "No, by God, if we get into a war over this Mexico business, I'll have none of it."

"What do you mean, 'President Johnson?'"

"Didn't you hear? He's been shot, Mr. Lincoln was. Killed dead."

"Somebody shot Abe Lincoln?"

"John Booth, the man who done it," said Orvis.

"The actor?"

"You heard of him?"

"I remember reading about him," said Noah, recalling a time before the war when minstrels traveled from town to town, entertainers like Blind Tom Bethune, troupes of actors in clever performances, before the armies had begun wrestling over Tennessee. "I think maybe he must have come to Nashville once."

As they walked, Noah tried to absorb this news. Everything was about to change, he was sure. But he did not know exactly how. He began to imagine the consequences. Lincoln dead? This was the man who started everything. Election of the sixteenth President and his slavery plank had doomed the country and forced it down the path to dissolution. Secession had been the only alternative.

Lincoln gone. Andrew Johnson, the former Tennessee governor, in his place, a man reviled by all Tennesseans loyal to The Cause.

Lincoln assassinated. Some irresponsible fanatic whose twisted sense of justice made him kill the man at the focus of his hatred. And in the process, any hope for restoring normal life in the South.

Lincoln dead. Reconstruction of the Union would be rockier for it, any generosity or understanding from the victors a lost hope, their patience at an end.

Prospects dimmed.

They walked in silence through a narrow lane, deep woods on both sides, quiet and majestic, new leaves shading a deep emerald carpet of spring grass, each man in his own thoughts. Noah at last said, "You lose some weight, Orvis?"

CHAPTER TWENTY-FOUR

Elm Grove Plantation, April 16, 1865

A soft breeze played in his hair as George made his morning inspection. He tipped his head back and bared his face to the faint sunlight as it cleared the eastern tree line. All about him, the land lay in bloom. Purple honeysuckle and bright orange-pink dogwood blossoms swayed lazily, their perfume carried on the wind, and he filled his lungs.

The people were already at work in the fields. Cletus and the others had dusty seed bags over their shoulders, bending and straightening, bending and straightening as they planted row upon row. Their unbroken rhythm reminded George of something, and he slowly counted a steady cadence: step, stop, pull, bend, dig, insert, bury, pat, straighten. Step, stop, pull, bend, dig, insert, bury, pat, straighten.

There was much to do at Elm Grove, and George sought to contribute. He found a routine to occupy both mind and body in extending the wall, stacking rock upon rock, and he chose it as his daily mission. It seemed a task suited to him. The perspiration felt natural to his head, and his injured arm felt suddenly alive as if thawing from long hibernation. For himself, the work lit a fire within, an aspect of fulfillment in the doing, one tally on the credit side, his personal Reconstruction.

On this day, Silas worked beside him and George was grateful for the company, the young man willing and strong. Bend and lift, bend and lift, they piled stones and layered gravel and bits of dirt, flat stones to the outside and smaller stones to the center. Sight along the headstone. Four feet per hour, the wall lengthened, running beneath the elms. Six rods, ten rods, nearly a hundred yards, waist high and straight. George removed his shirt and Silas did the same. The warm air clung to them as their arms flexed, muscles burned, and their sweat smeared to mud as it ran in rivulets down their bare bodies. Bend and lift, bend and lift, the two pounded a tempo. Bend and lift, another rock fell into place. Silas began to hum softly, the tune familiar, but George could not make out the words. Bend and lift, the song floating on the rhythm of their labor.

Horses on the road interrupted their tempo in frenetic counter-point as Federal cavalry turned into the plantation, disappeared for a moment under the elms, and emerged once more. A dozen mounted soldiers approached the house and slowed to a walk. An officer dismounted, let his reins trail, and stepped onto the portico.

George and Silas set down their rocks. "Halloo, Captain!" George hailed, gathering his shirt. "Come to bring news, sir? We heard the war is over."

The officer searched for the voice, found George, his mud-caked work trousers clearly not standard army issue. "Are you Sergeant George Van Norman?" His words were crisp and officious.

"I am." George saluted and swiped perspiration from his forehead.

The captain returned salute and stepped off the portico. He was tall and seemed older in his slow and methodical movements, a spot of gray at his temples, dirty gold braid on his epaulets. He removed his doeskin gauntlet, unbuckled the strap of his valise; insignia on it read: **6th IND**.

"I am to deliver this to you." He held out a package of papers wrapped in string and George took it. The captain swung into the saddle. "I also have…" He paused. "…other news." Astride their mounts, the other soldiers sat solemn and quiet. "President Lincoln is dead. Shot and killed day before yesterday."

Prepared to ask about news of the surrender, George was not sure what he had just heard. "Sir? What did you just say?"

"You heard me right, Sergeant. New president is Johnson, Andrew Johnson." The sound of horse droppings as the officer turned his mount. "A Tennessee man."

The captain signaled and the column began to move. George walked alongside, carefully avoiding the animal refuse. "Who? How did it happen?"

"Shot while he was at a theatre. They're saying it was agents of Jeff Davis."

The horses began to trot and George could not keep up. He shouted as the last of the men went by, "Any news of the Eighth Wisconsin?"

One man turned. "Who?" The soldiers passed under the elms and were gone.

Silas stood beside George, walleyed, hands nervously twisting finger knots. "Did that man say Massah Lincoln been shot?"

Bewildered, too much to absorb, George just nodded.

News spread rapidly at Elm Grove. Throughout the day, chatter came from the quarters, bawling and moaning and cries of anguish where a week before there had been celebration. Supper would be late, but the Wilson family would not notice. They remained inside, subdued and anxious, Eva with her needlework and Jesse idly spinning whirligigs.

By late afternoon, the breeze had died to a whisper. No rustle of leaves in the trees. Even the birds had no song. On the porch steps, George read the packet of papers delivered by the 6th Indiana captain. His orders were to remain at Elm Grove, to "keep the peace at all costs…" until further orders relieved him. There were requisition slips for drawing stores and a brief note from Lieutenant Ellsworth: All was well. The regiment was camped near Mobile but would march to Montgomery later in the week. Nothing more about the men, no mention of casualties, nothing about the end of the war or the assassination of President Lincoln. George stared at the pages without seeing, and tried to understand what madness could inspire such deeds and what outcomes would emerge. Where was the country headed?

At dusk, the door opened and Judge Wilson stepped quietly onto the portico. His suspenders hung loosely by his sides and he hitched his trousers before he sat. He smelled of brandy and old books, his hair in disarray. "I heard the news," he said. "It is a sorry thing, Sergeant."

George nodded.

"It was easy to damn Mr. Lincoln," the Judge went on. "Yet I'm sure it seemed to him that he could do nothing other than he did." He lifted a cigar from his shirt pocket and rolled it in his fingers. "For all his bumbling and his abolitionist leanings, I believe Abraham Lincoln was a good man and would have done right by the Confederacy." He rubbed his chin and added, "He had a certain political finesse that his successor does not. I know Andy Johnson, and on his best day, he is a horse's ass."

* * *

On the road to Columbia, Tenn., April 17, 1865

Dawn broke slowly, weakly, hesitantly, dusty clouds clinging to the sky as if to hide the morning; the moist air held a promise of rain. Silas stroked Bessy gently as he put her in harness. George loaded his haversack and rifle in the wagon, climbed on the bench, and snapped the reins. Bessy trotted purposefully along the gravel road beneath the elms.

They rode in silence, lonely and perplexed, their senses tossed from a place of great joy and expectancy to one of great sadness and worry in the span of a week. Huddled beside him on the bench, Silas sat rigid and George watched him flex and unflex his fingers. He suddenly shuddered and George thought the boy was fighting a chill until he saw the tears run down his ebony cheeks.

"Why they have to go and kill Massah Lincoln? Why they do such a thing?"

Silas broke down then in great racking sobs, his head between his bony knees. George had no answer. They rode quietly for another mile. The occasional hum of bees filled the dense air, with the distant gobbling of a spring turkey in atonal harmony.

At last, Silas lifted his head. "Tell me, Massah Van, did you fight with any of the coloreds, the ones they call 'Lincoln Soldiers'?" he asked. "Some of the darkie boys round here was talking about joining up with the Yankee troops and all. I was wondering if you maybe knowed some of them."

George thought for a moment. "I fought with some around Vicksburg, but they were mostly from the North," he said. "Got to know some at Milliken's Bend. We drilled with one group, the Eighth Louisiana. They were just as capable as any of the new recruits."

"I like to be a soldier sometime. I want to wear a fancy uniform—look so grand!—but I is too young. Now the war's over, guess I be thinking about other things."

They again rode in silence, through thick woods of mulberry and jack pine, beech and white oak. The air was thick with the smells. From time to time, Silas would ask questions. What makes clouds float? How come plants are green, but not people? Why is the road sunk into the ground? George followed with explanations of physics and photosynthesis, and how rain on a hill turns the road into a ditch, washing away the dirt, and nobody hauls it back again. He told Silas how to make ink using a little vinegar and the balls full of powdery black dust that dropped from oak trees. He showed him how to make a cat saddle—four hands clasping four wrists in a square—should he ever need to carry someone weary or injured.

"Massah Van, tell me about soldiering. What's it like being on a picket or marching with the other soldiers?"

Where to begin, thought George. Too many believed in the splendor of battle, typically those who had never fought. Battle was simply a loud, bloody, terrifying business. Yes, it was exhilarating. But for every minute of battle there was a month of boredom. And of sickness. Twice as many soldiers died of the alvine flux as were ever felled by the enemy. But vomit and diarrhea do not hold the imagination as do the glory and honor of battle.

He recited as if by rote the words of the manual, "When marching through enemy territory, we send out skirmishers a few hundred yards or so in front of the regiment. They form a line five yards apart, covering the front of the company. When we stop, one man hides behind a tree or a bush and two others sit down a few yards behind him. More are in the rear as reserves. If he sees the enemy, the sentinel fires. The other two jump up and they fire while the first reloads. Then the reserves come up and join in. If the enemy is too strong, they all fall back toward the camp, firing as they retreat. This alerts the camp and gives them time to get ready."

Silas's eyes were wide as saucers. "Did you ever kill any Secesh?"

How could he explain? To see a man walking and talking and enjoying the common frailties of life one instant, and in the next, seeing that same man reduced to blood and raw meat at the whim of chance and a minié ball. Instead, he said, "How would you like to learn how to shoot?" A tug on the reins and Bessy slowed to a stop.

The boy's face brightened. "I never shot no gun. I seen Massah Freddie shoot when him and me was a-hunting. That was afore the war."

George eased over the bench and jumped down, and Silas did the same. Bessy dipped her head and began gnawing at the roadside grasses. George pulled his Spencer from the wagon and assumed the profile of the drill sergeant. He removed the tube to empty the chamber and demonstrated the rudimentary procedures of loading, aiming, and firing the weapon. Silas watched carefully, eager to learn, and repeated each motion as well as any recruit.

On the ground, George found an old apple, soft and pithy, and stood it on a stump away from the road, thirty yards, maybe a little more. From a Blakeslee box, he withdrew a tin tube holding seven bullets, spring loaded. Silas cocked and aimed the weapon carefully. Slow squeeze on the trigger, earsplitting report, and the barrel jumped. His white teeth grinned through the puff of smoke. The apple had vanished, leaving nothing but a smear on the stump.

The day wore on and a soft breeze kept the bluebottle flies at bay. They passed several riders along the road, a family in a wagon, and two women in a carriage. A wave or a greeting often met with ambivalence at the sight of his Yankee uniform. Silas, who paid such behavior no heed, began to hum a familiar melody, and every now and then said, "*Doo-dah, doo-dah.*"

"What's that song? It sounds familiar."

"That's the horse racing song," said Silas, and he began to sing the words. "*The long tail filly and the big black hoss, doo-dah, doo-dah. They fly the track and they both cut across, oh, doo-dah day. The blind hoss sticking in a big mud hole, doo-dah, doo-dah. Can't touch bottom with a ten-foot pole, oh, doo-dah day.*" He knee slapped a tempo to the song, boisterous and joyful. George joined him on the familiar chorus. "*Gwine to run all night! Gwine to run all day! I'll bet my money on the bobtail nag if somebody bet on the bay.*"

Another verse, and when they finished, Silas said, "How you know that song, Massah Van?"

"Sang it around many a campfire with my friends."

"I thought that was a colored folks' song. We sung that while we was working in the Judge's fields. Do you know this one?" He cleared his throat. "Oh, it rained all night the day I left, the weather was bone dry. The sun so hot I froze to death, Susanna don't you cry."

George's guttural baritone mixed with Silas's clear tenor as they bellowed, "*Oh, Susanna, oh, don't you cry for me. I come from Alabammy with my banjo on my knee.*"

Singing made the ride seem shorter and George began to forget the events of the day.

"You know any more colored folks' songs, Massah Van?"

"Why do you say those songs are colored folks' songs?"

"Because they is. I once seen a minstrel show of colored folk that was on tour with Blind Tom, the piano player. Them minstrels sang all them Stephen Foster songs. Stephen Foster must be a colored man to write so much music for colored folk."

Bessy shook her mane and her bridle jingled. "Music is for everyone, Silas, black folks and white folks alike," George said. "But I think Mr. Stephen Foster is white."

Silas was quiet for some time but finally surprised George with, "What's it like to be white? I mean, you being free and all and being a white man in this here country, you can go whereas you please and do what all you please."

George took a deep breath to frame his answer carefully. He sat in the heart of the South with a young man who, until just days ago, had been owned by another man. "I believe I am the luckiest man alive, Silas. I live in the most powerful nation on earth, brought up by loving parents on our own land, a free man, free to go where I want and do what I want whenever I want to do it. Free to become whoever I choose to become, now that this war is over." He saw the wonder and, what else—envy?— in young Silas's face. "But you're free now, too," George added. "Free to go where you want and do what you want to when you want to do it. Free to become whoever you choose."

They approached the river and he remembered the riders' tracks that led to a cave, his feeling of helplessness. He snapped the reins smartly. "Tell me, Silas, what do you want to do with your life?" He asked more to introduce another subject than because he imagined the boy might have any serious plans.

"I'd like to be a teacher, teach reading to people of all races and colors." A smile lit his dusky brown cheeks, then dimmed just as quickly. "But I has to get some schooling to be a teacher. I ain't never had no schooling excepting what I learnt from them books of the Judge's."

"I didn't have much time for school myself. Too much work to do on the farm," said George. "You have a better education than you might think, Silas. I haven't read most of those books you've read, never heard of some of them."

It was Silas's turn to ask. "What y'all going to do, Massah Van, now the war is over?"

"I don't know. Just live at home for a while I suppose. I guess I'll find some work in town, maybe open a store." Remembering the offer from Ed Mason's father, he said, "I might go to work in the stockyards, you know, buying and selling cows, maybe some horses and mules, too."

"Lots of land round these parts," Silas said. "The soldiers what got killed? There's land here, be good for farming and such."

Another carriage approached, a tired-looking gray horse pulling an older couple dressed in black, the woman's face shaded by her bonnet. George nodded as they passed. The old man studied him, his eyes buried beneath tangled white eyebrows. Then a smart snap of his reins and the couple's old horse began to trot.

"I could come work for you," Silas said. "Be like Cletus, get a piece of the crop come harvest time. I ain't just a houseboy. I can do farming. While I ain't going to teacher school, I mean."

"It's something to consider," George said. Prices would be depressed; land would be a bargain. He had some money saved. Middle Tennessee weather was mild, the growing season longer than Wisconsin's, and its rich soil promised an abundant crop. "And thank you for offering your service. I could be assured of good help."

They rounded a bend and the steeples of Columbia's churches appeared in the distance. Silas began to hum *Nelly Bly* in high tenor.

CHAPTER TWENTY-FIVE

Elm Grove Plantation, April 17, 1865

S he dared not leave the lamp lit long. They were running short on terebine oil and could not depend upon more. Shortages had become commonplace—not enough cloth for sewing, nor enough pins or needles. Even food had become scarce, though not since Sergeant Van Norman had arrived. The only thing that remained abundant was wood for the stoves and in that she felt fortunate. Minnie Waters had lost all her firewood to the soldiers. Her letter sadly related the plight of her plantation near Pulaski. Yankees had taken her fence rails and even topped off trees on the grounds.

The army seemed to be training a society of thieves. Where they camp, homes are looted for every treasure, every object. No sooner do their tents go up than the boys are streaking in all directions, cabbaging boards for beds or floors, straw to stuff their mattresses, writing tables, stools, and carpets for their comforts.

Eva feared that now that the war was over, a host of bandits would be thrown upon society. Hundreds, thousands of vulgar men, reckless and irresponsible (not to speak of their uncontrollable licentiousness), men who, before the war, were perfectly acceptable members of society.

War, she believed, could be a great evil in many respects.

Dearest Mother,
It is over. Our great struggle for the right to govern
ourselves, the very hope for a new world of order and

comfort, has been dashed. *The facts are plain: We attempted to free ourselves from the Union and failed. We question not the constitutionality and rightfulness of our course — no, we thought our cause just and sacrificed beyond measure to make it successful. But we were beaten, and now we must trust our enemies to forge a merciful peace.*

Where once sprouted jonquils and iris, we have limestone tablets inscribed over our brothers and husbands and sons. For this alone, abhorrence and abomination would stand justified. Yet among the fallen is their leader, Abraham himself, struck down by an assassin in a most shameful and cowardly manner. I can find no consolation in this.

If it be true, "He who wrestles with us sharpens our nerve and strengthens our will," we require no such help from our antagonists. Our nerve has been brutally sharpened and our will sorely strengthened. We can only hope for similar strength and resolve from Mr. Johnson in peacetime that was exhibited by Mr. Lincoln in war.

Again, I revel in my despair. And were you with me, you would have none of it, I know. Your ideals remain a part of me as my blood. Affirmation becomes achievement becomes
Love

&

She put the letter with the others, quietly closed the drawer, and turned down the oil lamp. The darkness closed over her like a promise.

CHAPTER TWENTY-SIX

West of Columbia, Tenn., April 18, 1865

S ilas read the headlines aloud as the wagon rolled westward. "President Lincoln Assassinated," he said. "Attempt to Murder Mr. Seward. Full Particulars of the Affair."

"Go ahead and read it to me, Silas," said George.

Silas cleared his throat and read haltingly. "President Lincoln and his wife yesterday evening visited Ford's Theatre for the purpose of witnessing the performance of 'Our American Cousin.'" He looked at George. "I guess that's a show or something." He went on, "The theatre was densely crowded and everybody seemed delighted with the scene before them. During the third act and while there was a temporary pause for one of the actors to enter, the sharp report of a pistol was heard and a man rushed to the front of the President's box waving a long dagger in his right hand, and exclaimed, *Sic semper tyrannis.*" He stopped reading. "What's that mean, Mr. Van? *Sic semper tyrannis.*"

"It sounds like Latin," George said. "Something like 'Death to Tyrants,' I suppose." He scratched his upper lip where the mustache had grown full and thick. "Keep on reading. You're doing fine."

"Where was I?" He thumbed the paper. "He immediately leaped from the box, to the stage beneath and ran across to the opposite side of the stage making his escape amid the bewilderment of the audience, from the rear of the theatre, mounted a horse and fled." Silas looked up. "Sounds like the audience was in the rear of the theatre, don't it?"

George laughed. "Keep reading," he said.

"The screams of Mrs. Lincoln first disclosed the fact to the audience that the President had been shot, when all present rose to their feet. Many rushed to the stage exclaiming, 'Find him.' The excitement was of the wildest possible description, and of course there was an abrupt intermission of theatrical performances." Silas took off his hat to fan his face. "Whew! That's a lot of reading."

George started to grin but stopped abruptly as he looked west, where ominous clouds gathered. He heard thunder in the distance and smelled rain on the wind. Snapping the reins, George nudged Bessy into a trot. But with a wagonload of provisions, she soon tired and again slowed to a walk. Resigned to a wet ride, George let her have her pace.

"What else is there?" George was anxious to hear news of the world outside Maury County. "Read some more," he said.

"Here's something. All the medical men and the press recommend Doctor Strickland's mixture as the only certain treatment for day-raya and die-sentry." Silas stumbled over the words. "A combination of ass-trinjunt, absorbent, stimulant, and carminative and is warranted to ay-fect a cure when all other means have failed." Silas shook his head. "I has no idea what they is talking about."

George fought a losing battle for control of his face. His smirk turned to grin turned to guffaw. "That's 'dysentery' and 'diarrhea,' Silas," he said through a smile that hurt his still-tender upper lip.

Silas pouted. But George slapped the boy on his shoulder and said, "Day-raya," and laughed some more, and Silas joined in.

Coming toward them from the river bottom, George spotted a buckboard pulled by a well-trimmed mount, probably a former cavalry horse. Two men rode on the seat. One, a tall, thin man, wore the gray uniform of a Rebel. The other, sandy haired, had his hat pulled low over his eyes. As they passed, the tall one grinned, his front teeth missing. George nodded. Tethered behind the buckboard, two more horses walked, their saddles in the wagon.

George rode the wagon cautiously downhill to the bridge, Bessy taking her time. Silas turned in his seat and said, "Massah Van, those men in the wagon, they is stopping."

Over his shoulder, George saw both men at the side of the road, hurrying, unloading saddles from their wagon. All the goods he and Silas had picked up in Columbia would make tempting booty for bushwhackers. He snapped the reins and shouted, "Hey-ah, get on there, Bessy. Hey-aaaah!" The wagon lurched forward, lumbering over the bridge, its wheels rattling on the wooden planks. They bounded up the embankment, climbing steeply out onto the open road beyond. Sacks of flour and cornmeal tipped over and rolled about the wagon bed.

"They is saddling up," Silas said. He slid from his seat into the wagon, grasped the various packages, and held steady the small barrels.

Bessy showed her mettle. The wagon bounced freely, the rattle of the iron wheels on gravel, up, away from the river. Rounding a bend in the road where they were briefly out of sight of the two men, Bessy began to slow, tiring. Then George saw it, the cut-off he was looking for: stones piled on the road's edge, his mark left there months before.

He climbed off the bench and hurried Bessy down the overgrown dirt track. Silas slipped from the wagon and began dusting the trail, removing any sign of their passing. George climbed a small rise, then led Bessy around the long shelf of rock and into the cave entrance. Bessy snorted and Silas went to her, spoke quietly in her ear, and stroked her neck. The wagon was too large to fit deeper into the cave; they would be completely visible to anyone who rounded the rock wall. George leaned over the wagon and steadied his rifle on the gunnels. From the road came the sound of horses, galloping hard, passing, then fading westward. "They'll be back," said George quietly. "Soon as they realize we aren't there." He leapt to the rock wall, removed his hat, and peered over the top. Silas crept up beside him. "Stay here," George said and he stepped around the embankment and down the trail.

A moment later, he returned, out of breath. "They're coming back, but they haven't seen this trail yet." He hitched himself over the rock and lay on his rifle. "Stay inside the cave. Keep Bessy quiet, best you can," he said.

Silas said, "Yes, Massah," and did as he was told.

George waited, riding the rock wall, his rifle pressed to his shoulder. This would be the second time near this cave he had run from danger. It annoyed him. He had a notion to come back here with cavalry troops and clean up these renegades. Then he shook his head and almost laughed out loud. It must be like this all over the South. Soldiers were displaced, most with no homes to return to. Wandering colored folk looked for family members, a place to live, food to eat. Refugees took to the roads, white and black, and were just trying to survive.

Light faded quickly as the storm rolled in. He peered into the dimness but could not see beyond long shadows in the brush. Suddenly, the steady rhythm of hoofbeats became the rattle of bridles, and horses, at least a dozen or more by the sound, galloped by the cut-off. Could be a cavalry patrol, and George sighed as his rifle slipped from his shoulder. Still, he waited. A light rain began to fall, splashing off the rocks into his face. A clap of thunder formally announced the storm's arrival. He returned to the cave and removed his sack coat. "Well, Silas, I guess we'll stay here tonight," he said, and he unhitched Bessy. George stared into the gloom of the cave, but could see nothing in the fading light.

"Don't go in there," Silas said. "I heard tell of spooks in these parts."

Bessy gave a snort.

Silas said to her, "It's true! Could be a Swamp Wampus or some such."

George looked at Silas as if he had spoken a foreign language. "A what?"

"Swamp Wampus. I heard Cletus and some of them other folks talking about a Swamp Wampus with long fangs and big claws that eat pickaninnies like me."

"Hell, man, that's just nonsense."

"I sleeps here in the wagon just the same," Silas said. "Be all right."

Silas climbed into the wagon and George unrolled his haversack, found a level spot near the entrance, tipped his hat over his face, and quickly fell asleep to the drumming of the rain.

JUST BEFORE DAWN, SILAS SHOOK his shoulder to awaken him. George sat up, alert. "What is it?" He groped for his rifle.

"I heard something, Massah Van," Silas whispered.

George jumped to his feet. At the cave entrance, rifle in hand, he peered into the rain-soaked gloom.

Silas knelt beside him and whispered, "Not out there, Massah Van." He pointed into the black maw of the cave. "In there."

Silas retrieved a lantern from the wagon while George felt around inside his poke sack until he found his box of Lucifer matches, struck one and held it to the wick. Meager light traced the vague outlines of a huge space that tapered to a narrow passageway.

George walked slowly down the passageway with Silas behind him, his head poking like a feeding chicken. A soft breeze carried past them as they entered a cavern the size of a barn, with columns of rock like cathedral pillars along one wall, stone shelves forming a ragged staircase along another. To his right, the floor dropped away, walls twisting behind huge rocks and deep gullies. Silas pointed to the ground at the edge of the light: horse droppings. The smell of old hay lay on the stale air.

George stepped around a boulder the size of a field mortar and saw horse tack, several bits, harness, and leather straps. Lying on an old wooden bench was a neat pile of blankets next to a hand-tooled saddle, **EG** clearly scribed in the leather.

"Them's our blankets," whispered Silas. "And that saddle come from Elm Grove, too."

George examined the harness and tack, searching for one particular item. A steady breeze blew through a gap in the rocks, carrying a foul odor of decay and animal smells. He slowly approached the opening, rifle to his shoulder, listening. Silas edged closer to him. "Swamp Wampus," he whispered.

George rubbed his thumb along the stock of his rifle. A Swamp Wampus was no match for a Spencer Rifle. He peered again into the dimness and cautiously stepped forward. From behind him came a scuffling sound and Silas shouted. Echoes bounded off the walls from a hundred directions.

George held the lantern aloft but could not see Silas. Over a low shelf, around a boulder, George thrust the lantern, exploring a low opening. Nothing. "Where are you?" George shouted, "Silas!"

He peered down a fissure in the rock, a great gaping crevasse that swept away into the darkness, and heard a low scraping noise, like an adz in soft wood.

"Silas! Silas, where are you?" George swung the lantern in narrow arcs, trying to find the boy. But all that he could see were sharp edges and bits of rock and deep shadows that passed into forever.

Silas cried from below, "Massah Van!" his voice raspy and strained.

"Silas, I'm going to get a rope." He wanted to say, "Stay there," but realized the pointlessness and strode quickly to the cave mouth. He searched in the wagon for rope, but it seemed the one item he had not procured from the quartermaster. Bessie snorted as if to render assistance, and George tore the reins from her, nearly ripping the bit from her mouth. Back inside the cave, he wound the lengths of harness to the wooden bench and wedged it between two boulders. Hand over hand, he lowered himself into the crevasse. The bench slid with his weight before it held firm, and he dropped heavily onto a stone shelf.

"Massah Van?"

"Hang on, Silas." George lowered himself to the length of his tether and saw a hand reach from beneath a shelf of rock, blood clearly visible on its fingers. Bracing himself against the side of the cavern, he reached for the hand. Silas moaned as George pulled him from the pit. His face was crusted with dirt and blood, one eye already swollen shut, and in the darkness of the cave, he could see the boy's teeth broken in a jagged line. George had witnessed ghastly injuries, arms and legs shot off, men pounded to a bloody pulp by canister. But this was Silas and George nearly cried out with anguish .

HE TUGGED THE REINS AND THE WAGON skidded to a stop. George quickly carried the limp boy into the cabin. In his haste, he stumbled against the table and a white ceramic bowl shattered as it struck the floor. He set Silas gently on a bed with worn ticking and the boy cried out.

Eb and Mitsy gasped. To their startled faces, George said simply, "He fell." He could not bring himself to say more.

Mitsy mopped Silas' forehead with a damp cloth while Chryssy tugged at her mother's apron and began to cry. Eb went to work with mortar and pestle, grinding a poultice made of dried leaves and moldy bread with pinesap. "Old family recipe," he said as George looked on.

A row of jagged gashes streaked Silas's young face. Where he had scraped against the rocks, the flesh hung like an old dog's ear. George had patched and bandaged what he could, then pushed Bessy hard all the way back to Elm Grove. Now he could only stand by the sideboard and watch as Eb tenderly smeared the foul-smelling ointment onto the boy's open wounds.

George's shoulders sagged as the shame filled him, shame for the boy's wounds, the broken crockery, and for the muddied floor at his feet.

A knock came at the door and he opened it, grateful for the doing. They stood in a tight cluster, as if fearful of what lay inside: Eva wrapped in a wool shawl, Jesse, and the Judge. George told them of the retreat from the highwaymen, hiding in the cave, and Silas's fall. He spoke slowly and deliberately and had to stop often to swallow. Across the road, Cletus stood grooming Bessy in the shade of the smith house.

"Any broken bones?" asked the Judge.

George shook his head. "No, but his head took a beating."

The Judge just nodded. George felt an impulse to run, to escape, to somehow erase his memory of the incident, as if that might heal the boy. Impulsively, he turned toward the creek and began to walk. Eva followed. After a short distance, George said, "We sang Stephen Foster and I taught him how to shoot."

She said, "You hold yourself responsible, Sergeant? Why, next you'll tell us you started the rebellion." Her sharp comments seemed tempered by a voice deep and soothing and sincere. "Eb knows some things about medicine. He'll tend to the wounds. Silas should be all right in a few days."

They climbed the rocky shelf above the creek, stones cool to the touch. George sat with his back to a rock and looked at nothing. After what seemed a long time, the tightness began to fall from his shoulders and he breathed a long, heavy sigh. He noticed Eva's hand rested on his arm, but he did not remember her putting it there.

Below, the creek made a soft gurgling sound as it slipped past their perch. The air held aromas of magnolia and warm honey and something else: soap. Her hair lay clean and shiny. The long streaks of blue-black reflected the sunlight, pink and orange. He sighed once more. When Eva spoke at last, it was of trivial matters and soon George laughed, and while she spoke, he watched her. Her regal bearing lent her a self-confidence that he found soothing, reassuring. The humid air warmed him less than her presence. She sustained him.

The sky darkened and a chill breeze brought light rain that forced them homeward. They passed Eb and Mitsy's cabin, but did not stop. Across the road, Cletus stood in the shadows.

CHAPTER TWENTY-SEVEN

Hickman County, Tenn., April 20, 1865

"The way I figure it," Noah Turner said, handing his sister a dish to wipe, "I can't do anything till the courts are open again. I got Buck's deed, but no way to enforce it." His hands dipped in the dishwater, rinsing another dish. "And Buck ran off to join the army. Don't that beat a poke in the eye?"

Jenny wiped and stacked. "Mildred and Johnny never were none too bright," she said. "Can't hardly expect more from their children. Buck ran away to the army with the war over, and you tell me Jimmy got killed being stupid, too."

Noah saddened at the memory of young Jimmy shot out of the tree. "I told him to keep a lid on, but he opened up soon as the Yankees came waltzing down the road."

"And Mildred letting that phony preacher in for supper." She shook her head. "Times being what they are and all."

Noah said, "That whole family is up and wiped out by Yankees. Cousin Johnny at Murfreesboro, Jimmy at Nashville, and Mildred killed by a Yankee in her own home. And now Buck is gone, too, more than likely." He lifted another pot from the soapy water. "You, me, and Pa are the only Turners left in these parts, I suppose."

They stood in silence for a moment. Then Jenny said, "I'll wager Mildred didn't hide that deed. That was probably Johnny hid it afore he joined up."

Noah nodded agreement. Cousin Johnny had married Mildred when she became pregnant. A real "looker," she had a face that was pretty as any plantation princess, but a brain thick as a fence post. After twenty years of hard living on their small farm, she had grown old and spiteful, and it was rumored that Johnny had joined up to get away from her as much as any devotion to duty.

Jimmy Turner, the oldest son, joined up just in time to bury his father at Stone's River. Noah Turner had taken the boy under his wing—Jimmy called him "Cuz"– and taught him the science of soldiering. Impatient, impetuous, and importune, Jimmy proved to be a difficult student at best, though at Franklin, he had saved Noah's life with a quick bayonet in a stubborn blue belly. A pity Jimmy couldn't keep himself from shooting one last Yankee on the road from Nashville.

Would have, should have, could have. It was time to let the past pass, Noah thought. Time to worry about his future, Jenny and Pa's, too. His mind fading fast, Pa would need constant care, the kind Jenny could give him.

Noah would have to find work, build up a stake, use it to buy seed, and plant the farm. Then Mildred and Johnny's farm, too. Maybe turn the squatters to field hands, sharecroppers. The future still held possibilities.

They finished with the dishes and Jenny said, "Come set a spell. Minnie Waters has invited me for a visit. I spoke to Lang Doty and he said he and Hattie were going that way and I could ride along. We leave first thing in the morning."

CHAPTER TWENTY-EIGHT

Along the Natchez Trace, April 21, 1865

Eb sat awkwardly upon the old mare, his legs dangling, his feet too large for the stirrups. Bessy took no notice. Sergeant Van Norman cared for her, brushed her coat daily, found oats and hay for her, and the occasional carrot or sweet potato. The mare's old legs had grown stronger with the attention. Eb patted her neck softly and she shook her mane as if for the pure joy of it.

Eb pointed her toward a small clearing near the edge of the road where, beneath a spreading chestnut, a crude marker stood. A simple board angled from the ground, one word etched on its face, barely legible: **FLO**. Eb slowly dismounted, letting the reins fall. He hopped over to the grave and removed his hat.

For a long time he said nothing. Then, "Hello, Flo." He waited, as if expecting her to reply. "Been sometime, I know. But the war is over now and all us coloreds are free men. Free to come and go as we please. A fellow lent me this horse so I could come visit you a spell. And I don't need a pass or anything.

"You never knew freedom, Flo, but it is a wonderful thing. No one to tell you how to live your life but yourself. No one to whip you if you don't do his bidding. No one to buy you or sell you." He shook his head. "No one to own you."

High in the poplar and beech trees, the dry wind whistled gently and the tall grass swayed in rhythm with the rustle of leaves. Bessy grazed contentedly to the sound of Eb's deep voice.

"When we were young here at Watersmith, we used to come to this place on warm afternoons just like this, sit under this tree, talk of going away, going north and finding a new life." He scratched his head. "Funny how things change after a time.

"I got me a new woman now. Her name is Mitsy and she's a good woman. I know you would get along, you two. She's a good cook, too, just like you. We live with a judge and his family. We have made a good life, even have two children. Silas—he's Mitsy's boy, but a good boy—he just fell in a sink hole, but he's going to be all right. And Chryssy, well, she's just about the best little thing this side of heaven. Lots of spit and vinegar, too. Like you when we were little."

Bessy snorted and pawed the ground.

Eb glanced at the sky and breathed deeply of the warm air. "I have to go now." He knelt in front of the wooden marker, slowly opened his coat, drew out a small yellow flower, and placed it on the grave.

"You were my first love, Flo," he said. "You will always be my love."

THE ROAD CURVED SHARPLY AS IT climbed the piedmont. Huge boulders lay on either side in the thick woods. Eb worried about the growing darkness, a black man riding a Yankee horse alone at night, and urged Bessy to a trot, but she soon slowed and Eb was content to let her have her way. As he breathed deeply of the warm air, he couldn't contain a grin at the wonder of it: him alone on a darkening road with no pass, a free man.

Horses riding fast interrupted his reverie and Eb steered Bessy for the shadows of dense pines. He dismounted as two riders passed, galloping hard. One had a familiar look about him, heavy-set, his broad-brimmed hat pitched low over his features. The other rider, a smaller man, led a third horse. Something sinister stirred in Eb as he watched their backsides bob down the road. He set out again, hurrying now as the sky began to darken. Heavy clouds rolled in like a fog. But not fog. The acrid smell of smoke filled his lungs and he dug his misshapen feet into Bessy's flanks, urging her faster. Just beyond a tree break, gouts of dense black smoke spun and twisted in the air, shrouding the twilight sky. A small clapboard house rested between a stand of tall oaks. A faint glow of yellow light poked through the smoke coming from one window. A man lay in the open doorway, buried beneath a pall of thick smoke. Suddenly, the window burst and glass shards cascaded in a shower of glitter and fire. Tongues of flame licked the side of the wooden house, preparing to swallow it whole.

Bessy sidestepped, her mane twitching, ears flat. Eb slid from the saddle and bounded to the unconscious man. He knelt and lifted him easily, felt the sharp sting of heat on his face through the open doorway, then loped away from the fire and laid the man gently across Bessy's saddle. Another window burst and clouds of smoke rushed out before great pyres of flame overwhelmed them.

Bessy whinnied and pranced and Eb led the frightened horse away from the fire, hopping alongside. Smoke buffeted the trees and swelled their limbs. Sharp crackles and loud thumps gave way to a great roar as the roof collapsed in splintering wood and exploding timbers. Sparks leapt like fireflies into the evening sky.

He heard a groan and Eb stopped to lift the man's head. The face seemed swollen, the skin parched and stretched tightly over his raw cheeks. A trickle of blood fell from his hairline, another from his ear. The man groaned, "Uhhhh, where am I?" and slumped once more into the saddle.

Eb reached up. "You've had a rough go of it, sir. You should just rest easy there."

The man sat up, steadied himself, and rubbed hard on the back of his neck. "Who are you?"

"Name is Eb, sir. Eb Wilson of Elm Grove." Eb thought to show the man his pass, then remembered he didn't carry one. The man groaned again and Eb lifted the canteen from the pommel of Bessy's saddle. "I came by and saw your house afire. You were lying by the porch." He uncorked it, held it as the man drank, and watched the dribble carve gullies in the soot on the man's face. Under the soot were hard lines and spaces, a face worn by age and time and consequence. Eb did not know that it was a handsome face, as all white men looked strangely unpleasant to his way of thinking.

Suddenly, the man stopped drinking. "My pa!" he cried. "Where's Pa?"

"I don't know, sir. You were the only one I..."

"Pa!" the man shouted, and staggered to the ground.

The fire whipped and cracked and sang a wicked dirge of smoke and flame. The man staggered a few steps before he collapsed in the dirt, kneeling in supplication, his head bent forward between his long arms.

"My pa was in there."

"I am truly sorry, sir," Eb said.

The man lifted his head and ran his long fingers through his hair. "Thank you for stopping," he said as he struggled to his feet once more.

"Yes, sir," said Eb. "You're welcome, sir. Now you just get up on that horse and we'll take you where you can rest easy."

The man slowly mounted Bessy and began to plod away into the shadows. Eb walked alongside, stepping briskly, his gnarled feet padding softly on the moist earth. The man wore a tattered gray vest over a coarse shirt and heavy cotton trousers. His boots, worn and dirt-caked, were an honest farmer's boots. Eb had known many white men, guests of the Judge or young men courting Eva, and saw character on them as another might see a suit of clothes. He sensed their goodness instinctively. Or their malevolence. He felt no wickedness attached to this man, but a strength and selflessness, despite his circumstances.

Suddenly, the man turned his head and said, "What happened to your feet, Eb, if I may ask?"

"I was beaten by my overseer," Eb said. "Long time ago now."

The man pulled lightly on the reins and Bessy slowed. "I've known of whippings, even seen a man's legs chained together," he said. "But who would break a man's feet so he can't work?" He slowed Bessy some more. "Sort of at cross purposes."

Eb said, "This was a particularly cruel overseer."

They walked in silence for some time, Eb step-hopping alongside the tall stranger astride Bessy. Woods gave way to open country. The sky turned purple, the edge of the land melting into the gray dusk. In his mind, Eb began to picture running away with Flo on a night like this a long time ago. They had been spotted by a woman hanging out her morning wash, then surrounded and caught, and dragged back to Watersmith at the end of a rope. Some days, he still heard Flo crying inside his head.

But on this night, Eb walked these same roads a free man. Free to come and go as he pleased. Free to own property, free to choose his own house, free to choose a wife, even to marry. Free to live and work and follow his notion of happiness. Free. His step-hop quickened and he nearly laughed out loud.

NOAH TURNER RODE WITHOUT SPEAKING. Blood had crusted in his ear and he rubbed at it. Beside him walked a man big as a tree, a man hacked and beaten by a system of cultural arrogance and racial intolerance, the very system for which Noah had fought so hard and long to preserve.

But this man, this black man, had saved his life.

So much had changed. Slaves were now Freedmen, free to walk the roads at leisure. No pass. No curfew. Free as any white man. There was trouble in that notion, but at the moment Noah did not understand why.

His head ached, his face burned, his arms hurt, and his stomach felt like sour apples. The horse's graceless gait, like she was about to dance, added to his discomfort. Each breath made his head sting where Slive had struck him. He had never seen it coming. One minute he was standing in his doorway, lying on the ground the next. Bushwhacked by Slive and that other fellow, the young soldier with the fancy boots he had interrupted in mid-shit so long ago. Carter, a dog-robber, no place to go, no food, no home. No honor. Slive fed off the weak and the wretched. He scooped up the dregs of society like so much fodder at the base of a trough.

Noah Turner understood well. He had been one of them.

To no one, he muttered, "Goddamn you, Slive. This is not the end of it."

"What's that, sir?" Eb asked.

"Nothing. I'm just talking to myself."

"Did you say 'Slive'?"

"He's the fellow set fire to my home, killed my pa," Noah said.

"Master Slive," Eb said slowly. "Yes, he is the one I saw on the road."

"You saw them?"

"Yes, sir, just before I found you. Two men, but three horses."

"That was my horse they took." Noah turned in the saddle to peer back into the gloom of the road, but it caused his head to ache and he slumped once more as the horse plodded on.

Some time later, darkness complete, they finally turned up a tree-covered lane. There stood a large white house, much larger than Jenny and Pa's, with tall pillars and porticos along three sides.

"Hello, Eb."

A soldier, a Yankee by his accent, rose from beside a small tent, and Noah Turner felt something familiar stir inside him.

"What do we have here?" asked the soldier.

"This man lost his home tonight, Sergeant," said Eb. "It burned down. I brought him along."

Noah dismounted and stared at the sergeant who had captured and then released him four months before. Same square jaw, same dark eyes serious of purpose. New mustache. The sergeant showed no reaction, no recognition. And no wonder. Noah imagined he must have looked quite different then, unkempt, unshaven, hair long and tangled, rags for clothes, disheveled in defeat. Now here he stood, clean shaved, heavier by twenty pounds—Jenny's cooking to thank for that—and his face black with soot.

Noah rounded Bessy and faced the sergeant. "Hello, Sergeant," he said. Still no reaction. "Name is Turner." He held out his hand.

* * *

Along the Natchez Trace, April 22, 1865

They hitched the old mare to the wagon at first light. Noah Turner rode on the bench with the sergeant. A Negro named Cletus sat in back with a lone shovel as the buckboard jostled on the rutted road. Noah noticed the fancy repeating rifle that hung loosely in a makeshift holster. He was tempted to heft it and site down the bore, but decided to let it pass.

The sun rose like a bloated orange suspended in the tenuous mist, the sky still dark as a pool in the west. The wagon splashed across a swollen stream and onto the pike, its wheels tracing lines in the dew, the first tracks of the day. At the edge of the road, a field mouse sniffed the moist air, then darted into the undergrowth. A pale mist drifted to lie in shadowy skeins across fields that for three years had lain fallow, but now burst with barley and corn and tobacco sprouts. Somewhere, a mourning dove made a hollow call.

Noah was not able to appreciate this perfect spring morning in the heart of Tennessee. He had other matters to engage his mind. After arriving at Elm Grove, Noah had been given food and a spot of sorghum whiskey before meeting with the Judge, who offered sympathies but stopped short of promising assistance, feeling more inclined to adjudicate rather than enforce the law. It was the sergeant who, though he still had not recognized Noah Turner, offered to accompany him back to his home.

"Right decent of you to help out this way, Sergeant," Noah said.

"That's all right, Mr. Turner," George said. "I suppose my orders to keep the peace at Elm Grove can be stretched a bit."

Noah pointed and said, "Turn here at the crossroads."

They crested a rise and fell toward a broad valley that meandered through deep woods of oak and poplar and beech. In a puddle, a pair of jays pecking for an early breakfast made way as Bessy ambled through.

Noah eyed the Yankee at his side and wondered, What sort of man is this young soldier? As his prisoner, Noah had simply been allowed to walk away. An unusual fellow, this Sergeant Van Norman. He was the first Yankee Noah Turner had ever known face to face.

"By the way, Sergeant," Noah said. "How are Mr. Pooler and Mr. Rutherford? I hope they've recovered from their wounds."

George stared at him, his brow furrowed and mouth agape. "Hell, man! What do you know about Will Pooler and Jake Rutherford?"

Noah grinned, his big white teeth splitting his face. Then he threw his hands in the air and said, "Monkey up a tree?"

George looked to the sky as if the clouds held an answer. "Monkey up a tree?" he muttered.

Noah watched the young sergeant's forehead twist into a knot, thought he saw the instant of recognition, and slapped his thigh as George began to smile. "Much obliged to you once again, Sergeant Van Norman!" And Noah Turner tipped his head back laughing and nearly fell from the bench.

"Damn you, Mr. Turner, I thought you told me you lived just beyond the battlefield," said George. "Hell, man, we're a long way from Nashville."

Noah cleared his throat. "Well, I suppose it's time to 'fess up to the corn," he said. "I gave up my own place when the war started. My wife was dead—no kids to help out. This here farm we're going to is where I grew up. Belongs to my pa." He paused, remembering his father asleep in the house when Slive came. Noah had done a poor job taking care of Pa. What will Jenny think? "My sister, Jenny, she's been taking care of him since I joined up. Jenny was away when Slive came a-calling. She was due back yesterday, and if she finds the homestead all burnt, there ain't no telling what she might do, where she might go." He pointed again. "Here, head south from here," he said.

Bessy turned at the tug on her reins, scuffing her hooves on the winding valley road. George said, "And who was it you say set fire to your house?"

"Fellow name of Slive, has a small spread on south of here, across the valley." He brushed the hair from his forehead. "Said I stole his horse. We came to arguing and wrestling and we must have knocked over a lamp." He nodded his head aimlessly. "Went up so fast," he said.

"Did you steal his horse, Mr. Turner?"

Noah remembered the night raid on the Union encampment, though he understood that was not the sergeant's meaning. "No," he said. "I even had a clean bill of sale for her."

"Then we should be able to enforce its return."

"I said 'I had' a bill of sale. It got toasted with the rest of my kit. The Judge says without that bill of sale, there's no way to prove that horse is mine."

The sergeant rubbed his lip. "We'll salvage what we can, Mr. Turner."

Noah nodded. "I hadn't much to begin with, but Jenny had her whole life in that farm," he said. At his back, Noah felt the rising sun clear the treetops, felt the warmth on his shoulders. They rode in silence past another abandoned farm and a pasture overgrown with thistle and hogweed. A solitary corn plant, bent and broken and browned, thrust its leaves above the weeds. The absence of sound, neither wind nor bird, amplified the noise of Bessy's hoof clops and the rumble of the wagon.

Ahead, smoke lay suspended in the trees, its acrid pall wafting over the men's dour expressions. The wagon pulled to a stop and Noah sat transfixed, his watery eyes surveying the piles of ash and cinder. The lone chimney, braced against the scorched scene, stood sentinel over the still smoldering tangle of soot and rubble that had been his youth.

At last, Noah stepped from the wagon. The sergeant pulled the rifle from its makeshift holster and followed him over the fallen timbers, some still smoking and hissing beneath his boots. There was nothing to save, nothing Noah could see that was not blackened beyond repair. Little was recognizable. Parts of things lay twisted and curled in places where they didn't belong, bits of a lifetime black and hideous, as if the very pit of Hades had swallowed all that was held dear and then vomited it back into this pile of burnt lumber and blistered memories. Noah stooped to pick up a lone tin pan, warped and curled from the heat, its patina an oily rainbow beneath a film of soot. He lifted an old washtub and uncovered the remnants of his Government Issue haversack, its straps cracked but intact, the remainder burnt to scraps.

They found Pa and gently wrapped the charred remains in and old tarp, then carried him to a spot between the oaks where Cletus dug a hole. A few rocks, a few shovelfuls of dirt, and Noah removed his borrowed hat. The sergeant stood quietly as Noah Turner paid his respects. "I'm sorry, Pa," he said quietly. "It weren't your doing and I mean to make it right."

A muffled yelp interrupted his words. "Massah Van? Massah Van?" Cletus shouted. "In the barn, Massah Van. They is something in the barn."

He had forgotten about the barn. Noah nodded to his pa once more before he ran into the yard and up the dirt path. George followed, chambering a cartridge.

"In there." Cletus pointed into the dark recess of the barn.

George skidded to a stop and surveyed the scene: doors agape, whitewash blistered, the dry barn wood miraculously had been spared from the inferno by chance and location and a favorable wind.

Cletus said to George, "It come from in here, Massah Van."

George poked his head through the open door, pausing to let his eyes adjust to the gloom. Noah ducked past him, searched the back corners, peeked into stalls, peered behind an old buckboard, its wheels gone, its yoke broken. Quietly at first, then louder, came a rustle of straw and a muffled thump, and Cletus pointed his finger straight up. "Monkey up a tree," thought Noah, and he hand-signaled that he would climb the makeshift ladder while the sergeant aimed his rifle at the loft opening.

Hand over hand, Noah climbed the wooden rungs nailed to the sideboards. He poked his head above the loft floor carefully, ducked away, then up again and looked around. "Jenny," he said and quickly jumped over the last few rungs.

They descended the ladder and she gave a muffled cry when she saw the Yankee uniform. Noah quickly made introductions. She nodded politely, shook George's hand, and then rattled Noah with questions about the fire, the house, and their belongings. Noah answered as best he could as they walked through the rubble and ash that had been their home. Jenny squatted and turned over bits of ashen lumber and blackened pots and pans, but no other thing of value could be found, and the four mounted the wagon to return to Elm Grove.

As they pulled away, Jenny turned to look one last time at the charred wreckage, at the lone blackened chimney marking just another abandoned farm. Noah marveled at her hair, deftly piled on her head, neatly pinned. Even after spending the night in a hayloft, there was a cleanness about her. Soot on her boots and straw that clung to her skirt were superficial; the skirt had been fresh the day before, the boots scrupulously polished.

The wagon rumbled slowly north and Jenny related how she had visited with her friend, Minnie Waters, who told her about Watersmith and the man called Slive.

"The very same Slive who burned the house?" asked George.

"Yes," said Noah. "Slive, and another man, Carter."

Jenny told how Minnie had lost Watersmith when Slive produced a deed signed by her Aunt Anna (Mrs. Henry) Waters giving him sole ownership to the land and everything on it. "Bogus" is what Minnie had called it, referring to the deed as a "bodacious subterfuge." She had reserved several other decidedly unladylike descriptors for Slive himself.

Jenny had known Anna Waters as a good customer, had delivered store merchandise to Watersmith numerous times before the war. It was where she had first met Minnie and they had become friends. But she did not remember Slive. And who would, Minnie had said. The man was homely and stupid and had kept out of sight mostly, until the war. Then Slive became the farm boss and immediately there was trouble: a bad harvest, horses missing—the Yankees must have taken them, Slive had said—beatings and runaways, any number of maladies, none of which would have happened had her Uncle Henry remained in charge. Then Aunt Anna got sick and no doctor could tell them what ailed her. Minnie had taken her all the way to the hospital in Nashville. It was upon their return that her Aunt Anna had confided her will. With Henry and the boys dead, Anna would leave Watersmith to Minnie, her nearest kin.

Minnie had stayed with her Aunt Anna at Watersmith until the end, making the meals, nursing her, mopping her brow, combing her hair, changing her bed sheets. Minnie was away on errands when the old woman died. Slive had her wrapped in linens and ready to lay in the ground before Minnie had said a decent farewell. Then he banished Minnie from the house, showed her the deed, all signed and legal-like, and Minnie had no choice but to go home to Pulaski.

Noah listened, but it seemed like idle gossip to him. He didn't care. His intent was revenge, plain and simple.

Jenny explained that she had returned the day before with the Dotys and found the house in ruins, Pa and Noah gone. She hadn't known what to do. It had been past nightfall, and the nearest neighbor was too far in the darkness, so she had slept in the barn. Then she had hidden when she heard them coming, her perch in the hayloft betrayed when a rat defending its home startled her.

She stopped suddenly, turned to her brother, and asked, "How's Pa?"

CHAPTER TWENTY-NINE

Elm Grove Plantation, May 14, 1865

G eorge removed his Hardee hat, drew his sleeve across his forehead, and stood for a moment on the portico. Even the hottest days in Wisconsin had never been like this. The thick evening air chafed him and made his hands sticky. A sigh in the elms gave hope to a breeze and George shook his hair just for the cool of it.

Behind him lay row upon row of crisp green—early signs of corn and tobacco and barley and rye, vegetables of all kinds. Long lines stretched over three small hills like threaded spools. Cletus and his kin were up every morning before light, in the fields past dusk. Many days, George and Noah worked alongside them, or hauled muck from the creek, or tacked new boards to the tobacco sheds. The work was hard, just as he remembered. But the reward took shape and form, as Elm Grove had begun to reveal her hidden luster. And George felt a part of it.

He wiped once more at his brow. Across the road, beyond the wall, the tall grass waved at him, beckoning. He hefted his rifle and stepped off the portico.

"Sergeant Van Norman." Eva hailed him from the door. "I should like to go for a walk. Would you be so noble as to escort me on such an exquisite evening as this?" she asked, wrapping a colorful shawl about her shoulders.

"Yes, of course, M'lady," said George, mimicking her formality. "And, where would Your Highness choose to venture?"

She slipped her arm through his and he nearly burst out laughing. She blithely chattered on as they set out, either ignorant of the mockery, or polite enough to ignore it. "We must check on the progress of the tulip trees," she said. "It's very important to watch the buds. They should be trimmed back if they develop too quickly. You can double the number of blossoms that way, sometimes more. We should watch the boxwood, too. See if the flooding has hurt it. We had a wet spring and I'm worried. Though God knows, we need the water after that terribly dry winter. Do you believe in God, Sergeant Van Norman?"

Tulip trees, spring flooding, the deity? Her capacity for flitting from topic to topic was maddening. Yet he followed perfectly, track upon track, the ideas connected somehow, not linear, but sideways it seemed.

"Of course you needn't answer if you find it impertinent of me to ask," she said. "Everyone should go to church, don't you think? We used to go every Sunday until the war. Our preacher went off with the army."

"God seems to have an important influence upon some people." George said. "But in so many different ways."

They passed beneath the elms and he admired the canopy. Spring arrived here earlier than he remembered back in Iowa County, yellow-green buds bursting from chocolate-brown scales, blocking out the sky under a natural arch that framed the roadway. Such artistry must be God's work, he thought. "This elm grove is truly beautiful."

She said, "That isn't how it got the name, you know."

"Oh? How did Elm Grove get its name?"

"For my grandfather and grandmother, Edward and Louise McFadden. E, L, M. Grandpapa planted these elms when he built the house."

Someday, George thought, he would like to own some land somewhere and build a house worthy of a name.

Emerging from the row of trees, they turned onto the main road and George picked up the thread of a topic. "Some men in the regiment say they have a hard time believing in a God who would allow war and killing." He scratched his moustache. "But they are the same men who say a prayer just before battle. It's hard to figure."

"Did you attend church services before the war, Sergeant?"

"My father is a deacon at the Methodist church back home," he said. "I suppose I went to church because I had to. Now I find it difficult to believe in any particular faith." A peculiar statement, he supposed, being mindful of what his parents might think. He had lost his inherited faith. Not consciously. But somewhere near Corinth, it had simply fallen from him like a heavy overcoat he had shrugged off, knowing its warmth and bulk could not protect him.

"Why Sergeant Van Norman, you do believe in God, don't you?"

He bit at his scarred lip and thought for a moment. He did not know her religious leanings and did not wish to offend in any event. "I believe in a greater power, I suppose. But I can't say I believe one God is any greater than another. There are in this world many different ideas of God. Belief in one seems to deny the teachings of another. Who is to say one is right and another wrong?"

"I suppose only God can say."

"But which God?"

"I see your point," she said. "Some folks follow the Pope in Rome. Others don't even celebrate Christmas. People in India worship cows. Isn't that the silliest thing? Someday I should like to go to India. And Rome and Paris, too. Oh, I would love to see Paris."

She babbled on for over an hour, no subject lasting more than ten yards, some less than a few steps. Occasionally, she would ask his opinion, but often did not wait for a reply. Women love to hear themselves talk, George reasoned, and this one needed little provocation. From time to time, he made listening noises: the grunted affirmation, the arched eyebrow, or the sage-like nod of the head while humming softly.

He sensed she found security against the oppression of great events by absorption in her surroundings. She rambled from book binding to basketry and phrenology to kleptomania, all somehow connected, bits of ideas transformed, emerging and rising, only to be discarded for the next. She prattled on about familiar things that even she knew were of minor importance. But George let her tell him every detail on her mind and then discussed them with her in perfect gravity. This woman, haughty and self-absorbed, myopic in her belief that only the Southern Cause was just and that Tennessee was the center of the universe with Elm Grove its capital city, was after all his hostess and he was her guest.

Beyond the ford, along a thickly wooded path, they emerged behind the row of drying houses as the sky melted into a deep lavender and dusk descended on Elm Grove. They returned to the house just as the clouds lost the last rays of daylight.

"I do believe I have completely talked myself out, Sergeant. Why do you let me chatter on like that?" She teased him the way a woman will, testing her charm on this farm boy from Wisconsin, coquette accompli. "You'll just have to set with me a spell and do the talking for the both us," she said.

She stepped onto the portico and settled onto the pine bench, then motioned for him to sit in the chair beside her. Eb quietly opened the door, set an oil lamp on a table by Eva's side, and bid goodnight. The last of a purple ribbon disappeared from the horizon and the night closed around them, circumscribing their space, their intimacy. A moment later, light spilled from the side of the house as Eb and Mitsy left by the kitchen door. They stood framed for a moment in the soft lantern glow, Eb with his great hand behind Mitsy's waist, until they reached their quarters.

"They seem so much in love," George said quietly.

"Mm-hm," she agreed.

"How long have they been married?"

"I don't know. Most often, the people simply pair up. There never was any legal ceremony. After little Chryssy was born, they just started living together."

"He told me how he came to have those feet of his." Eb, the young blacksmith, tortured with his own tools. "Seems he was beaten by the same Slive who set fire to the Turner place."

"Eb had another woman before Mitsy, before he came to Elm Grove. Papa told me once that Mr. Slive lost an eye to Eb's Flo—that was her name. I guess she didn't want to allow any favors to the overseer." Her pursed lips were exaggerated by the shadows. "Disgusting beast," she said.

George rubbed his lip. Was the overseer disgusting for forcing himself on the slave woman, something most Yankee soldiers had thought common practice among slave owners? Or did Eva think it disgusting that Flo would put out the eye of her master?

"Mr. Waters sold Eb to us for nearly nothing because he was of no use as a farm hand. Papa made him a house servant, and Mother taught him manners and proper diction." She sighed wistfully, gratification in her tone. "The truly good owners were the best thing that could happen to slaves. Raise them up and give them dignity and self-respect, protect them. Give them homes and food and … family. That's what they are. They become your family. Why, Jesse and Silas have grown up like brothers, hunting and fishing together, reading the same books …"

"Except Jesse doesn't work in the fields."

"Well, no. But if they acted up, why, Mother or Mitsy would tan their backsides just the same."

George ventured into a dangerous topic and he worried for her reaction. "No one can honestly defend slavery," he said. "Except perhaps on the selfish ground that it shows a profit."

Eva said, "The government, the Federal government, imposed a tariff at the expense of farmers, both North and South." Doctrine heard from her father and his friends most all her life, George supposed, repeated as if her own. "As a consequence, farmers in the North are forced to live a life of endless toil. You've often told me so yourself."

He nodded. Up before dawn, fetch water from the spring, feed the livestock, plant or cultivate or harvest depending upon the season. Chores, endless chores.

"Under slavery, a farmer here is still a gentleman," she concluded.

George ignored the insult, allowing as it was unintended.

"It was good of your father to allow Mr. Turner and his sister to stay with you," he said, changing the subject..

"These are terrible times, Sergeant Van Norman. We Southerners are known for our gracious countenance."

Vanity masqueraded as pride, gratuitous and somehow irritating, despite her modest intent. "Most Southerners have not been so gracious, at least not that I have noticed." He added, "Until arriving at Elm Grove, of course."

Her eyes flared. "You Yankees are the intruders, come into our country, disrupting our lives, and destroying our homes. You're like a plague of vermin!" She breathed deeply, forcing herself into calm. "Though I confess, Sergeant, you have been an exception."

An uncomfortable silence ensued.

"I suppose not all Yankees spend their lives selling wooden nutmegs and cheating their grandmothers," she said at last.

"Yes," George said. "Repeat a lie often enough, even wise men begin to accept it. Most of what you have been led to believe about Yankees is just as false as the lies we were led to believe about Southerners."

"Minnie Waters says Mr. Slive stole her inheritance." Eva shifted the subject. "She says her aunt left her Watersmith. Jenny asked me to speak to Papa about it, to see if there is anything he can do."

"What did he say?" George followed her perfectly.

"Right now, the courts have no power. The courthouse is not even open. It's still occupied by Yankees," she said.

The clapboard building in the town square, George remembered, served as headquarters for the army operating in Maury County.

"But if Mr. Slive has a deed all signed and legal, Papa thinks there won't be anything anyone can do."

"What about a will?"

"They never found one. And Minnie is not even allowed into the house to look for one."

"Mm-hm," George nodded. "Tell me about Watersmith," he said. "Is it as big a place as Elm Grove?"

"Oh, no," said Eva. "Not nearly as large as we have here. Maybe half this size." Pride appeared evident in her tone. "But very pleasant in its own way," she added politely. "Mr. Waters, God rest his soul, raised tobacco mostly. Had a dozen slaves. Maybe more. Some horse stock, too, I believe. Naturally, the army took all the horses. And the land was about used up, I heard tell—tobacco will do that to the best land if it is not allowed to rest from time to time—so there may be little of value there now."

"How well did you know the Waters family?" George asked.

"Everyone knows his neighbors in these parts. We saw them from time to time, though we did not mix socially. Mr. Waters came from a good family. They have a beautiful place near Pulaski. That's where Minnie lives with her parents. Mr. Waters is her father's brother, but Mrs. Waters was always a bit different—came from a working family as I recall—and Mother did not find her to be…" she searched for the proper words, "…'our kind' as she would say. 'Mrs. Waters is from the mushroom aristocracy'," she mimicked.

"The what?"

"Mushroom aristocracy? Those are the silly people who believe that social status is attained by marrying it," Eva explained. "They climb a staircase of moneybags to their social position. But in their manner and in their speech, it is clear they have sprung from mold of a questionable nature."

George grinned and nodded. He knew many mushroom aristo-crats back home, women who married rich men. Some of those men had gone off to war and would not be returning, their riches left to the mushrooms.

"But Minnie and I have been friends for years," she went on. "I see her when we travel to Pulaski and she has been here many times, too."

The flicker from the lantern made her face seem animated, her features etched in shades of orange and lavender. It was the most interesting face he had ever seen, never the same, as if the lines and curves of it shifted slightly after each expression; her emotions remained undefined. George wondered about this proud defender of Tennessee aristocracy who sat with her slender arms wrapped around her knees, rocking gently in the cool evening air, a whirligig of words one moment, placid and introspective the next. Was she a woman of mystery, of intrigue? Or was hers simply the dogma of Southern heritage, refined by charm and politesse and, what? Virtue? Yes, perhaps that was it. Simple virtue that glowed beyond the flawless texture of her skin, the gentle curve of her neck, or the faint lift of her bosom when she spoke. It was that virtue that shone through her eyes. When she looked at him intently, as she was doing now, a sense of excitement engulfed him, and he smiled at nothing, or perhaps at everything, despite himself.

Suddenly, she asked, "What prompts a man to grow a mustache?"

He wrinkled his nose. "It hides a scar," he said. "From a wound."

He felt Eva inspecting him. He fidgeted in his seat and brushed aside a strand of hair dancing above his eyebrows. The first moth of the season darted over the lantern, and Eva said, "Thank you for the walk, Sergeant." She stood. "It was a most pleasant evening."

He opened the door for her. "You understand, of course, that you will need to accompany me again tomorrow."

"Oh, I will, will I?"

"Yes, we completely forgot to inspect the boxwood and the tulip trees." George tipped his hat. "Goodnight, Miss Eva," he said.

FROM THE DOORWAY, EVA STUDIED THE MAN, his open face crowned with wavy chestnut hair, one forelock dancing above wide-set brown eyes that framed a strong nose. An appealing face. Handsome? Perhaps. Rugged? Yes, but also something else. Honest. It seemed totally absent of guile, incapable of deceit. But that silly mustache. Whatever scar it hid must certainly be more appealing. It occurred to her that this mirrored the struggle all around them, the country's struggle for newness, for reform and recovery. Reflected in a silly mustache covering an ugly scar.

Eva smiled uneasily. He was close enough to smell, his odor like freshly hewn wood, deep and smooth and all encompassing as rainwater. She felt his nearness affecting her like a torrent, a physical emotion rolling through her like fog on wind. She quickly put her hand to her throat, to feel her pulse through her fingertips, to ensure her heart still beat. She felt an overwhelming need to belong in his world, wherever it might lead, and realized there was something unfolding here. But what? Not love. No, of course not. Long a sordid source of anguish and regret, she nearly panicked at the prospect. No, not love, which comes only once. Hers conferred and lost to time and war and the weakness of men. Her one love given to The Cause, and destroyed by the invaders, invaders much like this man.

But no. Different. This man conflicted with everything she had ever learned about Northerners. A man of spirit to be sure, but witty, kind, and generous. He seemed a pillar of decency.

My God, she thought. What would Mother think? A Yankee!

CHAPTER THIRTY

Elm Grove Plantation, May 15, 1865

George sipped his morning coffee on the same bench where Eva had sat the night before when proper businessmen and acquaintances of the Judge—Mr. Porter and Mr. Arnell, and others whose names George could not remember—arrived in carriages drawn by good horses with colored drivers. They wore dark suits and stovepipe hats and spoke to each other with earnest voices, their exact words lost in the thick summer air.

George wore work clothes rather than his Yankee uniform, but still they had eyed him curiously as they stood on the portico waiting to be announced. When they left, they had nodded politely and Mr. Arnell even spoke to him, called him "Sergeant," and commented on the warm weather. George tipped his hat as the man boarded his carriage.

One of the men had left behind his newspaper, and George read the reports, how the President's funeral train pulled out of New York City's Hudson River Railroad station and begun the poignant journey to Springfield, Illinois. First to Albany, then Buffalo, Cleveland, Indianapolis, and Chicago—Abraham Lincoln's body was solemnly hailed and wept over by grieving citizens, veterans, and politicians. Bonfires lit the 1,700-mile journey and mourners who had stood for hours in cold rain bowed heads as the train passed. Shock and grief paralyzed the nation. Confederate President Jefferson Davis's capture in Georgia a few days later had done little to appease Northerners. Nor had the capture and execution of the assassin, John Wilkes Booth, in a tobacco barn in Virginia.

He turned the page to read about President Johnson's Grand Review in Washington, held to help boost the nation's morale. The Army of the Potomac, 80,000 strong, had marched with impeccable precision, twenty abreast along Pennsylvania Avenue, said the accounts. The following day, it was General Sherman and his 65,000-man army. For most of the soldiers, those parades were their final military duty. After the Grand Review, the Union's two main armies had both disbanded. The soldiers had all gone home.

George swallowed, a taste of burnt tea in his throat. There would be no Grand Review for armies in the Western Theatre. No "Hip-Hurrah!" from a grateful nation. Soldiers west of the Alleghenies had fought just as gallantly as those out East. "But no, we're stuck here until the South recovers. Hell, man! That could be years!" He tossed the paper aside and marched down the driveway, no particular destination in mind, just to be going.

At the main road, he passed pedestrian traffic, a rare sight during wartime, but now active and bustling: an old couple in a dusty carriage with faded green fringe, colored families carrying bundles and baskets, two women alone in a buckboard, and soldiers, some on horseback, but most simply walking like himself, Union and Confederate alike.

He did not tip his hat or venture a nod as they passed, felt no community with them. Head bent low, arms pumping in march tempo, he stalked like some furtive specter. Once, as he passed a woman and her two small boys, he heard himself curse audibly. They scurried from his path.

He reached a low swale and, cresting it, he stopped. Plodding up the hill on a sweat-stained chestnut gelding was a lone horseman wearing a Yankee uniform and the distinctive, squared hat of the Eighth Wisconsin.

"George!" said a familiar voice.

"Well, I'll be damned."

Ben Entriken dismounted and said, "How are you, George?"

"Fit as a fiddle, and…"

"And fat in the middle," said Ben.

George said, "If you're still chasing Hood, you are definitely lost."

"Doc Murdock sent me to Columbia for supplies. Lieutenant Ellsworth thought you might need someone to laugh at your jokes, so I borrowed this horse, and here I am."

Renewed by the sound of Ben's voice, the touch of familiarity, the sense of home, implacable forces vanished from his heart. The two men joked and blustered as if they had seen each other just yesterday, and George returned to Elm Grove with changed faith.

In the shadows of the portico, Noah Turner, tall and lean, hat pulled low over his eyes, stood against the railing.

"Mr. Turner," George called. "This here is Ben Entriken. You might remember him. We took a walk together some while back, after your cousin laid up some of our friends."

"Good to see you again, Corporal. Noah Turner is my name."

Ben Entriken stared at the older man. "See me again?" he said to George.

"Monkey up a tree?" And George laughed along with Noah.

Ben Entriken studied the tall stranger. "Have we met?" he asked.

"In a manner of speaking," Noah said, and George explained.

Jenny stepped onto the porch and Noah quickly introduced his sister, who simply nodded to Ben's "How do you do, ma'am?" before she and Noah went inside.

Jenny returned with two cups of hot coffee and bid good evening while George sat with Ben and watched the last light drain from the sky. They leaned on their elbows and drifted from nonsense to philosophy like whimsy on the wind, and their laughter fell like rain. George felt a clarity in his thinking. It was how it used to be, before the war, when George would string the poles while Ben cut bait—endless summer days when tomorrow meant nothing at all.

Dusk crept up from the east and erased the last vestiges of color from the trees. "There are changes coming, eh?" Ben said. "I don't know what they're going to be, but they're coming. Colored folk wandering all over. Rebels pass you on the road like dosey-do. And here we are talking all smiley face with a man who once tried to kill us."

"This whole country is going to be different."

"I've been hearing officer talk. They don't put a lot of stock with Johnson, saying he doesn't have the mustard."

"Folks around these parts are saying the same," George said. "Life is likely to get worse before it gets better."

"That will take some doing," Ben said with a yawn. "What do you say we call it a night?"

They crawled into George's tent, the familiar gray canvas spread over rope. A light breeze stirred the warm air and they lay on their bedrolls.

"What'll you do when you get out?" George asked.

"I think maybe I'll find me a government job, be a clerk in the court or deed recorder or something like that."

"I thought you liked doctoring," said George. "You care about folks and you have a knack for it, if I am any measure." He stretched his arm and rolled his shoulders.

"Fact is, I don't have the stomach for it," Ben said. "Oh, not the blood—seen enough of that so it doesn't bother me. Truth is, I never much liked the schooling part, remembering body parts and such. Mrs. McGillicuddy always said I wasn't much for class work. *Ray's Primary Arithmetic* about scared me to death." He slapped at a mosquito. "What about you? You always had a head for numbers and the like. What are you thinking about doing when you get home?"

"I've been thinking I might like to try my hand at business," George said. "You remember Ed Mason?"

"Sure." Ben rubbed the stubble on his narrow chin. "Leg wound, died at Nashville. The fellow that recommended you to his father's business. Stockyards, wasn't it? Well, that's great," he said. "You're a lucky guy, going home to a good job all waiting for you. You know anything about the stockyards?"

George fingered his mustache. "I like jackasses," he said, and they laughed and slapped at the mosquitoes long into the night.

* * *

Elm Grove Plantation, May 17, 1865

George awoke when an elbow fell into his ribs. Beside him, Ben mumbled something, and George knelt to peer at the dawn. The same drafts that rattled the tent flaps brought a crisp to the air that had the elm trees chattering. Already, the people were in the fields, Cletus and the boys tending weeds, their heads barely visible above the corn sprouts. Mitsy cooked breakfast, the open kitchen window beckoning with ripe smells of fried bacon and warm bread.

George slapped his friend's shoulder. "Fall in, soldier," he shouted.

Ben leapt to his feet, stumbled against the stakes and jigged sideways before he fell heavily, George laughing all the while.

"Where'd you learn to dance?"

"Damn you, George!"

Such was the character of them, Ben Entriken and George Van Norman, once of Iowa County and the Eighth Wisconsin Volunteers, now travelers in a strange land.

After breakfast, they walked Elm Grove, talking like old timers. George showed Ben the new crops that had been planted and the work that had been done on the tobacco barns. He showed him the rock ledge by the creek where he and Eva often sat, though he did not mention Eva. Ben talked of the regiment and the men of Company H. George was relieved to learn that "Swede" Anderson, the boy who lost his hat at Nashville, had recovered from his head wound. Despite the comfort he drew from his friend, George hurt for more. A notion had found a place in his thoughts and he needed to examine it, display it for view. "Ben, I've been thinking I might stay on here after we muster out."

"Here? At Elm Grove?"

"Not exactly here," said George. "But there's good land around these parts, and they're saying prices back home will be sky high with all the boys coming back. The growing season is longer, and the winters are nothing. All winter here, I kept waiting for it to get cold and it never did." The words tumbled and fell and he looked at Ben expectantly.

"Winter back home can be brutal," Ben agreed.

George stooped to pick up a clod of earth. "This is good soil." Mashing it in his hand, the orange-brown loam spilled through his calloused fingers. "I could make a go of it here, I know it. Find a piece of land. Be a gentleman farmer." It was, he admitted, the "gentleman" that brought appeal to farming. The work was hard and the hours long, but Southern farmers seemed to have acquired a position of importance in the community. And farming was an occupation he understood. Not like the stockyards. George Van Norman, gentleman farmer. The sound of it settled in his mind and he breathed deeply, the earthy smell dizzy in his head.

"Yankees are not popular in these parts," Ben said. "Folks here…" he gestured, indicating Elm Grove, "… are nice enough. But how do you think the locals will feel about a Yankee moving in, especially after the whuppings they took at Franklin and Nashville?"

George accepted this, felt it would pass with time. How much time, he did not know as he had not yet decided about the Southern mind. How long to bury grief? How long to forget?

Noah Turner appeared from behind the stable, a leather harness over his shoulder and tools in hand. He nodded at the two men before he stepped inside.

"Let's ask Mr. Turner what he thinks about your idea," Ben said.

"Not just yet, Ben. I need more time to think on it."

Mitsy called them for dinner and they talked no more about it.

At the table, Jesse asked questions and Ben answered in his smiley way and had the boy laughing and asking more questions. Jenny told stories about her store-keeping days, and Noah told his share, too, only George noted most of them were made up.

The Judge asked about the regiment, of plans for mustering out. Ben said he knew of no plans, just administrative duties and peacekeeping in and around Montgomery. Eva sat quietly and George noticed Ben looking her way now and then.

"This reminds me of old times," said the Judge. "Family gatherings and plenty of food." And on their faces, George recognized the look of old times. He felt it, too.

When the dishes were cleared, George and Ben sat on the porch with their coffee and watched the children play in the yard. Their screams and laughter drifted on the warm air, reminding George of afternoons on his family's farm. As day faded to dusk, the washtub was brought out and, one by one, the children were subdued and scrubbed and readied for bed.

The evening breeze died to a whisper and Ben asked, "Is there another reason you might be thinking of staying here? You wouldn't be getting the sugar for Miss Eva, would you, George? I've seen the way she looks at you. She's got a sweet tooth on you, too, or my name isn't Benjamin Patrick Entriken, eh?"

"Patrick?"

"Don't change the subject. Is she why you want to stay on?"

George explored the scar inside his upper lip with his tongue, a habit he had when he thought on things. "It's good land, and plenty of it, that's all," he said. "But I do confess," he eyed his friend sideways, "she is easy on the eyes."

Ben slapped his thigh. "Hah! I knew it."

In the morning, they rode to the train depot. A porter gathered Ben's bedroll and belongings, his haversack brimming with delicacies from Mitsy's kitchen.

"Keep your head down." George bid farewell as Ben boarded the train, then turned up Garden Street. He tried to think what supplies they might need back home. Home? Was Elm Grove home? The question hung in his mind as Bessy ambled through town, past the courthouse to the sutler's.

CHAPTER THIRTY-ONE

Elm Grove Plantation, May, 17, 1865

Noah Turner sat on the edge of the porch, drew his knife, and began to whittle on a stick. So much had changed. All that was new had been presented for his understanding, and yet there was so much that he did not understand. It was as if the world had turned on its head, up is down, left is right-side out. Not that long ago, the very thought of Yankees had brought a chill. But one Yankee, this enemy named George Van Norman, had become his friend. When George and Ben got to joking, why, Noah had laughed along and returned jabs in kind.

Most perplexing were the high opinions he had come to have for Cletus. Before the war, Noah had supposed that all coloreds were slow in mind, body, and spirit. But Cletus was smart, careful, and even-tempered. After the Judge had ordered seed on credit at the First Union Bank of Tennessee (an irony of sorts), he had asked Noah to take charge of the planting. Noah and Cletus worked side by side in the fields. They tilled the rough loam, hauled stones to the road, and dragged mud slime from the creek for fertilizer. They sweated the same sweat, ached the same aches. They drank from the same water jug, and in the end, would earn the same wage. That's how it was.

Cletus and his family lived much the same as they always had. But now they did so by choice. When word spread—the promise of shelter and regular meals in exchange for labor—the quarters quickly filled, colored men and women with no place to go. Then a white family named Beauchamp moved into one of the ramshackle huts, side by side with the coloreds. Noah stroked the stick aimlessly and tried to find the meaning in all of it while wood shavings curled at his feet.

Elm Grove had begun to show progress. And while he felt a measure of pride in the doing, the land wasn't his. There was a time when Noah Turner had been a man of property. But his old farm held no attraction. Nothing but memories of flood and failure—and Eliza. When the cancer finally claimed her, he had lost all interest in the land. The farm wasted away just as she had. In the days that followed, he had tried to avoid thinking about her. Thinking hurt. It seemed to him easier never to think at all if he could manage not to. So when war came, he welcomed it as a respite from grief. Officers would do his thinking for him. He could simply follow.

Noah retrieved another pine stick, drew the blade against the soft bark, and tried to imagine what lay beneath it, what lay ahead. He was forty years old and starting over. His work at Elm Grove would earn a small stake, some money for seed. But where would he plant it? Mildred's place belonged to Buck, wherever he was. Pa's house was gone, but the land was really Jenny's. To rebuild would require more than a year's earnings at Elm Grove. A new house, furniture, everything could be replaced in time. Except Pa.

The blade cut deeper, and short thick flakes of tinder peeled from the stick and fell at his feet. He cursed between clenched lips and tried to understand the lingering resentment that lay buried deep in his mind. A resentment not for the loss of his wife, or the loss of his farm. Not even for the loss of the war, for which he could identify no blame. The bereavement that gnawed at him hardest was for the loss of his home, the house he knew as a child, where oaks he remembered as mere whippets had recently shaded the whole yard. Home. That final refuge, that sanctuary. The life that once had been his. Where the last ember of his youth lay smoldering by Pa's grave.

Noah sought a reason for such melancholy. It took only a moment to realize the root of his despair: Slive. It was Slive who stood between him and happiness. The foul malevolence that was Slive must be brought to justice. But what justice? Could Slive be made to suffer the pain and grief that he had inflicted upon others? What recompense was due? How do you square things with a man so undeserving of justice?

Pine shavings thickened on the porch boards.

AT SUPPER, JUDGE WILSON SAID, "Mr. Turner, you are a first-rate farmer, I daresay. The fields are planted. Even the tobacco is beginning to take hold. Corn sprouts are already knee high." The Judge handed him the platter and Noah took a generous slice of smoked ham (compliments of the Union stores in Columbia). "The stable is in good repair, as are most of the outbuildings."

Jesse said, "And he's got Cletus painting the house. He started yesterday."

"You don't say." The Judge stuffed a forkful of ham into his mouth, chewing vigorously.

"He may have the carriage fixed soon," said Eva. "As soon as the part arrives from Milwaukee. George said he would see to it at the post office while he is in Columbia. It seems that Yankees make all the parts for every type of machine there is."

The Judge nodded.

"I saw that nice Mr. Arnell here today with Mr. Carmack," Eva said. "Mr. Arnell always has a kind word for the taking."

"He asked to be remembered to you, my dear, though he had some very unkind words for Mr. Carmack, I'm afraid," said Wilson. "Mr. Arnell is introducing a bill to prevent ex-Confederates from taking part in state elections." He frowned. "Seems he wanted my endorsement. Such foolishness. Carmack and I firmly oppose it, of course."

Noah said, "Does he mean to keep all Confederate soldiers from serving in office?"

"Worse than that. You won't even be able to vote, if he has his way," said the Judge. "Why, that would keep more than half the state from casting ballots. Only the loyalists would make the laws." He suddenly slapped his hand on the table. "It's nonsense. Utter nonsense!"

"Is such a law likely to pass?" Eva asked.

"The Assembly is packed with Unionists, my dear. Yes, I'm afraid it is possible."

Noah looked at Eva and saw his despair mirrored on her face. Such is his fate, he thought. Can't vote, can't hold public office. Work the fields of another man's land alongside the coloreds.

"Samuel Arnell has an uncanny ability to disarm opposing arguments," the Judge said. "His courtroom style has always impressed me, though I do not agree with his politics." To Eva, he said, "You may be pleased to know he also supports women's suffrage."

Noah dropped his fork on the plate. "You mean to say Mr. Arnell would let women vote but not a man simply because the man supported Secession?"

"It would seem so, though I daresay the women supported it, too."

Jenny asked, "What about the coloreds? Will they be voting?"

Candlelight flickered in the warm breeze as Mitsy entered with more bowls of food, and the question went unanswered.

"The cavalry are missing some more horses," the Judge said. "Seems they lost another dozen to a raid near Kingston Springs." He said to Noah: "There's trouble among the coloreds, too, I am told. Some local boys dressing up as ghosts, screaming about some creature that's going to swoop down and eat them, a swamp dragon or some such."

Noah had heard as much from Cletus. Masked riders warned of a Swamp Wampus, some fantasy creature that lived on the blood of pikkininnies. Ridiculous, of course. But the people believed in all sorts of nonsense. Noah had also learned from Cletus that the "ghosts" wore dirty work boots. This, he thought bitterly, had Slive's mark all over it.

"Good thing we have the sergeant here, I suppose," Eva said.

Jesse said, "Eva, Eva, Eva, climbing in a tree. Eva says to George, 'You can't catch me'."

"Hush up, before I swat you!" she said, but Jesse just smirked.

"Sergeant Van Norman is a gentleman and a scholar," Judge Wilson said in his most judicial tone. "I am proud to make his acquaintance."

Eva smiled and nodded at her brother.

"Even if he is a Yankee," said the Judge.

An awkward silence followed, and Jenny said, "Noah was a first-rate farmer before the war came. Not so big a place as this, but he knows how to make the land produce. Learned some of it from reading books, too. Tell the Judge about that fellow Ruffin, Noah."

It was true. Noah Turner had worked no harder than other men, but had always fared better in his fields. He had no formal schooling, but he felt what little education he had was all the more his because it had been born from experience. For Noah, the work itself held more appeal than simply absorbing information from some heavy-handed teacher as passively as a mule absorbs blows. Forty years on a farm had taught him most all the valuable lessons life had to offer. Ruffin's was one of the few books he had bothered to read.

"I'm familiar with Edmund Ruffin," said the Judge. "The Roberts farm was the first to use his methods, I believe. We rotate crops here, too."

"It's more than rotating crops, sir" Noah said. "Ruffin says the land can spoil if it has too much acid. Some of it comes from rot. Some of the soil around here is just plain sour. Lime acts to offset that acid. So at our place, we ground up limestone and spread it on the fields. That first year, we doubled our yield."

"I daresay, I am pleased with the progress being made here." The Judge dished up a potato. "And that rock wall seems nearly a mile long!"

Noah slathered butter on warm cornbread and marveled with pleasure as it melted. "That would be the sergeant's doing," he said. "He and Silas have been working on it."

"How's Silas doing?" Jenny asked of Mitsy as she brought a fresh basket of cornbread.

"Doing just fine, ma'am, just fine, and thanky for asking." The kitchen door closed with a swish as she bustled from the room.

"Truth is," Noah said quietly, "His face won't ever impress the ladies. The fall in that cave cut him pretty good and the scars will stay."

The remainder of supper was eaten in silence. Noah glimpsed Cletus as he darted past the open window, brush and bucket of whitewash in hand.

CHAPTER THIRTY-TWO

Hickman County, June 9, 1865

J esse led the way, with Silas, his face a patchwork of pink scars and purple scabs, close on his heels. George followed. Hemlock poles strung with mosquito string were slung over his shoulder. Marching through piney woods and across a low valley, they sang songs and played at sword fights with tree branches. In the deep pool of a stream no wider than a city street, they dropped lines, wooden bobbers floating by whim and current. George sat on his heels and baited hooks while the two boys reeled them in. The sun played warm on his face. Water over the rocks made hushed melodies. By mid-afternoon, they had a sink line full of pan fish and at least six trout. As the sun dipped below the trees, he called the boys to shoulder their poles and head for home.

George led them out of the hollow, up a steep embankment to a rocky ledge where they paused to watch two doe pass through a small clearing a hundred yards distant. The deer hesitated at the edge of the trees, their ears back, white tails bobbing. Behind them, a huge buck emerged from low brush. Eva's deer. George felt his heart quicken. The buck looked up and down the narrow meadow, its massive antlers standing three feet or more above the distinctive black spot on its forelock. The two does ambled beneath the cover of hickory and chestnut. Overhead, Canada geese made chevron flight, and the deer turned his magnificent rack in homage.

chestnut. Overhead, Canada geese made chevron flight, and the deer turned his magnificent rack in homage.

George folded his arms and smiled. Warm evening sky, smell of honeysuckle and tulip tree blossoms on the balmy air, and fresh fish in the haversack. It may never be better than this, he thought.

"Ain't he big?" Silas whispered.

"He sure is," George said.

"Ain't he beautiful?" said Jesse.

The great antlers swung and the deer seemed to look their way, then quickly sidestepped. There came a loud crack and George ducked from reflex. The huge buck staggered and fell, stood unsteadily, then fell once more and lay still.

"What was that, Massah Van?" Silas whispered.

"Sh-sh." George pulled the boys to the ground—hand motion: lie still—finger to his lips: be quiet—and then slowly slid sideways down the ledge to a crack between two boulders. The buck lay motionless in the narrow meadow of fresh spring grass. Nothing moved. George crouched and took off his hat. Out of the trees, a large man appeared, a chestnut jacket over a body made for work, his hair sticking stiffly from an old felt hat. He carried a long-barreled rifle, wisp of smoke still hanging from the muzzle.

Silas beside him said, "That's Massah Slive." A tremor in his hoarse whisper made George turn. The boy's eyes were wide as plates. "He be the same one what burnt Mr. Turner's house up?"

"That's Slive?"

"Yes, sir, and he done shot that buck plumb dead."

Jesse stood to get a better look. "Is he the man who killed Jeff Davis, too?"

Slive stooped over the fallen animal. Blood sprayed as his long-bladed knife slit the belly. Slive knotted the rope around the buck's huge antlers and threw the end over a heavy limb. Hand over hand, he dragged the deer up, slimy blue and purple spilling from its insides.

Silas gasped. Jesse turned away. On the still air, George caught a faint odor of blood, the tang of cordite, a smell like battle. Silas slumped his shoulders and sat down. Jesse moaned, then emptied his stomach.

"Is that what it's like in the war when a man gets killed?" Silas whispered hoarsely.

They hid their eyes from the grotesque evisceration and George led the boys quietly over the ledge, down the far side, away from Slive, away from Eva's deer. Eva's deer! It will be a sad message to deliver. He imagined rich black tresses framing her oval face, her violet eyes clouded and desolate, her shoulders racked in sobs. He took a deep breath and grinded his teeth.

Thick clouds darkened the sky as they scurried down an over-grown path. Trees closed above them, heavy and dense. Tangled roots and vines snatched at thigh and boot. At a break in the trees, they jumped a small stream, and climbed the far embankment. George peered through the dimness, but could see little beyond a few rods.

"Where are we?" Jesse asked. "This isn't the right way."

"I ain't never been around here before, Massah Van." Silas yawned crookedly and sat down.

Elm Grove was east, thought George, and maybe south some. But which way was south? George searched for a guide star through the overhanging trees and saw nothing but thick clouds.

Upstream or down? Better to walk downhill, George reasoned, and they set out, following the edge of the streambed, strung together in the darkness.

"There any Swamp Wampus in these woods?" Silas asked.

George stumbled blindly, rocks and mud and water challenging any misstep. After what seemed like a long time, they stopped and rested on the embankment.

"We're lost," Jesse hissed.

"We're headed in the right direction," George reassured him. "Just follow this streambed until we hit the pike, then head east."

"That's not the way we come."

"No, but it will get us home. Now, come on. Everybody up. Silas, grab the fish poles. Company! Right face. Forward, march!" He did not see Jesse roll his eyes at him in the darkness.

The narrow stream meandered in no particular direction, and a half hour later, they had not come to the pike, or any road at all. A light rain began to fall and the troops were soon wet and discouraged, and Mitsy would want an explanation about being late for supper. The stream finally gave up and dissolved into a broad meadow below a low ridge, its craggy top dotted with spruce. To one side, more woods stretched into darkness. Rain began to beat heavily, dropping from the spring leaves, gathering in small rivulets that ran from the brims of their hats. George decided to seek shelter at the ridge and wait until morning to find the road home. "This way, boys," and they marched across the meadow at the double quick.

George examined the base of the ridge, a sheer rock face rising above them. He found a spot among some alder and told the boys to rest a moment while he gathered sticks and pine boughs to fashion a crude shelter. A "whoop" startled him and Silas jumped.

"What was that noise?" Jesse whispered.

"Just a bird," said George. "Stay here. I'll be right back."

"Massah Van?"

"I'll be right back, Silas."

Silas sat beneath the bushes in the darkness, his face betrayed by white eyes bobbing and searching.

Pine branches were plentiful and George soon had an armful. Returning to the clump of alder, he nearly bumped into the little man. "Gah!" His load of lumber clattered at his feet. "You startled me," he said. The fellow was short, rail thin, long hair matted to his head, his face creased and brown. He wore dark trousers, rags really, torn at knee and cuff. He had no shoes. George put him somewhere between thirty and sixty. "Who are you?" George asked.

The man said, "Whoop!" And then he smiled broadly. There were gaps in his teeth, and those that reflected any light were brown or gray.

"Who are you?" George asked again.

The man hopped on one foot, pointed to his head, then at George. And he smiled again. George couldn't help but smile back. There was something disarming about the queer little man. His eyes were wide, rainwater clinging to bushy eyebrows. He gestured to the boys and put his hands together by the side of his head, pointed to George again, and smiled his gap tooth grin.

George gathered his sticks and found the boys hiding under dense undergrowth. Jesse was already fast asleep, but Silas peered at him from between the brush. The little man waved and said, "Whoop!"

"Seems we have a visitor, boys," George said. "But he won't tell me his name."

Silas whispered, "Name is Dudley. I seen him before. When Massah Freddie and me was a-hunting once."

George turned to the stranger. "Mr. Dudley, my name is George Van Norman." He held out his hand. "Pleased to make your acquaint-ance."

Dudley stared blankly at George, then at his hand. He hopped on one foot, pointed to the boys, put his hands together by the side of his head, and pointed to George once more. More pointing and gesturing, at Jesse, at Silas, up at the ridge. Hopping on one foot, the man turned in a circle and clapped his hands together. "Whoop!" Then he motioned for George to follow him and he bounded into the darkness.

George dropped his bundle of wood, roused Jesse, gathered up poles and canteen, and followed the odd little mystery. At a gap in the trees, the fellow abruptly turned toward the ridge.

"Folks around here call him 'Crazy' Dudley," Silas whispered. "I wonder if he seen the Swamp Wampus."

Dudley disappeared behind some thick bushes and George hurried the boys along. Ahead, the little man stood on a mound of rock, pointing to a split in the cliff face behind him. Another "Whoop!" and he disappeared into the crevice. George followed, slowly squeezing his frame sideways between the rock walls for ten feet before the fissure widened into a narrow canyon. There they came upon a field with neat rows of corn disappearing into shadows. The group scurried between the rows, careful not to tread on the new shoots. Beyond the corn were more crops, beans and barley, and others George could not identify in the darkness.

They crossed a narrow gully and climbed a gentle slope. Through a stand of cedar and sedge, George saw the outline of a small cabin. Dudley opened the door and motioned them to enter, the light from a tiny fire casting deep shadows.

Inside the single-room hut, Dudley darted about, fussing with piles of old papers. He poked a log into the hearth and the room came alive. Animals stared with blank eyes from every corner. Deer and raccoons hung from the walls; an opossum and another animal that looked like a weasel were suspended by string above the stone fireplace. On the mantel, four tiny woodcarvings stood beneath a framed photograph. A single table and chair sat in the middle of the dirt floor. A bed made of little more than ticking stuffed with straw covered by a ratty blanket lay next to the hearth. Against the footboard leaned a rusted washtub. A small dresser, drawers hanging open, held what spare clothing the man possessed. Books and newspapers littered every surface and spilled onto the floor. George noticed a well-thumbed copy of Thoreau and *The Life of Joseph Bishop*. On the table, he read the *Nashville Times & True Union* masthead, dated April 17: "President Lincoln Assassinated. Attempt to Murder Mr. Seward. Full Particulars of the Affair. Etc. Etc. Etc."

"Crazy" Dudley, well read and well informed, poked and prodded the fire into a blaze that soon had the tiny cabin comfortably warm. Jesse and Silas curled up on the bed while George sat on a stool and "talked" with Dudley using hand gestures and words written on a slate. He learned the man's name was Arthur Dudley; the photograph was of his parents and brother, all of whom died from smallpox some years before the war.

But the little man clearly understood transcendentalism and crop rotation and the deity and myriad other topics. He explained that the canyon was not visible from the broad meadow where George and the boys had been found, and so he seldom had visitors. That seemed to suit him just fine. He lived in the canyon, raised his own food, or caught his own meat in trap lines he built by hand. Books were stolen, newspapers retrieved from discard piles. He showed George assorted bits of leather or tin scraps he had found and shaped to make tools or utensils. Whittling seemed a particular passion; the four figures on the mantel were meticulously detailed images of a man, a woman, and two children. Next to them rested a Bible. In it, Dudley showed George the history of his family: births, marriages, and deaths of at least forty people, notes crammed in the margins, lists and dates neatly penciled in block letters. The Bible and his few books seemed to provide all the companionship he required. God told him when to plant and where the pheasant could be found and which mushrooms were good for eating.

Dudley was a simple being living off the bounty the earth provided, hidden by the twists of nature and time and a limestone canyon, untouched by the war or politics or the madness of men, a king in his own little fiefdom. And George felt a certain envy for that. Dudley had a home and all the comfort and companionship he required. The only thing he lacked was the ability to hear.

Before he finally lay on the cabin floor and shut his eyes, George asked Dudley to thank God on his behalf.

CHAPTER THIRTY-THREE

On the Road to Columbia, Tenn., June 10, 1865

George pulled on Bessy's reins to stop the wagon. Noah Turner jumped from the bench and disappeared into the underbrush without a word. It had been that way with Mr. Turner of late. He brooded. He had spoken in clipped phrases as he had hatched a plan to "rescue" horses from a cave, recruiting George to the task. George admitted these horses might be those he had heard were stolen from Yankees camped at Kingston Springs. He surely imagined it to be the same cave where Silas had found the blankets and saddle, as Noah's descriptions met his own.

George breathed deeply of the thick air and rubbed his sweating hands, an excitement blooming inside him as if before a battle. And something more: a sense of atonement. He was returning to the place from which he had twice retreated, taking ground now, not giving it.

The plan was simple: George would go in the front entrance of the cave while Noah shinnied in through the back. If they found U.S. Cavalry horses inside the cave, George would ride to Columbia and return with the authorities. Noah served as insurance if anything went wrong.

Things went wrong before they started. George wanted no part of Noah's scheme to "bushwhack the bushwhackers."

"I didn't ask to be a provost," George had said. "But if those are my orders, I will enforce the law, not be a renegade from it."

They had argued, Noah demanding a horse for the one stolen. "Besides," he said to George, "Elm Grove needs horses to work the fields. All the stock was taken by Yankees in the first place."

For which the Judge would be compensated. And so the argument continued and, in the end, George had agreed to investigate, nothing more. Then they had missed the turnoff and had to turn back; new foliage had obscured George's rock marker. They finally found the overgrown dirt track, and George waited while Noah circled around the far side of the hillock to find the crevice that led to the back entry of the cave. Rifle in hand, George crept down the path. He peered around the rock wall to see the familiar mouth of the cave, a gaping maw carved by millennia of water and wind, a hole in the side of a hill tall enough for a man to stand and large enough for a troop of five or six. He checked his pocket watch and decided to give Noah another minute. A troop of five or six? Who would he want with him? Mike Mansion and Bill Illingsworth, for sure. Sandy Cluxton and Bill Craven. The toughest men in the Company. The ones you stood hard by in a fight. He'd want Jesse Cole, too. And Lieutenant Sherman Ellsworth, the man who had entrusted George with this miserable job of guarding a plantation. What would Sherm think of this little caper, George wondered? Teaming up with a Rebel deserter to recover Union cavalry horses?

He checked his watch once more. Time to go. He stepped cautiously around the rock wall, rifle first. Movement in the cave opening stopped him. A big red horse shooed a fly. It fit the description of Turner's horse, he noted as he continued. He patted the big animal gently, then crept around its flank and through the long grotto where he and Silas had spent the night. There, he stopped and waited while his eyes adjusted to the darkness, crouching, listening. The pungent odor of dung and mildew and old straw kindled memories of another time: Iowa County and haylofts and pretty girls with pink ribbons. He breathed deeply, filling his lungs with the familiar aroma. The cave had been empty when he was here with Silas, but there were horses here now. George knew it before he saw them. A faint rustling and then a snort confirmed it.

The vast room was dimly lit, shadows casting an unnatural pall on the cavern walls. He searched for the source of light, spied a small lantern on a rock shelf, and the hair on his neck began to itch. The room was quiet as a crypt, no sound but his breathing. He scooted behind some boulders and stepped in a mound of fresh dung, hoping it did not portend his luck. Still he saw no sign of a guard. A horse gave a soft whicker as George slid between two of the big animals. There, on the left flank of one, George saw it. He removed his glove to confirm with his fingertips: **U S**

As he stepped back to count the number of horses, George dropped his glove. When he reached to pick it up, he saw the boots. There was only a moment to lurch before the blow struck. It slammed him hard against a horse and he fell amid legs and hooves and dung on the cave floor. Horses whinnied and sidestepped, trying to avoid him as he struggled to regain his feet, spinning, his knees buckling sideways.

The boots, shiny in the dimness, came toward him, and he moved by instinct, crab-legged, beneath the horse, and fell outside the arc of the man's swing. He tried to kick out with his feet but another blow landed hard and he grasped at a wrist and missed. Another blow across his ear sent him reeling. He struck out, flailing in the darkness that closed about him, but there were too many arms, a knife, and blood, everywhere blood. The energy fell from his limbs and he tumbled into the rocks, twirling and falling, as if into a deep well. And darkness, like the cave, spread through him. Everywhere, darkness.

NOAH TURNER CURSED. IT WASN'T supposed to go like this. He had wanted to take the horses, not just look at them. Maybe take Slive in the bargain. But the damned sergeant had his own way of doing things. Stubborn sonofabitch. They had argued, and the best Noah could finagle was the rope he had used to sneak in the back entrance of the cave.

He had no trouble finding the opening just beyond the ridge of rock. He had tied off the rope on one of the nearby chestnut trees and then slid warily into the gap, down the steep hole to the ledge above the cavern floor. Below him stood a row of horses. He counted eight altogether. A man hunkered in the lamplight, a lone guard. It was Carter. The man's fancy boots gleamed absurdly amid the dirt and horse droppings that littered the room.

Noah dropped the rope and silently began to lower himself hand by hand to the rocky shelf below. A horse snorted as he jumped the last few feet to the floor and squatted in the shadows. He crawled behind a rock shelf and peered around a boulder, but Carter was gone. He looked to either side, quickly over his shoulder. Carter was nowhere to be seen. Noah took two quick strides and flattened himself against the cave floor behind a low bench piled with tack. From there, he saw George enter the cavern, saw him dart between the horses, saw Carter slip past him.

An easy thing, really. Carter, concentrating on thumping George, never saw Noah move in behind, never saw the knife, never felt the blade across his throat. Henry Carter simply rolled his eyes up as if to examine the underside of his brain, and fell dead.

CHAPTER THIRTY-FOUR

Elm Grove Plantation, June 10, 1865

Knit one, purl two. Knit one, purl two. Eva sat alone in the drawing room between floor-to-ceiling windows hung with bright chintz. The windows caught the late afternoon sun and warmed her. It was her favorite place to knit and she welcomed the activity, grateful to Mitsy for teaching her the skill. Mother had preferred that Eva do the fancy embroidery work, but such work required concentration and so she chose the mechanical click of the needles. To keep her fingers busy was curiously steadying. Knitting also seemed to serve purpose, an accomplishment, stockings or a sweater.

Knit one, purl two. A bluebird landed outside the window, strutting as if to display its bright azure and orange plumage. She wondered, now that the war was over, if even the land seemed happier. The dogwoods had never looked better. Trumpet flowers were everywhere, laurel dotted the hillsides, and the tulip trees were covered with yellow- and copper-colored blossoms. Spring in Tennessee seemed more lush and fragrant this year. A gentle breeze fluttered the curtain and the bluebird flew off.

Knit one, purl two. Knit one, purl two. Finish this row and change the yarn, a darker blue this time. She needed to stay busy. It kept her from thinking about the men, Sergeant Van Norman and Mr. Turner, on their dangerous adventure. Knit one, purl two. She dropped a stitch. "Good gracious, they should be home by now," she said aloud.

Eva put aside her needles and her yarn to gaze transfixed at the sun-drenched fields. All were in tidy rows of emerald green that stretched to the hills beyond. She had longed for that, the neat rows of crops that appeared after a long winter. It had been years since a full crop had been sown at Elm Grove. She looked again at her needles. Knitting a sweater with summer coming seemed ridiculous. But the colorful yarns given her by Sergeant Van Norman, no, George—he had asked her to call him George—called for winter wear despite the weather. She would craft something from them he could use when he returned to Wisconsin. And what little she knew of that faraway place was simply the cold. Wasn't that silly? She was nearly twenty years old, and George was the first Yankee she had ever known. To Eva Wilson, George Van Norman seemed a figure from another world.

Eva marveled at the way Papa listened to George. George, with his clipped phrases and nasal twang. Yet when he spoke, Papa paid attention. This somehow gave her a delicious pleasure she did not fully understand. She found George intriguing, even beguiling, the way he made her laugh, his unexpected charm. From their many walks together, she had learned there was meaning in every intonation, every lift of an eyebrow or tilt of his head. The way he paid easy compliments made her cheeks sting. His very presence filled her with wicked dreams.

Knit one, purl two. Knit one, purl two. The afternoon sky began to fade and Eva once again set her knitting in her lap. Minnie's letter had announced she would arrive in the morning. Eva looked forward to her visit, someone to talk to at last. Jenny Turner was sympathetic, but older; she somehow seemed a generation removed. There was George, of course. But he was why she needed a woman to talk to.

Oh, where were they? George and Mr. Turner should have returned hours ago. She set her needles on the sill and went upstairs.

Dearest Mother

A host of complications reminds me how I do miss your counsel, though truly my troubles pale when compared to those nearest to me. Minnie so deserves her property returned, and it would only be justice to find a new home for Noah and Jenny Turner, and perhaps a store to occupy Jenny's mind.

Vividly I remember how you worried during Father's frequent absences. Chores you found to keep busy concealed your anguish from you alone, for you could not deceive me. I find similar distraction in the yarn and the needles, and for similar reason.

Such distress visits me now. A man has incited passion where I thought none could again find purchase. Yet, purchase he has, the very hub of my heart. It worries me that his absence has me distressed so, and this distress further worries me. I suffer such conundrums poorly.

And this: What is this thing, love? Does a bee love the flower? Does a bird love the sky? Is not our heavenly worship love? Our dedication to The Cause? You and Father are my dearest loves of all. Yes, and Jesse, too, the scamp; he cheers the darkest mood.

But this is love of another kind, displaying none of the same traits or enthusiasms. This love has the taste of pheasant dipped in sorghum jelly and roasted to crisp amber. It has the smell of dogwood blossoms in spring, the electricity of a thunderstorm at the mere mention of his name. It breeds excitement, obsession. And yes, passion! I feel it burn again where only ash remained from what once was a conflagration.

I thought such love comes but once in a life. Or may a woman truly love again? This one calls me beautiful and I ask of my glass the reason why. Some beauty here must reside or he could not find me so. He creates a friction that warms me. He turns the soul within my soul.

Alas, conundrums have no answers. Perhaps Jenny will not have her store, Minnie may never again set foot on her beloved Watersmith. And perhaps love with Sergeant Van Norman (George, indeed!) is nothing more than an evanescent dream.

Clearer now for your counsel, this thing called Love,

&

A commotion in the yard drew her attention and she fumbled at the desk, its deepening stack of letters rustling softly as she slammed the drawer.

"HALLOO, IN THERE," CRIED A FAMILIAR VOICE. "Need some help here."

As Eva rushed to the open door, Noah Turner pulled up in the wagon, a red mare tied to the gunnels. But George was nowhere in sight and Eva, eyes searching, felt her fear growing. She breathed deeply and tried to control her panic.

Eb held a lantern high over his head and peered into the wagon. "Sergeant Van Norman!" he cried, and Eva nearly collapsed on the portico.

The sergeant lay still on the pine boards. Dust muddled with blood crusted in a flaky maroon-black coating over his face and clothing. Beneath his head, a spot of brighter crimson slowly spread on the wagon bed.

Noah said, "He'll be all right. Took a little knocking around is all."

Eva gasped. There was so much blood everywhere! Noah Turner's words seemed dangerously understated.

"Eva, fetch some water," said Jenny Turner.

Eva obeyed. She hurried through the house, grateful for something to do. There had indeed been need to worry. She had sensed it. This dangerous adventure, the men playing their "soldier" games, arguing over how to retrieve the Yankee horses. Her soldier, sublime in his whitewashed shirt and neatly-parted hair, now lay before her, his head a bloody pulp.

She burst into the kitchen and rummaged through the cupboards for rags. Mitsy stood transfixed until Eva cried, "It's Sergeant Van Norman. He's been hurt." With that, Mitsy burst into activity. She poured hot water from the stove into a deep bowl and snatched scissors from a drawer. Eva returned to the porch with Elm Grove's medical supplies, such as they were. Mitsy, close behind, huffed audibly when she saw the blood caked about the sergeant's swollen face.

"What's this?" the Judge demanded. "More bushwhackers, Mr. Turner?"

"Afraid so, sir," Noah said.

"Here, I'll take those," Jenny said to Eva.

"Thank you, Jenny, I'll be all right," and Eva clambered into the wagon to kneel over the injured man. Eb held the lamp while she carefully examined the lacerations about George's head and the crusted blood on his face.

Noah Turner said, "Not all that blood is his."

The Judge drew him aside. "I notice the bushwhackers seem to have given up a horse. Would you like to tell me what happened, Mr. Turner?"

While Noah spoke quietly with the Judge, Eva gently ministered to George's wounds. She squeezed out the rags and the water ran to deep red. Mitsy left to search for more. It was true; most of the blood was not George's. He had a lump over his eye the size of a chestnut. Several deep cuts over his right ear oozed blood and she dabbed at these with her cloth. Jenny brought a needle and thread from Eva's sewing kit, and Eva delicately stitched the gaping flap of skin together. George moaned and tried to sit up, but fell back again.

"Eb, fetch a board from the stable," commanded the Judge. "We need to take him upstairs where we can care for him properly. Jesse, you help Eb. Jenny, ask Mitsy to boil more water. Eva, you fetch some blankets and towels. We'll put him in the back bedroom." Frederick's old room.

Jesse followed Eb out the door and Jenny disappeared into the kitchen. But Eva remained on the wagon with the sergeant's head cradled in her lap. Her father looked at her sternly and was about to speak when Eva gave him a gentle shake of her head. Eva was no longer within her father's jurisdiction. Her father said nothing and she returned to her patient, gently mopping his face and smoothing his hair.

Eb and Jesse brought an old stall gate from the barn, rusted hinges still clinging to its edge. George groaned as Eb lifted him onto the rough wooden door, and Eva nearly cried out. She scurried ahead to her elder brother's old room, ghostly and dim, a lone lamp casting eerie shadows on the faded wallpaper. It had not been disturbed since her brother's departure; dust had gathered like tiny tumbleweeds along the baseboards and in the fringes of the rug. She gently shook out the bedding and turned down the linens.

Before rolling George onto the bed, Noah Turner tugged gently at George's blood-crusted shirt, but it was stiff and stuck to his skin. Eb worked to strip his shirt and George's long sinewy arms reflected in the lamp glow. Eva stood by, transfixed—George's broad chest, matted with hair, was muscled and taut—until she felt her father's presence, caught him frowning at her, and she slipped quietly from the room.

CHAPTER THIRTY-FIVE

Elm Grove Plantation, June 11, 1865

I n his dream, George saw a leg, soft peach with swirls of alabaster and pink rosettes, a disembodied leg, the surgeon's handiwork he supposed, maybe Private Ed Mason's leg, lost at Nashville. But he saw no blood, just the leg, and swirls of pink and alabaster, and sleep, deep and renewing. Sleep.

Awakening, he saw a hand resting on the bare leg, a delicate wrist, somehow familiar. He blinked hard to focus, the leg bare from ankle to thigh, the hand across it Eva's. Not a dream but real, more leg than he had ever seen in a lifetime of boyhood imaginings. Asleep, Eva sat in an overstuffed chair by his bed. The skirts of her robe had fallen open, her ivory limb pearlescent in the ambient light of first dawn. Was he dreaming? George raised up on one elbow, the pain in his head dull and throbbing. No, this was real. To be certain, he slowly reached out his hand to put one finger on the delicate skin inside her knee.

She stirred, but did not awaken, and he decided to lie still and simply admire her with her long ebony hair loose across her shoulders, delicate bones framing her slender neck. The thin cotton robe had settled closely about her slight frame. The mound of her bosom heaved gently with each breath, dots of a darker color visible through the thin fabric.

An involuntary shiver shook his body. He breathed deeply in a conscious effort to calm himself. Her feet were bare on the tufted rug, toes curled under, neat and trim and clean. Her ankle, for he could only see the one, was tiny, seemingly thinner than a mere twig, her calf slender and curving to her knee, its tiny oval cap suspended below her thigh, her beautiful thigh, alabaster and rose petals and heaven. Cinched at her waist was a cloth belt of the same bolt as the robe.

He looked again at her sleeping face. And gasped! Her eyes were wide and staring at him, awake and comprehending. She stood slowly and came to him, and her robe fell from her shoulders, and the room began to spin, and his head throbbed and he did not care, and she knelt over his legs and he shuddered, felt her skin against his, and he heard her moan, or not, whose voice it was he could not tell, and the bed began to move, and the sky opened. And the angels sighed.

CHAPTER THIRTY-SIX

Elm Grove Plantation, June 11, 1865

George awoke to distant voices. The fogginess in his head perplexed him. Some inner sense told him not to clear it or it might well fall off. The mist slowly settled and bits of memory fell into place. And then he smiled, and he would have smiled longer had it not made his scalp ache.

His eyes followed the sunlight that slanted across the polished oaken floor from the split between window draperies. Slowly, he gathered himself over his feet and stood, leaning against the bedpost, and pushed aside the drapes. Below, the Judge waited in the yard as Eva tucked her skirt and boarded the covered carriage. Newly repaired by Noah Turner, this was surely the phaeton's first excursion since the last of the horses had been stolen years before. Cletus snapped the reins, and Bessy lurched forward. It was Sunday and the Wilsons were churchgoing people.

George dressed with care so as not to loosen the heavy bandages that covered his skull. Several times, he had to steady himself against the bedposts. A tapping inside his head, as if someone were knocking to get out, reminded George of the damage he had endured. He took a few tentative steps across the broad hallway and nearly fell on the stairs but for the baluster, his chest catching for breath and his face shiny with sweat. At last, he emerged from the house and squinted in the bright sun. A smell of fresh-turned earth filled the air that breathed cool against his cheeks. Distant voices drifted placidly, and his eyes scanned the vacant lawns.

Beneath the elms, Silas and Noah Turner labored on the rock wall. They worked with demonic energy, their motions fluid, their bodies limber and strong. Heavy stones tumbled and fell with celerity. George smiled once more.

"Well, looky here," said Noah. "Good morning to you, young sergeant. And how are you feeling this fine day?"

"Like ten miles of bad road," George said, patting his bandages. "But better for your asking, thank you. Good morning, Silas."

"Massah Van?" Silas dropped the stone he had been about to place on the wall. "You is alive, Massah Van!"

George smiled again and felt the tapping in his head grow faint. Silas reached for a clay jug and uncorked it, offered it to George.

"You hit your head and got killed," Silas said. "But you has come alive again!"

George drank slowly from the jug.

"I has read about such stuff," said Silas. He lifted another rock and set it into place. "We all be fixing this here rock wall. Massah Tuna doing a right fine job, too."

George stared at Silas.

"What's the matter? I say something?"

"Mr. Tuna," George said, "May I offer my assistance?"

"Sure, have a rock." Noah lobbed him a stone no larger than his fist. "Good enough work for you today."

Silas squinted his scab-lined face at the two men, scratched his head, and moved further down the lane.

Noah lifted and stacked, lifted and stacked. The man deftly packed gravel for mortar, laid out stones for the sides, and gathered larger rocks for the base. He seemed a man made from the soil, his face lined like rows of corn, his temperament solid as the wall. He carried with him a pride, one that George had witnessed among farmers he had known, one that seemed natural to all men who lived by the soil and the weather and the fickle turn of nature. On their few starved acres, in their rude hovels or cabins, even the lowliest of farmers was still his own master. Farmers cultivated admirable qualities: strength from labor; courage, no matter how it was demonstrated; stamina, if only to prove you could drink more still whiskey than the next man; valor with no thought of consequence; dignity at all hazard. George understood such qualities. He saw them in Noah Turner.

He breathed deeply once more, felt the thrumming in his head, and summoned some hazy recollection of shiny boots and horses in a cave. He asked for details, and Noah told him. The red horse, Noah claimed, was his (though the animal carried a Union Army brand), the bill of sale lost in the fire.

"I tossed you in the wagon and lit out." Noah dragged a sleeve across his brow.

George sat on the low wall and closed his eyes. His head swam and he struggled for balance until, unbidden, George glimpsed the leg, Eva's ivory limb, and he felt the air rush from his lungs in a sudden gasp. Sweat ran down his nose and spilled to the earth and he stared at nothing and saw everything. The land, the house, Eva. Everything. A rock clattered into place by his side. He turned to see Noah watching him, and George realized he had been grinning.

"I am in your debt for what you did yesterday," George said. He bent to retrieve a rock, laid it atop the wall, and squared it with a poplar limb.

"It was a thing that needed doing."

George rested another stone on the wall, wiped his brow, and adjusted the bandage that covered his ear. "If this Slive fellow is responsible for those stolen horses, we must bring him to justice."

"He is strong and he is quick, Sergeant," said Noah. "He will best the man who takes him head on."

"Then we shall have to outsmart him, Mr. Turner." He lifted a stone with increased energy. Noah stacked another alongside. Silas placed another.

And the wall grew by rock and yard.

THE SUN HAD NEARLY REACHED ITS ZENITH when a grand carriage swept past them and rolled up the drive, an old black man and a boy in livery on the box. Two matched chestnut horses, their coats shimmering with sweat, led the magnificent coach of polished wood, its side lanterns gleaming. The boy leapt to the ground before the carriage had rolled to a stop and placed a stool beneath the carriage door as it opened. From within the dark interior, a lavender parasol of ruffled lace emerged and opened like a flower on a spring morning. With it came a delicate ankle adorned in stockings to match the parasol. It lighted upon the stool and was immediately draped by a flowing dress of pale yellow satin.

George stopped mid-rock. Noah stood transfixed.

"Who is she?" asked George.

"I don't know, but I aim to find out." Noah tucked in his faded shirt, finger-combed his hair and reset his hat, then strode toward the house.

At the portico, Eb, looming larger than usual, eyed the masons warily. In his deep bass voice, he announced her name was Minnie Waters and she had come to call on Miss Eva. Proper introductions would be provided after she had brushed the road dust from her clothing.

To George, Noah said, "He means she needs to use the sinks, so we got a minute to gussy up."

Inside, Noah bounded up the stairs at full leap. George made a quick critique of his reflection in the hall mirror. Staring back at him was a dirty face and head covered in soiled bandages. From beneath the dressing, his hair poked at angles. George stared with dismay at his dirt-crusted fingernails and wondered if he had time to rinse them in the horse trough. But then Eb approached with the visitor. George smiled a weak greeting as Eb spoke his name. She held out her hand and he took it, dirty fingernails first, and felt her warm touch. The faint odor of lavender stirred his conscious to stupor. Her words hummed against his ears.

George had seen wealthy Southern belles in Jackson, women little better than useless critters, too high and mighty to be civil, half the time pretending not to see you tip your hat, noses so high in the sky they seemed not to notice you at all, treated you like the dregs of society. Minnie was not like that at all. There was something immediately quizzical and amusing in her face, the upward slanting brows, curving lips that seemed about to smile, the mere suggestion of a dimple in her cheeks. She held herself proudly, square of shoulder and of chin. She looked like a queen.

He liked her immediately. Her smile was not too cordial, her greeting composed. She was so impeccably neat that George felt even dirtier, clumsier, and more repugnant. At any moment, he feared she might wrinkle her nose in distaste. Yet she did not. In the parlor, he spied a chair as though it were a safe harbor, and politely waited while she sat so that he could, too. As the youngest of ten children, George had resisted intimidation by virtue of age—she was perhaps five years older than he—but he was not impervious to the grandeur of royalty. He squirmed uneasily, and the tapping inside his head became a drum roll.

Fortunately, before he was required to speak, Eb introduced Noah Turner. George marveled at the man's transformation. Noah's clean white shirt nearly glowed. His dark piped trousers were tucked smartly into polished boots. His hands and face were washed, his hair neatly combed. He presented an image of a gentleman gambler on a Mississippi riverboat. Hardly the filthy, emaciated Rebel sharpshooter who had ambushed the regiment outside Nashville. Noah eased into polite conversation with Minnie Waters, and George could only listen and wonder at the flowery language and courteous mannerisms that flowed like soft wax.

Mitsy served coffee (compliments of the U.S. Army) and confections, and when the Wilsons returned from church, Minnie Waters greeted Jenny, Eva, and the Judge as old friends.

"How are you faring in Pulaski?" Judge Wilson enquired. "Has commerce resumed? What news from the courts?"

"We have been fortunate that the war passed us by," said Minnie. "Though some of our neighbors have not fared as well. Papa sends his kindest regards and a dozen messages, which I insisted he write down. Such complicated matters task my memory, I swear," and she proffered several letters on thick, cream-colored paper. To Eva and Jenny, she said, "But first, I have just come from the city and must share the social gossip." She put her hand lightly on Eva's elbow. "Come, my dears, do let us take a stroll in the gardens and enjoy the spring blossoms." She politely nodded to George and to Noah, but George thought her eyes lingered on Noah a moment longer.

They wandered off into the house talking their girl talk and Noah Turner, beaming like a joker, said to George, "I'm in love."

"It looks good on you," George said.

CHAPTER THIRTY-SEVEN

Elm Grove Plantation, June 11, 1865

The three women talked in lively tones as they strolled beneath the tulip trees. Through the yard, Minnie's parasol cast its muted shadow over her shoulders, layered petticoats creating walking space between herself and her companions. Eva fairly skipped along beside her, delighted to be in her company. Jenny cast a sidelong glance and just shook her head. They wandered beyond the stable and Eva grew even more animated as they walked, her steps lighter, the path smoother, as if she had suddenly freed herself of gravity and floated above the land. Her inner spirit had been restored, lost during so many long months, years, sequestered at Elm Grove. She felt near to bursting and had to gasp for breath.

Minnie Waters was to Eva more than friend and confidante. It was as if life itself had returned to Middle Tennessee. Now, there could be balls and society seasons once more. Oh, not so fancy as before. There had been a war, after all. And many of the most eligible men would not be there. But there were some. More importantly, it was time. High time, after all. Time to put away the mourning clothes in exchange for silks and satins. Time to rejoice and renew. It was spring, and Minnie Waters had arrived.

Gossip filled the air thick as soup. Tennessee's aristocracy was scrutinized and words flowed in whispers and titters of laughter. Minnie held forth on Mr. Porter and Mr. Taylor, and by extension, the mistresses Porter and Taylor. She spoke of society's snubbing of Cornelia Arnell because of her husband Samuel Arnell's Radical Republican policies and his unpopular stance against former Confederates. She explained that making outcasts of former friends came hard to her, but she suffered fools grudgingly, and, as Mr. Arnell had shown his mettle, then Mrs. Arnell must suffer as well. Such were the politics of polite society.

Eva liked her father's friend, Sam Arnell. She felt he valued the opinions of women more than most men, and she worried for him.

"But enough of this idle gossip," Minnie said. "Tell me what puts such a glow in your cheeks, Eva."

"Oh, Minnie, sometimes I feel as if the moon and the stars are my own personal property, and the whole world is alive just for my benefit."

"My, my, my, we are in a festive mood," said Minnie. "It seems the end of the war has had a most positive effect on your demeanor."

"Not so much the end of the war, as the Reconstruction," said Jenny, in her straightforward way. "Eva is in love with Mr. Van Norman," she said. "And I believe he is with her as well."

Eva blushed, for she had not yet admitted this to herself. She had most certainly not considered that George might feel the same.

"Van Norman? I know a Van Norman family in Bedford County," Minnie said.

"This Van Norman lives right here at Elm Grove." Jenny laughed. "You just met him."

Minnie stopped abruptly. "But that exceedingly handsome gentleman I understood to be your brother. You cannot mean that other dirty ragamuffin who should not have been allowed on the furniture?" She put a hand to her mouth. "You mean that ... fellow inside? Oh, my," she said, her eyes wide. "Though I am sure he is a fine gentleman."

"Yes," Jenny said, "despite his appearance. He works hard here at Elm Grove, and yesterday, he helped Noah get his horse back. He took a beating for it. You saw the bandages."

Eva said, "And he brought us grains and meats and other treasures—a keg of flour, sugar by the pound when there is none to be had anywhere, coffee—real coffee—and candies for the children. He brought me a beautiful bolt of burgundy silk. I intend to make a grand party dress."

"Where does he find such things?" Minnie asked. "He isn't a bushwhacker, is he?" She peered hard at Eva. "I would hate to think of you dallying with the likes of that rough lot."

"No, no, nothing of the kind," Eva said. "He acquires it quite legally from the army stores and Yankee sutlers."

At last, Minnie understood. "A Yankee," she said flatly.

Her words ripped through Eva's gay mood like the wrapping off a present. Minnie had been careful to remove any tone of distaste from the word, but the implication was clear. The politics of polite society. What other reason could she have for such reproach? Minnie knew of Eva's love for Tom Harden. But Minnie also knew he had been lost at Chattanooga over a year ago. Wasn't that ample mourning period for a young woman, especially in these dark days?

"Yes, a farm boy from Wisconsin," Jenny said. "Though not such a boy at all."

"He was First Sergeant of his regiment before he was wounded," said Eva. Minnie said nothing, so Eva plunged on. "He seems so sure of himself, somehow."

Jenny said, "I believe something happens to men in wartime. They acquire a quality, not wisdom so much as an inner confidence."

Minnie smiled and said, "Ordinarily, I imagine men never quite get over being boys."

"Any man who has sent men into battle is never just a boy again," said Jenny.

Eva nodded in agreement with this explanation, understood its simplicity: a competition. Playing at war, boys become men. Just as man has always fought for the hand of his fair maiden, men see war as the ultimate display of manliness, the splendor and the glory. The process transforms them, matures them beyond that of any peaceful effort, those in command most of all.

The conversation drifted to dressmaking and fabrics and eye-of-pearl buttons and Eva's thoughts wandered. Could it have been that way with Tom Harden? Could her handsome lieutenant, just a boy really, have been transformed into a man of wisdom and conviction? Perhaps someday she might talk to soldiers who had known him, learn what he had been like as a commander of men. Perhaps learn what happened to him. A moment of sadness swept through her like a hot wind, the same sense of isolation that struck whenever thoughts of Tom invaded. He had left a wound as deep and open as a great branch leaves when a sudden storm rips it from the trunk. How long to heal? Could such a wound ever mend? Eva shuddered and scurried to keep pace with her friends.

Minnie said, "Well, Eva, tell us what Sergeant Van Norman is like."

Her thoughts turned to George and her mood quickly lifted, the way he made her feel, the sense of value, of consequence. "When we're together," she said, "I feel refreshed."

"Refreshed?" asked Minnie and Jenny in chorus.

Eva chose her words carefully, unsteady, unsure of her sentiment. "You know the way it feels when it rains at night after a hot day, and then in the morning, the sun comes out and all the dust has washed off the flowers and they're all so shiny and bright and beautiful, and dew on the leaves sparkles like so many jewels?" She nodded, satisfied. "That's the way he makes me feel."

The women giggled and laughed and walked on and talked for another hour.

SUPPER FOUND THEM GATHERED OVER smoked fish, cornpone pie, and creamed peaches. George marveled at the starched civility of Southern decorum, a sharp contrast to the boisterous table he had known as a young boy. Even in Noah Turner, there seemed a profound transformation, a dignity and politesse George had not previously witnessed. As guest of honor, Minnie held court to the Judge's right, opposite Noah. Beside her, George sat mesmerized by her delicious odor. Once, as she spoke of her household and parties of years past and the handsome beaus they attracted, she patted his arm gently. It was a small gesture, but he felt an immediate kinship, a trust, as if royalty had touched him.

Mitsy served and the aromas ascended into his bandaged head and swam there—fresh spring beans and warm biscuits overlaid with Minnie's delicate perfume. His reverie was interrupted when talk turned to Watersmith and the onerous Mr. Slive.

"Judge Wilson, I do wish you could tell me some favorable jurisdiction that might return me to Watersmith," Minnie said. "That plantation was my grandfather's and my uncle's after that. It is part of our family."

"Mr. Slive is a land pirate, plain and simple," said Eva.

"It would appear so." The Judge nodded as he spoke. "He seems to have made a habit of ignoring civil law. But until the court is recalled and the legislature reconvened, only the Union Army has any jurisdiction."

"Around Elm Grove, that would be Sergeant Van Norman," said Noah.

"None of us holds a high opinion of Mr. Slive, ma'am," said George. "The Turners lost their home to him."

"So Jenny tells me." Minnie's soft voice had a soothing quality, like the rustle of wind in a forest. "I feel simply awful about your father," she said to Jenny and Noah. "A dear, sweet man."

Jenny bowed her head and Noah nodded politely.

Minnie said to Noah, "Eva tells me you had an adventure yesterday. Please do tell us what happened."

"Not much to tell," said Noah. "Sergeant Van Norman and I retrieved a horse, that's all. One stolen by Mr. Slive. Judge Wilson notified the authorities, and the Yankees reclaimed their horses."

"I am pleased to witness this alliance between North and South." Looking at George, she said, "If you are the emissary of Reconstruction, one can feel secure knowing one has such gallant allies."

Amused by her flattery, George said, "Simple military strategy, Miss Waters: unite two parties by offering a common adversary."

She smiled her bemused smile and the conversation moved on to other things. George nodded and smiled at the appropriate moments, slowly chewing his fish so as not to embarrass himself and choke on a bone. His head ached and his mind wandered and he remembered—just two days ago was it?—catching these fish with Silas and Jesse …

"… my Aunt Annie passing on …" Minnie said.

… *lost in the woods* …

"…wouldn't allow me to pay last respects …"

… *rescued by Crazy Dudley, who isn't crazy at all* …

"…has a legal deed signed by some Union general or another …"

… *finding stolen horses in the cave* …

"…said there was no will…"

… *bushwhacked, nearly drowning in a sea of blood* …

"…her private papers in a strongbox somewhere…"

… *awakening to Eva* …

"…told me the combination…"

… *Eva, in his arms* …

"…still won't allow me inside…"

What had Minnie said? "Mr. Turner, Mr. Turner," George stammered between her sentences. "Do I remember you telling me about a safe in Mr. Slive's study, one that hadn't been opened for some time?"

"Yes, I suppose I did."

"And Miss Waters," George went on, ignoring her tart expression. "You say you know the combination?"

"Yes, Sergeant Van Norman. My aunt made me commit it to memory. But you see, Mr. Slive won't allow me in the house."

George curled his napkin and leaned back in his chair. The deed, the safe, the combination. Slive.

He suddenly sat forward and said, "Mr. Turner, I have a plan."

CHAPTER THIRTY-EIGHT

On the Natchez Trace, near Watersmith Plantation, June 12, 1865

S un dappled the forest floor in spots of color and form as Noah Turner picked his way carefully through the bottoms, following the Natchez Trace. He rode comfortably on the big steed, Red's barrel steady between his knees. At the river, she fretted at the bit and Noah loosed her reins. The horse trotted easily then, avoiding the deeper mud holes. Half a mile below the railroad cut, he turned west into thick woods where the forest soared into a great canopy, ash and walnut and hickory, a trio of oak spreading across half an acre or more.

A woodchuck scurried for its burrow as Noah dismounted and looped his reins around a sapling. He weaved his way between the trees, the woods heavy and stifling. Over a low hill, he glimpsed the Watersmith grounds and stopped to observe. The main house sat in a clearing, the barn off to one side, the smokehouse just visible beyond. A single elm leaned away from the house as if trying to flee. In the driveway, Cletus stood by the carriage.

Noah squatted in the tall brush at the edge of the road. From the front doorway, George emerged with Jenny. The sergeant was dressed in a black suit with a ruffled shirt and black tie. On his head was a stovepipe hat, shiny and perfectly blocked. He carried a carpetbag of maroon and gold. Jenny wore a simple skirt of dark blue, a brown vest over her linen blouse, her auburn hair neatly pinned beneath a laced bonnet. Behind them stood Slive, coarse and brutish, his massive frame filling the doorway.

Ten minutes. George promised him ten minutes if they could lure Slive to the smokehouse. Or the barn. Either one. Jenny, posing with her carpetbagger investor, was looking to launch a meat-packing business, and needed locals to provide smoked pork, fish, and chickens, lots of chickens. Jenny knew about smokehouses, could feign interest in Watersmith's capacity and resources. Masquerading as her Yankee investor, George would rattle on about return on investment and profit potential and throw in some numbers and percentages to demonstrate his bona fides. Noah just needed them to keep Slive outside for ten minutes.

This was George's plan. He seemed to have a knack for planning, always considering options, consequences, contingencies. It was his special gift. But Noah had thought of one contingency that George had not: Coogin, the brutish overseer of Watersmith, slow-witted, maybe. But there was nothing wrong with his eyes. It was Jenny who suggested she drop a kerchief, her signal that the house was empty.

Raising his head, Noah could see them talking, George with Jenny, Jenny to Slive, Slive to George and Jenny. Crouched behind the hedgerow, Noah searched the grounds but saw no sign of Coogin.

Slive disappeared inside, returned in a moment with his hat, drew the door behind him, and stopped abruptly. A spot of white drifted slowly to the earth from Jenny's hand. The signal: all clear. Slive bent to retrieve it, Jenny with a hand to her mouth. Slive gave a slight bow, the gallant gentleman, accommodating.

One more swift glance over his shoulder and … Noah dove for cover. Coogin, his little round hat bobbing over the hedgerow, crossed the road to the house, waddling, portly when everyone in war-torn Tennessee was lean. He tossed a greeting to Slive and the four exchanged introductions while Noah remained hidden. Finally, Slive and

Coogin led the others up the dirt path toward the smokehouse. For the moment.

Noah squeezed through the hedge, running to keep the house between him and Slive. Cletus saw him and nodded. Noah signaled and Cletus walked quickly from the carriage. "Let me know if you see them coming," said Noah.

"I can have Bessy put up a ruckus like you never saw," he said.

Noah nodded and was about to open the front door when Cletus said, "Massah Turner?" Noah paused and Cletus said, "He be the Swamp Wampus man."

"The what?"

Cletus looked up the path along which the group had disappeared. "Massah Slive? I seen him when the ghost man chase us, burn my home and telling about the Swamp Wampus and all. I recognize his boots."

Noah nodded to Cletus and opened the door. Inside, he walked the long hallway cautiously, his heavy heels echoing, before he felt the relative comfort of the carpeted study. He found the safe tucked behind the row of books and set to work, spinning the dial to the right, then back the other way. Too far! He cursed softly. Deep breath. Still plenty of time to get the safe open, grab everything and go. Just relax. Retrieve the deed for Watersmith and Minnie will think you a hero. He rubbed his hands, spun the dial, found the marks, back, forth, tumblers falling into place. Last mark…

Outside, Bessy let out a screaming wail, like two cats fighting.

He froze. The front door opened and footfalls echoed on the oaken floor. He stacked the books, his breath coming in gasps, and dived beneath the desk. Footsteps outside the study door now crossed the carpet, coming toward the desk. Noah held his breath, blood pounding in his ears. He saw his hat on the floor beside the bookcase, thought surely anyone could see it.

Then a hand, meaty, an arm, covered in filthy cotton flannel, reached around the desk, inches from Noah's nose, opened a drawer and withdrew a ring of keys, jangling as they backed across the desk. A moment of silence, then footsteps in the hall, a door opening and shutting.

Moments later, clutching a bundle of papers to his chest, Noah slipped out the door, tipped his hat to Cletus, then ran pell-mell across the yard to the hedge, and was gone.

SLIVE DROPPED HIS HAT ON A CHAIR, stepped into the study and put the keys back in his drawer. His mind wrestled with the man and woman who had just left, weighing their business ideas, chewing the possibilities. Strange, those two, he thought. That Yankee fellow didn't know nothing about nothing. Couldn't tell a smokehouse from an outhouse. The woman, that storekeeper, now she knew business. Knew land. Smokehouse production and profits. Him? Bloodsucking Yankee scum. Dead soldiers not even warm in the ground and here come the bottom feeders, maggots sprung from the carcass of the loser, come to pick up what bits of rubbish they could find. Carpetbaggers.

He leaned back in his chair and laced his fingers behind his head.

Well, William Slive ain't no rubbish. This carcass still got some kick. Just need to figure out an angle. Better play them for a while, see how it lays out.

But save a little something for William Slive.

He had just propped his boots on the desk, his eyes heavy after the long day, when he reached to scratch at his ankle. There, on the floor, a sheet of paper lay by the bookshelf. Slive snatched it from the carpet and peered at the words on the page. Gibberish. He turned up the lamp. There was his name, but different: S-L-A-V-E. There were more words, something about money—he recognized money words—some names, a signature. He eyed the bookshelf carefully, the row of books, big red ones on the left, others to the right, thought he remembered it the other way round. Behind the books was Mrs. Waters' old safe.

Who knew about the safe?

* * *

Elm Grove Plantation, June 12, 1865

Papers lay strewn across the long dining table like autumn leaves on a meadow, yellow and brown and crisp. Stacked among them, George found paper money—some Confederate, worthless—but also some Union greenbacks. Crafty old Mrs. Waters, prepared for whichever side won.

The others gathered over the documents as Noah Turner spread them, shuffling and sorting the scrawled writings.

Examining an old parchment, Jenny said, "Sergeant Van Norman was most persuasive."

George reflected on his role as a carpetbagger, one he realized might strike all too true if he were to remain in Tennessee. He said, "Your performance as a shopkeeper and butcher is what took him in."

Jenny, who with her husband had spent so many years tending their store, replied, "No talent required, Sergeant Van Norman. Simple negotiation with a clever supplier."

"I'm sure Papa's old carpetbag must have looked quite at home with you, Sergeant," Eva teased.

"Mr. Slive was convinced it was packed with money." He laughed. "All I had inside were some dirty shirts."

Jenny leafed through another set of papers. "I thought I was going to die when Bessy wailed like that."

"I'm grateful she did or Slive would have had me square," said Noah.

"Cletus says he always keeps liniment in the wagon for the horses," George said. "When Slive went back for the keys, Cletus stuck some under her tail, and Bessy didn't like it one bit."

Eva clapped her hands and laughed out loud, matching the expression on Minnie's usually placid face.

"Here it is!" Noah lifted a single page from a stack. "Last Will of Anna Smith Waters," he read. "It's dated July 7, 1864."

Minnie put a hand to her pale throat. "That would be soon after Cousin Del and Cousin Tru were killed at Kennesaw," she said. "With all her people gone, she drew up a new will."

She read, her eyes moving carefully, gathering in the words, her aunt's intentions. Finally, her shoulders heaved and she let out a long sigh; the single page drifted to the floor. "Oh," was all she said as she hurried from the room. Jenny and Eva hastened after her.

George retrieved the paper and began to read. "It's all hers," he said, and showed it to Noah. "We should ask the Judge to review it, but it appears that Watersmith belongs to Minnie, with ten acres to Slive."

"Slive?" Noah inspected the document.

"Must be for his years of faithful service," George said, but he wondered what services a man like Slive might render to deserve a ten-acre reward.

CHAPTER THIRTY-SIX

Maury County, June 21, 1865

A baking summer sun lay across the pedegral and Noah Turner drove Bessy slowly, George perched on the bench beside him, the wagon heavily loaded with flour barrels, smoked hams, boxes of dried fruit, and sacks of potatoes stamped in bold black letters: **Wisconsin**. There were also carriage hardware and spare felloe plates, two shovels, a pitchfork, and a Dole's hub-boring tool laid beside the gunnels. In Columbia, the quartermaster had laughed at Sergeant Van Norman's requisition sheet, enough supplies for a company of men, but he stopped abruptly when he saw Noah's faded butternut shirt and gray trousers. The sergeant had talked easy with the quartermaster, showed the proper paperwork, and they had loaded up and were headed back to Elm Grove in little more than an hour.

Watching George, Noah had marveled at the ease with which the young man could command respect, how he seemed at ease with the mix of people, a trifling compliment or gentle cajole depending upon circumstance. Other men seemed grateful to do his bidding.

As they passed through town, Noah reflected on the many changes brought by the war. There seemed to be hundreds of people whom he had never seen, people who ignored him or who only saw him as one sees cows grazing in a field, without notice. Where formerly he would nod to men on the street, tip his hat to women with hoop skirts and parasols, now even the square was filled with strangers, rough fellows who frightened the ladies, and men in tattered old uniforms who often as not were unsteady with drink.

Worse were the dapper characters with sharp greedy eyes from Cincinnati and Cleveland and Chicago. These were Yankees, with their clipped speech and glib manner. Not like George. These were transients, come to the South for fast money and political power, who carried their worldly belongings in bags made of carpet. Speculators and opportunists. Calculating, devious, dissolute. Adept in addition, division, and deceit. No, not like George at all. George was different. Not here by choice, but by circumstance. Not a "carpetbagger" at all.

In the Columbia town square, an auctioneer's chant spilled over the crowd. Beside the platform, a corral held dozens of mounts. Rather than leave them to the farmers who needed them for plowing and planting or pulling their wagons and carriages, the Army sold surplus horses to Northern traders for a pittance. Those same Yankees were reselling the beasts to locals for a handsome profit, the very same locals from whom they had been requisitioned, or stolen. George said, "When I muster out, I'll leave Bessy with the Wilsons."

The wagon rolled through the outskirts of town. Sun baked their heads and arms, the heat rising oppressive and dull. Bessy's feet beat an unsteady rhythm while cicadas hummed atonal harmonies, each one in passing taking up the refrain.

"Orders I received in town are to remain at Elm Grove," George said. "No timetable has been set to muster the regiment."

"What's the rush? You got no need to drag a leg out of here."

"Thank you kindly, Mr. Turner," he said. "But my kin are in Wisconsin." Unconsciously, George fitted his speech to Noah's pattern. "Soon as I muster out, why, I'm fixing to drag a leg straight home."

Bessy's lazy gait rocked the wagon. The heat dried the air and blistered the hard-packed dirt. Cresting a rise, the fresh breeze touched his face and Noah breathed deeply.

"Maybe there's another reason you might want to stay on."

"How's that, Mr. Turner?"

"Plenty good land here about, I suppose. But could be there's a pretty little woman back there at Elm Grove has her eyes on you," said Noah.

"Just another string to my bow," George said with exaggerated remorse. "The truth is, I've been making promises to fine young women all over Dixie."

Bessy snorted.

"Who's to say I don't have a pretty girl or two back home?" George thought briefly of Elizabeth.

"Well, do you?"

George had no answer. "What about you and Minnie Waters?" he said. "Seems you might be fixing to jump the preacher with her now, doesn't it?"

Noah rubbed his chin. "I admit she's a mite easy to get used to," he said. "But there's a barrel of difference in our ways, and a barrel more in our ages. To think she might agree to have an old farm boy like me, well, it would take a heap of learning for me to know which fork is which, and whether Nottingham is a race horse or a table linen. No, you and Miss Eva seem a better match."

George rubbed his lip. "Well, I do believe she is smitten with me."

Noah grinned and raised his face to the warmth of the sun and the music of the crickets. This was a day for promenading with a beautiful woman, a woman like Minnie. Composed and proper and petite. But what did he have to offer a woman who had everything: genteel family, fine clothes, wealth and social position. And soon, mistress of Watersmith, which didn't look like much now, but could be grand again with some honest effort. Noah began to wonder what Watersmith was like, what crops were grown, what promise the soil held. He thought of someone who would know and at a crossroads, he said, "You mind if we take a little detour on the road home, visit an old friend of mine?"

George simply shook his head and leaned back on the bench, fingers laced behind his neck. A shadow drifted languidly over the wagon, a white-tailed hawk riding the wind as a trout rides a current.

* * *

Roberts's Farm, Hickman County, June 21, 1865

Place looked different since he last seen it. Crops in the field. New fence. House got a fresh coat of paint. Fancy bric-a-brac in the window. Even the porch looked swept.

Slive dismounted, dropped his reins over the hitch post. Coogin did the same. Slive dragged his muddy boots up the porch steps, rapped his gloved knuckles on the heavy oak door, then peered in the window. "Orvis! You in there, Orvis?"

No reply.

Coogin slapped his bowler hat on his thigh and a thick cloud of dust shimmered in the hot afternoon sun. "Gone."

"I can see that," Slive scowled. "Go check in the barn while I look around back."

After a minute, Coogin found Slive at the back of the house looking in another window. "Horse," he said, and jerked his thumb at the barn.

Slive looked toward the fields behind the house, neat rows, freshly tilled. Tubby young Orvis been to working, from the shape of things. With his mam and pap gone, he must be here alone. But where? Not in the house, not in the barn, can't see him in the fields. It ain't Sunday so he ain't to church. Where else is there?

Slive searched the grounds and his eyes fell on the privy. He stepped up to the small outbuilding and rapped hard on the door, shaking the tiny shack. "You in there, Orvis?" He leaned into the door. "Come on out, Orvis. I can smell you."

For a moment, silence. Then, "Be out in one minute, I will," came a small voice.

Coogin grinned, whistling softly between the gaps in his yellow teeth. Slive leaned on the side of the clapboard outhouse and began rocking it back and forth, threatening to overturn it and its contents.

"Hold on there," cried Orvis. "I'm coming."

"Orvis, you remember when you was working for Mr. Waters out to Watersmith?" Slive still rocked the outhouse. "Remember when you used to do the numbers? Tallying up this and that?"

The door opened a crack and Slive stopped the rocking.

To Coogin, Slive said, "There he is." Oily and unctuous and cruel. "Everything come out all right, Orvis?"

Coogin laughed heartily as Orvis emerged from the little structure.

"Hello, Mr. Slive, Mr. Coogin," Orvis said, hitching his trousers. "Something I can do for you?"

"Well, damn, Orvis, but you is right skinny." Slive gazed in amazement.

"Shrunk up," Coogin said.

Orvis eyed Coogin's rotund physique. "Hard work and long days on the march is what done it." To Slive, he said, "What you want to know about Mr. Waters for? I did their books, that I did, for five, six years before the war. I did them a good job for a fair wage, I did. Mrs. Waters, she can tell you."

"She can't tell shit," Slive grunted. "Been dead near a year."

Orvis stared and his shoulders drooped. "Sorry to hear that, I sure am." He began to walk toward the house. "Sorry indeed, she was a right proper lady and a fair-minded boss."

So Orvis didn't know about Mrs. Waters being dead. Don't mean nothing. He could still know about the safe. "Hold on there, Orvis." Slive grabbed his sleeve. "Where did she keep them records?"

"Is that what you're after, the records?" Orvis shook his head. "Know nothing about that, I don't. Mr. Waters kept a strongbox somewhere, but I never saw it."

Slive considered: was Orvis telling the truth? Who else knew about the safe? Besides that damn niece, and she ain't been around of late, run back to Pulaski. Nobody. Nobody knew about the safe except Orvis. Called it a strongbox. Same thing, sure.

Orvis went into his house and Slive followed, Coogin behind. Inside, broad windows lit the hall. The drawing room walls were painted to mimic ornate plaster molding. A design around the chandelier had plump little cherubs swimming in a sea of plaster garlands. Heavy oak furniture of an earlier time dotted the room; hooked rugs covered the polished wooden planks; a heavy iron stand holding two umbrellas and a lace parasol rested in the corner.

Same shit at Watersmith, thought Slive. Fancy shit. Good for nothing except gathering dust. Orvis thinks he's a swanky pants now he's got his folks' fancy house and all. Scrawny little toad.

Slive picked up some loose papers from a small writing desk. Words, couldn't read any of them. He tossed the papers back.

Orvis quickly stuffed the pages inside the desk, scrambled into the hall as if to usher the two men to the door, and nearly tripped over the iron umbrella stand.

Coogin followed, but Slive waited at the writing desk where Orvis had hidden the papers. He opened the desk, drew out the papers, and scanned them, looking for a familiar word, some numbers, something. There, S-L-A-V-E. He recognized that word again. Same kind of writing that was on the paper on the floor of his study at Watersmith. Names and money and such. Same damned papers. Orvis's folks never owned no slaves. Orvis must have been in the safe, the scurvy little shit.

Orvis said, "Mr. Slive, those are private documents." He puffed out his lean frame. "Downright rude, I believe, to go reading another's personal papers."

Slive sat heavily in a spoke armchair that nearly bowed under his weight, his mind working out the possibilities, figuring consequences. His brain, as much soup as animal, began to roll roughshod over things small and remote, until William Slive hung balanced between reason and retribution.

This pudgy little bookkeeper had stolen Mrs. Waters' will from the safe at Watersmith, Slive's safe. The will that could cost him his property. Watersmith was his and he would be damned if this slimy little carp-faced kid was going to take it from him. It weren't right and William Slive aimed to make it right. He spied the heavy umbrella stand, its cast-iron countenance holding possibilities. Instinctively, he rubbed at his eye, remembering a time long ago, the woman who fought so viciously, and her man who ran but would run no more, his feet mangled and twisted.

Slive leapt to his feet and waved the papers at Orvis as Coogin stepped behind the frightened man. "What's these papers say, Orvis?"

Orvis tried to back away but Coogin pinned his arms and Slive slapped him across the face, hard. "Sit down, Orvis," he said.

Coogin threw Orvis into the spoke chair and held the boy's skinny arms as Slive lifted the heavy umbrella stand. "Orvis," he hissed. "Most all your life you been toting up numbers like counting on your fingers. If you want to keep on toting, you better tell me about these here papers." Before the young man could reply, Slive brought the cast-iron stand down hard on his hand. Orvis screamed.

"You was the only one what had reason to be in the safe." And he swung the stand again against Orvis's bleeding hand. "Where's the will,

Orvis? Tell me what you did with the will." He pounded the heavy umbrella stand again and heard distinctly the crack of bone.

Orvis began to whimper, "I don't know, I don't know, I ..." Then he hung his head as if sleeping. Slive lifted the stand for another blow. But he stopped when he heard a wagon roll into the yard.

THEY VEERED ONTO A DIRT TWO-TRACK that wound past thickets of brier and loblolly. The smell of turned earth filled his head and Noah Turner breathed deeply. He appraised each field as they rolled by, row upon row of new plantings, wheat and corn and sorghum. A small vegetable garden bordered the road with sprigs of broad beans, sea kale, chives, and horseradish. Behind them were eggplant, lettuce, and cucumbers. Farming was for Noah Turner a passion. He loved the land, the whims of rain and wind and blazing heat, cherished the sense of attainment that came by producing food from dirt and sweat and courage. He respected others who shared his ardor.

Orvis Roberts was one. Meticulous Orvis. Noah was sure the young man would have his farm in order by now, even with his mother and father gone. The Roberts's family property had always yielded more than others. Not that their land was any better or worse, nor did they work any harder. But the Roberts had Orvis, and Orvis knew numbers.

Some folks called him a genius, the precocious little pudge who could add columns of numbers in his head, remember multiplication tables past twelve. The man had compared notes and records year to year, studying crop results before he was old enough to wear long pants. Other farms had known good years and bad, and so had the Roberts. But to others, it was simply good times or bad. Orvis knew why. He could tell you just how much each crop had produced, which crop should yield the highest prices next year, and why.

Turning in the drive, Noah admired the corn in long straight rows, more fields of deep green beyond. Barn boards needed paint, but none were out of rank, and two had been recently replaced. Behind the barn, the chicken coop lay downwind of the house so the odor would not upset the evening meal. A new fence framed the yard and the house was in good repair. Strangely, the door stood ajar.

George said, "Mosquitoes will be a bother tonight."

Noah jumped from the wagon as George lifted his rifle from its holster. Stepping to the porch, Noah cried, "Halloo in there, Orvis. You at home?" No reply.

Noah eased his knife from its sheath, used the butt end to rap on the door. It swung inward noiselessly. Once inside, he stopped to listen, but heard nothing. At his feet, umbrellas lay scattered on the carpet. From the parlor, he heard a low moan and he eased his head around the corner. There, in a spoke chair, sat Orvis, ashen-faced, eyes closed, his hands bloody mangles. The bones were broken and twisted, some poking through skin at sharp angles. On the floor, an iron umbrella stand lay stained red with blood.

Noah sheathed his knife and knelt by the injured man. "Orvis, tell me what happened." From outside, he heard George hail him and he shouted in reply.

Orvis, groaned again, sat forward in his chair and vomited.

"Whoa!" George cried as he entered the parlor. "Guess I could fetch some water," and he departed quickly in search of the pump.

Head between his knees, Orvis began to mumble. Noah bent forward to hear.

"…I didn't know … Watersmith … Mr. Slive…"

"Slive? Where?" he cried. "Here? When?" He grasped his friend by the shoulders. "Orvis, did Slive do this?"

The man lifted his head. "… some papers." Groggy, his eyes stared unfocused. "… the will." His head bobbed lazily and he closed his eyes, his breathing shallow, mouth agape.

George shouted and Noah ran to the voice. As he reached the kitchen, gunfire sounded from outside and George dove through the door, his rifle clattering on the wooden floor. Noah rolled behind a table and squatted on his hams.

"In the barn," George said. He removed his tattered hat and lifted it to the window with his rifle barrel. "I heard a noise while I was at the pump." The window suddenly shattered, knocking aside his hat and throwing bits of glass across the floor.

"It's Slive. He's here. He's looking for the will. Where's the pistol?"

"In the wagon."

"I'll try to flank him." Noah scampered through the house and out the front door before George could respond. There were ten yards of open ground to the wagon. Noah risked one look toward the barn, and…

Gunfire erupted from inside the house, three, four, five shots in rapid succession, holes ripping into the side of the barn. Noah dove under the wagon and scrambled up the far side, Bessy stepping nervously. He peered over the wagon gunnels. No sign of the revolver among the sacks and barrels.

Suddenly, horses burst from the barn, running hard. Racing for the road, Slive passed near the wagon and didn't look back. Coogin galloped close behind, leading a third horse. Noah groped among the sacks for the pistol, came up empty, grabbed for something, anything, the tools, a long handle. He snatched it up, reared back, and flung it as Coogin raced by.

The pitchfork intercepted Coogin across the face and he screamed, lost his grip on the trailing horse, nearly fell but managed to recover, his horse carrying him past the corn rows and out to the pike without slowing.

CHAPTER FORTY

West Alabama, August 1, 1865

The lurch of the train awakened George as it pulled from the station and began its slow kick-kack. Wind blew through the open window in warm gusts, and bright sunshine lit the Alabama sky. He rubbed his eyes and fished in his kit for his canteen.

A soldier carrying a small haversack ambled down the aisle. He wore a sturdy chestnut-brown shirt tucked neatly into his gray trousers, a Confederate kepi covering his long hair. He eyed George warily, chose the vacant bench opposite, and stuffed his kit beneath the seat. Another soldier going home, George guessed, and he lifted his canteen in salute. The man looked at George, nodded, took the canteen, and drank in slow gulps.

"Smoke?" The man slid out his haversack, opened it, and produced two hand-rolled cigars, lit one, then the other, with a match from his pocket.

George nodded, took one to his lips and drew slowly, inhaling carefully. The Rebel sucked hard, then leaned back and blew long, blue-white streams toward the ceiling where they hung in milky waves. "Seen some action?" he said.

"Corinth, Iuka, Vicksburg," said George, the roll of towns that would be forever named for battles. "You?"

"Four years with Bobby Lee. Gettysburg to Petersburg, every-where in between." He tipped his ash onto the worn wooden floor. "Four years."

He said no more and George left him to his thoughts.

The soft kick-kack grew to monotony, mesmerizing. They passed through bottomland littered with bushes and trees of especially deep green, their branches fingering in all directions as if they belonged to another world, as if gravity were different here. At the base of the valley was a sluggish, winding stream not unlike the Pecatonica back in Iowa County, or the creek at Elm Grove.

Wind swept through the window and brushed George's hair from his brow. Such thinking wearied him. He tipped his hat over his eyes and slumped into the seat. Yes, the creek at Elm Grove, where the wind had swept her velvety hair, too, floating it above her narrow shoulders, exposing her long neck. Her face, delicate, expressive, intimate, as if she were listening to the wind whisper her name, tiny and hushed: Eva, Eva, Eva. Kick-kack.

* * *

Elm Grove Plantation, July 29, 1865

George lay in the sparse grass. They had come to calling this place "theirs," this rocky outcrop over the creek, their destination on long walks together. He yearned for her daily chatter, a soothing balm, like sunshine or birdsong. But on this day, Eva sat subdued, her mind in some incorporeal place, a place far away. George had seen this before and knew that some part of her would always be remote, mysterious and vacant, unknown and unavailable. But he had thought it through and he knew that it did not matter.

Overhead, bright puff-clouds drifted across the pale blue sky, miasmic shapes of horses and cannons and soldiers marching in neat rows, parading for his personal inspection on the late afternoon air. His minded drifted, too, wrestling with the possibilities, the circumstances, vaguely aware life decisions awaited him, but unsure of the questions. His imaginings were built upon the only experience he understood: the army.

Some general once said that topography was strategy, timing was tactics, and decisions were made based upon forces available. The whole essence of war was simply a big game, one in which you played the best hand you could once it had begun. Decisions made from knowledge of strategy and execution of tactics coupled with the wisdom of experience. To struggle and to risk and to win. Or lose.

Could those not prove an analogy for life? Topography and timing and a series of decisions like crossroads, choosing one path and forever ignoring that which might have been down another, each road leading to a new crossroads and new decisions? A simple matter of timing and tactics and geography?

And luck. Soldiering caused George to believe life's recipe was also a good part luck. Life: a matter of chance so fragile that a casual bullet fired at random by a stranger in an instant took away. Yet, to hide amid restraint and take refuge in the anodyne was to invest nothing, to risk nothing. A man might be alive at a hundred in such banality, but he would not have lived.

To George's way of thinking, to truly live meant to enjoy, to prosper, to respect yourself, and to earn the respect of others. Enjoyment in your labor, the labor that affords prosperity, a prosperity to be shared with family and neighbors, their love and respect to be enjoyed. The great circle of life. The recipe for happiness, save but one ingredient. Enjoyment and prosperity and respect were best when shared. Even a beautiful sunset was made more beautiful when there was someone with whom to share it, someone to nudge and say, "Beautiful sunset, don't you think?" and to hear her agree.

To truly live, then, meant to love and to be loved. To allow oneself vulnerability to loss and grief. Despite all hazard. Despite all consequence. Such rational argument gave George a sense of slow amazement, a contentment sprung from resolve, an incredible and overwhelming sense of rightness.

He reached out his hand and Eva grasped it willingly. She sighed heavily and nestled beside him.

"George Van Norman, you do make the time pass more easily."

What was this? He felt a sudden tension, a brittleness, as if touching glass. Were these words about nothing, or could they be some cipher with deeper meanings? "I believe I'm blushing," he said.

"Oh, don't you mock me." She sat up to face him, her skirt tucked beneath her. "What I'm trying to say has me … anxious."

George carefully removed his hat and rolled to face her.

"I've never known anyone like you before." She plucked aimlessly at the yellowed strawgrass. "I can't explain it. A few months ago, I was … I didn't know you, I hadn't even heard your name. Now, everything seems…" She reached for the words. "It's as if I've been changed somehow."

He felt the air stir between them.

Eva took a deep breath. "What I mean to say is, well, that I wondered if you had considered… I wanted to ask what plans you have for when the army let's go of you, when you get your muster papers, and what you had in mind to do, and… oh, stop your grinning at me. Heaven knows this is hard enough without …" She swatted at him playfully.

As Eva stood and began to pace, George felt the brittle sensation again, and he consciously worked to bridle the emotion in his body. Finally, he stood and put his hand on her shoulder. "Eva, what would you have me do? I'm a Yankee in the South, a carpetbagger. That little charade at Watersmith was painfully true."

She turned then, her hair whirling about her shoulders. "You are not! You aren't like other Yankees. Even Papa says so—oh, George, he's awfully fond of you—and so does Noah Turner. Carpetbaggers are selfish and cruel. They drum up support from the darkies so they can win their vote and control the government. They meddle in local business and politics. They set up companies and make money and such off poor Southern folk like us."

George, surrounded by the vast wealth of Elm Grove, considered the irony in this, but noticed she had not meant to be ironic. "And how would I be different?" he asked. "I would be a Yankee farmer living on Southern soil growing a money crop under a Southern sun." The logic of his love for Eva made sense to him; the logic of a life in the South was harder to absorb.

"You would be selling that crop to Yankees," she said, following his train of thought. "So you would be making money off them, not Southerners." She nodded. Problem solved.

Nothing to return to in Wisconsin, it was true. Brother Peter had already mustered out and laid claim to the family farm; his brother Jacob had bought up another piece adjacent. George didn't know what he would do. There was Ed Mason's father and the stockyard business, but that was in Racine. He had never been to Racine.

"Have you ever thought about living in the North, Eva," he asked.

She barely hid her look of alarm. "It gets so cold there." She held her elbows. "I think I would just die of the chill."

George nodded. Wisconsin winters could be cold beyond cold. "But the summers are better than any place you could imagine. Warm days and cool evenings perfect for sleeping. The fields all fertile and green. A thunderstorm will come up on a moment's notice and the lightening puts on a show to beat any fireworks." He spoke rapidly as a man keen for his subject. "The fall is prettiest of all, when the leaves turn and the geese fly and steam rises off the creek."

"Oh, George, it sounds beautiful, it does. But I know I just couldn't leave here." She sat on the ground as if to confirm her position, and idly patted her hair into place. "This is my home. It's all I've ever known, ever wanted. Just a little house here in Tennessee, a few hired hands to take care of things."

His head swam with the possibilities, life as a "gentleman farmer" in Tennessee. An overwhelming sense of belonging engulfed him like a powerful tide that could purge the rubble and bones from every part of the world. And all George wanted was some sense of order in his little corner of it. And Eva. Yes, that he knew. George wanted her more than home or summer or thunderstorms. "I should speak to your father about this," he said.

Eva leapt to her feet. "Oh, will you?" she said. "Oh, George, that's wonderful. Just wonderful."

He thought she might begin skipping through the grass and he grinned because he, too, shared her fervor. Instead, he reached for her hand and pulled her to him and they fell into the grass, her body across his body, her arms firm as wires engulfing him. He kissed her and she kissed him and they lay under the evening sky until the stars began to wink.

CHAPTER FORTY-ONE

Elm Grove Plantation, July 30, 1865

E b wore a gray morning coat with black piping that fit poorly on his massive frame, and a gray silk cravat that matched his top hat. His shoes: ferryboats hand-sewn of deer hide dyed black and nearly as wide as they were long. George served as witness and wore his uniform, his buttons and boots scrupulously polished. Even his Hardee hat had been cleaned and blocked. Eva wore a dress of deep blue with a wide lace bodice and streamers of navy and violet. Her glossy, blue-black hair was piled atop her head and fashionably curled, pinned with silk ribbon and purple flowers.

Mitsy wore white. Jenny and Eva had painstakingly labored over the wedding dress, last worn by Eva's mother. Eva would have preferred to wear it herself one day, but knew it could never be made to fit her tiny frame. So she graciously offered it to Mitsy. She and Jenny laughed and giggled as Mitsy tried it on and pranced about the room, her bare feet slapping against the floorboards, pantaloons variously showing and, finally, hidden once the dress was let down. In it, she looked truly stunning, her coffee skin in sharp contrast to the white-on-white watermark taffeta, the long sleeves and wide jeweled neckline framing her shoulders. Crowning her head was a soft veil covering a coronet of dried flowers.

"I ain't never been so pretty," she said, and began to weep. "I be glad my Eb getting hisself such a pretty wife."

That morning, Judge Wilson had informed Eb that he and Mitsy would need witnesses to make their wedding legal. Approaching George, his hop-gait slower than usual, Eb had "ahem-ed" beside the tent where George sat folding laundry, and asked politely if George might be so good as to witness their vows. George replied that nothing could please him more. Eva would serve as maid of honor.

Gathered on the portico, freshly decorated in garlands of red and blue, Jesse and Silas sat quietly with Jenny and Noah in a row of hastily arranged dining room chairs. Orvis Roberts sat beside them, his hands wrapped in thick bandages. Behind them sat Alice and Cletus and the others. Chryssy carried a bouquet of fresh flowers gathered that morning: ageratum and daisies mixed with black-eyed Susans and bladdernut buds.

"Dearly beloved," began the Judge. "We are gathered here in the spirit of God and the presence of these witnesses to join Eb and Mitsy in holy matrimony…"

As Judge Wilson spoke the words, George watched Eva—beautiful, glowing, her long neck shimmering in the sunlight, her chin high, proud. He imagined himself before the Judge someday. She spied his gaze and smiled, as if she shared his thoughts.

"I do," said Mitsy.

Could they make a life together in the heart of the South? George wondered. So different than the life he had known, the weather, even the land itself, red clay and sandstone, so unlike the glaciated gravel and loams of Wisconsin. Could he be happy as a gentleman farmer in rural Tennessee? He nodded imperceptibly in self-assurance.

"I do," said Eb.

"By the power vested in me, I now pronounce you man and wife. Eb," said the Judge with a broad smile across his face, "you may kiss the bride."

Eb hesitated. "Right here?" he whispered.

The Judge nodded.

That was enough. Eb swooped up Mitsy in a great bear hug and kissed her full on the lips, her feet dangling a full two feet off the floor, a shoe dropping quietly to the wooden planking. Immediately, Silas jumped up and slapped Eb on the back; Jesse let out a whoop and Jenny clapped her hands.

George took Eva's hand. A message passed between them unspoken, as if he could feel her vibrate inside himself. Somehow, he felt compelled to speak, but did not know what to say. The Judge, busy congratulating the wedding couple, did not fail to notice George and Eva, but he smiled at this nonetheless. As the others went inside to begin the festivities, George saw Cletus walk back to the quarters. Eva saw him, too, and nodded, understood, and George marveled at how she guessed his thoughts, and at how he discerned hers.

In the grand hall, they had lemon drinks and corncakes that Mitsy and Eva had prepared earlier. Jenny served as hostess, which struck George as odd, but Eva had tacitly agreed to play the guest in her own home on this one day.

In the Judge's study, Mitsy and Eb dutifully signed their marks on the appropriate spaces, Eb's mark a distinctive flourish, easily legible, Mitsy's less so. Marriage documents would be filed in the recently opened courthouse, one among hundreds of colored marriages to be duly registered, the first time in Tennessee history Negroes could legally wed.

Chester Beauchamp sawed a fiddle while Silas strummed his banjo. Several of the new hands got to dancing and Noah took a swing with Mitsy, moving forward and back. Mitsy lifted her skirts and showed some fancy footwork, her petticoats bouncing in tempo. The Judge sat at the edge of the room patting the rhythm on his knee. He caught George's eye and smiled, gently nodded.

The music rose and fell. Shoes got to beating a rhythm loud as drumming, and no one heard the rider approach until the knocker sounded. Eb naturally started toward the door, until George stopped him. "I'll get it, Eb. You have the day off," he said.

George opened the door to a Yankee soldier, a boy no older than nineteen with the air of timidity that comes when interrupting strangers. George stood speechless, the soldier seeming so out of place. Beside him, Eb said, "May I help you?"

"I am looking for Sergeant Van Norman," said the visitor.

The music stopped and the shoes fell silent. The dancers grew quiet. The young corporal stood in the hall under the bright gaslight and looked around at the circle, his Adam's apple working in his thin neck.

George suddenly realized the significance of this visitor. "I'm George Van Norman," he said.

The boy said simply, "Orders," held out a packet, and without waiting for further word, turned on his heel and was gone.

George looked dumbly at the envelope. All eyes in the hall were watching him, but he took no notice.

A hand fell upon his shoulder. "Why don't you use my study?" said the Judge.

CHAPTER FORTY-TWO

Elm Grove Plantation, July 30, 1865

Dishes cleared, guests retired to their quarters, Eva sat alone in the drawing room, knitting, waiting for George, waiting for what news the young soldier had delivered. Knit one, purl two. Knit one, purl two. Waiting. How she hated the waiting. Waiting for Mother to get well, waiting for Frederick to return, waiting for word from Tom Harden, waiting for victory. Forever waiting for what would never come.

Knit one, purl two. Eva's wooden needles ticked a rhythm to her racing mind: this would be different. Papa would give his blessing. He must. George is a good man, and Papa would come to love him in time, just as she loved him. But the waiting infuriated.

She concentrated on tying off an end. The boy had delivered George's orders, of that she was certain. Then George had requested to speak to Papa. It could mean only one thing. But oh, the waiting.

The needles flew and her mind raced in tempo, filled with domestic imaginings. She pictured a small farm at first. There was good land to the south, past the river, some bottomlands that would make good farmland once the cedar and sedge in the fields could be cleared. Hire some coloreds, perhaps some soldiers who could work the crop, a nanny for the children and ...

Omigoodness! Children? She nearly dropped a row of stitches.

Eva paused to set the knitting in her lap and gaze from the window at the golden light of the receding day. Children?

GEORGE SAT STIFFLY IN THE WINGBACK CHAIR. The Judge extended his hospitality. Cigar? No, thank you. Brandy? Not tonight. Best to maintain temperance under such circumstances. "I have orders to return to my regiment," he began.

In the lantern light, the Judge's white hair glowed about his head. A dollop of amber liquid circled in his brandy snifter. "So I assumed," he said.

The redolent smell of tobacco filled the room, and George remembered when he had been in this same leather chair listening to Judge Malachi Wilson speak of slavery and sharecropping and the efficiency of war. It seemed a long time ago. "I have appreciated your hospitality here at Elm Grove, sir. You have been most gracious," he said.

"It is we who should be grateful to you, George. You and the army stores have allowed us to remain quite comfortable these last few months, while many families around here have gone wanting."

"Yes, sir. Thank you, sir." While his mind was not afraid, his hands showed a tremor and he felt a sudden chill. "I mean, you're welcome, sir." George shifted in his chair.

The Judge scratched a match on a pipestone, lit his cigar. "You nervous about something, George."

The room felt close and stifling. His stomach growled noisily and he squirmed in his seat to settle it. The Judge studied him and George met his eye. "I have come to ask for your daughter's hand, Judge." He swallowed hard. "I am hopeful you will permit me to marry Eva," he said.

A smile creased the older man's face and he leaned back in his chair, cigar smoke spiraling above his head. "My, my, my." Inhaling deeply, the Judge made sucking noises, and the end of the cigar glowed brightly. "I declare, George, you are a right fine young man," he said. "In these unsettled times, no one can tell much about the future. It seems the more extreme the circumstances, the more often young hearts will turn to other young hearts for their happiness."

"I assure you, sir, it is not circumstance that has drawn us together," George said. "Circumstance has simply presented the opportunity."

"Yes, yes, of course." Ash dribbled to the Judge's coat and he cupped it carefully, deposited it in a small tray on his desk. "Tell me about your plans."

Practical matters. George was prepared for this. "I have no claim on my family's farm," George said. "I do have an offer of a job back home, but Eva prefers to stay here in Tennessee."

"Hm-mm." The Judge let him continue.

"There are many abandoned farms around these parts. I have some back wages due me." Perfectly logical when he had thought it out, but it seemed to lose something in the saying.

"Hm-mm." Nodding.

"I believe I can make a good home for Eva and me, a good home here in Tennessee. We've talked about it. We'll find a place near Elm Grove. We can visit as often as you like." He blundered on. "I know how to farm and raise a crop. I know about hogs and cattle and horses…"

"I believe you." The Judge interrupted. "I believe you, George." He poured more brandy and watched the liquor circle in his glass. "You know, George, this war is different from other wars. Historically, war has been waged between countries, or over differences in religion. In almost all cases, the winner has subjugated the loser." He rested the brandy and relit his cigar. "But this war pitted countrymen against countrymen. The winner cannot, must not, subjugate the loser."

George said nothing. He did not know what to make of this line of conversation.

"This will breed resentment among Northerners. Mothers who have lost their sons, wives who have lost their husbands, will demand retribution. Small politicians will stir the voters to vindictiveness. And the Northern merchants will seek opportunity here among the vanquished. Spoils of war, I suppose." Smoke billowed over his head in great plumes. "In the South, those same wives and mothers will stir the hearts of their children, and their children's children."

He sat opposite George, leaned in close and George could smell brandy on the air. "The fighting has stopped, but here in the South, this war may be a long time ending."

George sat dumbly, swallowing hard. Deep recesses of his mind urged caution. He sensed that, by his desire to remain in the South, Judge Wilson labeled him a carpetbagger and that Eva was simply the opportunity he sought.

The Judge leaned back in his chair, retrieved his brandy once more. To George's puzzled expression, he said, "Happiness takes three things." Three fingers held aloft. "Vocation, geography, and partner." A smile creased his face. "The vocation is up to you. You are a capable young man and I have every confidence you will do well in whatever endeavor you choose." George nodded. "As for partner, Eva, I have no doubt, will multiply your happiness tenfold." He leaned into George. "But this geography carries great concern," he said. "It will not befriend you. Men will shun you. Widows and mothers will dislike you outright."

He set aside his brandy and George felt compelled to speak, but did not know what to say.

The Judge leaned into him. "Yes, this geography concerns me," he said.

CHAPTER FORTY-THREE

Elm Grove Plantation, July 30, 1865

Knit one, purl two. Tick. Tick. What is taking them so long? Tick. Tick. Tick. Her needles made a hummingbird flutter.

"Eva, I swear you are the noisiest knitter I ever did hear," Jenny said, wringing her apron.

Eva stared at her hands as if they were not her own, then set down her yarn. Jenny sat beside her. "They've been talking in the study nearly an hour," Eva said. She glanced into the hallway, but her father's door remained closed. "What do men find to talk about?"

"Man talk never amounts to much anyway," Jenny said. She carefully smoothed the apron against her skirt. "Do you think he will be leaving soon?" she asked.

Eva said, "I suppose so." Then added, "But just to muster out. Then he'll be returning." She wanted to blurt out hopeful news, the unexpected love she had for this Yankee, his unexpected love for her. Her mind rested upon this new thought: I am in love. And then the words nearly burst from her lips. "We're to be married, Jenny."

Jenny's eyes grew wide. "Are you sure? I mean… oh, Eva." She bent to embrace the younger woman.

"He's in there now, asking Papa." And they both looked to the shuttered study.

"Shouldn't he be asking you first?" Jenny teased.

"Oh, silly. Of course he did." Though she could not recall his exact words.

"Where will you live? What will you do?" Jenny asked.

"Why, we'll will live right here in Tennessee," Eva said. "George is a farmer, you know, and there are farms all around here that have been abandoned, and…" The pain in Jenny's eyes stopped Eva. "Oh, I'm so sorry," she said. "I'm so sorry."

"It's all right. It's a chapter in my life that has ended, at least for now," Jenny said. "I suppose it is best not to think on it too much. But when I do, I mostly smile for the good times we had there."

Eva lifted her knitting, but set it down again. She locked her fingers together and looked once more down the hallway.

Jenny asked, "Have you thought what it might be like to marry a … someone like him?"

"You mean a Yankee? Yes, I have, and I don't care. When folks get to know him, well, they'll see what a kind and decent man he is. You know yourself. He helped Noah get his horse back. He helped Minnie, too, helped get her house back." How could she explain? Did Jenny understand how George was willing to sacrifice for her, leave his home, live among his former enemies? For her, for Eva?

"But he is a Yankee."

Eva stood and her needles dropped to the floor. "He is a good man who simply was born in the wrong place. If he had been born here, he would be just as respectable as could be." As she spoke the words, Eva imagined George as a Confederate officer, noble and dashing. Then, the image shattered as she remembered another boy who wore that uniform. Anger and grief and disappointment clutched at her and she said, "Only he would probably have gone off to war and never come back and… oh." She put her face in her hands and cried, "What's taking them so long?"

"DO YOU UNDERSTAND WHAT I'M TRYING TO SAY, SERGEANT?"

Eager, willing, but sincerely confused, his shoulders sagged. "No, sir," George admitted.

The Judge slowly inspected his cigar, struck another match, and sucked greedily, puffs of smoke drifting to the ceiling. He set it down again and lifted his brandy while George waited. "George, George, George."

George sat up straight, awaiting the ruling he was sure the Judge was about to make.

Instead, "George, George, George."

More waiting until George felt himself suffocating and consciously filled his lungs when he realized that he had somehow forgotten to breathe.

"I have no doubt your intentions are noble," the Judge began, "And I have no doubt of my daughter's feelings for you." Smoke wafted about his head and the air thickened as he spoke. "Of course, Eva herself will make the decision, but I shall put no obstacle in the way..." He sucked once more on the cigar and George wanted to jump from his seat. Until the Judge said, "Save one."

George sagged into the chair as if struck.

"I want you to wait a year. One year." The Judge waved a digit for emphasis. "Right now, feelings are raw, tempers hot. Every calamity around here—or throughout the South for that matter—will be blamed upon the Yankees. This feeling of oppression—of shame—will fade with time, I'm sure. But were you to settle here now, you would face intolerance from most, and torment at the hands of some."

The Judge took another sip of brandy as George awaited his summation.

"Wait one year," he said. "Your passion for each other will survive, I daresay. One year. Then return and you shall have my blessing, my congratulations..." He sucked once more on his cigar. "...and my daughter."

George folded his hands as if to hold himself from panic. Each breath came thick and smothering, as if he were buried deep under a quilt. He felt as if struck dumb, all thought and reason having been lifted from his head. He could find no words against this case.

The Judge rolled brandy in his glass. "Men will be coming from the North, men who will suck the life from what is left of the South. Gobble up goods and property, or steal them, whichever is more convenient. Every form of ugliness you can imagine." His thick voice sounded as if from a deep pool. "I don't want you tarnished with the same brush," said the Judge.

These were words for which he had argument. "I'm no carpetbagger, Judge," George said. "I seek no political office, no advantage of any sort."

"No, no, no." A wave of his hand. "You misunderstand me. Do not assume because I point out the obvious—you are a Yankee, after all—that I would suggest you are connected to the disreputable activities of those smarmy connivers." He puffed again on his cigar. "Not at all. I simply mean that these are desperate times. We are only now just reopening the courts. Sheriffs must be appointed, disputes decided. Criminals are everywhere. Corruption and malfeasance at every level. And it is very likely that you—or rather, what you represent—will be held accountable. And by extension, Eva." He waved his cigar in the air for emphasis. "Eva would suffer most of all, the target of gossip and slander. A lost soul."

George felt bitter with disappointment. He wanted to cry out, to slay the dragon that gripped him, that tore at his bowels as it reached for his heart. His chest heaved and he struggled to keep his seat. The Judge's words sank deep into his mind and festered there. He studied them as if there were some escape, but he could find none. There was common sense inherent in the Judge's words. A defeated society would seek to blame its oppressors, or the agents of those oppressors, for every malady that befell them. Despite the "noblest of intentions," George was a

Yankee and, to the Southern mind, an agent of those who defeated them, a member of the legion that slaughtered their sons and brothers and husbands.

The Judge drew on his cigar. "It's your decision, George," he said, though George knew full well it was not. "There's no rush. Give it some time."

"Judge..." George slowed his breathing. "I wish to have your blessing. I will speak to Eva." He stood on shaky legs and walked quickly from the room, afraid to slow lest he should fall.

EVA FUSSED WITH HER NEEDLES AND looked once more down the hallway. "Sometimes, I remember what it was like before the war and I remember long walks on warm evenings with... someone else. Remembering still hurts."

"I'm sorry, Eva," Jenny said. She gently put her hand to Eva's shoulder. "I know George isn't like that. Not like a Yankee at all, hardly. He's a wonderful man." Quietly, as if to herself, she said, "I also know what it's like to lose someone."

Eva sighed. Then as if with enormous effort, she inhaled deeply and said in one long breath, "I know I have no right to mourn my loss when so many have lost just as dearly as I have, yet I do. But lately, the grief somehow seems more distant."

"We all grieve in our own way," Jenny said. "Women just take longer than men. Maybe it's because women give life that we grieve so deeply when it's taken away."

Eva considered this. Is it as much a woman's natural instinct to grieve as it is to nurture? "How do men find it so easy to kill one another?" she asked.

Jenny said, "I would hate to think Mr. Darwin is right, and it's all just a matter of natural selection!" Eva laughed and Jenny belly-laughed so hard she stumbled and that made Eva laugh even more, and they hugged and nearly fell over each other until the study door opened and George marched through the hall and out the front door without so much as a look in their direction.

SHE FOUND HIM ON THE ROCKY KNOLL. His elbows rested on his knees and he thumbed his mustache the way she had come to expect whenever he fell deep in thought. "Are you all right?" she asked, though she had a sense of foreboding that she did not want to hear the answer. "What happened? Tell me."

George sighed, tossed a pebble into the stream below and watched the ripples disappear in the current. "This sure is beautiful country," he said as she sat beside him. "Good weather. Good soil. Good farming country."

"George, what did he say?"

He tossed another pebble into the water. "Your father said we have to wait a year."

She jumped to her feet. "No! No, no, no, no. Why? No, we mustn't. We can't." She waved her arms as if to fly away.

George tossed another pebble, and another. His calm infuriated her all the more and she made a concerted effort to be still. At last, she sat beside him. "Did he say why?"

"Geography," he said.

"Geography?"

"Geography," he said again. "I am a Wisconsin Yankee in Secesh Tennessee. I certainly won't be the most popular man in town. And you'll suffer as a result. And that isn't right."

"But it isn't like that. You're not like that. Anyone can see that. You're..."

"It doesn't matter," he said. "Don't you see? It really doesn't matter. People will think what they're going to think. I'm a Yankee, plain and simple. For every sheep that gets stolen or fire that gets started, somebody will want to know where I was." He stopped to throw another pebble.

"But that's not right. It's…"

"And it won't just be me, it'll be you, too. You'll be left off the guest list for parties, treated shabby by the neighbors, shunned by the community. Because of me."

A coolness swept through her in shallow breaths. "Well, that's not …" If Cornelia Arnell could be shunned because of her husband's politics, perhaps Eva, too, would be turned away by her friends. She remembered Minnie Waters' reaction at learning George was a Yankee and clasped her hands to stifle a shudder. "Well, it's wrong," she said. "It's wrong."

George said, "Right now, spirits are high. So much has changed. People fear the unknown." His voice seemed far away and she strained to hear. "Maybe in six months or a year or so, things will be different, folks getting settled in, reacquainted with living normal lives again."

"But it's the waiting!" she said. "I can't stand the waiting."

George arced another pebble to the water. "You can't wait for me?"

She lifted her head. "It's the waiting," she huffed. "I just can't stand the waiting."

"It's just a year, Eva."

"You said six months." She wiped her cheek on a sleeve.

"Well, yes, six months. To a year."

"Well, which is it?" she said. "Six months? Or a year?"

"Six months, I'll be back in six months. It'll give me time to visit with my family. Get things planned out. I'll be back before spring planting. I promise."

Eva put her head to her knees and stared into the deep water. It seemed she had been waiting for something most all her life. She picked up a pebble and threw and it splashed amid the rocks. "Spring comes early around here," she said. "By January sometimes."

His laughter ran only a moment, but it was enough. She sighed and lay back on the warm grass. Dusk crept over the land and the first stars awakened, blinking uncertainly as they secured their spot in the darkening sky. Wind shadows danced off the heavens and Eva imagined they were spirits flying: the ghost of dear Frederick; the ghost of her mother, sad and gaunt; the ghost of Tom Harden marching off to war. Ghosts of a thousand lifetimes chased away like a whisper, pursued by faint awareness of passing time. It was not war, or fire, or mayhem she feared. It was the waiting, the settling beneath a sky composed of dust ground from the small stones of time. Waiting.

"Do you ever wonder," she asked, "why men seem to grow more handsome with age, while women seem to whither and wrinkle like old prunes?"

George held her then, the smell of her hair thick in his senses. "Your beauty is enduring, Eva. It comes from within. It will last forever."

Together, they lay on the promontory until the night covered them like a blanket.

CHAPTER FORTY-FOUR

Elm Grove Plantation, July 31, 1865

awn and the last day of July already promised to be warm and sultry, dew clinging to the leaves like honey. His tent was struck and rolled, his few belongings stowed in the wagon. Bessy waited patiently in harness for the ride to the train station.

He shook hands warmly with the Judge and said his good-byes to Jesse. Noah climbed into the seat and adjusted the reins. Silas sat on the tailgate, feet thick with grime, dust clinging to his ankles. Mitsy appeared at the door and said Eva would be down shortly, she was feeling poorly this morning, but to please wait.

George went to where Eb stood on the portico. They shook heartily, George's hand lost in Eb's much larger one.

"When Mr. Turner and Silas return," George said, "Bessy is yours." He reached in his pocket, handed Eb a square of paper. "It's legal, signed by the Judge."

The big man's eyes moved slowly across the page as he read the words that made him a man of property. Then he nodded, and breathed long and deep.

At last, the front door opened and Eva emerged looking pale, her shoulders wrapped in a shawl despite the weather. "Sergeant Van Norman," she said, and retreated into the house. George followed.

Alone in the hall, she reached her arms around his neck and kissed him. She clung there and said, "Oh, George, I'm so afraid."

Her eyes glistened and her raven tresses hung limply. He brushed a strand from her face. "I'll be back before the last frost is off the grass," he said.

"There's something I want you to have." From the folds of her skirt, she withdrew a long ribbon-like piece of silk, blood red with a generous fringe. She wrapped it about his neck and kissed him once more. "I made it for Frederick. It was returned to us after he was killed." She stepped back to look at him. "It makes you look even more handsome. And dashing."

He fingered the soft fabric. Then he gripped her arms and held her close enough to inhale the perfume of her hair. "I love you, Eva," he said. "Wait for me."

He saw her smile as he backed through the doorway, saw her nod as the heavy oak closed softly behind him.

THE WAGON ROLLED OVER THE DUSTY ROAD, noise of the insects rising and falling with their passing. George rode the bench while Noah held the reins. Silas sat on the tailgate, feet hanging over as if trolling for dreams. At a crossroads, a smithy performed his magic, a fountain of sparks rising from ringing hammer blows. In a yard, chickens scratched for seeds and geese hissed and strutted until their stiff wings scraped the ground. At farms, white men worked beside colored, sweat of their labor equal reward. Everywhere fields once fallow were gone to bounty. It was good country, thought George, made better by the pride of knowing this was to be his home.

Carriages, old but well maintained, passed them and travelers stared curiously at the farmer riding with the Yankee soldier, a darkie hanging off the back. Noah nodded or tipped his hat to the ladies, and to some who weren't. George smiled and tipped his hat to everyone. These were to be his neighbors and friends. Without the uniform, he felt certain he could become one of them. George believed the men of

Maury County, whether staunch Unionists—and there were a few—or those loyal to the Southern Cause, would soon accept him as their own. Left to their natural affairs, men are rudimentary animals, live and let live, at peace among their neighbors who face the same joys and hardships, content to lament amicably. over politics and taxes and the heat of the day.

The road dipped into a cool hollow and Bessy trotted easily, her crooked gait smoothing to a graceful rhythm. In a deep glade, a spring boiled from the slopes of a steep hill to form a rivulet that Noah claimed trickled all the way to the Duck River. They paused in the shade while Bessy drank and Silas cooled his toes in the water.

Soaking a kerchief, Noah rubbed his neck. "Hot one today." He carefully folded the square of fabric, put it atop his head, and secured it with his hat.

"What are you doing?" George asked.

"Old Indian trick," Noah said, climbing into the seat. "The evaporation keeps you cool."

In his regiment, many of the men had suffered this Southern heat poorly, fallen ill, or simply passed out. Here was a simple remedy. George knew know how to build a fire ring to escape a grass fire, or a snow tunnel to survive a blizzard—solutions to common problems in Wisconsin—and he vowed to learn the lessons of overcoming mundane maladies in Middle Tennessee.

The road undulated through bony hills dotted with scrub pine, crested a ridge where they passed George's stone marker for the cut-off to the cave. Noah pointed and George nodded. The wagon rolled downhill to the river bridge, wheels rumbling on the dry planking.

Noah said, "Red is the color of love." He tapped the reins and Bessy sidled off to allow another wagon to pass. A tip of the hats and he continued. "It's a token of devotion. I knew many a man who wore his sash in battle as a charm against the hazards of war."

"And did it work?" George asked.

Noah replied, "Sometimes." As he laughed, George had a desire to reach over and touch the man, but he did not.

Passing around a bend, they entered the shade of deep woods. The wind fell to a whimper and the cicadas were strangely quiet. Suddenly Silas shouted, "Massah Van? Massah Van!"

George turned in the seat. "What is it?"

"I seen somebody in the wood. Back there," Silas said.

"Who?"

"Can't tell. Just somebody. He be sneaking around, ducking down like, and then he be gone."

Before Noah had stopped the wagon, George leapt from the seat, rifle in hand. Brush raked his arms and face as he scampered into the underbrush. He jumped a fallen log and landed heavily on a patch of scree. The gravel gave way and George fell noisily into a shallow ravine. Footsteps rattled nearby and he rolled onto his back and cocked his rifle.

"Whoop!"

On the edge of the ravine, a squat little man waved a dirty hand. George sucked air with a soft whistle and lowered his rifle. Crazy Dudley grinned at him, his mouth a mix of laughter and misplaced teeth. George waved and struggled to his feet and led Dudley back to the road.

Silas climbed from under the wagon and waved. Noah emerged from the shadow of the trees. "Halloo, who we have here?"

"It's all right, Mr. Turner." George put his arm over the little man's shoulder. "This here is Dudley."

Noah muttered a greeting and sheathed his knife.

"He doesn't hear you," George said. "Deaf. He's the one I told you about. The boys and I waited out a storm in his cabin."

"Whoop!" Dudley grinned.

George stepped toward Noah Turner and patted him gently on the arm, smiled at Dudley, patted Noah some more until the man backed away in annoyance.

Dudley nodded and patted Silas. Silas patted him back. Dudley patted him again and Silas responded and they both patted each other and dissolved in laughter, until Dudley suddenly stopped. "Whoop!" He pointed down the road. Then he fanned his arms before him, held up two fingers, peeked around his hands, and hit himself on the head with his fist.

George furled his brow and Dudley repeated, "Whoop!" Pointed down the road, fanned his arms and held two fingers again, struck himself on the head. Manic gestures, but nothing more than a grunt and occasional click sound from his tongue.

George said, "He's trying to tell us something."

"You think so?" said Noah.

George concentrated on Dudley as he fanned and pointed, his eyebrows working, his mouth contorting with each gesture. "He says two men … up ahead between … in the road… they're hiding… waiting …" Dudley struck himself, and George turned to Noah. "I think he's warning us there are a couple of bushwhackers up ahead."

Eagerly, the little man spread his fingers by his ears, then shot an imaginary rifle, again fingers to his ears, then fell to the ground.

"Looks like he's shooting a deer or something," Turner said.

Dudley aimed his rifle, patted his chest, and pointed.

Silas stared, white-eyed and together, he and George said, "Slive!"

CHAPTER FORTY-FIVE

Elm Grove Plantation, July 31, 1865

From her window, a gentle breeze cooled her and brought with it the faint smell of wood smoke. Below, near the back garden, Cletus was burning old husks and tree fall.

She felt crisp and alive and a warmth from within that had nothing to do with the August heat, grateful that whatever nausea she had felt upon awakening had left her. Now her whole body tingled. George loved her, had told her so, the source of warmth, the heat that would sustain her through the chill of his absence. Come spring, he would return, just as the Canada geese always return to Bethel Pond. Yes, George, too, would return.

But it was the waiting. The waiting!

Perhaps she could speak to her father, ask him to reconsider, persuade him of her love for George, of her profound unhappiness in his absence. But no, his judgments were always final. "Once the decision is made," he would say, "you should never look back." In her twenty years, she had not known him to change his mind once made up.

But oh, the waiting. How she hated the waiting. Whenever Mother had had to wait, Eva had heard her murmur a verse:

> *Let us then be up and doing,*
> *With a heart for any fate;*
> *Still achieving, still pursuing,*
> *Learn to labor and to wait.*

"Learn to labor" indeed. Her fingers had grown calloused where the knitting needles rubbed. Just how many socks or sweaters could she make? Perhaps dozens before his return, she supposed. In the meantime, little to do but wait.

She opened her drawer and took out paper, dipped her quill.

Dearest George:

I trust your arrival home proceeded without incident, and hearth and home were all as you remembered. My hope is this letter will find you well, but suffer only in the heart until your return to me.

She paused to read her words, frowned at the crude sentiment, then tore up the page to begin again.

My Dear George:

You have not been absent but a few hours and I ache for that interval. Not because you don't convey my heart beyond all earthly joy. Ardor knows no bounds for the woman enchanted by your spell. The interval creates the great burden: Time.

Time, that most precious of commodities, that cannot be earned nor saved, only spent. I did little appreciate those hours we so squandered in bliss on summer afternoons, wandering in the orchard, conversing on the porch, trivial time I would forfeit a coach and four to suffer now.

Time becomes the great antagonist, as each hour seems a week. Yet, each day becomes one day you are closer to my heart, each moment surrendered as forfeit gladly given for the moment of your return.

Such brazen affection becomes not a fair maiden. And
though I may know no earthly fame nor hope for words of a
poet, know this: you are the love of
my life.

I eagerly await our reunion, with all my heart, and all
my

Love,

&

By habit, she went to place the letter in her drawer and saw the stack of
paper, her many letters to her mother. The curtains swayed and the smell
of wood smoke again drifted on the gentle breeze. Eva put the letter to
George aside, reached into the drawer and gathered up the pages. She
swept down the stairs, past her father's study where he conversed with a
local merchant, past the drawing room where Jenny knitted by the
window, through Mitsy's kitchen and her pots and pans and sacks of
food marked "U.S. Army," and out into the yard.

The sun, high in the sky, beat on her brow, no breeze now to cool
her fervor. She followed the smell of the smoke, found Cletus there
leaning on his shovel, and she stepped close to the brush fire.

"Afternoon, Miss Eva," Cletus said.

She stared transfixed at the red glow of the flames, oghams and
cursives rising in great billowing clouds, yellow cinders popping and
twisting into the afternoon sky.

"You all might want to stand back a little, Miss Eva," Cletus said.
"Be a shame to smudge that pretty dress."

Bright flame fixed in her eyes, gripping, and served only to harden
her resolve as if by some plutonic force.

Cletus watched as, one by one, she fed pages to the blaze.

CHAPTER FORTY-SIX

On the road to Columbia, Tenn., July 31, 1865

William Slive thought there was something peculiar going on. Something amiss for sure. He and Coogin had heard the wagon on the road, then hidden in the woods when that Turner fellow—thought he was dead in the house fire—rode past with that carpetbagger. Except the carpetbagger was wearing a Yankee uniform. Something not right about that at all.

Slive and Coogin had cut through the woods to the creek, then ridden fast to where the pike turned north before it dropped into the Duck River Valley. At the top of a rise, they waited by the sunken road, their horses tied out of sight beneath a stand of hemlock. Coogin, his face rutted by ragged lines of crusted scabs, sat on a rock and picked a stone from his bare toes while Slive looked over the ground.

Good a place as any. Get a fair look from up top, use Coogin to distract them. Then hold them at gunpoint. Maybe find some papers on them with the writing that says "Watersmith" and all. Maybe find out what they know about this will business.

Yeah, the will business. Something suspicious going on, for sure. Courthouse sent him a letter that said to vacate Watersmith. Slive even had to hire a smartass lawyer to read the thing. Said that damned niece had come forward with a legitimate will. All verified and legal. Now how'd she get that? Ain't one anywhere in the house when he went through.

And that business with the safe. What was that paper doing on the floor, that bill of sale for some slaves? Looked like somebody had been into the safe. But who? Coogin didn't know nothing about no safe. Orvis sure didn't know. Orvis couldn't have hid nothing, not when William Slive got done with him. But then the niece showed up with a will. Some damn suspiciousness was what it was.

Seems that horse thief Turner and that carpetbagger fellow were in cahoots. And that carpetbagger was dressed up like a Yankee soldier. Or maybe he was a Yankee soldier who had dressed up like a carpetbagger, come to Watersmith all high and mighty, wanting to know about butchering hogs and renting the smokehouse. Something damn dubious was going on here. Something mighty irregular.

And William Slive aimed to get even.

Slive checked his pistol, a Colt Navy Buntline with 12-inch barrel he had taken from a dead Yankee. By propping the barrel against a tree, it was accurate up to a hundred yards. Stuffing the heavy gun in his belt, he re-hitched his pants, took one last look down the road, then drew his knife, a D-guard Bowie with worn wooden handle. He carefully scored it across his forearm. Blood flowed easily from the wound, a long gash but not deep.

"Lie on the ground over here," he said to Coogin, who dutifully obeyed. "Just lie still here when they comes. I'll be up there," he said, pointing to the ledge some six feet over their heads. "Here, put your hat on so they can't see your ugly mug."

Rubbing his arm across Coogin's back where he lay, Slive left dark streaks on the rumpled work shirt. By Coogin's head, he set a hefty rock and smeared it with more blood. At the sound of a wagon, he quickly wound a dirty kerchief around his wound and scurried up the embankment.

NOAH HELD THE REINS LOOSELY, the Colt revolver in easy reach as the wagon bounced up the dusty gravel road. Ahead, the lane cut between two ledges like a canyon, one side the height of a man, the other towering tall as a two-story house. Perfect spot for an ambush, and Noah drew the revolver from beneath the bench.

Beside him, his head buried beneath the sergeant's Hardee hat, Silas whispered, "Massah Tuna?" Despite the heat, Silas shivered inside George's uniform. "I's scared."

"Buck up, soldier," Noah muttered quietly. "You're doing just fine."

Another one of George's ideas, switching clothes with Silas. "Always wanted to wear a uniform, be a soldier boy," Silas had said as he buttoned up the dark blue shirt. George would follow behind, try to capture Slive for the authorities. Easier to just shoot him, thought Noah. But George had this stubborn way about him, and Noah let it go. Maybe there might be room to improvise later.

Approaching the gap between the bluffs, Noah saw an old sack by the side of the road. No, not a sack. It was a man. They drew nearer and Noah saw dark streaks on the homespun shirt. Bessy snorted, her ears laid flat.

"Whoa!" The wagon stopped and Noah eyed the prone figure carefully, stalling to give George time to get in position. He remembered a day not so long ago, Pa poking in the dirt for potatoes. Pa, burned in the fire, his home and everything he and Jenny owned, gone up in smoke. To hell with the plan. If Slive was around, better to just shoot him outright. For Jenny and Pa, and for Orvis. Yes, and for Eb and Cletus, too. Slowly, Noah climbed down, revolver held to the side of his leg. A bird cried out from the fields behind him as he moved closer. That's when he saw the hat. There was something familiar about that hat. Noah bent to lift it from the man's head.

Coogin swung his meaty arm in a great hook that knocked Noah from his feet and pitched him into the sidewall. His revolver clattered in the road. In an instant, Coogin landed a blow to Noah's stomach; a second came at his head that he managed to block. Pushing off from the rocky wall, Noah knocked the man back and dove for his knees. They fell in a heap, tangled legs and leverage and Coogin bounced to his feet, snatched up a boulder, lifted it high in the air, steadying it for a crushing blow as Noah rolled to face him.

A loud bang like a single drumbeat, and the stone fell in the dirt. Coogin dropped to his knees, stared at Noah, then turned to Silas, hidden under the wagon, the pistol smoking in his two-fisted grip. Coogin hung there for a moment, his dull mind slowly comprehending, before he pitched over in a great cloud of dust.

Noah sat up carefully, rolled his neck and breathed, deep and slow. He looked at the dead man, Coogin's eyes staring blankly from his scarred face, his tongue dragging in the dust. Noah cursed, took another deep breath, slapped hat to knee and stood.

From under the wagon, Silas screamed, "Massah Tuna!"

There was a loud bang like a cannon, a single shot. Then two more further away, but Noah did not hear these.

ON HIS BELLY, A SKIRMISHER IN ADVANCE of the regiment, George inched his way along the wall of earth. Stay low, keep to cover, slip behind those rocks, come up along the embankment. "He is quick and he is strong," Noah had said. Surprising him from behind held the least risk. But which side of the road? Dudley hadn't known. George had chosen the higher side, guessing Slive would do the same.

This had been the plan, his idea to hide Silas under the Yankee uniform, George's turn to take the "back door" as Noah had done for

George at the cave. The cave. It seemed so long ago now, before Eva and he had…

Movement, there in the tall grass!

George flattened himself in the heavy brush and tried to peer through the undergrowth, but could see nothing. There was no noise except the soft rumble of the wagon on the road below. George heard Noah say, "Whoa!" But his attention was riveted ten feet ahead where something waited, tipping the grass, something scuffling along the ground, edging toward the road. George peered over the brush and brought his rifle to his shoulder. Suddenly, a brown mass rose up in a flap of feathers and a loud squawk and George gasped, startled as much by the wild turkey hen running off as she was by him.

He lowered the rifle and worked to slow his breathing. More noise came from the road, men grunting and scuffling, and he crawled the last few yards to peer over the edge. There, Noah and another man wrestled in the dust. Silas lay beneath the wagon, just as he had been told, his feet sticking out the other side. But where was Slive? George quickly sighted along the ridge across the other side of the road. Nothing. Along his side. Nothing.

He heard the shot and brought his rifle to aim down onto the road. Sitting in the dirt was Noah, legs splayed, the other man on his knees. Who had fired the shot? George sighted on the man as he toppled over, felt relief as Noah stood and began to brush himself off. George stood up and was about to hail Noah when a shout from Silas stopped him. There was Slive, large and ominous, standing on the bluff on the far side of the road, long-barreled pistol in his two-fisted grip.

"No!" George shouted. Slive's pistol jumped and Noah sat heavily. George fired once and Slive spun around. George cocked and fired again to put him down.

Quickly George slid on his heels down the embankment to kneel over Noah. Silas scrambled up beside him, the revolver still in his hands.

George said, "I'm sorry." It seemed so inadequate. "I was on the wrong side."

"Story of my life," Noah said weakly.

George peeled back Noah's shirt and the blood spilled down his side onto the dusty earth. "Silas, get me my haversack." Silas dropped the pistol and went to rummage in the wagon. "And bring the canteen." He helped Noah to sit up and Silas held the canteen while the wounded man drank, coughed, and drank some more.

"Whoop!" came a shout behind them and George turned to search for Dudley. A shadow loomed overhead and Noah Turner raised his arm and fired, the pistol report deafening beside George's ear. Slive tumbled from the ridge and landed in a cloud of dust at their feet. He struggled to rise. Noah shot him again, and he lay still.

Noah coughed. He lay back, coughed again, and whispered, "Is he dead?"

Silas kicked the body hard. "Yes, sir, he dead."

But Noah did not hear him.

George sat heavily, and silently cursed the dust and the heat and the shadow that fell across his heart. He held his lips tight, as if to hold in his despair. His face twisted and his chest began to heave under the strain. From where it sat by his feet, he retrieved the round little hat, grasped it by the edges and ripped it into pieces. Then he thrust it aside and covered his head between his knees.

Dudley helped Silas roll the two bushwhackers into a shallow ditch and throw a layer of dirt over them. Silas bent and removed a spur from Slive's boot. He gave it to George. "This belong to Miss Eva," he said.

No words were said over the makeshift graves; George could think of none appropriate. He wrapped Noah's body in a piece of oil cloth and they loaded him onto the wagon. Silas would carry him back to Elm Grove once he had delivered George to the train station.

For several miles, Dudley rode on the bench beside George. Then suddenly he leapt from the wagon with a whoop and a wave and was gone. Silas and George rode on in silence, deaf to the stiff breeze that rose to buffet the trees, oblivious to the first raindrops as they began to fall in great gobs.

CHAPTER FORTY-SEVEN

Demopolis, Ala., August 1, 1865

A t Demopolis, George changed lines, a smaller train, less crowded, same slow kick-kack. One full day after leaving Elm Grove, he stepped off the train in Uniontown, Alabama. The one-room station featured a ten-foot bench of rough boards freshly painted with an immense motto: VISIT THE SICK. The stationmaster, telegraph operator, and freight manager were all Union soldiers. Two black men stood by; one offered to tote George's goods, but saw he carried only the haversack and a small case and backed away, until George beckoned him.

"Where can I find the Eighth Wisconsin?" George asked, and pressed a coin into the man's hand.

"They's a heap of Yankee camped out that away," the man said, and pointed a long bony finger up the dusty road. George gave him another coin and the man agreed to show him the way.

"It's Van!" someone shouted at his homecoming, if home was where the regiment lay. George did not feel so sure anymore. These men, his family for so many years, seemed separate from him now. They represented his past. His future, and his heart he knew now, lay in Elm Grove. Despite the garrulous greetings he received, George felt somehow ill at ease. He could find no solace in the routine of camp life, the neat rows of tents, supper at the appointed hour.

"Company H is to do guard duty tonight, George," said Lieutenant Ellsworth. "See to it, will you?"

"Yes, sir," George responded. Guard duty? Guard what? This poor farm turned to dust bowl by the tramping of a thousand feet? And why? The war was over; who were they to guard the camp from?

"I'd guess you had more than your share of guard duty lately, eh?" Sherman Ellsworth said. "Good to have you back, George."

"Thanks, Sherm. Good to be back," George said, though he did not feel it, his spirit dampened by his longing for Elm Grove and Eva. He thought, too, of Noah. It surprised him at the loss he felt for the man, no less than he felt for many of his friends in the regiment, this man who had been "The Enemy."

He would not forget his family and his friends, some in his regiment, others left behind in unmarked holes. Yet, his true home, family, and friends had become those he had left at Elm Grove: Eb, Mitsy, and Silas, Jesse, and the Judge. He had grown to love—and be loved—by these good people. He was truly convinced that "home" was Elm Grove.

"Could be your last day in the army, boys," George said to the men posted to guard duty. "Make it a good one. You muster out soon. Until then, you're still a soldier."

The days passed in routine and ritual, boredom the enemy from which there was no guarding, monotony broken by games of chance—Sheepshead or Chuck-a-Luck—and of baseball. But too often, sweltering heat discouraged exercise. Forays into Uniontown were also discouraged to avoid conflict with local townspeople. Some men wagered on which date the regiment might finally muster out. Delays due to transport, supplies, and paperwork all contributed to the soldiers' frustrations. And every day they drilled: battalion formation, company formation, skirmish tactics. Discipline and the practiced drill of the methods of war, a war that was over. The soldiers just wanted to go home.

Except George. He ached for Eva. His mind swam with images of their walks together or sitting quietly at their "special place" often without talk but simply enjoying the nearness, the other's very presence. He often imagined her violet eyes, soft and yet piercing all the same, as if she could see through him, but chose not to. He remembered her words, her rapid-fire speech, her flitting from topic to topic, and him following perfectly. Her husky voice, intoxicating, played in his mind. "Handsome" she had said, "And dashing." And always when he thought of Eva, he remembered the leg, the night when she had first come to him. He smiled at this, a lopsided grin.

He had not worn the sash since that first day for fear it would be sullied by sweat and dust, but kept it tucked neatly inside his haversack, separate from the hardtack and bits of dried pork, protected in a scrap of gum blanket. He had shown it only to Ben Entriken. His friend had remarked he had seen others like it occasionally when a Rebel soldier was brought to hospital. Was it of some significance, he had asked? George simply replied that it was a gift and said no more. With the sash he kept the spur, a gift for Eva upon his return to Elm Grove.

The interval seemed an eternity. Six months, he had promised. Six months to allow the wounds of prejudice to heal, for Southern wrath to mellow. Even in six months, it would not go easy for him. He knew this. He would be held accountable for every atrocity that had befallen the defeated South, every injustice, every misdemeanor. It did not seem fair, yet life was not always fair. It was never easy. This he knew. And sometimes, it ended all too soon.

That was the great tragedy. Factories could be replaced, farms renewed. But how many men would never know another sunny afternoon? Would never have children, or grandchildren? Would never know love?

This line of thinking nagged at him as a scab on a sore. It brought him to intense worry and frustration, and he took to brooding as he marched about the camp, until at last he reached a resolve, a judgment that gave him profound peace. Life was not fair. It would never be easy. So when the opportunity for happiness arose, it was all the more important to seize it. Timing and tactics, the strategies of war, were fit lessons for life. George must return to Elm Grove. He must seize his opportunity. And he must do it now. Later might be too late.

His decision made, the return to Elm Grove as soon as he mustered out, George secured the necessary paperwork.

"Think of your parents," Lieutenant Ellsworth had said when he learned of it. "Don't they want you to come home?" George had considered this, but he decided that, with nine other children, his parents had enough to manage without him. It was the right decision, he was sure of it, even without the Judge's blessing. His mind set. Now it was simply a matter of getting through the next few days, until the regiment mustered out.

Sitting with Ben Entriken one warm evening before the mosquitoes drove them to their tents, George said, "I was thinking about going home for a few months, see the family. But I've decided to stay right here. Or back in Tennessee anyway. There's some land near Elm Grove—some land I'd like to buy, maybe grow some corn, some cotton."

"You sure you don't want to talk with Mr. Mason about that job in the stockyards? Could be a good job," Ben said.

George just shook his head.

Ben said, "There wouldn't be a woman involved, eh?"

George offered his lopsided grin.

"As I suspected, eh?" Entriken said. "Is that it then? Is that what you want for your life?"

"I am what I am, Ben. Born a farmer. Raised to farm. It's what I know."

"And Eva?"

"Sealed the deal," he said.

"You are what you are, George. One part dreamer, one part hard work, more than a few parts tomfoolery, eh?"

"Don't forget wisenheimer," George said. "A big part is wisenheimer."

"George, you know the Johnnies might make it pretty hot for any Yankees who don't go back North, eh?"

George B Van Norman

2 Lyt, Co.N., 8 Reg't Wisconsin Infantry.

Age........years.

Appears on **Co. Muster-out Roll**, dated

Demopolis Ala, Sept. 5, 1865.

Muster-out to date   Sept. 5, 1865.

Last paid to   Feb. 28, 1865.

Clothing account:

Last settled Sept. 24 1864 ; drawn since $19 $\frac{99}{100}$

Due soldier $............$\overline{100}$; due U. S. $............$\overline{100}$

Am't for cloth'g in kind or money adv'd $............$\overline{100}$

Due U. S. for arms, equipments, &c,, $............$\overline{100}$

Bounty paid $210 $\overline{100}$; due $190 $\overline{100}$

Remarks: Veteran. Desires to be mustered out in the south with the intention of remaining

Sam roll

Book mark:

Hodge

(861)   Copyist.

George thanked him, understood his motive—protect those you cherish, comrades in arms. It was the glue that held together every unit of fighting men the world over. It would last through their lifetime.

At dress parade on the evening of September 4, 1865, Lieutenant Colonel William B. Britton gathered the regiment:

"Head Quarters, District of Montgomery, Alabama. Special Order Number 21 to the Eighth Wisconsin Veteran Volunteer Infantry. Lieutenant Colonel W.B. Britton, commanding, will, after having turned over all land transportation and animals to the quartermaster department at Demopolis, Alabama, proceed without delay to Madison, Wisconsin, reporting to the Chief Mustering Officer of the state for final payment and discharge. By command of Major General Henry Davis."

Britton folded the paper slowly, slid it into the breast pocket of his dress jacket, carefully removed his glasses to the same pocket, stood erect, and brought his arm up in salute. "Dismissed," he said.

A great "Huzzah!" and Hardee hats were tossed wildly in the air. The regiment was going home.

In the morning, George boarded the rail cars for Demopolis, where he marched up Franklin Street to Ash, turned in his government property, and received his official discharge.

THE REGIMENT WAS IN JOCULAR MOOD. Laughter filled the crowded train as men lounged on rows of rough wooden benches, cattle cars converted to troop carriers, two windows on each side where they gathered to smoke and tell stories. They were finally going home, four years (nearly to the day) after enlisting.

The train passed through Birmingham without slowing, swung north and crossed into Tennessee, rattling across the Elk River bridge. Late in the afternoon, they approached Columbia, where the engine was scheduled to take on fuel and water.

George walked slowly through the train car. These were to be his last moments with those he had marched with and slept with and fought with for four years, and he made it a point to speak to each man in the Company.

"Good luck, George." "Hey there, Van, you take care of yourself, eh?" "Fit as a fiddle and fat in the middle."

Ben Entriken said, "You're a risk-taker, George. I envy you. You know what you want." They shook hands. "I know you'll find it, eh?"

CHAPTER FORTY-EIGHT

Columbia, Tenn., September 5, 1865

The train chuffed into the station and he waved hale and hearty to a chorus of jeers and cat calls and "Keep your head down, Van." With little more than his haversack and small carrying case, George stepped from the train into his new life. Opposite the tracks, a dozen sparrows lifted from the trees in formation, a great sweeping arc celebrating the sunshine, or perhaps his return.

Inside the tiny station, he inquired about obtaining a horse and the stationmaster called for a porter to lead him to the livery.

"Massah Van!" George recognized a familiar voice. "That you there, Massah Van?" Silas reached to take George's case but George dropped it to the ground and wrapped his arms around the boy in a great bear hug.

"Silas!" George stood back to look at the boy all dressed in a bright green uniform topped with a pillbox cap, its brass insignia, **Southern Railroad**, glinting in the sun. The scars on his face had faded to thin, pink lines. On his feet were a pair of boots, the first George had seen him wear.

Silas stared at him wide-eyed. "What you doing back here, Massah Van?" he asked. "I thought you was gone north to be with your family."

"I was," George replied, still grinning. "But I just couldn't wait to see you again, so I came back." He slapped the boy on his shoulders. "Looks like you finally get to wear a uniform."

"That's right, I does." He flashed a toothless grin. "How about that?" He stood proudly. "And I is living on my own and going to school now, too, at the Freedmen School."

Chuff-chuff of the engine keeping up steam, and George had to speak up to be heard. "How is everybody? Tell me everything on the way to the stable. I'm anxious to return to Elm Grove."

Silas stopped suddenly, the grin washed from his face. "You ain't heard?" he said. "You ain't heard about Massah Tom?"

"Who?" George stood still.

"Massah Tom, Miss Eva's … uh, she and him was fixing… before the war, I means …" Silas seemed lost within his own mind, unable to speak.

But George understood. Tom, Eva's betrothed, Tom Harden, Confederate soldier lost at the Battle of Chattanooga, presumed killed. Presumed. No word in over a year. George pushed his hat back on his head. "What about him?" George asked.

"He come back from the dead," Silas said, his eyes wide and staring. "Just like you done. He got killed, and then they took him to the Choozits place. And now he come alive again."

Choozits? What was Silas trying to say? "Silas, let's go sit down here on this bench." As if leading a child. "Now, tell me about Mister Tom, and what is a Choozits?"

Staring at the floor, Silas shook his head slowly, uncomfortable with the telling. "Massah Tom, he was Miss Eva's man afore you come along," he began. "He got hisself killed in the war, but then he come alive again. Raised up by some fellow name of Choozits. They kept saying he was at Massah Choozits, Massah Choozits. Some kind of miracle place or something. I ain't sure." Silas rubbed his eye. "But he come home, Massah Tom did, and Miss Eva, she was so surprised and what all."

George studied the boy's words. Not dead. Severely wounded, taken prisoner, and shipped north to a hospital ward in Massachusetts. Tom Harden, come back to Elm Grove. Back to Eva.

"Massah Van?" Silas looked up at George, tears flooding his eyes. "I's sorry to be telling you this." He swiped feebly at his eyes but gave up and put his head between his knees and cried great alligator tears.

Not sure what to say came out as, "It's all right." George gripped the boy's shoulders, searching for words. "Nothing's wrong, Silas. I'll speak to Eva and I'm sure it will be all right." He sat with Silas on the bench and rubbed his lip where the scar lay buried beneath his mustache. Not so sure at all, but resolved to find out. Did Eva still love him? Or would Tom Harden's return re-ignite some ardor long smoldering?

Approaching from behind his desk, the stationmaster said to Silas. "Say, what is going on here, boy?" The skinny old man had the air of a bureaucrat, his eyes vacant and flat behind pince-nez glasses. He glared from Silas to George and back.

"It's all right, sir," George said. "We're old friends."

The man stared blankly, surely wondering who this uppity Yankee thought he was and why would he have an old friend who wasn't so old at all. And a darkie at that.

Chuff of the steam engine, and George stood. "Come on, Silas. Let's go find us that horse. I had better get out to Elm Grove before Miss Eva decides she doesn't want me anymore." George pondered his own words. Was it possible she would not want him? Could her devotion have dissolved while his grew more committed? Only one way to find out. "Let's go, Silas," he said as he reached the station door.

"You don't understand," Silas wailed.

George stopped once more.

"They be married!" he cried. "Miss Eva and Massah Tom!" Tears fell freely down his brown cheeks. "They was married last week. The Judge done it, just what he done when he married Momma and Eb. He said all them same words and all: 'Dearly beloved' and 'Does you take this man' and like that."

Sting like a hot poker staggered him and George sat once more.

Silas sat beside him. "Massah Tom is on crutches now, but his leg is going to heal and they say he be up working again by harvest." Babbling now, the boy's words were lost in the thick stuffiness of the station. George, stunned, tried to comprehend.

"Miss Jenny and Miss Minnie be living at Watersmith now. They in business or some such thing. And Jesse got hisself a new dog, calls him Robert E. Lee. That's a better name than Jeff Davis, sure enough. I sees the Judge in town from time to time. He be here on business, or maybe judging stuff, I guess..."

Silas went on, but George did not hear. A dull numbness settled on him, energy drained, faith depleted. A dozen questions flooded his mind. Eva married to someone else? How could it happen? And so suddenly? Was she planning to tell him? Or just let him return in six months, only to discover her happily married to another man. Perhaps she was simply going to write him a letter: "So sorry things didn't work out, but I suppose it is best this way. Tom is, after all, a Southerner..."

"All aboard!" Hail from the conductor drifted on the warm air.

"...and Massah Roberts, his hands is mostly better. He be working with Cletus and his people. They say they going to have a good crop of smoking tobacco, and some cotton, too. They got beans and peas and corn and 'taters..."

"Silas," George interrupted. "Silas." He grasped the boy's shoulders, looked at him squarely. "Don't tell anyone you saw me here."

"What you going to do, Massah Van?" Silas said.

"I'm going home," George said. "Like I was supposed to. I'm going home to Wisconsin."

George gathered up his haversack and bag and stepped into the sun; Silas fell in behind him, stoop shouldered and snuffling.

"It's all right, Silas," he said. "I'll be back. Just remember what I said."

"All aboard! Last call!" Another chuff of steam and the whistle sounded a long blast.

George stepped aboard the last rail car, waved to Silas as the train engine hissed and the smokestack huffed and the sound of metal grinding on metal signaled their departure.

Silas walked alongside, wiping his runny nose on the shirtsleeve of his new uniform. "I know she love you, Massah Van. I know she do." He quickened his step to keep pace. "Something else, too." He shouted as the train gathered speed and George strained to hear.

"Miss Eva," Silas said, running to keep up, words coming in gasps. "Miss Eva," he repeated as the train pulled away. "She going to have a baby."

Silas stopped and George left the station behind, left Silas standing on the platform, left Columbia, and Elm Grove. And Eva.

Epilogue

The regiment reached Madison, Wisconsin, on September 12, 1865, receiving final pay and discharge papers the next day. As an organization, the "Live Eagle" Eighth Wisconsin Volunteer Infantry disappeared and was absorbed into the bustle of post-war America.

George Van Norman returned to the family's farm in the tiny town of Moscow, Wisconsin, but did not stay long. With his accounts near to bursting, he began a successful business career in nearby Spring Green, buying and selling horses and cattle, shipping goods to Milwaukee and Chicago.

On October 28, just seven weeks later, he married Elizabeth Atkinson, whom George had met while in Madison on furlough. In 1874, he and Elizabeth moved to Milwaukee, where he became successful in the livestock commission business at the Union Stockyards.

Together, they had three daughters: Jane, Alma, and Lizzie. Elizabeth Atkinson Van Norman died shortly after Lizzie (great-grandmother to the author) was born.

A single father of three daughters, George married a second time to Cornelia (Nellie) Parsons in 1876. Their first child—a boy—died five days before his mother in 1878.

By the age of 35, George had lost two wives and his only son. He married Minerva (Minnie) Amelia Booth, a distant cousin to John Wilkes Booth, in 1881.

Business prospered and in 1891, George founded the South Milwaukee Company, a real estate development firm that he ran in addition to his stockyard business. In 1893, he entered the meat-packing business with O.F. Mason and William Plankinton. O. F. Mason was the father of Ed Mason of the Eighth Wisconsin, Company K, the corporal who suffered "a spitfire in the leg" at Nashville and died under the surgeon's saw.

Others of the regiment also went on to successful careers as farmers and businessmen. Jessie Cole became an ordained minister; Sandy Cluxton and Bill Craven returned to farming; Ben Entriken accepted a position as Chief Time Clerk in the Government Printing Office in Madison, Wisconsin, at $1,200 annual salary.

Tennessee was the first Confederate state to be re-admitted to the Union on July 24, 1866, partly through the efforts of Judge Wilson's associate, Samuel Arnell of Columbia.

Despite his professional commitments, George Van Norman never forgot his friends in Tennessee. Several times he had occasion to visit Elm Grove and was a welcome guest of the Judge. But he never again saw Eva. Having learned she was pregnant, Eva married Tom Harden rather than suffer banishment from society. She remained the first great love of George's life.

In 1910, George and Minnie retired to Old Oak, a substantial estate outside Milwaukee, where George passed away quietly in 1924; he was 81 years old.

In his will, among the bequests, George left a substantial sum to Grace Harden of Tennessee, b. Mar., 1866.

The spur and the sash have been handed down through the generations; they now rest in a prominent display in my study.

Robert Grede
Milwaukee

RETROSPECTIVE

THE EIGHTH WISCONSIN "LIVE EAGLE"
VETERAN VOLUNTEER REGIMENT

I n its four years of service (1861-1865), the regiment traveled over 14,000 miles: 4,200 by rail, 4,800 by steamer, and 5,200 on the march.

The 2nd Brigade, consisting of the 8th Wisconsin, 5th Minnesota, 11th Missouri, 47th Illinois Infantry, and 2nd Iowa Battery, logged more marching miles than any other brigade in the war.

The 8th Wisconsin took part in thirty-two battles, inscribed upon its battle flag. In addition, the regiment fought some forty skirmishes, many so sharp as to deserve the name of battles.

Fredericktown, Mo. Oct. 22, 1861
New Madrid, Mo. April 7, 1862
Island No. 10, Mo. April 8, 1862
Farmington, Miss. May 8, 1862
Corinth, Miss. May 28, 1862
Iuka, Miss. Sept, 14, 1862
Iuka, Miss Sept. 19, 1862
Corinth, Miss. Oct. 3 - 4, 1862
Jackson, Miss. May 14, 1863
Champion Hills, Miss. May 14, 1863

Vicksburg, Miss. May 22, 1863

Mechanicsburg, Miss. June 4, 1863

Richmond, La. June 14, 1863

Fort de Russy, La. Mar. 14, 1864

Grand Ecore, La. April 4, 1864

Pleasant Hill, La. April 9, 1864

Cloutierville, La. April 23, 1864

Potter's Bridge, La. May 7, 1864

Mansura, La. May 16, 1864

Moroville, La. May 17, 1864

Bayou de Glaize, La. May 18, 1864

Lake Chicot, Ark. June 6, 1864

Carmargo Crossroads, Miss. July 13, 1864

Tupelo, Miss. July 14 - 15, 1864

Hurricane Creek, Miss. Aug. 13, 1864

Abbeville, Miss. Aug. 23, 1864

Nashville, Tenn. Dec. 15 - 16, 1864

Spanish Fort, Ala. March 25, 1865

Fort Blakely, Ala. April 9, 1865

Of the total 1,643 men who served in the Eighth Wisconsin Regiment, 255 were lost by death, 60 deserted, 41 transferred, 320 were discharged from service, some 177 severely wounded or disabled, 3 were declared missing, and 964 mustered out.

Survivors of the 8th Wisconsin gathered at Milwaukee in 1889 in one of the nation's largest reunions of Union Civil War veterans. Following is an excerpt from the local newspaper of that reunion.

Robert Grede

THE MILWAUKEE SENTINEL
Friday, August 30, 1889

MILWAUKEE—Over 200,000 veterans and their families visited Milwaukee this week as part of the National G.A.R. reunion...

Among the encampments was the Eighth Wisconsin Volunteers, guests of Mr. & Mrs. Geo. B. Van Norman, prominent citizens...

"Camp Van Norman" was located at the spacious residence of comrade Van Norman, 966 National Avenue... Comrade Van Norman's elegant home was turned into a sleeping room for the ladies, of whom about 70 enjoyed his generous hospitality, while his mammoth barn, 40 by 80 feet, which had been especially fitted up for this occasion, furnished sleeping room for 200 comrades.   Quite a number of the old 8th were on hand Tuesday and more were arriving all through the week: Col. Britton, Capt. Willoughby, Lieut. S.K. Ellsworth, Surgeon Murdock, Patrick McFarland, Thomas Green, Russell Brownell, D.R. Lewis, Jessie Cole, J.M. Williams, Benj. Entriken, and Will Pooler to name but a few. 208 officers and men reported for duty.   Among the many pleasant events of the week was the visit of the regiment's old commander, Gen. A.J. Smith of St. Louis... In the course of his remarks he said he held a higher regard for the Eighth Wisconsin than for any other regiment that he ever had the pleasure to command.

Thursday afternoon...the regiment gathered on the spacious front lawn to a say a few well chosen, eloquent words to Comrade Van Norman and his lovely wife, Minnie, and charming daughters, Jennie, Alma, and Lizzie...

At 5 p.m., seven omnibuses arrived and the entire party were conveyed to the lakefront to witness a [mock] naval battle, where the ever-thoughtful Van had, by special arrangement with Capt. Pabst, secured reserved seats.

Friday ... was spent in final partings and handshakes and kindly regard, and love for the old boys of the Eagle regiment revived and intensified with the hope that they might be spared to meet in many more happy reunions.

ACKNOWLEDGMENTS

Every author is helped in his efforts to fashion a readable story, and I am no different, forever grateful for the kindness of strangers and friends alike.

In particular, I would like to thank all the folks at the extensive American Civil War collection of the Wisconsin Historical Society; the Director of the Maury County (Tennessee) Archives, Bob Duncan, and his supportive staff; Joyce Mayberry and the late Gill Thompson of the Hickman County (Tennessee) historical society; and American Civil War re-enactor, R.J. Samp, who reviewed the manuscript for historical accuracy, and helped me avoid being "farbie." While their contributions are numerous and significant, any inaccuracies are mine alone.

Many family members helped both create the myth and fill in the voids: my grandmother, Elizabeth Wait Grede, George Van Norman's granddaughter, from whom I first learned the story; my father, Edward A. Grede, whose recollections were invaluable; my mother, Mary Jane, the English teacher; siblings Dick, Don, and Libby for their contributions; Cammy and The Nate who watched me write and wondered when their dad could "come out and play."

Larry Watson opened up the world of fiction to this "hack" ad man; Mary Beth Tallon at Marquette University Press brought structure and depth; Terry Firkins taught me how to make it sing.

A special thanks to Kira Henschel, who rescued me from the wilderness with her insights, her strength, and her willingness to compromise.

And of course, Karen, for her patience, her creativity, and mostly for just being Karen.

And lastly, that wonderful woman in Centerville who runs the restaurant on the southeast side of the Square—she stayed open late one Sunday evening to serve a lonely traveler. Thank you.

PHOTOGRAPHS

The Van Norman family on their farm in western Wisconsin, circa 1860. George Van Norman is leaning on the fence (far right). A brother and sister are to his left. Seated, George's father is to the left, grandmother in the center, and mother to the right.

George B. Van Norman,
carte de visite, 1869

George B. Van Norman, circa 1916

George B. Van Norman,
circa 1923

Four generations, circa 1921 (left to right):

♦ George B. Van Norman (1842–1924), the author's great-great-grandfather

♦ Burton C. Wait (1870–1962), the author's great-grandfather, who married Elizabeth Van Norman, youngest daughter of George

♦ Arthur L. Grede (1895–1976), the author's grandfather, who married Elizabeth, only daughter of Burton C. Wait

♦ Edward A. Grede (1920–), the author's father

♦ Henry Grede (1865–1942), the author's great-grandfather

♦ Alvin Wait (1844–1924), the author's great-great-grandfather, father of Burton C. Wait. Alvin lost his leg at the Battle of Peachtree Creek

"There is someone here I have not met."
—George B. Van Norman

ABOUT THE AUTHOR

Robert Grede has been a carpenter, musician, teacher, author, speaker, entrepreneur, consultant, and dad. For fun, he writes string quartets. *The Spur & The Sash* is his first novel.